Learning CURVE

DICKSON UNIVERSITY BOOK ONE

max
monroe

New York Times & USA Today Bestselling Author

Learning Curve (Dickson University Book #1)

Published by Max Monroe LLC © 2024, Max Monroe

Editing by Silently Correcting Your Grammar
Formatting by Champagne Book Design
Cover Design by Peter Alderweireld

AUTHOR NOTE

So…this book is *something*. In fact, if pressured, we might say this book is *all the things*.

Imagine…being wrapped up in the comfort of visiting a dear friend while simultaneously being lit on fire while season one of *Grey's Anatomy* and *One Tree Hill* (the most addictive seasons of both shows, in our opinion) and every episode of *Friends* play at full volume at the same time. But, like, you can concentrate?

Never mind. Let's try a different description…

There's angst. There's DRAMAAA. There are emotional twists that will leave you breathless. There's hilarity and spice and the kinds of friendships that last a lifetime. It's all-consuming and real and so dang raw we swore we were living it in real time.

This is a story of two people who have every reason in the world not to be together but can't resist each other no matter how hard they try.

Learning Curve is going to take you on a ride. It is, hands down, our most bingeable book. Once you start, you won't be able to stop. Trust us, we wrote it. We *lived* it. We still find ourselves going back for more.

Just buckle up, okay?

All our love,
Max & Monroe

Disclaimer: *Learning Curve* is a New Adult Romance that is book one in the Dickson University Series. It is highly addictive, and while you think you might know what's coming, let us be the first to tell you that you don't. This book is a complete **stand-alone**, but if you've read Max Monroe's Billionaire Bad Boys Series and/or Winslow Brothers Collection then you will see some of your favorite familiar faces a lot.

****TW: This book does contain sensitive topics.

DEDICATION

To new beginnings.

To learning the hard way.

To a book so thick—*and dramatic*—it almost killed us.

And to all the readers who've been requesting a spin-off series with the Billionaire kids all grown up: We had to wait until the characters were ready, but we promise, they've arrived in high style.

This one is for you.

Learning
CURVE

PROLOGUE

Scottie

We're both in my bed, completely naked, and I want to give myself to him.

Soul, heart, virginity—he's the one I want to have it all, even when I know it's the worst idea I've ever had.

He traces the lines of my body with his heated gaze. Goose bumps form on my skin, and I glance down to where he's hard and aroused. For *me*.

I feel immediately powerful.

Finn is the kind of guy who can have any girl he wants but chooses to be alone. He's complicated and complex, and there's so much I don't know about him—so much no one knows about him.

I *want* to know about him, though, which is what got me into this kind of trouble in the first place.

We're dynamic. We're kindred. We're meant to be. I feel it in my bones. But how long can you shoulder the guilt of secret betrayal before you burst at the seams?

His perfect brown eyes will turn hard and cold. His smile will disappear. Everything he thought he could trust will be gone.

This is so much bigger than this moment, and yet, I can't stop. I have to have him.

I just hope it doesn't mean I lose him forever.

1

The buzz of a busy New York City pounds against my back as I push through the doors of Graham Hall, my home for the foreseeable future.

It's move-in day at Dickson University, and I, one of the university's newest freshmen, have officially entered the next phase of my life.

In a sense, I feel free. My last "phase of life" was shittier than ideal. Still, there's a whole other element to the excitement of college when you're me, and the burn in my chest glows hotter and hotter every day.

The strap of my oversized black duffel digs into my shoulder. It's heavy, filled with everything I own—which, admittedly, seems like hardly anything at all as I weave through the dormitory hallway teeming with wealthy pricks and their parents.

Sofas, mini refrigerators, computer monitors, and TVs the size of my childhood basement battle for space in the hallway of the tiny, male-only building located at the far northwestern corner of the entire campus.

I'm alone, as normal, and that draws more than a few stares on the way to my room. Deep navy-blue doors spaced twenty feet apart line the gold-painted halls. No doubt, the color choice is a nod to the university's colors.

Dickson is one of New York City's most prestigious universities. A fucked-up guy like me shouldn't belong here, but I fought to make it happen anyway. I maintained a perfect GPA for the last two years of high school, despite everything going on at home, and wrote a personal statement that took a month and a half to finish to earn an acceptance letter and enough financial aid to cover the basics.

Everything depends on this.

"Hey," one guy wearing a Yankees baseball cap says, giving me a jerk of his chin as I scoot past him and an older man I'm assuming is his father as they try to cram a couch through his dorm room door.

I give the head nod back, but I don't need to bother with anything else—he's already back to what he's doing before I'm finished with the simple motion.

Two doors down, I find my name on the wall beside a wide-open threshold.

Finnley Hayes

On a sigh, I take the black Sharpie marker I got in my welcome packet out of my jeans pocket and scratch out the l-e-y until the sign reads **Finn Hayes**.

Underneath is a second name—**Ace Kelly**—belonging to my university-random-generated roommate. I might be more nervous about sharing the space with someone if I weren't one of five rambunctious kids. I'm used to having people on top of me all the time, and I'm used to not having a choice about it.

One roommate is child's play, compared to what I dealt with growing up.

The room looks empty at first, save several boxes and suitcases and a shitload of electronics on one of the desks, but when I step inside, a voice proves my assumption false. I turn around just as one of the hottest middle-aged ladies I've ever seen pops out from behind the door. "Hey," she says casually, her dark brown hair and vibrant blue eyes standing out immediately. "Are you Finnley?"

"Finn," I correct, loathing the sound of my full name coming from such a hot mouth, even if she is old.

"Ah, Finn." She nods, and her mouth curves up into a smile that only makes her lips look fuller. "Yeah, that's way more fuckable."

My eyebrows shoot up. My mom would never dream of saying something like that to a college kid she didn't know. But she probably wouldn't have her tits halfway out of her shirt either.

She holds out a hand. "I'm Cassie Kelly, your roommate Ace's mom."

I take her hand and shake it, careful to keep my eyes on hers. In my peripheral vision, I know her tits are bouncing up and down with the movement. "Nice to meet you."

With as polite of a smile as I can manage, I turn away from her and head for the other side of the room where my empty, bare-mattress bed is waiting. I toss my duffel on top and start unloading the essentials. A set of sheets and a blanket, the laptop computer I spent the last two years saving for, and my seven sets of jeans and shirts. I leave the underwear and socks at the bottom of the bag and shove it under the bed.

When I turn around, Cassie Kelly is watching me surreptitiously. She's only bashful for half a second before owning her nosiness. "Where are your parents?"

"Busy," I say simply, though fuck knows the truth is a lot more complicated than that.

She frowns but nods. A loud curse sounds outside the door, followed by two of the tallest people I've ever seen coming through it, carrying some kind of futon. I'm six one, but these dudes have several inches on me.

"Ace, for the love of everything, could you stop dropping this fucker?" the older man says as they finally make it inside the room.

"It'd be easier if you weren't running me over the whole time," my roommate responds. With the same black hair, brown eyes, muscular build, and towering height, they're clearly father and son. A sprinkle of gray hair mars the black at the older man's temples, but other than that, they're practically twins.

When they reach Ace's side of the room, they drop the black futon unceremoniously onto the cream vinyl tile floor of our dorm with a thud. It takes a few scoots, but they manage to stuff it into the only available corner near his bed.

"I fucking told you we should've hired movers," Ace says, swiping sweat off his brow.

"Aw, poor Ace," his dad says through a laugh. "His wittle baby muscles hurt."

Ace rolls his eyes. "Says the old man who is going to spend the rest of his night in his fucking hot tub crying to Mom about how old he's getting. Probably going to lube up your decrepit muscles with Aspercreme too."

"Lubing up with Aspercreme? Have I taught you anything, Acer?" his dad retorts. My eyes bounce back and forth like ping-pong balls. "That's the most dangerous game any man can play."

"You talking from experience?" Ace counters. "Tell me you've lubed your balls with Aspercreme, and I'll never let you live it down. All I have to do is make one phone call to Gunnar. You and I both know his response will cause long-lasting pain."

"You tell your crazy-ass brother I lube up my balls with Aspercreme, and I swear I'll—"

"Thatch." Cassie cuts off their ongoing verbal judo with a hard shove to his shoulder. I stopped watching her the moment they came in, but I have a feeling she's had at least one blue eye pegged on me the whole time. "Stop fighting with your spawn and say hello to his roommate."

Thatch, evidently, turns toward me and smiles. "I'm just going to apologize in advance for you being stuck in a dorm with this shithead."

"Shut up." Cassie hits Thatch in the shoulder again and turns her attention to her son. "Ace, this is Finn."

Ace's response is a jovial grin I've never had the pleasure of sporting, especially not in the middle of a family bicker session. It's a grin only someone with a glamorous life can have.

"Hey, Finn. Nice to meet you."

I jerk my chin up in return.

He looks behind me at my somewhat lacking display of belongings, but I'll give him credit; he doesn't make a big thing of it. "Don't mind us moving all this shit. We should be done soon, and my parents will get the fuck out of here."

"I spent my whole pregnancy and the first ten years of your life not dropping f-bombs, and yet, somehow, it's the only thing that comes out of your mouth." Cassie slaps her son on the back of the head, but he laughs. It's an obvious affection.

"No offense, Mom," Ace says and wraps her up in a big hug. "I'm just saying you can't stay forever."

"Watch me," she fires back, and I have to smother a smile. Cassie Kelly is very obviously a woman who does what she wants, when she wants.

"We won't be here long," the big man named Thatch assures both Ace and me. "You can use your dicks to explore Dickson U all you want in just a couple of hours."

"With condoms!" Cassie exclaims, shifting her smacking over to her husband again. "Good grief, Thatch. Have some decency."

"The kid chose this college because it has the word 'dick' in it, and you think he's thinking with anything else?" He snorts. "Get real."

"Excuse me! He did what?" Cassie's eyes go wide as she turns her attention back to Ace. "You did what?"

"Mom, relax. Dickson is a great university. Does it really matter why I chose it?"

The three of them start bickering again, so I take out my headphones and put them on. Nine Inch Nails seethes in my ears as I do too, all the things that have added up to this moment running through my mind.

My rich, ridiculous roommate may have chosen this college on a whim, but I came to my decision a little differently.

Almost two years ago, on the day before my seventeenth birthday, while my dad was gone on a bender, I stumbled upon his journal from several decades prior. I thought it was just a place he used to scribble his shit music notes at first, but a couple of pages in, the contents changed entirely. Instead of writing songs, he detailed all the ways he'd screwed it up—how he'd abandoned his young family, changed his last name, and run away to start over. After years of fucking around completely, drinking, doing drugs, and committing any manner of crimes, he finally decided to settle down…with my mom.

In the span of five years, they had my older brother Reece, then me, then the twins, Jack and Travis, and last but not least, our baby sister Willow. And that was that. He never looked back.

Jeff Hayes moved on, but the world Jeff *Winslow* had created prior to me and my siblings didn't. He has a whole other set of kids—ironically, four sons and a daughter, too—who are an entire generation older than us, and one of them is a professor here. In fact, he's the head of the English Department, and my first class on Thursday is with him.

Professor Ty Winslow is in for the surprise of his life, and as much as my dad is the asshole in this scenario, I can't wait to give it to him.

I guess I'm an asshole too.

Thursday, September 5th

Finn

Rain pelts me in the face as I make the stroll from my dorm in Graham Hall down 120th Street in the direction of where the Newton Building sits on the corner of Broadway. This is my first official class of the semester—English Lit with Professor Ty Winslow.

Other kids run and shriek like the water will melt their skin away, but I bask in the feeling of each cool drop on the heat raging inside me. A brewing ball of anticipation and excitement and a tiny sliver of anxiety churn in my stomach as I think about the look on my target's face as I turn his world upside down.

From all my research on the Winslow family, I know that Ty Winslow's had an easy time with money and an even easier time with getting whatever the fuck he wants. He and his brothers are all wealthy—though, I'll admit, he's the least silver-spooned of all of them—and it appears they've never known struggle, thanks to their cushy life here in the city.

Ty taught at NYU before transferring here to head up the whole English Department at Dickson, and his younger brother Jude owns and runs a PR company for some of the most lucrative clubs in New York. Flynn was by far the hardest to find any information on, but he's got a huge penthouse in the city and some kind of high-profile name in the engineering world. Winnie, the baby sister of the group, is married to the owner of the New York freaking Mavericks pro football team, for goodness' sake. And the eldest, Remington, is an investment broker and day trader with a net worth even Google has an estimation for—like he's some kind of celebrity or some shit.

My three brothers and sister and I, it seems, would have been a lot better off if our dad had abandoned us too. Instead, he drank heavily and got mean nearly every night, and our mom is a hollow shell of herself because of it.

I shake my head to clear it. I don't need to think about that bullshit. I need to think about how I'm going to deliver my first blow to my half brother.

A gust of wind blows as a girl runs past me in her navy-blue cheerleading uniform, a guy in front of her with combed dirty-blond hair already in the alcove of the building, standing and laughing at her as she sprints through the rain. She turns back to say "Excuse me!" as her elbow brushes mine, and a crack of lightning and thunder a mere hundred feet away startles her just as she's finishing the motion.

Her feet tangle on each other, and she trips, falling hard on the water-pooled, concrete sidewalk in front of me. I wince, knowing how much that must have hurt on all her exposed skin. The dude in the alcove laughs harder, like a total dickhead. "Come on, Scottie," he calls carelessly. "Get up. We're gonna be late."

I can feel my jaw tick as I step up to the girl and squat down beside her. "You all right?" I ask softly as the rain picks up, coming down even harder. Water drips off the tips of my hair and pauses on the end of my nose before running off to join the rest on the ground.

She's crying a little but trying not to when she looks up at me, her gaze piercing me right in the chest. Her features are somehow soft and bold at the same time. Plush lips, flushed cheeks, and full, perfectly shaped dark eyebrows that are the exquisite frame for her long-lashed doe-like green eyes.

A tear slips past her right eyelid, mixing with the rain that's already on her olive skin, and I find myself discreetly reaching out to brush it off. Crinkles form at the corners of her eyes at my touch, and she blinks up at me, her gaze searching mine through the sheen of tears.

She's as mystified by the gentleness of my touch as I am, and a feeling of unsettling familiarity churns in my gut.

Has someone been rough with her?

"Scottie! What the hell?" the asshole in the alcove calls again. "You're getting drenched, and my shoes are still taking on water under here. Just get up and come on."

It takes everything I have not to walk straight over and punch the random fucker in the face, but I don't, and that's all that counts. You see, the Hayes men have a history of solving shit with their fists—I guess we learned from the best—but I'm trying to turn over a new leaf.

I ignore his obnoxious self-importance the best I can and ask my question again. "Are you all right?"

She hesitates a beat and then nods, so I stick out a hand and wait for her to take it. When she does, a shiver runs through me. I guess the chill of being waterlogged is finally getting to me.

"I'm always a klutz—" she explains, her sentence cutting off momentarily thanks to an anguished inhale. I follow her gaze to the spot on her leg where her knee is gushing blood.

"Shit," I murmur just as Prissy Pete arrives with the hood of his Dickson Football-emblazoned rain jacket held up over his precious head in agitation.

"What the hell, Scottie? You're bleeding."

It's an accusation, not an attempt at comfort. I nearly roll my eyes.

"Come on," he says again, but this time, he drags her up from her seated position straight into a run.

She glances back at me apologetically as she trots to keep up with him on a limping leg, but I just jerk up my chin. Like my older brother Reece always says: *Not my rodeo, not my horses.*

It doesn't matter if this particular horse is beautiful.

I've got bigger fish to fry, and the grease will start sizzling in about ten minutes when I come face-to-face with Professor Ty Winslow for the first time ever.

Scottie

Dane keeps a grip on my wrist as we scurry down the wide hallway of the Newton Building and head into the auditorium-style room of our first class—English 101 with Professor Winslow.

It's the only class we have together, and I don't know why I'm relieved about that fact, but I am. Maybe because it'll be easier to concentrate.

Dane Matthews has been my boyfriend for the past two years. The clichéd star quarterback and cheerleader couple of our high school, we started dating when we were juniors, and now, we're both attending Dickson University together. I'm still a starting cheerleader, but Dane is no longer the star quarterback. He barely got on the team as a walk-on, and seeing as Dickson is a Division I school and their current quarterback, Blake Boden, is a sophomore—who was highly recruited out of Southern California and rumored to have a magic arm—the odds of Dane becoming the star quarterback again are slim.

Though, I'd never say that to Dane. He'd lose his shit in a nanosecond.

College as a whole is overwhelming so far, and this is only the first day of classes. But since moving in a week ago, it's been a constant rotation of cheerleading practice, orientations, and meeting new people. Plus, I've never lived in a big city, and New York is about as big of a city as you can get. I can only pray I'll finally know my way around the campus by the time I start my second semester.

All it takes is two steps inside the lecture hall to remind me of just how different my life is about to be for the next four years. My private high school in Upstate New York was *small*. There are more students sitting in this massive room than in my graduating class.

"Scottie, what are you doing?" Dane asks as his grip on my wrist stops my forward progress to the front of the room. "Let's sit back here."

"But I want to sit a little closer..." Truth be told, I forgot to put in my contacts this morning, and Dane hates when I wear my glasses. He says it reminds him of our sixty-year-old high school librarian, Donna Lanser.

"Don't be ridiculous. Let's sit right here."

"Dane." I lean toward him to whisper in his ear. "I don't have my contacts in. I need to sit closer so I can actually see."

"Don't be a nerd, babe." He laughs and drags me toward two seats in the last row.

I want to tell him he's being an asshole, but I clamp my lips shut instead. Lord knows my calling him out will only make him more annoyed with me, and since I'm now going to have to use my glasses for this class, I decide to pick my battles.

As I sit down beside him, setting my backpack on the floor between my feet, I unzip the front pocket to grab my glasses, but when I don't feel the familiar texture of their leather case, anxiety starts to fill my chest. *Shit.*

"I don't have my glasses," I whisper toward Dane, but he just shrugs.

"Can't say I'm disappointed to hear that. You look way hotter without them."

Looking hot is the absolute last thing I'm worried about right now.

I rummage through the other pockets of my bag and still come up empty-handed. On a sigh, I lean back in my seat and try to figure out my next move, but in my periphery, a head of familiar dark hair catches my eye—the mystery guy who witnessed my clumsy butt tumble to the sidewalk in the most unladylike fashion.

I don't know his name, but he was incredibly kind, despite my having run directly into him in my haste to get out of the rain. He also, as it happens, has the most soul-piercing brown eyes I've ever stared into, the kind of chiseled jawline that Paris Fashion Week would eat with a spoon, and muscles that stand out effortlessly in his rain-soaked T-shirt.

I'm not the only female in the room to notice, though I probably shouldn't. Several pairs of eyes look in his direction as he walks near the professor's desk. He's a little blurry, but from what I can tell, he has a gray backpack swung haphazardly over his shoulder and his dark jeans are just the right amount of tight—fitting like a glove over his firm butt but avoiding the horrible skinny-jean look on his long, toned legs.

He runs his hand through his dark hair as he chooses a seat near the front—*lucky duck*—and sits down in an empty row. Besides me, he appears to be the only person who wants to sit so close to our currently empty professor's desk.

I blow out a breath of air, its contents beleaguered, and glance over at Dane. He's busy staring down at his phone, Instagram front and center on the screen. He must not be aware that I can see what he's doing, because the first thing he does is like a girl from our high school's bikini pic. And then, I see him do the same thing three more times, but for three different girls I've never seen before.

My older sister Wren would say that's a huge red flag, and it instantly makes me miss home. I was close with a lot of girls in high school, but now that we've gone our separate ways to college, it's almost comical how quickly we've lost touch. Besides some of the cheerleaders I've met through tryouts and practice, Dane is the only person I know at Dickson.

And he's too busy staring at IG tits and ass to even notice you.

I open my mouth to say something about it making me uncomfortable, but another voice fills the void first.

"Hey, girl." I look up to find Nadine, a fellow cheerleader, taking a seat beside me.

I smile. "Hey."

"So…" She pauses as she eyes me up and down with one raised eyebrow and a mouth that's curled into a combination of a snarl and a smile. "Why are you wearing your uniform?"

Unlike me, she's wearing jean shorts and a tank top. Her blond hair is voluminous, seemingly untouched by the rain, and her lips are painted red.

"Uh…" I pause and shrug, a little embarrassed. "I don't have any time to head back to my dorm before pictures."

"So, you went full-on cheerleader glam for your classes?" She narrows her eyes and snorts as she grabs a notebook out of her backpack. "You're a better woman than I am. I'd feel like such a dumbass if I had to do that."

I don't say anything in return because what can you even say to that? *Thanks for the insult?*

Nadine prattles on about the professor who's going to be teaching this class. "Word on the street is that he's crazy-hot. McKenzie had him her freshman year and said she could hardly keep her jaw off the freaking floor."

McKenzie is a sophomore and one of the captains of our squad, and Nadine's been trying to kiss her ass since day one. Though, I wouldn't say it's actually benefiting her. Coach Jordan is the one who is in charge, and she currently has Nadine placed on the team as an alternate.

"Who's crazy-hot?" Dane chimes in, looking around me to meet Nadine's eyes.

"You," Nadine teases, and Dane laughs like she just said the funniest thing he's ever heard in his life. "And Professor Winslow."

"Who's Professor Winslow?"

"Oh my God, Dane." Nadine squeals out a laugh so hard it makes her boobs bounce beneath her incredibly tight tank top.

My boyfriend doesn't miss a single jiggle, but I'll admit, neither do I. They're unbelievably obvious. "He's our professor for this class."

Dane smiles at her, and suddenly, the thought of spending the whole class sitting between the two of them while I can't see sounds like a nightmare.

"I really think I need to sit closer, Dane," I interrupt their little powwow. "I'm not going to be able to see anything he writes on the board."

"You can copy my notes."

"Copy your notes? You didn't even bring a notebook. Or a pen."

He smirks like he's the smartest man in the room as he taps the side of his head. "That's because I keep it all stored up in here. Big brain shit, babe. Big other shit, too." He winks at me, but I don't miss the way his eyes glance Nadine's way after he insinuates he has a giant dick.

Which, from what little I know about the male member, he doesn't. From what I hear, six inches is average. Dane is lucky to be five and a half on a good day.

Nadine laughs and twirls a strand of her blond hair with her finger. She also adjusts her breasts so they're resting—and being pushed up—on her arms.

Apparently, the possibility of a big dick is her version of catnip.

I know I should be jealous right now. I mean, he is my boyfriend and he's being completely shameless in his attempt to impress a girl on my cheerleading squad. And part of me, I suppose, is. But this class and my cheerleading scholarship that requires a 3.5 GPA to keep it dominate the rest of me. I need to be able to do well, and Dane's notes, invisible or not, aren't likely to help. He's a C average student at best. To be honest, I'm still not entirely sure what he had to say in his essay to get in here.

"I'm moving to the front," I tell Dane and offer an apologetic smile Nadine's way. "Sorry, but I need to scoot past you. Mind standing up so I can get out?"

She stands up, but Dane stays sitting down, making no moves to follow me.

"See you after class, you little nerd," is the only thing Dane says to me as I swing my backpack over my shoulder and head for the middle aisle of the lecture hall. He does, however, offer a slap to my ass as well. Nadine laughs at his stupid hijinks, and I choose not to glance back in their direction as I descend the stairs to the front.

Instead, I focus on finding a seat in a now-crowded room. The best option, as it happens, is located right next to Mr. Soul-Piercing Brown Eyes because it's perfectly centered with the whiteboard. If it were even one row back, I guarantee it would have been taken by a drooling girl by now, but I guess even a hot guy isn't enough incentive to get picked on by the professor on the first day because the seats on both sides of him are empty. Unless, of course, you're a nerd who forgot her glasses like me.

"Sorry," I apologize as I bump his desk with my backpack when I swing into the seat beside him.

He offers a small smile and nod in my direction, a silent *no problem*, but when he holds my gaze for a good five seconds, my knees buckle. My ass plops down into the cool wood on a smack, avoiding grace entirely. *Real nice, Scottie.*

Too embarrassed by my repeated blunders to face him directly, I pretend to be super busy looking at something on my phone when a text message from my dad rolls in.

Dad: I hope you have a great first day, kiddo. Love you to pieces.

I know a lot of people probably feel like their dad is the best dad, but my dad actually is. He's kind and caring and has made it his life's mission to keep Wren's and my life as normal and happy as possible. Which, if you knew my mother, you'd know it isn't an easy mission at all.

He also worked eighty hours a week as a welder at the steel factory so he could afford to send my sister and me to private school.

Mom didn't help at all with money—in fact, most of the time, she spent it—but she didn't help much at home either. He did it all as best he could in the little free time he had.

Me: *Thanks, Dad. Love you too.*

I go to shove my phone back into my bag, but my poise is still on vacation, and I manage to drop the damn thing on the floor, facedown, with a loud bang.

Of course, my ongoing battle with gravity catches my neighbor's attention again, and I feel his eyes on me as I bend awkwardly around my desk to grab it. If it weren't for the case and screen protector, I'm certain I would've shattered it, but as it is, the only damage is a hairline fracture in the protector at the top by the camera.

"Is it fucked?" he asks on a near whisper.

My smile is self-conscious as hell, and I consider telling him I'm not always this much of a mess, but his phone vibrates on top of his desk and promptly removes his attention from me before I can open my mouth. I'm equal parts thankful and disappointed.

His fingers move furiously over the screen, and I set my notebook and pen on the foldout desk connected to my chair. I sit silently and awkwardly, waiting for him to be done and wondering how I can find a way to apologize again for the mess outside and thank him for his help.

A memory of his thumb reaching out to brush a lone tear off my cheek does the Cha Cha Slide in my head, and my mind takes an immediate, dirty-as-hell detour. *If a simple touch to the cheek is that memorable, what would happen if he touched me other places?*

My face heats from the inappropriate thought. *Jeez Louise, what is wrong with me today?*

"Good morning!" a loud, boisterous voice shouts from the back of the lecture hall, and it grabs both my and my seat neighbor's attention, along with that of everyone else in the room.

I look over my shoulder to find a man dressed in a perfectly fitted gray suit striding in with a briefcase. He has a full head of light-brown hair, but without my glasses, I can't make out much more about his features than that. But from the gasps and sighs around me, it's obvious I'll want to take another look on a good vision day.

"I'm Professor Winslow," he greets with a smile as he walks right past me and my seatmate to his desk. I immediately glance toward the back of the room to see if that horny bitch Nadine is flinging her underwear from across the room, but she's too busy giggling and bouncing her big boobs toward my boyfriend, whom she now sits right beside. Dane is eating it up like a chump.

Is he for real right now?

On a huff, I turn back around in my seat as Professor Winslow drops his briefcase down on his desk. But my elbow manages to make contact with my notebook and pen and shove both onto the hardwood floor of the lecture hall with a slap.

Of course, both items land right next to *his* shoes, and I offer an apologetic frown in his direction. "Whoops." I cringe. *Why can't I human today?*

He shakes it off without judgment, his brown eyes warm, and reaches down with one strong hand to pick up my lost items off the ground. His bicep flexes beneath his T-shirt as he sets them back on my desk, and I find myself wondering how much a guy has to work out to get muscles like that.

I've spent most of my life surrounded by football players, and I've yet to see anyone look as sculpted as this guy. I'd question if he was a student-athlete, but his vibe doesn't give off jock. It gives off...I don't know...mysterious bad boy.

I haven't a clue why, because "bad boys" are notoriously single animals and the absolute last thing a *not-single* girl like me needs, but it only makes him more appealing.

"First day of college," Professor Winslow states with another smile that has some of the girls in my class fanning themselves with one hand. "How are we feeling?"

"Like it's too early for this shit!" someone yells from the back. Professor Winslow laughs.

"I love when the smartasses make themselves known on day one. Makes my job easier."

Holy shit. Cursing and engaging with the class clown to do anything other than send him to detention? College is definitely different from high school.

Unable to stop myself, I glance behind me to see how other people are reacting and then over to my mysterious neighbor. Unlike the rest of us nervous, excited newbies, he looks angry.

Man, I hope he isn't annoyed because of me.

Finn

I don't know anything more about Professor Winslow than the internet and the first five minutes of class have told me, but I already hate him.

The way the girls in my class nearly faint at the sight of him in his expensive suit. The carefree smile. The teasing jokes tossed toward my classmates.

He's the picture of a man whose asshole has had nothing but rainbows and sunshine shooting out of it since his mom was changing his diapers.

He grabs a black marker and starts to write something across the giant whiteboard at the front of the lecture hall, and my heart pounds hard in my chest. My half brother. Here in the flesh.

I still cannot fucking believe my dad has five other kids, and I've known for years at this point.

My fists clench with the effort to stay in my seat—to not jump up and shove the news of our relation right down his smug throat in front of the entire class. But I don't think it'll do me any good to blow my load this soon. I need to strategize to make sure it hurts as much as possible—to make sure he feels the way I've always felt.

My phone vibrates again on top of my desk, and Scottie the Cheerleader glances my direction furtively. She's a bundle of nervous energy, so I'm not surprised she looks this way with pretty much every move I make.

I check the screen, figuring it's one of my siblings—the most

common texters in my inbox—but instead, it's my roommate Ace...
again.

> *Ace: Dude. Why didn't you tell me the two blocks between our dorm and Newton are fucking SWARMED? I've lived in New York my whole life, and I feel like I've never seen this many people out at one time. Don't these assholes have anything better to do???*

I don't know what it is about Ace Kelly, but for the past six days, he's made it impossible for me not to be his friend. He's just one of those people who demands your friendship and does it in such a way that you find yourself going along with that plan willingly.

He's wild, boisterous, is always making jokes, and gets a thrill out of pranking people. How do I know this? Because I've already witnessed *three* of his infamous pranks, and we've been roommates for less than a week.

The two clueless dudes in the dorm room across the hall from ours came out of their place this morning dressed in their finest clothes—looking nervous as hell—because they're convinced the dean wants to have a personal meeting with them.

There's no meeting. Only Ace and his pranks.

Regardless, I don't bother telling him it's not my job to babysit him or wake him up for class. Given his personality, I feel like he's going to have to learn to swim or sink the hard way.

> *Ace: I think I'm, like, five minutes away. Has he started class?*

> *Me: He's writing on the whiteboard as we speak.*

> *Ace: SHIT.*

Phone returned to my desk, I move my eyes back to my target. My half brother who's had life by the ass and didn't have to experience our father's violent, drunken ways.

Lucky asshole.

My older brother Reece would be so pissed at me for coming to Dickson for the reason I did, but Reece can suck a fucking egg. He chose to go to college in California—thousands of miles away from home—and he's not the one who discovered our dear old dad has a whole other family.

I clench my fist and open it again but am shocked that the motion finishes with Scottie the Cheerleader's hand on mine. I'm startled by her touch, but to be honest, she looks startled too. Her hand is remarkably warm and soft.

I look down at where her fingers are gently placed over mine and then back up at her again.

"Here," she whispers and slides a folded-up piece of notebook paper into my hand.

Confused, I unfold it until I can see what's inside—a note in some of the prettiest fucking handwriting I've ever seen in my life. It's all swirls and clean lines and nothing at all like my chicken scratch.

I'm sorry about before. Outside. When I was a super klutz. You must think I'm a total bitch for running off on you without a thank-you. I swear, I'm not! I really wasn't trying to be rude. Thank you for trying to help me.

PS: I'm Scottie Bardeaux. What's your name?

Without even thinking twice, I pick up my pen and scribble a response.

Finn Hayes. And I don't think that. But I do think your knee is still bleeding.

I pass the note back to her and then reach into my backpack to snag a tissue. She's still reading my response when I tap the excess blood off her knee. She jumps a little when the soft cloth hits her skin, but other than that, she just sits there, her warm hazel eyes fixated on my face as I dry her scrape.

I don't know if it's a fucking cheerleader thing or a college girl thing, but Scottie Bardeaux is beautiful. Girls back home never looked like this.

She's wearing makeup, but it doesn't look like a ton—my ex used to cake the shit on like she was tarring a roof—and from this close, I can see that the hazel of her eyes is more green than anything else. It's just the gentle ring of brown in the center that makes them look the way they do.

Thank you, she mouths before putting her head back toward the paper and scribbling out another response. I watch the way her white teeth dig into her full bottom lip so intently that I'm startled when Professor Winslow's teacher's aide, Doug, drops a syllabus packet on the desk in front of me.

I don't bother reading it. My plans for this class don't quite follow the same bullet points as Professor Winslow's.

Scottie slyly slides the notebook paper back to me, and I've got the paper open to her new words in seconds.

Got any plans this Friday, Finn? The cheerleaders are throwing a party with the Delta Omegas at their house on Sorority Row.

I don't know why seeing my name in her handwriting urges the hint of a smile to form on my lips, but it does.

And while I'd love to do a lot of things with Scottie, going to some party with sorority chicks and frat bros isn't one of them.

I appreciate the offer, Scottie, but I'm not really a party kind of guy.

Her response is back on my desk mere seconds later.

Really? That's a surprise.

When I glance back at her, she's focused on Professor Winslow as he starts to talk about our first reading assignment—*Wuthering Heights*.

I should probably pay attention too, given the financial aid requirements for me to stay enrolled here, but finding out why she would be under the impression that I like to party seems like a higher priority.

Why is that a surprise?

She glances down at the paper and then back at me before quickly scrawling out a response.

You just look like trouble, you know? But, like, the good kind. Don't be mad. LOL

Is she flirting with me? I move my eyes to her, and even though she's not looking in my direction, I don't miss the way her cheeks are flushed pink.

I thought this girl had a boyfriend—*an asshole boyfriend, at that*—but when I glance toward the back of the class where I saw his douchey head full of blond hair when I first came in, there's a matching blond chick sitting beside him.

She's bouncing her tits like they're balls on a seal's nose, but his eyes are locked on me, a scowl sitting front and center on his lips.

What the fuck is happening? Is she using me to play games with her boyfriend?

Scottie's quiet demeanor, attention on the lecture, and the fact that she hasn't noticed my silent interaction with her boyfriend at all only makes me more confused. Truthfully, I don't think she's glanced back in the fuckface's direction a single time.

I turn back to the front, pen poised over the paper to tell her I don't want to be a part of whatever fucked-up thing she has going on, when the sound of the lecture hall doors slamming open with a loud bang grabs my—along with everyone else's—attention.

Ace jogs in, a backpack slung over his shoulder and his dark hair a mess on top of his head. He's wearing jeans with a wrinkled T-shirt, and his long legs eat up the aisle as he moves toward the front of the lecture hall.

"Can I help you?" Professor Winslow questions, squinting toward Ace's entrance.

"Sorry, Ty…I mean, Professor Winslow!" Ace calls out as he keeps moving up the rows of seats. "Running a little late this morning."

"Ace, I'm sure I don't have to tell you that this is—" Professor

Winslow starts to comment, but another bang from the lecture hall doors slamming open stops him midsentence.

"Sorry, I'm late, Professor W!" Ace Kelly's big-ass dad calls from the top of the stairs.

Ace is just plopping down in the seat next to mine when his brain registers his father's voice. "What. The. Fuck?" Ace mutters, horrified as his dad's humongous legs eat up the distance toward us in a heartbeat.

"Acer! Save a seat for me, bud!"

"Thatch Kelly, to what do I owe the pleasure of this massive disruption to my class?" Professor Winslow questions and crosses his arms over his chest.

"Well, Prof, I've decided to go back to college," he responds like it's the most normal thing in the world. "And I figured, what better time to do it than now."

"You're taking this class?" Professor Winslow asks, a smile just barely on his lips.

"You bet your academic ass I am."

I glance back and forth between the two of them in abject realization—they know each other. My roommate's dad is *friends* with my stupid half brother.

Thatch gestures to the girl in the seat next to Ace to scoot over, and she does, not knowing what else to do, I imagine. He takes the seat next to his son, and Ace just sits there, glancing back and forth between his dad and me.

"Dude. Am I hallucinating?"

I shake my head.

"My dad is really here? This isn't a fucking nightmare?"

I nod.

"Fuck me."

"It's gonna be a good year. Right, Acer?" His dad gives him a soft nudge of his elbow as he makes a show of getting notebooks and pens and shit out of his backpack that literally still has the tags on it. He even has a fucking stapler and paper clips. "Me and you in college. Hell yeah!" He meets my eyes with a big-ass grin. "Hey, Finn. Good to see you, man."

I smile, completely despite myself. Seeing Ace this close to a mental breakdown while his dad full sends it is hilarious.

"Dad, what the fucking fluff is happening right now?" Ace asks, his voice shaking in a whisper.

"Oh, c'mon, son. You're going to have to start calling me Thatch around our peers. Don't want them assuming I'm some boring-ass old man. I'm the original dick-swinger, you hear me?" His words may be meant for Ace, but they're loud enough for the whole class to hear them.

Guffaws and side-splitting laughter take shape all around us.

"Oh my G-od," Ace whispers, horror making the benediction at the end catch in his throat. "Are you having a stroke? Does Mom know you're here?"

"By Mom, I'm sure you mean my hot-as-balls *girlfriend* Cassie—*whom I just so happen to be legally wed to*—and yes, she knows. Hell, she's so jealous, I wouldn't be surprised if she's enrolled by the end of the day. Though, she is *pissed* she missed rush week. Sorority sparkles and TikTok dances are her jam." His laugh is hearty. "You think we can get her a late entry, Ace Face?"

Ace stares at his dad, each gulp of his mouth turning his skin more ashen.

"Yeah, okay, you think on that," Thatch says and flips open his notebook. He leans over Ace and whispers to me, "Did I miss anything, Finn?"

"Do not even humor him with a response," Ace snaps at me and shoves his dad's big head back toward his seat.

"Oh, come on, bud. I can't make a bad first impression for my first class."

"Your first class?" Ace questions. "As in, you have more classes?"

"Oh yeah. I made sure we have the same schedule," Thatch updates and chooses one of the twenty pens he has sitting on his desk to scribble something in his notebook. "By the way, I'm going to own your ass in accounting."

Every student inside the lecture hall is one hundred percent fixated on Ace and his dad's conversation, including me, and I realize it's been that way for several minutes without interruption. When I steal a glance at Professor Winslow at the front of the room, I note that he's outright smiling now.

I roll my eyes. He's trying so hard to be cool that he's just letting this sham play out in its entirety. It's annoying.

Ace is at a loss for words finally, opening his notebook and turning to the first blank page, when his dad leans over to his face and whispers in a boom that's loud enough for all to hear, "Prank champion."

Ace's face is a mask of shock, horror, and undeniable awe. Thatch bursts into laughter.

"You're shitting me?" Ace questions, and Thatch just waggles his brows in amusement.

"Remember this summer? When you paid NYU acting students to pretend to do an FBI-style raid on my office? Consider this payback, baby."

This family is fucking nuts.

Students shout and cry out, and kids stand up and charge toward us to high-five Thatch one by one. It's mayhem.

Professor Winslow lets the madness and absolute hysterics of an overwhelmed class roar for a full minute before taking command again. "All right, everybody. Time to relax," he orders, waving his hands up and down for both the volume and for people to take their seats again. His voice is a rumble as he adds, "Thatch, with all due respect, get the hell out of my classroom."

"Cool your nuts, Ty," the giant man-child says in reply. He pulls out his phone and snaps a picture of Ace. "Just needed to get a photo of this amateur's face before I go."

Thatch stands, shoves all of his notebooks and pens and shit back into his backpack and pats Ace on the shoulder with a hard but loving hand. "Don't mess with the king."

Ace is laughing and shaking his head at the same time. "You're such a dick."

Thatch winks. "Never forget that I've got friends in all the right places." And just like that, as quick as he came, he's gone.

Ace looks back toward our professor and glares. "Thanks a lot, man."

Professor Winslow is still grinning. "Maybe next time, you won't be late to my class."

Ace nods and rolls his eyes before whispering toward me as he pulls a notebook out of his messenger bag. "I hope you know that you're officially an accomplice to my next crime."

I quirk an eyebrow.

"There is no way in hell I'm letting my dad get away with that bullshit without retaliation."

My attention is pulled back to my desk when Scottie grabs the sheet of notepaper from it and scribbles something down before shoving it back over to me.

Now you have to come to the party on Friday. You and your friend Ace. No excuses.

And at the bottom of that note? Her number.

Ace sees it immediately, the nosy bastard, and snatches it from me. He's giving Scottie the thumbs-up before I can even process any of it.

She smiles and looks down at her desk to concentrate, her cheeks pinking up once again.

So much for telling her I'm not getting involved.

I t's almost midnight—two hours later than we originally planned to leave for the party I don't even want to go to—and we're still in our dorm room.

But, as I'm starting to learn, thinking I can do absolutely anything my way without Ace Kelly fucking it up this year is mistake number one. He's a force to be reckoned with, and after living with him for a week, I feel like I've gained a new, hugely dysfunctional, but somehow lovable extra appendage.

Honestly, I wonder if this is what my brothers Jack and Trav feel like being twins. Like there's just a whole other set of arms and legs attached to their own, doing shit that's unpredictable, or another brain theirs has to consult before taking action—because that's Ace in a nutshell.

"Do you like this shirt?" he asks, pacing in front of the mirror and then turning to face me with his arms held wide. "Or is too… like…I dunno…"

"Preppy?" I offer, staring in offense at the popped-up collar of his polo.

"No."

"Rich?" I try instead, to which he shakes his head.

"No, no. It's, like…what's the word I'm looking for?"

"I have no fucking clue," I answer honestly. "And I swear, if you make me think about it for another second before picking something so we can leave, I'm going to bed."

"Okay, okay," he placates, holding up a hand before disappearing behind his bed again to dig in the closet. I scroll my phone, pausing on TikTok for a while, then flitting to Instagram, and finally considering Scottie's number for a few seconds, wondering if I should text her to say we're running late.

Which is dumb. I hardly know her, she has a boyfriend, and I have zero business getting in the middle of any of it.

When Ace eventually reappears in a three-piece suit, I don't even blink.

He challenges my steely demeanor, looking for a reaction. I don't give it. For all I care at this point, he can wear a turtle shell and call himself Donatello.

"Okay. I think I'm ready."

I nod and clap my hands before dragging my ass off my desk chair. "Great. Let's go."

"Whoa, whoa, not so fast. We still have to wait for Julia."

I groan. "I'm not even sure Julia actually exists. *Julia this, Julia that.* All you've done this week is talk about this girl, and I've yet to see her."

He frowns. "I haven't talked about her that much."

I guffaw, and he rolls his eyes.

"We grew up together. Our parents are best friends."

"Ah, yes. Richie Rich playdates. Who else was there? Macaulay Culkin?"

"What?"

"Come on. You haven't seen that movie?"

Ace shakes his head like I'm crazy, but I can picture a whole list of eighties and nineties movies with perfect nostalgia. We didn't have the money for streaming service bullshit, so we watched my mom's VHS collection on an old VCR when my dad was out of town. When he was home, he hated the sound of anything that resembled children.

Ironic for someone who fathered so many of them.

"Whatever. It doesn't matter. If she's not here in five minutes, I'm leaving her ass."

"My, my, another threat. How surprising. Who hurt you, Finn? Really? Because your coping skills could use some work."

I flip him off and groan, dropping back into my desk chair to wait yet again. My friends from high school would have taken me at face value and gotten their shit together because I intimidated them. It was part of my pseudo-persona, I guess—being a tough guy who didn't take any shit.

But Ace Kelly is so immune to my powers, I think he might have some of his own. Between that and the fact that he manages to keep me liking him even when he's a royal pain in the ass, I'm going to be trying to figure him out all year.

The sound of a soft knock on the other side of the door comes ten minutes later, and I drag Ace right through it as soon as he pulls it open. Julia has blond hair and blue eyes and a gentle laugh that grabs my attention.

She's not surprised by the lack of greeting or the fact that my grip on Ace's suit jacket collar is making him crow-hop or even that he's in a suit to begin with, confirming that Ace hasn't been lying about their growing up together.

She knows his shit and then some.

Still holding Ace on his toes with my arm stretched up high because the fucker is taller than Jack with the beanstalk, I hold out my other hand and introduce myself. "Hi, Julia. I'm Finn."

"Nice to meet you," she returns with a smile. She's pretty—so pretty, in fact, that I'm not at all surprised anymore that Ace seems kind of obsessed with her.

"Next time, don't be so late," I chastise unabashedly. Maybe two hours ago, I would have had more patience to be less rude, but right now, it's gone.

A small crimson dot spreads into a circle in her cheek, and her eyebrows draw together. "Late? I thought I was early. Ace told me twelve fifteen."

"Twelve fifteen?" I drop my hold on his collar instantly and turn toward him. He stumbles a little before laughing and shaking out his jacket.

"You can't go to a party at ten o'clock, Finn. That's nerd behavior."

"I do what I want."

He laughs again, this time hitting a note so carefree, I almost lose it. "Oh, I know. I can tell you've got that quality, a fine gentleman like yourself. That's why I took matters into my own hands."

"Ace!" Julia comments, stepping forward to slap him on the shoulder.

He glances at his watch. "Now, we *are* late, and if you punch me, you'll fuck up my suit and I'll have to change again, making us even later, so I suggest we just go."

What was that I said about liking him again?

"Come on, Ace," Julia chides, pulling him along like a puppy. "Finn's patience with you seems to be depleted."

"She's observant," I mutter, and both she and Ace laugh. Remarkably, the sound of it puts me back in a good mood, and we're on our way.

To a party on Sorority Row to see a girl I have absolutely no business seeing. God help me.

Scottie

Steam filters off the grass in front of the Delta Omega house as some of the frat lackeys hose down the slip 'n slide again with water and bubbles. The air is cool, but the ground is still warm from the sun of the day, and the difference in temperature shrouds the front yard partiers in a cloud.

I let the curtains fall back into place and turn back to the party inside. It's loud—so much so I can't even make out the song that's playing—and there are bodies everywhere. Some people are dancing, some people are chugging beers out of helmets with funnels, and a whole other contingent is playing flip cup on the dining room table.

I shove through a group of giggling girls and head toward the group of cheerleaders that's congregated in front of the kitchen, glancing back toward where I've just come from more times than I'd like to admit on the way.

I am at my first college party, action all around me, and I can't keep my eyes off the stupid door.

A frat guy snags a stack of pizza boxes from an Uber Eats driver, and two more groups of scantily clad girls trickle through the door on arrival, but still, there's no sign of Finn Hayes.

"You waiting on someone, Scottie?" Nadine questions, her eyes narrowing on me as I make it to my teammates.

I shake my head. "Just wanted to see what they were doing out there. Two Delta Omegas just did the slip 'n slide together in their bras."

Nadine laughs at that. "I bet that had the tongues wagging."

"Come have a drink with me!" Dane slurs as he roughly wraps his arm around my shoulders, fresh from the kitchen with a new drink. His big frame makes me trip over my shoes, and he laughs when my hip bone careens into a nearby chair. So does Nadine.

I wince from the discomfort. *That'll probably leave a bruise.*

"Uh-oh…looks like your boyfriend is shit-faced, Scottie," Kayla, one of the cheerleaders I came to the party with, comments. It could be catty, but from her tone and what I know about her, she seems to be saying it sympathetically.

"Don't be such a downer, Kay," Nadine purrs and flashes a wink at my lazy-eyed and loose-lipped boyfriend. "Let the man have some fun."

"Damn straight, sweetheart! Let the man have some fucking fun!" Dane agrees enthusiastically.

Nadine giggles, but I don't see the humor. Instead, I stand on my tiptoes to whisper into Dane's ear. "Don't you think you've had a little too much to drink? Don't forget you're in season right now. Technically, we both are."

Once you make any team at Dickson, you have to sign a contract that pledges you won't drink or do drugs of any sort while in season. If the university finds out you've broken that contract, they'll kick you off the team. And they're allowed to test any time they want to.

"Damn it, Scottie," Dane snaps back, shoving me away from him hard enough that my back impacts the wall this time. His gray eyes grow dark with annoyance as he stares down at me. I don't think he's actively trying to hurt me, but the booze has pretty much ensured he's not feeling remorse either. "Why do you always have to be such a killjoy?"

"Hey there, buddy," a different male voice chastises from behind before stepping in between us. "Go easy on your girl, yeah?"

"Suck my dick, Boden," Dane retorts to *the* Blake Boden, his teammate and nationally recognized starting quarterback for the Dickson Dragons.

Blake's gaze moves to mine, a concerned warmth making his

eyes look like the Caribbean, and I shake my head toward him. It's a silent *I'm okay*, even though I'm not necessarily feeling it.

At the end of our senior year, Dane really got into drinking more heavily, and sadly, it only seems to enhance every asshole bone in his body. We wouldn't have lasted two years if this was the way he'd always been, but the majority of our relationship was different. We were different.

He was different.

He used to pick flowers for me from the front of the school and write notes to me during class, and every Friday night, we did movie night in his parents' basement, just the two of us. I still have the fake movie stubs he made me for all of them.

But when he acts like this, I have to fight my inner-child instincts to go fetal and cower in the corner. He reminds me too much of my mom before my dad divorced her and took full custody of my sister Wren and me. Our mom always turned into the worst kind of drunk when left to her own devices.

She's been to rehab too many times to count—her latest stint having just finished up a month before I graduated. Wren and I still haven't given in to her requests to see us. She says she's really turned over a new leaf this time, but after seeing her as nothing but a mean drunk for most of my life, her words don't hold any power.

Blake Boden eyes me for a long moment before three bouncy Delta Omegas wearing Boden jerseys that have been cut to reveal everything but their nipples drag him toward the large living room of the house, where a makeshift dance floor has been created in front of the DJ.

I watch as Blake smiles down at the girls, dancing with all three of them in a way that makes it apparent this isn't his first time handling more than one woman. I guess that's how it goes when you're the star quarterback of the school. Add in the fact that Blake is single and has the kind of shaggy strawberry-blond hair and blue eyes that would make most girls my age describe him as *stupid hot*, I have a feeling he rarely spends his nights alone.

"You coming, Scottie?" Dane asks, unconcerned with Blake Boden on the dance floor or any of his own transgressions against me. I shake my head. "I don't think so."

He lets out an annoyed huff, but that's squelched when Nadine pipes up, her voice a classic eager beaver. "I'll go, Dane."

"Hell yeah! Someone who wants to have some fucking fun!"

And off they go, my boyfriend and another girl, straight into the kitchen where there's more booze than I've ever seen in my life. It covers every counter and available surface, and coolers line the whole back wall.

"You okay?" Kayla asks, placing a gentle hand to my shoulder, and I nod.

She leans closer to search my eyes, a twinkle in her deep brown eyes and perfectly white teeth. "You sure?"

"Promise." I shrug it off with a smile that feels foreign on my lips. "He's just drunk, and Nadine's just Nadine."

Kayla laughs so hard at that, her whole head of spiral curls shakes—everyone on the squad knows how Nadine can be.

"How long have you been together?"

"Two years."

"And you both decided to go to Dickson?"

"Not exactly." I shake my head. "I got a cheerleading scholarship, and Dane decided he wanted to go here too."

"Interesting."

There's a small part of me that wishes Dane would've done his own thing. That there would've been a university that wanted to recruit him. But Ivy Prep's football team never garnered the kind of attention that our cheerleading squad did.

We won Nationals all four years that I was in high school. The football team, on the other hand, was lucky to end the season with a handful of wins.

"I want to tell you something, but I don't want to come across as rude," Kayla says and steps closer to me, wrapping her arm around mine. "Promise you won't get mad?"

I tilt my head to the side. "Well, that depends. I mean, if you're going to tell me I look like a troll tonight, then consider my claws out because I spent an hour trying to get this smoky eye right."

"Shut up. You're gorgeous."

"And so are you." I nudge her playfully with my elbow.

"I don't want to talk bad about your boyfriend, but…"

"But what?"

"He's, like, really careless with you."

I furrow my brow.

"I just think you deserve better. That's all I'm going to say." She raises both hands in the air before pretending to zip her mouth shut. "Consider my lips sealed from any more commentary for the rest of the night."

I'm at a loss for what to say—mostly because I feel a burning embarrassment at the thought of being a girl who has to be told she deserves better—but an interruption by one of our fellow cheerleaders shuts down the conversation entirely before I have to say anything anyway.

"Ladies, it's time to dance!" Tonya exclaims, grabbing us both by the wrists.

On a giggle, Kayla goes along willingly, but I find myself staying rooted to my spot. "You guys go ahead. I'm going to run to the bathroom. I'll catch up with you soon."

"Scottie, your cute ass better make its way on the dance floor soon, or else I will come find you!" Tonya calls toward me, and I just laugh, holding up both hands.

"Be there soon. Promise."

Once the two of them get lost in the sea of writhing bodies, I lean my back against the wall and let out a deep exhale. Normally, I'd be one of the first people on the dance floor, but tonight, I don't know… I'm just not feeling it.

Surely it's just been a long week with lots of adjusting. Between practice and classes and Dane being a bit of a dick lately and simply trying to figure out this whole college thing, my anxiety is at an all-time high. It doesn't help that the Delta Omega house is filled with more people than the whole of Ivy Prep—which was K-12—and my nervous system is telling me I need to go back to my dorm, put on some pajamas, and binge-watch *One Tree Hill*.

Music pounds through the speakers that sit on either side of a local DJ who is currently doing a mashup of "Party Rock Anthem" and a song I've heard a million times in stadiums.

The one that goes *whoa oh oh oh-oh*.

When the beat drops and the lyrics *Shots! Shots! Shots!* echo inside the room, I don't miss Dane in the corner doing exactly that. One, two, three, he downs the small glasses of amber liquid in quick succession and pounds his fists against his chest like he's Tarzan.

Good grief. My annoyance makes a pit form in my stomach, but the small crowd of people around him is verbally celebrating his dumbassery with chants and fist pumps. Nadine claps and cheers so hard, I fear her tits might make a bid to escape her crop top like cats coming through a newly opened door.

Nadine Jones, put simply, doesn't like me. Sure, she's flirtatious with everyone, but I'd have to have been born yesterday not to understand Nadine's underhanded comments and blatant seduction of my boyfriend stem from our current situation on the cheerleading squad—I'm the only freshman with a starting flyer spot—exactly what Nadine was gunning for. So, unless something happens to me or one of the other flyers, she's stuck at alternate.

Cheerleading can be cutthroat, so this isn't something I haven't experienced before. It just sucks that it's another thing I have to deal with while I'm trying to adjust to college life.

And truthfully, I'm not good at the whole drama thing. I'm a people pleaser to my core. A lover, not a fighter, and the type of person who clams up in any type of confrontational situation. It's like my brain misplaces all its words for a few days and then finds them again when I'm revisiting that confrontation in my mind.

I'm the queen of "I wish I would've said that," just like Meg Ryan in *You've Got Mail*.

Dane appears to be pouring himself another round of shots, and I can no longer witness the drunken clown show. I pull my phone out of my jeans pocket to check the time—**12:30 a.m.**

Still no sign of Finn Hayes.

Yeah, I don't think he's coming. And I think it's time to go home.

On a sigh, I start to head for the mudroom of Delta Omega's massive three-story brownstone to grab my purse, but before I can round the corner into the hallway, someone shouting, "Ace Kelly!" fills my ears.

I spin on my heel, my eyes going straight for the front door.

Ace Kelly and a super-pretty blond girl who's in my calculus class named Julia Brooks are there, and someone else is right behind them.

Dark hair. Warm brown eyes. With my contacts in tonight, I can see both just fine.

Finn Hayes. Here. In the flesh. *And looking as hot as ever.*

Did he come here because I invited him? Or did Ace drag him here against his will?

It takes every bit of self-control I have not to run directly to the door to find out. Frankly, I don't know that it would have held out if it weren't for Kayla grabbing me by the hand and pulling me into a quiet hallway back behind us.

"What's going on?" I ask, trying to pay attention to her and split focus with the door at the same time. It's out of my eyeline, though, so I have no choice but to behave pretty quickly.

"Girl, I hate to be the bearer of bad news, but Dane and Nadine just made a bet with someone to take three more shots each."

Well, hell. If that isn't karma telling the girl with the boyfriend that the hot guy she's crushing on is going to have to wait, I don't know what is.

7

Finn

We're not even through the front door of the fancy Delta Omega house when I have to dodge the first elbow to the face. It's not some crazy partygoer, though, but my roommate, announcing his presence like he's a member of the royal family.

"Ace Kelly in the house!" he cries obnoxiously, garnering the shouts of an apparent fan club shortly after. I'm not surprised he's popular—he's charismatic and rich. But I am surprised by the number of people who already seem to know who he is within the first week of school.

With a roll of her pretty blue eyes, Julia steps around him, and I take that as a cue to do the same. When she smiles back at me, I'm reminded why Ace does nothing but talk about her. Her features are almost delicately feminine, and her eyes are a crystal-clear blue ocean that seem to go on for miles.

"Come on, Finn. Let's go get a drink. You're going to need it, living with Ace."

I chuckle and follow her gratefully, not bothering with the tedious explanation of my general aversion to alcohol. It's not that I'm righteous or sanctimonious or some bullshit—you just see it a little differently when you grow up with a mean-as-fuck drunk.

She shoves her way through a group of writhing bodies first, me following behind, and takes a cup of beer from the guys at the keg on the far side of the food bar. They eye her longingly, dicks perking in their pants like ears on a dog, and I find myself crowding her back possessively. Maybe I'm fucked in the head, but for some reason, I'm feeling protective of Ace and his feelings, even if he doesn't realize them yet.

Because for all he says they're just friends, I sense there's more brewing beneath the surface. I've only known Ace for a week, but six out of seven cumulative days have been spent on the topic of Julia. A guy doesn't talk that much about a girl without deep feelings being involved.

If I got paid a dollar every time he brings her up, I'd be a rich fucker too, and all my problems would be solved.

The tallest one of the drooling suitors is still an inch or two shorter than I am, so my back crowding makes him change the way he's looking at her entirely. The determined scowl on my face may be another reason his hot-girl hope bubble has been popped, but Julia, thankfully, doesn't seem to notice any of it.

She hands me the first beer and takes another. "Thanks," I remark, relegating myself to the idea of just holding the cup until I can find somewhere to put it down.

Julia lets me turn her away from the two of them—which I finish out with a wink over my shoulder—and guide her back out into the living room through the crowd. She turns to smile at me gratefully when we're not being absolutely choked by bodies anymore, and I actually return it. Just like Ace, she's got an undeniable magnetism.

Ace comes bounding over, and I step aside to allow him the space to flail. Julia laughs, and against my will, I do too. He's just that kind of guy.

"Oh, man," he pouts. "You got beer without me?"

"Here," I offer, holding my cup out. "You can have mine."

Ace wraps an arm around my neck and pulls me toward him. "Aw, schnookums! You're the best." I shove him away jovially, and he laughs.

"You want me to go get you another one, Finn?" Julia offers.

I shake my head. "I'm good."

Neither she nor Ace pushes the issue, and I allow myself to like them both a little more, despite my better judgment. It's not that I don't want the full college experience or that I don't want to make any friends at all. I just have a bigger, conflicting goal while I'm here, and if Ace's parents are friends with Ty Winslow, chances are good that Julia's are too. And I'm not so sure they'll like me after I eventually follow through with my plan to turn his world upside down.

Sure, it's a half-baked plan at this point, but once I open the can of we-have-the-same-dad worms, there's no way Julia and Ace will still want to be friends with me.

Because friends don't hurt friends, and everything inside me wants to hurt Ty Winslow. I want to see the look on his smug, my-life-has-been-a-cakewalk face when he finds out we both have the same deadbeat dad. I want to see him feel an inkling of what it's like to have our shitty father actually stay in your life and the kind of destruction that causes.

My phone buzzes in my pocket twice in two short bursts, and I pull it out to read the text. It's from one of my younger brothers.

Travis: At tne Grto, Cver for me?

The Grotto is a really sketchy, unofficial club where underage kids in our town hang out because they don't ID, and they can drink and screw around without the cops showing up. I find it creepy as fuck, since it's in the catacombs where old New Yorkers are buried.

Drinking may not be my thing, but Travis and Jack—my younger twin brothers—can't seem to get enough. Before I left for college, I was normally their DD, their protector, and their get-out-of-jail-free card. Frankly, keeping the two of them out of trouble has been a full-time job ever since they hit puberty.

> **Me: I'm at Dickson, Trav. You're going to have to find someone else to cover for you while you're at the Grotto. And for the love of everything, DO NOT DRIVE DRUNK.**

> **Travis: Akl good. I wont drve.**

"Fuck."

"What's wrong?" Ace asks, surprising me. His goofball act is absent from his face. Julia turns to us, attentive too.

"Nothing." I shake my head and shove my phone back into my jeans. "Just one of my younger brothers getting into trouble like usual."

He and Julia both let out huge exhales and nod simultaneously. My eyebrows draw together, but Julia rushes to explain. "We both have crazy younger siblings too. Though, my sister Evie is Taco Bell mild sauce compared to Ace's brother, Gunnar."

"Dude." Ace runs a hand through his dark hair. "My baby bro is off his rocker."

"More so than you and your dad?" I question with a knowing smirk. Ace doesn't get defensive at all, instead nodding with wide eyes while Julia laughs herself sick.

"Tell him about Gunnar's fourteenth birthday, Ace!"

"That crazy fucker paid off the window cleaning guys of our building to take him up to the 69th floor so he could stand outside our living room windows in his underwear with the words *Birthday Boy* painted on his chest."

"And if that isn't already crazy enough," Julia chimes in, and the most adorable snort leaves her nose. "He timed it perfectly when Ace's parents were throwing him a surprise party. Everyone was standing in the living room, waiting to yell 'Surprise!' but Gunnar was behind everyone through the windows."

"Julia's mom about had a stroke when Gunnar started pounding on the glass instead of coming through the door," Ace states, smiling over at her.

"And your mom literally grabbed a butcher knife from the kitchen and threatened to cut his balls off if he didn't get his feet back to pavement!"

"And that's just the tip of the iceberg." Ace laughs.

"How sure are you he wasn't involved in the whole *Titanic* debacle?" I ask teasingly, making Julia snort beer through her nose.

Ace offers the sleeve of his suit coat to Julia without hesitation, adding, "I'm terrified for the day he starts college."

"Me too. And your parents are going to be out of their minds. They're worried about you, and you're only a fourth of his crazy on a good day," Julia teases. "The number of times your mom *and* my mom have texted me about you since we moved in to the dorms would make your nipple hairs stand on end."

"What?" he questions, putting his hands over his nonexistent boobs out of reflex. "What the hell are they saying?"

She pulls her phone out of her purse and shows the screen to both of us. It's a text conversation between Julia and Ace's mom, Cassie.

> *Cassie: Is Ace still alive?*
>
> *Julia: Yes.*
>
> *Cassie: Is he planning on pranking Thatch back after that idiot showed up in Ty's English class?*
>
> *Julia: Also, yes.*
>
> *Cassie: Son of a bitch. Maybe we should've sent him off to a college on the West Coast. Watch him for me, okay? Honestly, leash him if you have to. I'm not above leashing my kids.*
>
> *Julia: I thought they only did that with toddlers with a run-into-traffic tendency?*
>
> *Cassie: And? You've just described Ace, sweetheart. Anyway, I couldn't send him to the West Coast because I need you together, and we both know your stage-five-clinger mother would've spent the next six months crying her eyes out if you were so far away.*
>
> *Julia: Speaking of my mother, I think it would be REALLY*

great if you take her out for some drinks so she's too busy to call and text me every 10 minutes.

Cassie: *I'm on it, Jules. Love you, girl.*

"Letting my mom secretly keep tabs on me? You're a sneaky little turncoat, Julia."

She narrows her eyes. "Like you're not texting with my mom too."

"Hey, I can't help that Georgia and I are besties." Ace smiles over at her like a guy who would lick the ground she walked on if she asked, and I silently wonder when he's going to become aware of his feelings for her.

But when he wraps his arm around her shoulders and sways her playfully from side to side, I get the feeling that denial is his coping mechanism of choice. The two of them are in sync, and it's not just because they've known each other forever.

"Hey, Scottie!" Julia exclaims across the room suddenly, startling Ace's arm off her shoulders when she shoves her hand into the sky to wave. I turn slowly to look, though my heart is pacing anything but slow, and lay eyes on the girl who invited me here tonight in the first place.

She's standing in the back of a rowdy crowd, but for some reason, I can see her perfectly.

Her long brown hair is pulled up in a fancy ponytail with loose strands curled around her face, and her fit body is covered in a tight black dress, a jean jacket, and black Converse sneakers. Her eyes shine in the DJ's lights.

Fuck. She looks incredible.

She notices Julia first and then me, her gaze flicking theatrically in a double take. It takes a minute and several mini conversations of explaining herself, but eventually, she maneuvers herself away from the boisterous crowd that includes her douchebag boyfriend and the flirty blonde who sat beside him in our English class.

I can't seem to find it in myself to look away as she closes the distance between us, no matter how much I know I should. Several idiots gawk as she crosses the room, but I'm not surprised. Scottie's petite build and uniquely striking face are hard to resist, especially for a bunch of dudes with low impulse control.

When she arrives, her eyes on me, Julia smothers her in a hug so intense the two of them end it in giggles. Ace and I look on like a couple of schmucks, but Julia quickly includes us.

"Scottie, do you know Ace and Finn?"

"Yeah! The three of us have English class together," Ace confirms. "Scottie here is the one who invited Finn tonight." He waggles his eyebrows at Julia. "Remember…I was telling you how Finn has no friends except for the one girl—"

I knock the back of my fist into his stomach, a gentle warning, and he stops immediately. Julia smiles and laughs.

"I'm kind of sad your dad isn't actually enrolling," Scottie jumps in to tease, and Ace groans.

"Trust me, you're not. He's a caricature of a human."

"Says the apple under the tree," I say with a gravelly chuff.

Scottie's eyes meet mine and then flutter to Julia and Ace too. "I didn't think you were coming tonight…any of you. It got late."

I tilt my head toward my three-piece-suit-wearing roommate. "Someone had a bit of a clothing crisis."

"That wasn't the only reason," Ace counters, but someone yelling both his and Julia's names steals his focus. A few seconds later with a brief excuse to us, the two of them are heading toward a guy I've only seen on ESPN before, Blake Boden. Evidently, Ace knows our star quarterback in a more personal sense.

"I'm glad you came," Scottie says, her voice a mere whisper now that we're alone.

"Yeah?"

"Yeah." She nods, and a piece of hair falls in front of her face. My fingers reach out to tuck it behind her ear before I can stop them.

My stomach feels like a lead-filled helium balloon—simultaneously in my throat and my toes. Her eyes lock with mine for a long beat, the unspoken connection between us tethering just the two of us to a moment and making the crowd disappear.

But the contact is broken suddenly and violently, when a body barrels into hers, making her sway so hard she almost falls.

It only takes a second for me to realize it's her boyfriend—a brutal reminder of how little business I have stealing moments with her at parties.

"Wha the fucks, babe?" he slurs. "You over here flirting with this dude in my face?"

"Dane," Scottie says placatingly.

"She wasn't flirting, man," I correct, stepping closer to him. "Just saying hello."

He tosses his head back on a laugh as he roughly wraps his arm around Scottie's shoulders. "And what's a friendly hell-o it was."

Every bone in my body wants to get nose-to-nose with this drunk fucker and tell him to stop being so fucking aggressive with Scottie, but a loud cry across the room startles our attention. The flirty blonde from the back of English class is on the floor and holding her wrist with a grimace on her face. Several girls help her stand on unsteady feet.

Scottie shoves out from under Dane's arm and runs toward them. Dane follows, and against my better judgment, so do I.

"We told you not to drink so much, Nadine," a girl I don't know says to the blond flirter, who's actively crying now and still holding her wrist. "What if it's broken? What's that going to do to our season?"

"I'm an alternate this year," Nadine grits out. "Scottie has my position covered, remember? So, what's it even matter?"

"Nadine, you know how important you are to the team," Scottie consoles, which is more than I can say I would do, given the way she's behaved every moment I've been around her.

"Ugh, this shit is so boring now," Dane complains. He grabs Scottie's arm forcefully then, dragging her in the direction of the door with no warning. Her face flinches, and I step forward without even thinking. Next thing I know, I'm right in the middle of their mess again. "What the fuck? You just about ripped her arm off."

"She's fine," he says with lazy, bloodshot eyes. "And she's my fucking girlfriend. Not yours. Lay off."

A potent mix of anger and adrenaline dumps into my veins, and I clench my fists at my sides at his complete lack of remorse and concern. *This motherfucker.* He's just as vile as my deadbeat dad.

My vision tunnels, homing in on his stupid face, but a gentle hand on my shoulder pulls me back before I can shove that anger straight between his eyes.

I don't even realize it's Ace until he steps in front of me. He's lucky I didn't turn and swing on him.

"I'm Ace Kelly," my roommate says, introducing himself to Scottie's boyfriend. "You're Dane, right?" Sticking out his chest, Dane unwraps his arm from Scottie so he can shake Ace's hand. Julia steps into the hole he left, carefully pulling Scottie back from the staggering asshole and over toward me.

"You okay?" I ask just as another guy takes a spot at my back and says the exact same thing. When I turn to look, I'm expecting anyone but Blake fucking Boden.

Scottie shakes her head once and then again before finally smiling at both of us.

"I'm okay," she says then, but I know that face—I've fucking lived it.

She's anything but.

"**R**eally," I say again, willing myself to be more convincing. "I'm fine. It's no big deal. Everyone's just had too much to drink."

"Not everyone," Blake corrects, staring daggers at Dane. Nadine is still hysterical, while Kayla and Tonya try to do damage control.

"You don't seem drunk at all," Finn asserts, and I roll my lips into my mouth before explaining. It shouldn't be embarrassing to be sober, but under the immense pressure of college eyes to "be cool," it is.

"We're not supposed to drink during the competition season, and I can't jeopardize my scholarship." I also have a lifetime of dealing with a drunk mother that's tainted my view of alcohol, but that's not the kind of thing I share with strangers.

Blake nods. "I'm not drinking either."

"You're not?" I ask, my voice a little relieved, even to my own ears.

He shakes his head. "Of course not. Coach would kick my ass."

"Pussies," Dane taunts, having overheard the conversation despite Ace Kelly actively talking to him to keep him busy. "It's just a little booze. It's no big deal."

"It *is* a big deal," Blake Boden challenges. "We've got one girl hurt and one who you practically yanked in half. It's time to cool it."

"Fuck off, Boden."

I blush at how freaking embarrassing he's being, and I shove through Tonya, Kayla, and Nadine to grab Dane's hand. "Come on.

It's late anyway, and you have practice tomorrow morning. Let's go sleep it off."

Dane turns cocky then, trying to save face. "Come on, baby. You know we aren't gonna sleep if you put me in a bed."

"Dane!" I snap, really over his shit tonight. He's lying to make himself look good, and I hate it. This is *not* the guy I've been with for the last two years. We haven't even had sex because I'm not ready, but again, none of this is the kind of stuff we need to be telling *strangers*.

"All right, all right. Fuck. Les go, then." It's a slur of compliance, but compliance, nonetheless.

I glance back to Finn and Blake, mouthing an apology. Blake smiles and gives me a salute, but Finn stares me down so hard—his eyes an intense mix of concern and confusion—that *I* end up bumping into Dane. He laughs. "I may be drunk, but you're the fuckin' klutz," he taunts.

"Dane, stop."

"You fuckin' stop, Scottie. You're not my mom." Dane is in my face now, the smell of booze emanating from his every pore and stinging my nostrils. "I wish you'd get the giant stick out of your ass and try to have some fucking fun."

This is not the Dane I loved. Not the Dane I knew. This is not the Dane I owe my loyalty to. I am done with a capital D. If he wants to be a total dick to me, then the last thing I'm going to do is help him.

"You know what?" I shove him away from me. "Find your own way to bed."

"Don't be a bitch," Dane sneers.

"Hey!" Finn says then, completely startling me by being *right there*. Blake and Ace are both behind him. "All she's done is take care of you tonight, so maybe you should treat her with a little more respect."

"Fuck that!" Dane declares in front of the *entire party* full of people, his voice loud and unmistakable. "If she wanted to take care of me, she'd actually let me fuck her. Two years with this bitch and the best I can get is a fuckin' hand on my cock."

"Wow." Nadine starts cracking up. "That's pathetic."

Deep, overwhelming embarrassment runs through my entire body as Nadine continues to cackle uncontrollably while several others laugh. Tears threaten in the corners of my eyes, and the urge to get the hell out of here is overwhelming.

Julia and Kayla look on sympathetically, but I don't dare look at anyone else. I can't. I am *mortified*.

Finn

Scottie takes off at a run, through the living room and toward the back of the house. I look on, everything inside me wanting to chase after her but knowing I shouldn't. For the sake of her embarrassment, and because of everything I know about myself, she's better off without me. Kayla and Julia head in that direction instead, while I look on, my spine rooted so straight, my jaw aches.

Nadine takes over coddling Dane, her whining about her fucked-up wrist playing supporting actress to telling him how amazing he is, and the two of them toddle off together out the front door.

Blake is the first to say something to ease the tension after their exit. "I fucking hate that guy."

"Dude," Ace comments on a laugh. "He's the worst."

I find myself laughing a little at the truth of their statements, but for Scottie, I know nothing about tonight has felt funny. I don't know how a girl like her found herself in a relationship with a guy like that, but I only hope that she starts to see the light.

I stare in the direction she went, as though I'll be able to X-ray vision my way through the damn walls, but all thoughts of Scottie are cut off when my phone starts ringing in my pocket and I see my brother Jack's name on the screen. *Shit. Those motherfuckers better not have driven home.*

"'Lo?"

"Finneyyy," Jack croons, his drunkenness taking on a much more jovial state than that of dickhead Dane.

"Tell me you're not driving," I say by way of greeting.

"Well, see, the thing is…we don't wanna drive, really, but everybody else is drunk too. And if we don't leave soon, Mom's gonna freakkk—"

"Do not get in the car, Jack. Do you understand me?" I talk over him before he can try to tell me their clearly dumb-as-fuck plans. "I'm coming to get you." The last thing I need is for one of my brothers to get behind the wheel right now. I knew when I decided to go to Dickson—and with our eldest brother Reece in Cali—that shit like this could come up. I just didn't expect it to be a thing the first damn week of college.

"No. No. We gots it," Jack slurs. "Trav said you got school and shit."

I swear, these two will be the death of me.

"Jack, stay put until I get there." My words come out harsh because they need to be. "It's going to take me at least an hour because I have to take the train to my car, but *stay fucking there.*"

"But Mom will be—"

"Don't worry about Mom," I cut him off. "I'll handle it. Just keep your asses there."

"Sorry, Finney. Reallllyyy sorry, Finney Finney Bo Bennyyy."

"Jack?"

"Yeah?"

"Shut up."

"Ten-four."

I hang up with a sigh.

"What's going on?" Ace asks, and I look up to find him eyeing me closely.

"I have to go to Westchester to get my brothers so they don't do something stupid."

"I'm coming with," he says, and I shake my head.

"You don't need to do that."

"I know, man, but that's what friends are for." He pats me on the shoulder. "Just let me tell Julia I'm going."

"I want to come too," Blake Boden says then, surprising the shit out of me. "This party is lame anyway."

I shrug, too tired from all the other bullshit tonight to fight it. "I guess it's a group outing, then."

Looks like some people from Dickson are going to get a little glimpse into my real life a bit earlier than I expected.

10

Finn

If I didn't think Ace Kelly was rich before, I certainly do now. All thanks to his personal driver, Gary—whom he has on speed dial—the three of us made it to Westchester in thirty minutes flat.

I was set to take a train to Westchester and then hike the three blocks to the side street where I park the car I bought without my parents knowing. It's a Buick LeSabre from the nineties, but it gets the job done, and if my dad knew, he would have sold it for cash. Still, the whole thing would have taken me hours, and with Jack and Trav drunk and impatient, I'm actually thankful Ace butted in.

During the drive, I found out I'm not the only one who Ace's powers work on as Blake regaled me with how Ace won him over during their one elective class together—which is bookkeeping, of all things. Evidently, Ace sacrificed himself on the sword of their professor when Blake's checkbook balance was off by saying he'd sold him a black-market calculator that changes ones to fours. It's fucking ridiculous, but so is Ace. One stupid class together, and Ace has the star quarterback on his squad.

It's amazing, really. A case to be studied by historians in the next century.

As Gary pulls the shiny black Escalade into the dim parking lot of the Westchester Catacombs, all vestiges of the good-time guy I was on the ride here are gone, and the hard-ass older brother in me takes over.

My twin brothers Jack and Travis are screwing around at the

edge of the parking lot, while our little sister Willow sits on a bench near the entrance door to the stairwell that leads underground. Jack is wearing a damn parking cone on his head, and Travis is swinging his shirt around his head like a lasso.

"I'm going to kill them," I mutter as I hop out of the SUV before Gary has a chance to pull it to a stop. Music from the still-open Grotto vibrates the ground as I stalk toward my two idiot brothers.

"Finney!" Jack shouts at the top of his lungs. "You're here!"

"Hells yeah! Finnsishere!" Travis cheers, alcohol hindering his tongue's ability to enunciate.

Willow cringes on the bench, fully knowing that her brothers' theatrics aren't helping with my already volatile state. I don't bother with hellos. "You brought Willow to the Grotto? Have you two asshats lost your minds?"

"Don't be mad, Finn," my sister jumps in, standing up from the bench as she does and crowding me away from Jack and Trav. "I begged them to let me come out tonight. It's not their fault."

"Not their fault?" I snap disbelievingly, staring down Jack and Travis. They've sobered enough to stop screwing around in the parking lot and actually listen, but the parking cone is still on Jack's head and Travis is still shirtless with his T-shirt resting in his hand haphazardly by his side. "I'm gone for what? Not even two weeks? And you're letting our *sixteen-year-old* sister come to this sketchy-ass place so you can drink?"

"I'm not a child, Finn," Willow attempts to interject. "I'm more responsible than Jack and Trav, and you know it."

My sister may have a valid point about responsibility, but the Grotto is the last place a sixteen-year-old girl should be.

Travis is the first to break.

"Sorry, Finns. She begged." He holds both arms out wide, but that movement makes him trip over his own two feet.

"Yeah, Finn." Jack's head bobbles up and down. "Her jackass boyfriend dumped her, and she didn't want to be home alone while Mom was at work."

"Wait…what?" Travis questions, looking over at Jack before his eyes land on Willow. "Stupid Steve broke up with you?"

"What the hell?" Willow cries out, pointing an accusing index finger at Jack. "I told you not to tell anyone."

Jack is bashful, though the parking cone on his head really lessens some of the effect.

"Willow, why didn't you tell me?" Travis questions, his eyes softening around the edges.

"Because I'm embarrassed, okay?" she mutters, and I don't miss the fact that a few tears prick her eyes. "And you're a total hothead."

"Low, I swear, just say the word. I'll kill him." Travis steps toward her to place a gentle hand on her shoulder, proving that he is, in fact, a fucking hothead. "No questions asked."

"Travis," I chastise when I realize shit is going way off the rails. "Cool it."

"What? I'm being serious. No one makes my baby sister cry. I'll bury Stupid Steve's body in the backyard. I don't give a flipping shit."

"Tabasco Hot. Maybe Fire. I dunno. Too early to tell," Ace remarks from directly behind me, and I glance over my shoulder to find him and Blake standing there with amused smiles on their faces. Gary still sits behind the wheel in the idling Escalade.

I sigh. Run a hand through my hair. "Jack, Travis, Willow, this is Ace Kelly, my roommate. And Blake Boden," I halfheartedly introduce, hoping my brothers are too drunk to notice who Blake actually is before I get back to reaming their asses.

Unfortunately, Jack doesn't miss a beat.

"Oh, holy balls!" he shouts at the top of his lungs, his parking-cone hat falling off his head when he starts to gesture wildly with his hands. "*The* Blake Boden? As in, one of the best fucking college quarterbacks in the nation?"

Blake smiles and waves, the motion making him look like a young, super-muscular Ron Howard. *Gee golly gosh* might as well be the next words out of his mouth. "Nice to meet you, man."

"I just want you all to know I'm uncomfortable living in this kind of shadow. Blake, I don't know if we can be friends anymore," Ace teases, and Blake shoves him in the shoulder.

"Finn, your new college friends are hot," Willow says, propelling her breakup with Stupid Steve distinctly into the past.

"Low, you're too young," I interject without remorse. "And you two idiots—" I turn to Jack and Travis "—if I ever find out you brought Low here again, I'll be the one burying bodies in the backyard. We clear?"

"Yeah," Travis says, holding up two hands.

"Fine," Jack agrees.

"Finn Hayes. Aren't you a sight for sore eyes?" The distinctive voice is as aggressive as always, and my balls make a bid to climb halfway inside my body as I turn in the direction of it.

Dressed in a pair of cutoff jean shorts, cowgirl boots, and a crop top that barely covers her pushed-up tits, Sara Dean, my ex-girlfriend, flashes a flirtatious smile in my direction as she pushes through the door from underground and sashays toward us.

Son of a bitch. What a special hometown reunion this is turning out to be.

"Oh, by the way, Finn," Jack whispers, "your ex-girlfriend is here tonight."

Ace, the fucker, practically chokes on his own saliva, he laughs so hard.

I roll my eyes and force a neutral smile to my lips. "Hey, Sara."

Her hip sway is obnoxious as she approaches our small group, and she doesn't stop until she's directly in front of me, so close her breasts brush against my chest. "That's it? Just 'Hey, Sara?' C'mon, Finn. You've had your dick in me. Pretty sure I deserve at least a hug."

I'm annoyed at her for saying that shit in front of my sister, but she doesn't give me a choice, wrapping her hands around my shoulders and gripping tightly as she hugs me. Her face falls into a frown when I pull away sooner than she wants.

"Did you come to party?"

"No. Just here to get my brothers and sister."

"Who are your friends?" she asks then, eyeing both Ace and Blake up and down. Sara loves attention, and if I'm not giving it to her, she's willing to find it somewhere else.

"Ace, Blake, this is Sara."

"Sara. Receiver of Finn's dick. Got it," Ace says, the shit-stirrer. I glance at him over my shoulder, the obvious context summed up in a glare. He raises both his hands, a picture of innocence. I shake my head.

"It's nice to meet you," Sara says to Blake specifically, and it comes out like a purr. She licks her lips. "Why don't you come inside for a drink?"

Fuck no. It's time to end this shit. "We can't," I interject.

"Why not, Finn?" she questions, stepping closer to me again. "It's been a while since you and I have had some fun…"

A year ago, sadly, this shit would have worked on me. I was lonely enough and angry enough that wrapping myself up in Sara seemed as good an option as anything else.

But these days, for some reason, it doesn't seem like enough.

"We gotta go. Sorry."

She starts to open her mouth, but Ace surprises the hell out of me by cutting her off at the knees.

"While I'm always up for a good time, Sara, we need to head out."

She pointedly looks at Blake, and he nods in agreement.

"Maybe some other time."

"Boo." Sara pouts. "You boys are boring."

Thankfully, her best friend Maddie peeks her head out the door, shouting, "Sara! Get your bony ass in here! Rusty just bought a round of shots!" The call of alcohol on other people's tabs is too strong for her to deny, and Sara heads back into the Grotto with a little wave and more flouncing of her ass.

"Sorry we didn't give you a heads-up," Jack comments immediately.

"Yeah, man," Travis agrees. "She's here all the time now. I think she's still dating Zach King. You remember him?"

Of course I remember Zach King. He's one of the biggest pricks who went to my high school and the first guy Sara fucked after we broke up. I don't bother telling my group of current company that, though.

"Get in the Escalade. Now."

It's then that all three of my siblings notice the car we pulled up in. Their eyes damn near bug out of their heads at the sight, but they know better than to say anything at this point. Willow takes off at a run behind Ace, who is already leading the way, opening the back passenger door for everyone to climb in. Trav and Jack get in next, followed by Blake and me pulling up the rear.

"Where are we headed, Ace?" Gary asks from the driver's seat, completely unbothered by my drunken siblings as they fumble around inside.

Ace looks at me expectantly. He doesn't know our address, obviously.

"Thirty-two Oakwood," I instruct. "It's about four miles from here."

Gary is already putting the address into his GPS. "You got it."

"By the way, Gary, this little trip is under the radar," Ace remarks with a sly smile. "Don't want the parental units to get jealous that their life is way more boring than mine."

Gary laughs. "Roger that."

"I can't believe you have a fucking driver," Travis marvels, looking at Ace.

"Dude. You're like rich, rich," Jack adds, staring at Ace like he's a damn celebrity. "I want your life."

Ace just shrugs. "Gary's been with me since I was fourteen. And before you agree to Freaky Friday with me, you should meet my parents," he says with an overzealous laugh. "They're fucking crazy."

Willow bites into her lip and stares at her lap, and Jack and

Trav look straight at me. We know crazy parents too. Just not the good kind.

"Heard your dad showed up to Winslow's class on the first day to prank your ass," Blake comments, and Ace just rolls his eyes.

"Yeah. Rat bastard." Ace sighs and laughs at the same time. "All I know is that once I figure out my next move, payback will be a bitch for him."

Blake and Ace chatter back and forth about Ace's possible future pranks on his big-ass dad, and my siblings become less and less preoccupied by our shitty upbringing and more and more riveted by Ace's explosive storytelling. I don't miss the way both guys include my brothers and sister in the conversation, and I'm grateful for it.

A friend like Ace Kelly was nowhere in the cards when I was planning my first year at Dickson. And yet, I think I'd miss him. It's so fucking weird.

By the time Gary pulls up to the house, Jack and Travis think they're going to attend a college party—because Ace took it upon himself to invite them—and Willow's face might as well be the fucking heart-eyes emoji every time she looks at Blake.

I sneak them all into my house while Blake and Ace wait in the driveway, and I slip out the back door once I know everyone is safely in their rooms with their doors locked.

There's still a chance they'll have hell to pay in the morning if my dad noticed them missing, but if he's asleep now, he probably had no clue.

With my sister and brothers safely tucked away, there's only one person left to worry about tonight—the girl I have no business thinking about at all. Before I climb back in the car with the guys, I send her a text I probably shouldn't.

Me: Are you okay? It's Finn.

11

Scottie

The concrete steps of the pedestrian court in front of Beckley Theatre chafe at my bare thighs as I look up into the street-light so Kayla can grab the eyelash that's worked its way into the corner of my eye.

We walked while I cried for thirty minutes or so, and then Julia suggested we sit down somewhere we recognized so we didn't end up lost. It was a good idea. I've hardly spent any time on the east side of campus so far, and being this close to the football stadium will make it easy to find my way back to my dorm when I can get it together.

All my smoky makeup is caked beneath my eyes instead of on them—I can feel it—but Julia and Kayla have been nice enough not to mention it.

My breath comes out in a stuttered puff, the tail end of my sobs turning into uncontrollable shaking. Julia wraps an arm around me and rubs just as Kayla gets the offending lash.

"Got it!" she cheers, holding it up in front of me on her finger.

I laugh sardonically. "I think it's a little late to make a wish on it, though."

"I know you're upset," Julia says softly, squeezing at my bicep. "And you deserve to be after what happened back there." Kayla nods in solidarity. "But I promise you, the only one who looks stupid is Dane. Outing all your business in front of everyone like that?" She shakes her head. "After being so rough with you in public?" She leans her head into my shoulder and hugs me. "You deserve so much

better than that, and there wasn't a single person at that party besides Dane and Nadine who couldn't see it."

Embarrassment sits on my lungs, heavy and all-encompassing,
and it suddenly feels hard to breathe again.

I have two years of history with Dane, but with the way he's
been acting since we got to Dickson, all the history is starting to
feel like it never even existed. It makes me wonder if my memories
are clouded by rose-colored glasses.

Has he always been this way, and I just wasn't letting myself see
it? Or has he really changed into someone I don't even recognize?

I let myself think of high school and the way things used to be.
"He wasn't like this," I hedge carefully when the barrage of everything our relationship used to be makes me feel a little less crazy. I
don't want to defend him now—his behavior is unacceptable—but
once upon a time, I loved Dane for a reason. "I know most people
say that because they were ignoring the red flags, but I swear, for the
first year we dated, our junior year, he was so patient and kind. He
brought me flowers to school every day, even when his mom had to
take him to get them because he hadn't gotten his license yet, and
he liked that I applied myself in my classes. He used to joke that
he was going to be a house husband while I ran the world." I shake
my head as fresh tears form in the corners of my eyes and threaten
to fall. "I don't know what happened."

Kayla shrugs in front of me, grabbing my knee and squeezing.
"You outgrew him, and I think he knows that."

Julia nods. "If he belittles you, he thinks it'll make you slow
down. But Scottie, you don't deserve to slow down for anybody. The
right guy'll ride a rocket to the moon if you're inside it, you know?"

I nod. They're right. And I know it. I just can't believe it all had
to happen this way.

"You guys, I'm going to be okay." I stand from my spot on the
steps and brush off the back of my dress. "You can go back to the
party."

"Are you sure?" Kayla asks, standing up in front of me and dabbing at the mess on my face one more time.

I nod.

But Julia eyes me with concern.

"I promise. I'm okay," I say, my words only a little more resolute than I'm feeling. "It's time for the whole thing with Dane to come to an end. I'm tired of trying to find a way to fix him. I'm tired of giving him the benefit of the doubt. I'm just…tired. But no conversation is going to happen tonight, so for now, I just need to climb under my covers and rest."

A girl should feel safe and protected and loved by her boyfriend. Not like she's walking on eggshells all the time out of fear she's going to do or say something that will upset him.

"He's an asshole," I say out loud. Kayla's and Julia's eyes go wide, but they also both nod. "No matter who he used to be, now, he's, like, a really huge asshole," I add. "The other night, I was scrolling through TikTok, and this girl on my FYP was talking about how her ex was a narcissist, and everything she was describing is exactly what Dane does to me. Do you think he's a narcissist?"

"Girl, I'm certain he is," Kayla comments without hesitation. "He's always gaslighting you. Always doing whatever he can to make you feel bad. He's a dick. A total fucking dick. And with the way he acted tonight, it honestly makes me worried for you."

"Do you think the same thing?" I look at Julia. "I mean, this was the first time you met him…"

Julia nods. "My dad is like the chillest, most understanding guy on the planet, but if he found out a guy I was dating was treating me like that, I honestly think he'd end up in prison on murder charges."

"So, it's just as bad as I think it is." I cringe. "Good thing you're dating a guy like Ace. He seems like a real character, but also, a total sweetheart."

"Oh, *hell no.*" Julia laughs. "I'm not dating Ace. He's legit just a friend."

"What?" Kayla whips her head toward Julia. "Seriously?"

"I've known Ace my whole life. We're just friends."

"Are you sure?" Kayla questions. "Because I thought you two were together."

"Holy moly! Yes, I'm sure!" Julia exclaims on another laugh. "Ace and I aren't like that. We're just good buddies."

Both Kayla and I share a look, and Julia doesn't miss it.

"Stop it right now," she says through a snort. "We are just friends. Period. End of story."

"Okay." Kayla grins. "You're just friends. But when you end up marrying him, I'm going to remind you of this conversation."

Julia snorts. "You're insane."

A yawn makes my mouth gape and my cheeks shake, and Kayla gives my shoulders a squeeze. "You sure you don't want us to hang out with you tonight?"

"I'm positive." I pull her in for a hug. Then, I do the same to Julia. "You guys are the best. Thank you for taking care of me. I'll talk to you tomorrow."

"Oh wait!" Julia says and pulls out her phone. "I need your digits, girl."

It doesn't take long before we both have each other's numbers, and I'm heading back to my dorm while they go the other direction, back toward Sorority Row.

The walk to Delaney, the girls' dorm, is a short trek through Wheaton, where the teachers' offices are, and then a quick jog across Broadway. There are people everywhere, despite the fact that it's late, and I feel surprisingly safe even though I'm by myself.

The door on the Broadway side doesn't have a key scanner to get in when the doors are locked—a fun little fact I forgot—so I round the corner onto 116th Street to go in the entrance at the end of the building. I dig in my bag for my key for a full minute before finally finding it, and unfortunately, by the time I look up, there's no time to turn around.

Dane. He's sitting on the steps in front of the door, hard eyes on me as I approach.

"Where the hell did you go?" he questions, his mouth set in a firm line. He stumbles to his feet just as I reach the first step. "I've been waiting for you here for hours."

I know for a fact that it hasn't been hours—it's only been a little more than an hour since I left the party altogether. He's just too drunk from all the alcohol he's consumed tonight—I can still smell it wafting off him—to have any real concept of time.

"I don't want to talk to you right now."

"Scottie, don't be like that. Let me come up."

"No." I shake my head, and when he tries to grab my hand, I yank it away from him.

"What the fuck, babe?" he questions and steps closer to me. "Just let me come up."

I crowd the door, but I don't unlock it yet. "Good night, Dane." I don't know what I think he'll do—if he'll rush the door and overtake me or something—but he's been just unpredictable enough tonight for me to question it.

"Why are you being such a bitch?"

The tension in my shoulders and the knot in my stomach tighten like vises. I'm stretched to the max capacity, my heart feeling like it'll jump outside of my chest at any moment from pure desperation, and his words are my tenuous hold's undoing. This conversation should be happening tomorrow, when he's sobered up, but I can't do this anymore.

I need finality now.

"Dane, it's over." The words are harder to choke out than I expect. There's so much history, so much heart between us. But more than that, in this moment, there's fear. A whole hell of a lot of it.

And that's a giant red flag. I won't allow myself to ignore it.

"What did you just say?"

I swallow hard. "I said, it's over."

"You're breaking up with me?"

I nod.

"You're breaking up with me?" he questions again, a scoff leaving his lips. "Wow, Scottie. How fucking pathetic are you?"

I shake my head. It's so disappointing to watch someone you once loved become so cheaply callous. "Goodbye, Dane."

"So, that's it? Two years together and that's all you're going to say?"

With the way he's treated me for the last month and a half, I don't know where he finds the audacity to be sentimental about all the time we've spent together, but it *does* strike a nerve. I don't want it to, but it does. "We aren't who we used to be, Dane. Either of us. You crossed a huge line tonight, and regardless of the past, I'm unwilling to let it happen again. I can't be with you."

"You're such a bitch, Scottie." A maniacal laugh jumps from his lungs. He steps closer to me, and for the first time, real dread sends a chill down my spine and into a tingle in my toes. His previously mellow eyes are a harsh storm of malice, and I don't know what he's going to do next.

"Everything okay here?" an uncharacteristically strong female voice asks. I look around Dane's imposing body to see the source. It's a girl from my dorm, obviously coming home for the night. She's got copper-red hair and fairylike features, but I swear the tone of her voice made her sound six feet tall. I've never met her, but I've seen her around.

"Everything's fine," Dane slurs. "Mind your business."

The girl looks at me for a real answer, and I know by the way my teeth are chattering that my smile is shaky at best.

She reaches out to grab my hand, boldly putting her body between Dane and me. "Ready to call it a night?" She's asking, but she's not *asking*. We haven't stopped moving since she gripped me.

I don't dare look over my shoulder to see what Dane is doing. Instead, I clutch her hand probably way too tightly as she unlocks the entrance door with her keycard and puts herself between me and Dane.

As soon as we're inside, she slams the door closed with a click.

Dane stands there staring at me through the glass, but she doesn't let me be a part of it for long, dragging me up the stairs a flight and out of sight.

"You going to be okay?" she asks when we stop. Her honey eyes are so sincere, I can't stop myself. I reach out to pull her into an abrupt hug. She gives me more than I can ask for by squeezing me back.

"Thank you," I whisper into her ear. "Just…thank you."

When we pull away, she wipes a tear I didn't even realize I'd shed from my cheek with the edge of her sweatshirt sleeve. "Is that guy your boyfriend?"

I shake my head. "Not anymore." The words don't quite feel real, but they do feel right.

"Good," she says. "I'm Carrie, by the way."

"Scottie."

Her smile pulls down at the corners of her long-lashed eyes. "I hope to see you around under better circumstances."

I nod. "Me too."

"If you're good now, though, I'm headed to bed. I'm exhausted."

I crack a smile of my own—a real one. "Me too."

With one last wave, Carrie climbs to the third floor before dipping through the stairwell door to head to her room. I stay on the second so I can make a stop at one of the vending machines. I'm on the fifth floor, and vending is only on the even numbers.

I grab a bag of pretzels and some M&Ms and then jog up the three remaining floors of stairs, practically sprint down the hallway, and lock myself in my dorm room. Tonight, of all nights, I'm thankful that I don't have a roommate. I was supposed to, but according to my RA, the girl backed out of admission right before move-in day. All the other girls of Delaney are stuck sharing their space and their toilets with other girls. I have to go to the communal bathroom for showers, but I at least have my half bath to myself.

It's not long before I'm under my comforter, eating my pretzel and M&Ms mix from a bowl, and scrolling mindlessly on my phone.

With the weight of the evening, stupid internet content seems like the only way to shut my mind off enough to be able to sleep.

It's only when I close out all my apps to finally give in to exhaustion that I see the little red number two on my messages icon. I open it immediately, hoping it's not Dane.

The first is from Wren, babbling about some movie scene starring Glen Powell, which I'm sure will seem more worthwhile tomorrow.

But the other is from an unknown number and makes me sit up in bed with a scoot, turn on my bedside lamp, and put on my glasses.

Are you okay? It's Finn.

Finn. Holy shit. My heart pounds furiously inside my chest, tripping on itself every time I try to take a breath. My hands shake as I program his number into my phone and try to find the right words to say back.

Me: Yeah, I'm okay.

It's a ridiculously simple message that makes me roll my eyes, but it's the best I can come up with under this kind of duress. My head is still spinning from the whole freaking night. Not to mention, he texted this a while ago, so who even knows if he'll text ba—

Finn: I know you have friends, but if you're ever looking for someone you can come to when things get bad, you can come to me.

Me: When things get bad?

Finn: Scottie, your boyfriend shouldn't treat you like that.

Me: I guess it's a good thing he's not my boyfriend anymore, then.

Finn: You're done?

Me: He showed up at my dorm tonight after everything. I broke up with him.

Finn: Okay, then. Good.

Okay? Good? That's it? I bounce up and down in my bed, shaking my hands in a silent scream. Where the hell am I supposed to go from here? I can only think of one thing to say, and it feels unbearably pathetic. Desperate, I send it anyway.

Me: I guess I'll see you in class, then?

Finn: Yep.

Yep. Gah, why are boys so hard to understand? Is he just a short texter? Is he over it? What the hell is he thinking?

I take a deep breath in and close my eyes to calm down. *Scottie, you need to chill.*

Right. Well. Okay. I mean, whatever. At this stage of the game, I need to focus on myself anyway. Dane and I have been together for the majority of my transition to adulthood. Half the time, I'm not even sure I know who I am anymore.

For now, I need to think about me, so Finn Hayes's text messages and what they may or may not mean don't matter anyway.

Right?

Right.

Me: Goodnight, Finn.

Finn: Goodnight, Scottie.

12

Finn

"**W**ait up, dude," Ace calls from three floors up. I'm pushing through the stairwell exit door of our dorm, and I swear he was still asleep when I left the room less than five minutes ago.

Maybe it was a dick move not to wake him up when I know he's got the same class as me, but for all I knew, he was planning to skip.

I stop just outside and tuck my hands into my pockets, a windy chill in the fleeting summer air making me feel like it's going to be fucking Christmas soon—which I'm not looking forward to. I barely even set foot in my parents' house Friday night, but the smell of booze and stale cigarette smoke still lingers in my nostrils.

Guilt for leaving my brothers and sister behind while I attend Dickson is a daily struggle that was only renewed by stepping back into that world. I know I need to live my life, but I can't help but feel bad that both Reece and I aren't there.

The door bangs open with Ace's urgency, and I step out of the way just before he bowls into me.

"Sorry," he apologizes on a laugh, sliding his feet back into his shoes that flung off in his haste. His hair is disheveled and his eyes sleepy, but his mood is bright. "I thought I set an alarm when I got back from Julia's last night."

I waggle my eyebrows, and he rolls his eyes. "She was

trying to teach my stupid ass some calculus. I don't even know how I met the requirements to be in that fucking class. It's like hieroglyphics."

"Don't ask me. My dumb ass is still taking Algebra I."

Ace chuckles. "The only reason I've passed anything in the last ten years is because I've gotten Julia's help. She'd probably help you too, even with algebra. Or you could ask Scottie. She's in our calc class and seems pretty good at math too."

I hum but don't say anything more. Being obsessed with a cheerleader who just broke up with Asshole of the Year isn't going to get me any closer to my goals. Frankly, neither is being besties with Ace Kelly, but he doesn't give me any choice.

On the plus side, he does seem to have an amazing understanding of where my actual boundaries are. He hasn't commented on my parents' house or how obviously run-down it is or the fact that I refused his invitation to go out on Saturday night, and right now, he's not pushing the Scottie issue either.

We walk in silence for most of the trip to English 101, the courtyard teeming with just enough activity to stay engaged in people-watching. As we get closer to Newton, though, a crowd outside the front entrance piques both of our attention.

"What is going on over there?" Ace asks, transitioning his walk to a jog, his backpack slung over one shoulder. Reluctantly, I match his pace to keep up, trailing only slightly behind when we get to the crowd. It looks innocent at first—just a stupid gathering of people with no sense of awareness about blocking the concrete path—but when we get to the other side of them, it becomes painfully obvious why they're gathered.

Scottie stands facing away from us with her posture sunken and her arms crossed over her chest. She's in light-wash jeans and a simple white T-shirt, and Dane is in front of her, facing us, pleading his case as it were, football apparel on display as always. For the first time since I saw them on my way into class last week, he actually looks like he likes her. His face is gentle, and his words—though I can't really hear them from here—seem placating.

Ace and I share a glance before continuing toward the two of them. We're maybe ten feet away when I get a handle on what they're saying.

"Please, babe, just give me another chance," Dane pleads, and Scottie's long locks brush her shoulders as she shakes her head.

"Look, I'm glad you can see how you were acting now, but we're better off on our own. Too much has happened. We've both changed to want different things, and I can't go back. And I don't want to hold you back either."

"I can't believe you. All this time together, and you want to throw it away over one crappy week?"

"It's been more than a week," Scottie challenges softly, sending a hit of adrenaline zipping through my veins. It's the right response—she doesn't want to be with a dick like him in the long run. But he's not going to like it. I know from experience watching my parents what challenging a guy like Dane does to his ego.

"Two fucking years!" Dane yells immediately, confirming just how right I am. Gentle is gone, and in its place, the guy who's going to *teach her a lesson.* "Two fucking years of waiting for you to be ready to put out, and it's going to end now on some sanctimonious *wasn't what we had great, though* bullshit? Damn, Scottie. You're even more fucked in the head than I thought you were."

Her spine stiffens. "Maybe it's not me who has it twisted if all you can think about is the fact that I didn't put out. I thought we were together because you *wanted* to be with me. Because you loved me."

"Love? I'm a fucking *guy.* Hate to break it to you, honey, but guys love tits and ass, okay?"

Scottie's face falls, and the words "What the fuck?" fly out of my mouth on a harsh whisper.

Ace, sensing my building tension, no doubt, jumps forward

and puts himself in between the two of them. "Heyyyy, folks. I'd say this is probably a good time to go our separate ways, huh?"

"This is a good time for you to mind your fucking business, Kelly," Dane asserts, pushing Ace in the chest so hard that he bounces off me.

All I see is *red*.

13

Scottie

ce bounces off Finn slowly at first, and then faster as Finn helps him to the side. One second, Finn's five feet away, and the next, he's *right here*. I watch like I'm seeing a train wreck happen while I'm standing on the tracks.

Dane's eyes widen briefly as Finn gets in his face, towering over him by a good three or four inches. Finn's energy vibrates, so much I would swear I can feel it like a current in the ground, but for all intents and purposes, it seems controlled. If it weren't, I imagine Dane would be pulverized already. "It's time for you to get the hell out of here," he tells my ex-boyfriend unequivocally, his pronunciation clear and his message unmistakable. "Go to class or find somewhere to cool down, whatever. Just fucking *go*."

There's a beat of time—just one, where the air feels thick and I can hear the sound of my own blood in my ears—before everything shifts and turns on its head.

Dane's eyes narrow, and he swings an unexpected punch, landing his fist on the underside of Finn's waiting chin. Finn's head jerks violently, and I let out a scream just as Ace steps in front of me and holds me back with one strong arm, preparing for a fight.

Finn's control is beyond impressive as he settles onto his toes once again, almost as though the punch never even happened. "Feel better?" he taunts Dane, a barely there smile curling up his plump lips. I don't understand how it's even possible, but he almost seems like he *likes* to be hit in the face. Which is insane, so I know I must be imagining things.

"You get the one free shot, understand? The next one, though, is going to end with a whole lot of fucking hurt on your end. I suggest you get out of here before the urge to tempt it overwhelms you."

"Fuck *you*, asshole," Dane says instead, doubling down with yet another swing of his fist.

I gasp, and Ace grabs me by my arms and pulls me back even farther. My gaze, though, is glued to the action. This time, Finn blocks the punch, catching Dane's hand in his grip and twisting his arm behind his back. Dane's posture is completely deflated as he gets on his toes to keep from falling forward. It's humiliating and emasculating in a way I know he can't stand.

"Fuck," Dane cries out then, rage in every hard line of his face. "You can have the stupid fucking cunt!"

I hear a gasp behind me that sounds like Kayla and then nothing but the sickening crunch of Finn's fist landing a direct blow to Dane's face. It's audibly overwhelming, the thick sound of physical devastation. There's absolutely no way his nose isn't broken.

From there, things devolve quickly, the two of them going at each other with a savagery I've never experienced before. Finn's blows make contact every time, and I swear Dane looks more and more like a scared little boy as the seconds tick by. People yell and shout around us, but all I can see is the fight. Finn stands Dane up when he can't stand up on his own and hits him again, and both of my hands fly to my mouth in an attempt to stop the scream I know I'm emitting involuntarily.

I don't love Dane—in fact, the more I think about all the moments we've had recently, the more my feelings seem like hate—but watching Finn beat him up is like something out of an action movie. It's guttural in every possible way.

I know it's about me, but it feels...brutally personal for Finn too. His fighting skills are so much better than Dane's. Frankly, I've never seen anyone fight like *this*.

Ace, secure in the fact that I'm not diving headfirst between their meaty fists, steps in again, trying to separate them. At first, I think it's because he wants Dane to stop getting demolished, but when I allow my eyes to leave their clench for one second, I see the more likely reason.

Our teacher, Professor Winslow, is headed this direction at a run.

"Yo!" Professor Winslow yells. "Stop!" I have no doubt he'll be able to handle the situation when he gets here—he's a big, muscled-up guy. But Finn's physique looks like it won't be far off from matching it in a couple of years.

"Finn! Dane!" Professor Winslow shouts, this time from the middle of their fray. "Stop right now!"

Finn's careful control of earlier reengages first, and he steps back, wiping just one tiny speck of blood from his lip while Ace clasps him on the shoulder. Dane, on the other hand, is much worse for wear. His normally kempt, preppy face looks like it got run over by a truck, but that doesn't stop him from continuing to swing, hoping he'll manage some sort of cheap shot.

"Dean's office," Professor Winslow barks, his face hard. "*Now.*"

"Ty, Finn was just defending himself—" Ace attempts to interject, but he's stopped by a harsh look and a silencing hand.

"Not right now, Ace."

"But, Ty—"

"Ace," Finn says then with a firm shake of his head. "Don't worry about it."

Ace's eyes narrow. He's a good friend, but even in the short time I've known him, he's made it abundantly clear he's not the type to drop something just because someone suggested he should.

"Fine. But if you need bail money, I know plenty of investors."

Finn manages a small smile at that—so does Ty Winslow, though I'm thinking he's hoping no one notices—and everything gentle I've known about Finn since the first day I met him comes back into startling focus.

Finn Hayes is a lover, not a fighter. But boy oh boy, is it obvious he's spent some time moonlighting as the second anyway.

14

Finn

Anger brews under the entire surface of my skin as Dane, Professor Winslow, and I make the long walk to Dean Kandinsky's office in the Stewart Building, located in the middle of campus. It burns and sizzles and eats at me like a form of flesh-eating bacteria.

But it's not because of my impending trouble with the dean, and it's not because of that stupid fuckboy Dane.

It's because of Professor Ty Winslow and his sanctimonious need to talk to me like he actually cares, despite knowing absolutely nothing about what it's like to be me.

"I understand more than anyone that hormones practically have fists of their own at your age, but you can't be fighting on campus. Start an underground fight ring or take it upstate, but don't throw punches in the courtyard in front of my class, okay? I'm duty bound to take you assholes to the dean if you do it right in front of me."

Neither Dane nor I say anything. There's nothing to say. Dane is too busy pissing himself over the possibility of expulsion—I can see it written all over his pathetic face—and I'm fighting every instinct I have to break Ty Winslow's heart right here and now. To tell him the fuckup he just caught fighting on campus is his own blood and DNA.

But doing it in front of Dane would be entirely counterproductive, and I've been waiting way too long to throw this shit out there without having an actual plan now.

I blink hard to adjust to the dimmer lighting as we leave the sunny outdoors and enter the Stewart Building. In addition to Dean Kandinsky's office, it houses all the upper management of Dickson, including both the admissions office and counseling.

As most head cases would, I've pointedly avoided it up until this point.

Ty talks to the receptionist, while Dane and I take seats in the wooden chairs outside the dean's office, separating ourselves as much as possible. The molding in this little section of the building alone has to cost more money than my mom has made in her entire life.

The receptionist nods, and Ty goes straight into Kandinsky's office, I'm assuming, to explain the situation before we get in there. When the heavy wooden door emblazoned with the dean's golden plaque shuts behind him, I let go of a breath I didn't know I was even holding.

I look down at my bloody knuckles to pass the time, studying the split in the skin where I already had a scar from two years ago. I came home that night to my dad, drunk as usual, laying into my mom and Willow because they'd gone and gotten her belly button pierced. Dad said it made her look like a slut. I'd hauled off and hit him with no control, no plan, no thought whatsoever. I got in a good first shot, but I also got my ass beat.

Since then, I've practiced both control and technique, and I don't lose fights anymore. Dane's bloodied face proves it.

"Finnley Hayes," a gruff, annoyed voice of authority calls, startling my gaze up. Dean Kandinsky is in the doorway of his office, looking none too pleased.

I stand without hesitation and walk toward him, ignoring Dane's sneer as I walk by. The kid wouldn't know appropriate behavior if it hit him right in the nuts.

"Dane," the dean says then. "You get in here too."

Ty stands in the back of the office, his arms crossed over his chest while the dean instructs Dane and me to take the seats in front of his desk.

Dean Kandinsky considers me for a long moment before looking at Dane. There's familiarity in his eyes, as well as annoyance. I guess having some douchey kid ruin your chances at getting any more fat checks from their parents is a real downer.

"Dane, why don't you explain to me what happened?"

Dane, the pretentious asshole, turns on his rich-kid persona in an instant. "It was all just a simple misunderstanding, sir. I was having a conversation with my girlfriend, and—"

"Ex-girlfriend," I interject. "And it wasn't a conversation. You were harassing her."

Dane shakes his head. "See, this is a big misunderstanding if you think that's what was happening, Finnley."

Oh, this asshole.

Unexpectedly, a strong hand clamps down on my shoulder. I follow it upward to Ty Winslow, and my jaw tightens so hard it's a wonder it doesn't break under the pressure.

"I've had several firsthand accounts that there was an argument happening between Dane and Scottie Bardeaux when Finn arrived," Ty updates. "Finn stepped in to dispel it, and Dane threw the first punch."

"Sir!" Dane objects hastily. "I was just defending myself proactively from a much larger opponent."

"Right. And you calling Scottie a cunt for everyone to hear was just a bid for an Oscar."

Dean Kandinsky laments and rubs a hand over his bald head with rough movements. "All right, all right. Enough. You're both on probation. One more physical altercation on campus and you're out."

"Of course, sir." Dane kisses ass. "It'll never happen again, sir."

"I hope you mean that, Dane. Your father would be extremely disappointed to hear otherwise."

Uh-huh, I hum internally. *So, the dean does know his family.* Just as I suspected.

Dane and I stand, and Ty steps forward to address us again. "I'm going back to carry on with whatever class is left, but the two of you are going back to your dorms to cool off. I'll see you on Thursday."

My jaw flexes under the overwhelming PSI of my clenched teeth, but somehow, I manage not to say anything at all.

He nods to the dean and leaves, and Dane and I trail behind him on our way out of the office. Our footsteps sound on the expensive tile floors and echo off the massively arched ceiling like we're a stampeding herd. Still, I keep my head down and my mouth shut the whole time. I'm smart enough to learn when to quit. It's not until we push through the door of the Stewart Building that Dane proves he, on the other hand, didn't learn shit.

"This isn't over, bro. I promise you that."

I don't bother with a response as I keep walking without a glance or any recognition at all.

Funnily enough, it's more than over for me. I've never been more done inserting myself into a situation in my life.

15

I t's been over two weeks since Finn Hayes beat the shit out of Dane in the courtyard in front of Newton and just as long since he's spoken to me.

I tried to offer my notes after he missed our English class to speak with Dean Kandinsky, even showed up at his dorm, but he wasn't there and Ace told me he'd already gotten the notes covered.

I've also texted him, several times, just to apologize and check in, but all of it has gone unanswered. Not to mention, he always manages to sit on the opposite side of the room as me in Professor Winslow's class now, the seats around him filled by Ace and his lackeys, so I don't even have a chance to get close to him.

Oddly enough, I understand. Rumor has it Dean Kandinsky threatened expulsion, and to be honest, if Dane's family weren't friendly with him, he probably would have done it already.

But now that things have been quiet from my ex-boyfriend, I've had the time to consider all the things I know about Finn Hayes.

There's a gentle outer layer that covers a burning rage inside. From the first moment I bumped into him, he's shown a level of care and consideration for me that, with other people, I haven't even been able to earn. He has a willingness to stand up for what's right, even when it shouldn't be his concern at all. And at the end of the day, I want people like that in my life.

I know I don't deserve his attention or company after all my drama has put him through, but I can't say I don't miss the idea of having it—even as just a friend.

The front door to Brower Center squeals as I open it and step inside. Our dining hall is multilevel, with a cafeteria-style buffet on the first floor and a food court setup on the second. Only the buffet is open for breakfast, though, so I skip the stairs and head directly for the wide-open double doors in front of me. It's pretty empty this early in the morning on Fridays—I guess most everyone is sleeping in or in class—and while Kayla normally joins me, she's at home for a family wedding this weekend, so the trays are stacked almost too high for me to reach. A little tippy-toe action does the trick, though, and I take it to the metal track at the end of the buffet to start scanning my options.

I should eat an omelet to fuel myself for the day—it's going to be a long one since we have a game to cheer at tonight—but for some reason, today, the thought of eggs makes me want to throw up in my mouth. It's comical since just last week, omelets were my fixation food.

As I'm passing the waffle station and eyeing the syrupy, not-nutrient-dense-at-all goodness longingly, my phone buzzes in my purse. I pull it out to find a new text message from a number I don't recognize.

An unknown number.

It's not the number that Finn texted me from the night of the party and I saved, but that doesn't stop the small thrill of excitement that runs through me from the memory.

Unknown: Is this Scottie Bardeaux?

My eyebrows draw together. Quickly, I type out a careful response.

Me: Who is this?

Moving on, I shove my phone back in my purse, stop at the next station, and fill my tray with oatmeal and toast. It's boring but dependable. I grab an apple from the basket at the end of the buffet before I step up to one of the self-service checkout lines and pull my wallet out of my purse to get my Dickson U Meal Card, but my phone buzzes again before I can swipe it. I pull the phone out to check it, juggling the card and my tray in my other hand.

Unknown: *Your worst nightmare.*

What the hell? I glance around the dining hall, waiting for, I don't know, a murderer wearing a *Scream* mask or something to pop out, but all I find are a couple of students in their pajamas, barely awake as they shuffle to fill their bellies. *It's probably just some young kid messing around or something.*

Whatever.

I scan my card, grab my tray, and make my way around the drink fountain machine to the tables on the far side of the massive, open space.

I put my tray down on a table in the corner, jamming my feet into the space between the legs of the chair, and wince when I catch my open-sandaled toe on the metal bar that runs across the bottom of the table.

"Ow, fudgesickles!"

A dark head jerks up on the other side of the planter that divides the midpoint of the tables, and mysterious brown eyes lock with mine. Eyes I haven't had the privilege of seeing in what feels like forever.

Finn.

"H-ey," I say, my voice box just as startled by the sight of him as my brain.

"Hey," he says back, shifting in his seat before folding his textbook closed on the table.

"I stubbed my toe. Shocker, huh?" I tease, trying to add a little levity to the awkward tension, but he just jerks up his chin in a nod, opens his book back up, and starts reading again.

Really? He can't even make civil conversation? A wave of anger and frustration consumes me, sending me into a tailspin that's entirely out of character.

"Hey!" I say again, but this time, it's a snap. Agitated, choppy movements compound into me storming straight toward his table while he looks on. "Are you avoiding me?"

His rigid jaw breaks, bending his face into a hint of a smirk. "Well...yeah. Isn't that obvious?"

"Right. Yes. I mean, of course it is. But I don't—"

"Scottie, let me stop you right there, okay?" His hair falls just slightly over his eyes, and I have the most annoying urge to push it back for him. "I don't have a problem with you. In fact, I like you fine. Too much, probably. But I think—actually, I *know*—we're better off keeping our distance."

"Oh." *Ouch.*

"You and I are from totally different worlds," he adds. "You went to private school. I—"

"You and Ace are from different worlds too. His parents have more money than God."

He sighs. "Ace is a leech. I've tried to get rid of him, but I can't."

"Well, maybe I'm a leech too."

He shakes his head. "No, Scottie. You're above that shit."

"What's that supposed to mean?"

"You're just—" He stops midsentence and shrugs, shoving back in his seat and then leaning forward again, his eyes intense. "Look, Scottie, if I don't need you, you don't need me. *You* are *not* desperate. For *anyone.* Understand?"

"Finn," I whisper, but he's already shaking his head at me again.

"It's just how it has to be, Scottie."

I stare at him for a long moment, my eyes searching his, desperately trying to understand why he's doing this. From where I stand, it makes no freaking sense. It's like he's afraid to get too close to me.

Or maybe all your ex-boyfriend drama has turned him off entirely? It's not exactly made the first few weeks of school easy for him.

I guess the reason doesn't matter if his decision is final anyway.

"So, that's it?" I question, my stupid, betraying bottom lip quivering. I quickly dig my teeth into it to force it to stop. "You don't even want to be friends?"

"I'm sorry."

My heart thrums so hard in my chest, I'm afraid it'll escape. "Okay, Finn. If that's what you want, then fine. If you don't want me to need you, I don't."

When he doesn't respond, when he doesn't even look up in my direction, again, I can't stop myself from adding, "But mark my words…you'll regret it."

He looks up then, a smile touching his lips that's laced with the kind of all-encompassing sadness I'm afraid I'll never understand. "I know I will, Scottie."

The air I've just inhaled catches in my lungs and holds.

"But that doesn't change anything."

Finn

The afternoon sun bounces off the gold helmets of the Dickson Dragons football team, and the crowd goes from ear-bending volume to silent as they line up on the five yard line.

"Mark my words, we're converting on this down, and we're doing it on the ground," Ace states confidently, his eyes fixated on the field. "Blakey Boy is going to score this TD."

"You think Boden's running it in?" I question incredulously. With Blake's arm and more than a couple yards to go, I'm expecting them to throw it.

"Hell yeah." Ace flashes a smirk in my direction. "All those orange defensive fuckers are clearly preparing for the pass just like the rest of you chumps." He points to me and Julia and three of his other friends who surround us.

The Pennington Tigers are our biggest opponents in our division, and following their last possession and touchdown, the game is tied. I glance at the scoreboard—*24 to 24, fourth quarter, two minutes left on the clock, third down.*

Blake better make this one count.

He calls for the snap, and both teams jump into action. He fakes a handoff to Reggie Banks, our top running back, and his O line holds their position against the Tigers' defense. Boden cradles the ball to his chest, jumping over their strong safety as he dives for his ankles, and runs it straight into the end zone.

"Touchdown, Blake Boden!" the announcer shouts, his voice so loud, the stadium shakes. The crowd goes nuts with cheers and applause.

Ace fist-pumps the air and gives me a high five before free-falling into the people behind us, who catch him and laugh. The band dives into Dickson University's fight song, and we all sing along—Ace at the top of his lungs, of course.

"By Dragon's fire, you're dust to us! Dickson U, in Dragons we trust!"

"I fucking told you he was going to run it in!" Ace bellows, and we high-five again.

Tommy Slate hits the extra point with ease, and Ace wraps his arm around Julia's shoulder and playfully swings her back and forth while the instrumental crescendo builds once again. "Jules, tell our defense they better fucking hold the line!"

Julia laughs and punches him away with gentle hands while the cheerleaders run on the field, gold pom-poms in the air during the TV broadcast timeout. I watch unabashedly—because everyone else is too, and somewhere in my delusion of the last couple of weeks, that excuse makes sense.

Since the confrontation in Brower Center, Scottie has kept her distance from me. She hasn't texted or called or even looked in my direction in class, for that matter. She's done exactly as I suggested and moved on from me completely.

I'm such a fucking idiot.

Scottie smiles and claps her hands along with her fellow cheerleaders as they all shout something about the Dragons' defense in synchronicity. The crowd follows their enthusiastic lead, as they climb into some sort of stunt formation that sends Scottie shooting into the air like a freaking rocket.

"Holy shit!" Ace remarks, watching her as she flips in the air and lands in the arms of the girls below her.

They catch her with ease, and Scottie is back on the ground, clapping and cheering along with her team.

"Woo!" Julia cheers, throwing both hands above her head enthusiastically. "Go, Scottie! Badass bitchhhh!"

I had zero plans of coming to this game—rather, my strategy was to avoid it just like I have with all the others. Then I wouldn't be here staring at a girl I have no business staring at like some kind of sap.

And yet, because I'm Ace Kelly's roommate, I find myself here anyway.

You also find yourself having fun.

I don't know how or why, but wherever Ace Kelly is, a good-ass time isn't far behind. Though, the CIA would have to waterboard me to get me to admit that to him out loud.

As the cheerleaders leave the field and the game starts up again, I pull my phone out of my pocket to check to see if I have any missed texts from my siblings—at least, that's what I tell myself. But I end up scrolling through the one-sided conversation from Scottie from before our encounter at the breakfast buffet. Before I basically told her to stay the fuck away from me.

I sigh. I should have deleted these, but I didn't.

> *I'm so sorry for everything I've gotten you involved in. Please let me know if I can help with anything.*

> *I have notes from class if you need them. I can't believe you're in trouble because of me.*

> *Dane told Nadine, who told everyone here, that you guys are just on probation for now. I'm so sorry, but I guess it's good for once that Dane is a nepo baby. ☹*

> *I know you probably need some time. Reach out when you're ready.*

> *I hope you're okay, Finn. I'll always be sorry.*

Fuck, I'm such a dick.

My fingers hover over the keys for a brief moment before I start to type out a message.

I'm so bad for you, but maybe we could try anyway.

Delete.

I'm sorry I'm such an asshole. Maybe I took things too far. Let's be friends.

Delete.

I know it's my fault, but I miss you.

Delete.

This fucking sucks, but it's for the best. She's way better off without me.

"Yo, Finn, by the way, you already have plans tonight," Ace declares, pulling my focus away from my phone. I shove it back into my pocket.

"Huh?"

"Two words. *Computare Caterva*," he says quietly and then waggles his brows at me like I should know what he's talking about.

"Are those words English?"

"You haven't heard about Double C?"

"Ohhh. Double C. Yeah! I totally know."

"Really?" he asks excitedly.

I frown and shake my head. "I have zero fucking clue what you're on about right now."

"Ah, man. You are in for a treat. I can't wait for you to thank me later."

I roll my eyes. "Somehow I don't think that's how it'll go."

"Believe me, it will. I got you an invite into the most exclusive, top-secret thing on campus." He winks. "Be ready to go by eleven tonight."

No room for excuses. It's not a choice. And just like that, Ace Kelly, roommate extraordinaire, strikes again.

17

Finn

Through the darkness, Ace guides us across campus, past Newton and the dean's office in Stewart until we reach Nash Mathematics Center. There isn't much I know about this mysterious mission to what Ace claims will be the coolest part of our college experience, but I know if it's much farther of a walk, I'm giving up and going back to the dorm.

"Ace, I swear if you're taking me into some back alley to watch a bunch of dudes do a séance-style circle jerk or some shit, I'm going to kill you," Blake remarks, mirroring my thoughts impressively.

"Ditto on the killing."

"Cool your jets, boys," Ace chides, waving a hand before circling around to the back of Nash like a cat burglar in a cartoon. His stride is animated, and his toes are pointed as he high-steps.

In the center of the massive building, a set of cement steps that lead to nothing but more darkness makes Ace's eyes light up and his posture straighten. "This is it. We're here."

"We're *here*?" Blake asks, annoyed now. "What the fuck is going on?"

I still don't know why Blake Boden is with us, seeing as the guy just won one of the biggest games of the year and could be celebrating with his teammates while co-eds hang on his every word, but I'm not mad about it. So far, he's doing a hell of a job of asking all the questions I'd be forced to ask on my own if he weren't here. Plus, I thought the star quarterback of a Division I school with the kind of national attention that he has would be stuck-up or cockier than shit. Instead, he's kind of wholesome. Confident, sure, but not at all the kind of fuckface I like to beat the shit out of.

"Relax, Boden," Ace says, an ironic command, given our current location in front of a creepy, abandoned stairwell. "We'll go down in a sec. Just waiting on Julia to get here."

"Pretty sure Blake's primary concern isn't the holdup," I reply with a howl. "We want to know what the fuck's down there in your little mystery cave."

Before Ace can answer, Julia's hurried voice cuts through the stillness around us. "Hi, hi! Sorry we're late! We had a little wardrobe emergency, and—" She stops talking as the three of us turn to look at her, a small smile forming at the corner of her mouth before she continues. "Right. You dudes don't care about clothes."

Scottie is at her side, clinging to her elbow and avoiding any and all eye contact with me. She's no longer in the cheerleader uniform I saw her in this afternoon, sporting cutoff jean shorts, white Pumas, and a white T-shirt that reads "Feeling very IDGAF-ish" in black letters instead, and her hair is in a ponytail that cascades down her back. She's fresh-faced, like she showered off the heavy makeup from today's game that all the cheerleaders wear, and even more gorgeous than I'd let myself remember.

Yep. I'm still a fucking idiot.

"Scottie came along so I wouldn't be the only girl at the sausage fest," Julia remarks, making me smile despite myself. She's so carefree and funny—almost the way I would expect Scottie to be, given her silver spoon background. I'm always surprised by Scottie's grit.

But when Julia looks down the stairwell we're currently standing at the top of, her grin vanishes. "Um, is it just me, or is this giving murder-y vibes?"

"Wait...*that's* where we're going?" Scottie questions.

"Just relax, ladies," Ace attempts to reassure as he wraps an arm around Julia's shoulders. "It's all good in the hood."

"If I end up in a sex-trafficking ring because of you, Coach is going to be so pissed," Blake teases, making Ace roll his eyes.

"Come on. We have to get down there before we're late." Ace unwraps his arm from Julia's shoulder and takes her hand in his instead, walking down the stairs with her at the front of the group.

"I swear, Ace, if I didn't know where you were taking us, there's no way I'd be following along," Julia comments. "This is creepy as fuck."

"At least you know where you're going," Blake says through a barking laugh as he follows Ace and Julia down the steps. "Ace hasn't told us shit."

"Yeah," Scottie mutters. "I'm also in the dark."

"It's going to be worth it, Scottie! I promise!" Julia calls over her shoulder, but Scottie is still standing at the top of the stairs. I'm beside her, of course, but the power of her indifference is like a force field between us. A force field of my own making, I realize, but fuck if I don't hate the way it feels.

"You okay?" I ask, my feet refusing to leave her behind.

She nods, her eyes flicking to mine twice before actually settling there. She digs her top teeth into her bottom lip, hesitation to engage with me within her every movement. "I guess you could say I'm not a big fan of the dark."

Before I can even process what I'm doing, I reach for her hand, gently wrapping it in my grasp. Startled, her big doe eyes meet mine, and the urge to pull her to my chest and kiss her hits me like a fucking truck.

"Finn?" she asks, my name a whisper on her perfect lips. I'm confusing her; I know. Because I'm confusing me too.

"I got you," I soothe through a pointedly averted gaze. Focusing on anything but Scottie's eyes or her lips or the way she smells like vanilla and honey is the only thing I can do to keep my sanity right now.

She grips my hand tighter as I guide us down the stairs, and I hate that it makes a small smile form at the corner of my lips. I feel two times taller when she acts like she trusts that I can keep her safe.

Ace knocks on the closed door at the bottom of the stairs four times, a unique staccato making it obvious that it's some kind of code. It swings open five seconds later, a big, burly-looking guy with a fully shaven head peeking his upper body out.

"Name."

"Ace Kelly," my charismatic roommate says cheerfully, like this isn't the start of at least ten horror movies.

"Everyone else?" the big, scary dude asks then, his eyes narrowing.

"My friends."

Baldy's eyebrows draw together, and then the door slams shut, right in Ace's face. Blake starts laughing, and Scottie looks at me, her eyes wide in question. I don't have an answer, so I just shrug.

As Ace turns around to look at us, he appears nervous for the first time. "Nothing to worry about. I'm sure this is just part of the process."

I nod. "Right."

Scottie pulls her hand from mine and rubs her hands up and down her bare arms, looking over her shoulder and back up the staircase, our moment gone. "Jules, I think I'm gonna—"

The door slams open again, and the burly dude waves us all in with a frown on his face. Blake, shocked, pats Ace on the shoulder as he follows him in.

I gesture for Scottie to go ahead of me to give her some security now that we're not holding hands anymore, and she accepts shyly. I work hard not to watch her ass as she walks and, instead, settle for watching the sway of her dark locks as her ponytail moves side to side.

The hallway is dark as we pass the man at the door and proceed inside, and a dingy, metallic smell settles inside my nose. There's a dull roar of noise up ahead, but no light whatsoever that I can see.

Ace turns the knob to open the solitary door at the end of the hall, and a room full of paint and supplies illuminates. A single bulb is hanging from the ceiling on a small chain, and the sound of something even louder comes through the door on the other side. Ace tries the knob for that door but finds it locked. After a small shrug of anticipation, he does the special knock again, and the door swings open.

Scottie navigates through the piles of paint cans, and I follow behind to bring up the rear.

A girl with long blond hair and startlingly pretty blue eyes stands just inside, a clipboard in her hand and a scowl on her face. She looks a few years older than us and carries the kind of confidence that makes you feel like she's in charge.

"You're on my shit list, Ace," she says in greeting, and immediately, Blake smiles back at me with wild eyes.

"Hey, Lex. Good to see you," Ace replies, his posture relaxed now that we've successfully made it inside.

Her eyes are hard but beautiful as she glances behind Ace and Julia to Blake, Scottie, and me. "I see you took it upon yourself to just...invite people."

"They're trustworthy. I swear. Signed a blood contract and everything before I brought them."

She rolls her eyes. "Fucking hell, you're always a thorn in my side." She turns to Julia. "And, *you*. You should know better than this."

"Sorry, Lex." Julia is sheepish but not actually scared. It's obvious both Ace and Julia know "Lex" in some other capacity than whatever tonight is.

She grabs her clipboard and unlocks the pen from the top of it. "What are their names? I need them."

Ace points back at me. "Finn Hayes. And in front of him, Scottie Bardeaux."

Blake takes it upon himself to step up and hold out a hand toward Lex like a true gentleman. "I'm Blake Boden."

She glances down at his hand and then back up at his face before averting her attention away from him entirely and speaking to everyone. "You have to sign an NDA. Give fingerprints. And if any of you talk about Double C to anyone, I'll make sure they never find your bodies."

"You gonna murder us, Lex? Won't that make the family cookouts a little awkward?" Ace teases, and she glares at him. He holds up both hands. "Got it. First rule of Double C is don't talk about Double C."

She pulls out a cell phone and opens an app, flipping over Ace's hand and scanning his fucking fingerprint. His eyes go wide as she shows it to him.

"I can put this anywhere I want if I need to. Understand me?"

Holy shit, who is this girl?

Ace nods, a dutiful puppy on the leash of his owner. Still, he's also him, so he has a comment.

"Did you rob the FBI or some shit? How the hell do you have a thing that scans fingerprints, Lexi?"

"I made it in my free time in comp lab."

Ace nods as though that checks out, making Scottie actually look at me with frightened eyes. All I can do is make them back. I mean, I'm confident, but not enough to think I can somehow protect us from a girl who makes fingerprint scanners in her spare time.

"Do I need to give a blood sample too?" Julia asks as Lexi scans her hand.

Lexi is unfazed. "Don't tempt me."

"I'm Blake Boden," Blake repeats for the second time as she moves on to scanning his hand. "Not sure if you heard my full name over the noise."

"I heard you." Lexi doesn't even bother looking up in his direction as she pushes a button on the screen of her phone and drops his wrist.

"The name doesn't ring any bells?" Blake continues, undeterred and desperate. To be honest, I don't think I've ever seen him like this before.

"Last year, you threw for a record 3,995 yards, completed forty TDs, and only had three interceptions," she rattles off like it's no big deal.

"Wait…what? You know my stats from last year?"

"I know everyone's stats."

Blake's smile is sly and amused. "But you also know *my* stats."

"I also know you lost in the second play-off game like a chump."

Ace snorts so hard, Julia has to turn him around when snot flies out of his nose.

And Lexi just moves over to Scottie to get her digital signature for the NDA and take her fingerprints like she didn't just deliver a life-threatening burn.

Blake, rather than looking offended, makes gah-gah eyes at her the size of Texas.

I offer my hand as Lexi gets to me and watch as she scans my print, and then I quickly scribble a signature on the NDA when she shoves it toward me on her phone. As soon as she's done with me, she pushes back through the others and starts to walk down yet another dark hallway, rattling off information as we follow. "Computare Caterva is the most exclusive society on campus. No one knows we're here. No one knows what we do. And it *will* stay that way. When we're having an event, you'll get a text. It will just say the time and where to be. Bring cash if you're smart. Bring more cash if you're shit at betting, so the rest of us can profit."

There's a finality in her speech as she throws open the door at the end of the hall to reveal a sunken room full of no fewer than fifty people. Bodies writhe and people shout as they hold cash in the air for runners who circle the room to exchange it.

Ace and Julia move through the door expediently, but Blake pauses, holding Scottie and me up from doing the same.

"So, you need my number?" Blake questions Lexi, having paid attention to the entirety of her speech like the best student in the class. "For the texts? And, you know, anything else would be okay too."

She looks from him to us, including the three of us instead of answering him directly. "I already have your number."

"How?" Blake asks, mystified, and this time, she looks directly at him.

"Because I'm the smartest girl you'll ever meet."

"Well, smart girl, how about you give me your number?" Blake grins. "Feels like it's only fair."

"I don't date football players."

"Why not?"

Lexi smiles then, the first real smile I've seen her make since we arrived. What she doesn't do, however, is answer. "Have fun. If you lose your ass tonight, sorry about your luck. Though, if you're as smart as I hope you are, you know that betting is never about luck."

She walks away, and just like that, we're dismissed.

"I'm going to marry that girl," Blake whispers as he watches her move to the center of the room where what looks to be a boxing ring with a cage surrounding it sits.

I use my own momentum to push Scottie and Blake farther into the room, going up and around a group of people before climbing down into the sunken center to where Ace and Julia are standing in the back row. Students jostle back and forth as someone in the front stumbles and falls before their friends pick them back up to standing.

Ace spots us coming and turns to help Scottie jump down beside Julia first. Blake follows, though his eyes still wander the room, looking for Lexi.

"Yo, Blake," Ace says through a laugh when Blake trips off the step and falls into them. "How about you pick your jaw up off the floor and pay attention to what you're doing, dude? I'll never live it down if I bring the Dragons quarterback somewhere and get him injured."

"I'm going to marry that girl," he repeats as he stares at Lexi, who's now on the far side of the ring collecting money, one of her feet through the ropes, prepared to climb in.

"Do you even know who that girl is?"

"My future wife?"

"I'm not sure if you noticed, Blake, but Lex didn't appear all that interested in you," Julia chimes in, a little smile on her lips.

"Yeah." Scottie giggles. "Kind of seemed like she didn't give a shit about anything you were saying."

"Mark my words, ladies. That girl will be mine."

Both Scottie and Julia laugh some more, and Ace and I look at each other like Blake has lost his ever-loving mind.

"Listen up, everyone!" Lexi calls from the center of the ring, a microphone in her hand and her voice echoing throughout the room. "Tonight's official activities will commence shortly. But we're going to need a volunteer to step up to the challenge."

"What's the challenge, Lex?" a guy yells from the crowd.

She smiles. "A guy with big enough balls to fight Donnie Marks."

"Wait…he's a fucking ex-UFC fighter, Lex! Are you nuts?" another guy yells out.

"Looks like your balls are too small," she teases and glances out toward the crowd. "C'mon, you assholes, someone needs to step up. Otherwise, we might as well pack it in early."

"Dayum," Ace mutters when Donnie Marks steps into the ring. "He's a big motherfucker."

"Don't you dare, Ace," Julia states firmly as she pokes him in the chest with her index finger.

"What? You don't want me to fight him?" he questions with a grin on his lips. "I can hold my own, babe."

Julia's lips move down into a frown. "If you manage to hold your own, I will personally finish you off later."

"Wait…what?" Ace's eyes go wide. "Finish me off? Sounds kind of nice."

"As in murder you, you idiot!" she exclaims and shoves him in the chest.

"Are you sure that's what you mean?" He starts to open his mouth again, but Julia slaps her hand over his lips.

"Shut up, Ace."

He laughs. And then I'm certain he licks her palm because she jerks her hand away on a disgusted laugh.

"Ew! You're so gross!"

"By the way, whoever volunteers to fight Donnie gets ten percent of the betting pool," Lexi announces, and my ears perk up.

Ten percent of the betting pool? I look around the room, taking in the size and scope of the crowd and quickly deducing that most of the people here look like they come from families with parents who keep their bank accounts stocked full of cash.

You know, the opposite of my family.

I think about how I still haven't managed to find a steady job that fits into my class schedule and how Travis and Jack will need new basketball shoes and the fees that go along with their playing high school ball.

I think about how Willow wants to go to homecoming and probably has a dress in mind she knows she won't be able to afford.

I think about how our dick of a father spends all his money on booze and our mom's paycheck barely covers food and rent.

By the time I add my student loans into the poor-people-problems equation, I realize the decision is already made.

"I'll do it!" I call out over the crowd and lift an arm so Lex can see me.

"What?" Scottie damn near shouts, and she reaches her hand out to grab mine and pull it down from its raised position. "You're going to fight him for money?"

"Not all of us have life handed to us, princess." Deep down, I know she's trying to stop me because she cares, but she has no idea what it's like to walk a day in my shoes. I don't need her judging the choices I make in order to survive.

She stares at me, her eyes widening with both anger and fear. "Finn, this is crazy. Don't do this."

"Finn Hayes, right?" Lexi questions through the mic.

"That's right," I confirm loudly, which leads to Scottie letting go of my hand entirely.

"All right," Lexi says with a nod. "Come on up and show Donnie what you've got."

"Holy shit!" Ace whisper-yells, shoving me in the chest as his excitement gets the best of him. Blake claps me on the shoulder encouragingly, but Scottie, unable to stop herself, grabs my hand again and squeezes tightly.

"Finn," she pleads when I look down to meet her eyes. "Please don't do this."

What she doesn't understand is that I've spent most of my life… fighting for my fucking life. And for my mom's. And my siblings'.

When you have an abusive drunk for a father, you go through so much shit in your childhood that there isn't much that scares you anymore by the time you become an adult.

You learn to fight. You learn to take punches. You learn to survive.

Scottie's green eyes are imploring, and the desperation inside them breaks into my carefully crafted wall. I lean down to whisper into her ear. "I'll be fine." My voice is gentle in a way I know no part of me will be soon.

"Finn."

My name is anguish, her voice a plea. Everything in me is drawn to her need for comfort—to her level of care for a fuckup like me.

Digging my hands into the taut sides of her ponytail, I press my lips to hers and kiss her. It's a short kiss, but I make the most of it, savoring the soft plushness of her lips and the way her tongue tastes like the strawberry-flavored gum I always see her chewing in class.

"Just in case," I say on a whisper when I pull away. Her eyes shine with both surprise and fear as I turn for the ring and don't look back.

The guy she knows now won't exist anymore when I'm done with Donnie Marks anyway.

18

My lips tingle as my fingertips glide over the sensitized skin left behind by Finn's bewildering kiss.

After weeks of avoiding me and warning me away and acting like I couldn't even begin to know what I'm getting myself involved in with him, Finn Hayes kissed me. Out of nowhere and without forewarning and with all the passion I dreamed could be between us.

Out of my head and heart, I've shoved him away, just as he suggested I should, and stood on my own two feet. I've socialized and studied and thrown myself into *my* life at Dickson University. It's been almost amazingly difficult to move on from him—to coach myself into letting him go without ever having had him in the first place.

But with one kiss, all that progress is so done and gone, I'd swear it never even existed.

And now, he's going to do the stupidest thing I can imagine— fight a guy who apparently fought in the UFC.

I watch Finn climb into the ring with the pounding sense of impending danger clogging my chest. My hands are clammy and shaking, and I can feel the rattle of my fear in the chatter of my teeth.

"This feels like a bad idea," Blake comments, and Ace nods, agreeing.

"No shit. I'm nervous as fuck for him."

"Me too," Julia whispers as she grabs Ace's hand and rests her face on his bicep.

Convenient how none of them mentioned this shit *before* Finn took off to fight a guy who literally fought for a living not long ago. I'd love to tell my friends that, but a knot has lodged itself in my throat and words feel impossible under these circumstances.

I know Finn fought Dane like he could fight the world all at once without being fazed. But fighting a second-string football player from upstate with pretty-boy tendencies is a completely different animal from fighting a professional like Donnie Marks.

"Place your bets!" Lexi announces loudly over the din of excited hysteria in the room. People rattle off numbers and toss cash to both her and the runners, and somehow, she seems to keep up with it all.

"Fuck this," Ace says and presses a soft kiss to Julia's forehead. "I'm going up there. Even if it's just to give moral support. Stay here, Lia."

As he breaks away from the group and pushes through the people in front of us, I follow.

Julia yells my name and reaches for me, but I'm swallowed by the choking crowd of people before she can make contact. I glance back to see Blake pull her into the safety of his side, and when I turn around, I run right into Ace, who's stopped to face me. "Scottie, what are you doing?"

"The same as you. I can't just stand back there and watch." I stare at him as he studies me, his eyes narrowing. I know I'm just supposed to sit back and keep my mouth shut, but Finn Hayes just kissed me, for shit's sake. I'm not going to watch him get killed from a distance.

"Fucking hell," Ace mutters and grabs my hand, dragging me to the front so quickly I have to run to keep up. He shoves into the thick crowd, forcing our way into a spot right behind Finn where he sits in a chair in the corner of the ring, getting his wrists and knuckles taped by a guy I've never seen before. Finn's shirt is off, and his feet are bare, leaving only his jeans covering his long legs.

"You sure about this, Finn?" Ace questions loudly, but Finn doesn't respond. It's like he can't even hear us. His eyes are fixated on his opponent across the ring.

"Final bets!" Lexi announces. "Final bets!"

People hold out cash and shout toward several bet attendants in the crowd, one of whom I think might be my calculus TA, and my throat nearly closes on itself.

"Son of a bitch," Ace mutters and runs a hand through his hair before shouting toward Lexi, "I've got five hundo on Finn!"

"Ace!" I hiss. I can't believe he's getting involved in this right now. Lexi quirks a brow, pointing in our direction, and Ace snags five one-hundred dollar bills out of his wallet and holds them out toward the ring.

"What?" he whispers in my ear. "It's not like I'm betting against him!"

"You heard him, Connor," Lex commands a guy with auburn hair. "Five hundred from Ace Kelly." Connor grabs Ace's cash, and Lex records something on her clipboard.

I shuffle from side to side as people shove us from behind, and Ace glances over to the spot where we left Julia and Blake. Blake jerks up his chin, and Julia waves. All is good back there.

I shake my head. I sure as hell wish I felt like all was good up here. Lexi gives a nod to the guy with auburn hair, tosses him the mic, and climbs out of the ring to come stand by Ace and me as a bell rings and Finn and Donnie both stand in their corners.

My heart jumps into my throat and pounds there, choking me on my own saliva.

"You sure have a lot of confidence in your buddy," Lex remarks to Ace, and he nods.

"Fuck yeah, I do."

She eyes him closely and then smiles. "Good. Because I've got my money on him too."

"We want a safe, clean fight, boys," Connor announces into the mic as Finn and Donnie step toward the center of the ring. "No illegal shit, yeah? I went over the rules with you. Now, touch fists if you want."

Donnie and Finn nod before bumping fists.

"All right!" Connor exclaims. "It's time!"

Connor climbs out of the ring. A bell dings again. And the fight begins.

As Finn and Donnie circle each other, their eyes locked and their bodies in a defensive stance, vomit climbs the back of my throat to join my heart.

I don't know anything about UFC fights or fighting in general, but I do know that Donnie and Finn at least appear equal in height and weight. Also, now that I'm seeing him with his shirt off, Finn Hayes is *way more* muscular than my brain could even imagine.

His muscles tense and flex as he jockeys from side to side in a way that would make girls turn a ten-second TikTok into a twenty-minute video, but my body is too hyped up on anxiety to think about anything but hoping Finn walks away from this fight okay.

Donnie throws out the first punch, and Finn dodges it with ease. But when he tosses out three more punches before I can even process the first, he manages to make contact on the last one. A dead shot to Finn's nose. His head jerks back violently, and a shocked scream releases every vestige of air in my lungs.

Shit!

Ace wraps an arm around my shoulders and pulls me close, dwarfing me in the frame of his incredibly tall body. I shrink into the cover gratefully, leaving little more than my eyeballs exposed as Donnie flashes a dark smile.

Finn shakes off the punch with ease, his mouth set in a firm line.

"You still wanna keep playing, buddy?" Donnie teases, enjoying this little stroll through Dickson University's underbelly like a kid in a candy store. Finn doesn't respond, opting for stoicism instead, but when Donnie does some kind of jump kick toward Finn's chest, making contact and pushing him back to the cage, I have to cover my eyes.

"C'mon, Finn!" Ace shouts from over top of me, rocking my body forward along with his own. "You got this!"

I hold my breath for a few seconds, but Ace's muttered, "Shit," pretty much solidifies that I'm watching the rest of the fight from behind my hands.

I peek through my fingers occasionally, especially when Ace jostles and screams enough to knock me off-balance, but each time I catch Finn taking another punch to the face or a kick to the ribs, I shut my eyes again.

"Kick his ass, Finn!" I hear Blake's voice through the absolute crush of sound. I glance under Ace's arm to see Julia yelling too, but I can't hear her at all.

The rest of the crowd is starting to get louder by the second, the room appearing to be in favor of the UFC fighter. Money is on the line, and they want Finn's blood, classmate or not.

Finn dances backward before jabbing Donnie with a punch to the teeth, but Donnie swings back, and I close my eyes yet again.

A reverberating crack reaches my ears, and my heart sinks to my shoes. I squeeze my eyes tighter, so hard I feel the strain in my hair, but when I hear Ace shout, "Yes, motherfucker!" I sneak a peek through my fingers.

Donnie is flat on the floor, with Finn on top of him, wailing one punch after another into his bloodied face. Donnie's trying to block the assaults with his hands, but it's no use. Finn's punches are coming too fast and too hard for him to do anything about it.

I feel like I'm in the courtyard watching him beat the hell out of Dane all over again, only this time, it's more violent. More aggressive. More…primal.

Blood spurts from Donnie's nose and his face goes slack, and Lex calls over to Connor, "End it! Ring the bell!"

The bell rings, but Finn doesn't stop, working Donnie with an aggression that overwhelms his handsome features with vibrant agony. Like the violence embodies him and sickens him all at once. It takes Connor and two other guys to pull him off the bloodied UFC fighter, and I'm convinced they only succeed then because of Ace's sharp and cutting voice as he yells to get Finn's attention.

"Winner! Finn Hayes!" Connor announces into the mic, grabbing Finn's hand to raise it in the air while what appears to be a paramedic assists Donnie to his feet. The UFC fighter shoves him away, muttering something about being fine, and Ace fist-pumps the air in excitement, jostling me all over again as he drags me into the ring.

"Fuck yeah, Finnley! Fuck yeah!" Ace cheers, wrapping his arms around Finn and swinging him into a throat-choking hug. Finn's eyes meet mine over Ace's shoulder, blood coating his eyes, nose, and teeth as it runs down from a couple of cuts in his eyebrows.

Everything disappears between one moment and the next—the crowd, the boos from disappointed bettors, the commotion over on Donnie's side of the ring, and Lexi taking over on the mic. All I see is Finn, who overwhelms my thoughts during the day and my dreams at night.

I shove Ace out of the way and pull Finn's face toward mine by his chin. "You're such an asshole," I say to his face. "Do you have any idea what could've happened?" I shove at his chest, hard, both delusional enough to think I can actually move a guy who just beat up a UFC fighter and senseless enough to think it's safe. "How fucking stupid! You're damn right about us, you know that? We are different! We're so different, I don't even know—"

I'm prepared to say more, but he shuts me up entirely with another kiss. His mouth to mine, the metallic taste of blood from his busted lips reaches my tongue, and for some fucked-up reason, it makes me kiss him harder.

Clashing tongues, wrestling lips, and hearts on fire, we vie for supremacy in a fight of our own. Finn's hand at the base of my skull, I give in willingly as he finally takes control, tasting and taunting me so much my equilibrium spins.

Just as I suspected, there's something chemically catastrophic between us, and it'll either make us stronger or kill us trying.

"Hang out with me tonight," he whispers against my lips, his breathing shallow as I steal his air with gulps of my own.

I lean back to look into his eyes, searching for answers to all the questions I've had since I met him. Our game is a tug-of-war of hot and cold, but right now, his eyes look like glazed chocolate fresh out of the oven.

With the progression of the last few weeks—with how much I know I should protect myself from another temperature swing from Finn—my answer defies logic. "*Yes.*"

Trouble's on the horizon, shining like the bold colors of the sunset, but my heart shoves sensibility out of the car and recklessly pushes the gas pedal to the floor. Ready or not, I'm headed right for it.

19

Scottie

Julia sits on Ace's bed while he sits on the floor in front of her, her calves draped over his shoulders as though they're a footstool. Blake is splayed across their futon in the corner, while Finn shoves in behind me on his bed with a bag of popcorn. His face is clean after his shower, and his wet hair curls around the top of his neck. I toss the crust from my last piece of the pizza we ordered down into the box on the floor and flop back onto Finn's pillow, my stomach freaking tap-dancing from the highs and lows of the night.

"That motherfucker didn't even know what hit him," Ace regales again, pretending to be dazed by an imaginary punch and passing out. Julia laughs as her legs twist around his corpse, and Finn chuckles lightly behind me. I can feel the warm air of his breath in my hair, and it takes everything inside me not to turn around.

Blake pulls a photo album out from the shelf below Ace's bed and flips through it, pausing to hold it up with a guffaw as soon as Ace is done with his little show. "Hold up. You know Snoop Dogg?"

Ace shrugs like it's no big deal. "My dad helped him with some financials, and my mom did some photos for the inside of his last album."

"That's insane," Blake says with a shake of his head and a laugh.

Ace rolls his eyes. "Julia's dad is the reason half the celebrities in Hollywood are together, with his discreet version of the TapNext dating app."

Finn and I are both silent. I know he thinks my family life is different from his, but I think he'd be surprised by the fact that I feel like I can relate more to him right now than anyone else in the room.

Julia blushes before shoving Ace in the shoulder. "All our parents know famous people. What's it matter?"

"Well, fuck me," Blake cries, shoving to standing. "That's it. I have to go back to my apartment and cry over how uncool my parents are." He clasps his hands and looks to the white textured ceiling. "I hear you, Lord. I'm a nobody."

We all laugh—even Finn—at the thought of Blake Boden being a nobody.

Blake gives Finn, Julia, and me a fist bump before ruffling Ace's hair and leaving with a flick of his hand. I sit up and shuffle my back toward the headboard as Julia removes her legs from Ace's shoulders. "I need to go too," Julia remarks. "I'm exhausted."

Ace climbs to his feet, a yawn making his long limbs stretch nearly across the room. "I'm fucking wiped too. Just sleep here so I don't have to walk you back to Delaney."

"Scottie and I can walk together," Julia suggests, to which Finn pipes up.

"You can both sleep here. Scottie can sleep in my bed, and I'll take the futon."

I start to protest the idea, but Finn scoots up on the bed so my legs are crunched into him and his eyes are on mine. "People saw you with me tonight. People who lost a lot of money because I beat Donnie. I don't want you walking out there by yourself."

My head jerks back. The thought of someone being mad enough at Finn to hurt me never even occurred to me. He looks at Julia. "Same for you. I'll feel better if you guys just sleep here and wait for daylight."

Julia shrugs. "Fine by me." She turns to Ace. "Do you have a T-shirt I can sleep in?"

Ace digs in his closet and tosses out a shirt, and Julia smiles at me as she trots into the bathroom to get changed.

Finn looks at me as I shift awkwardly to take my shoes off. "Do you want a T-shirt?" he whispers gently, seeming to sense that I'm absolutely losing my shit inside. It took a year of dating Dane before I slept in his bed for the first time, and I wasn't feeling nearly the things I am now.

My whole body aches with the tease of arousal.

My nod is shaky, but it's a yes, nonetheless.

Finn climbs off the bed and reaches into a drawer on the side of the bed, pulling out a neatly folded black T-shirt and tossing it to me. I pull it to myself gratefully, a small smile curving the corner of my lips upward.

It smells clean, but it has a hint of him too. Like maybe he's worn it enough that the wash cycle never quite gets rid of his scent.

The bathroom door clicks open, and Julia emerges, the bottoms of her bare legs the only thing left in the dwarf of Ace's huge shirt. Her own clothes are in her arms, and she drops them at the foot of Ace's bed before climbing under the covers.

Ace is about to go into the bathroom to change himself, when Finn jumps up and grabs him by the back of his shirt between his shoulder blades. He looks over his shoulder back at me. "We'll go use the hall bathroom. Scottie, you can use ours."

Julia giggles as Finn drags Ace out the door and then smiles at me as I climb off Finn's bed on nervous legs. I close the bathroom door behind me and lock it, and then I pause to stare at myself in the mirror.

My lips are flushed, a slight lingering tinge of Finn's blood collected at the edges. I run the faucet to clean myself up, brushing my teeth with my finger and using the toilet, and then change into Finn's shirt, leaving only my underwear underneath.

My heart races, and my fingertips tingle with adrenaline.

At this rate, it's going to be daylight by the time I'm able to fall asleep.

Carefully, I open the door to the bathroom and walk over to Finn's bed, dropping my clothes at the foot of it just like Julia did.

Ace is back from the bathroom and in bed with her, and I swear, the two of them look like they're already passed out.

Finn isn't back yet, so I climb quietly into his bed and pull the covers up to wait for him. The door creaks open gently, and he steps inside in a pair of lounge pants and a clean T-shirt. Unlike the one on me, it fits snugly across his muscles.

He smiles gently as he flips off the overhead light and tosses his clothes in his hamper at the head of the bed and then turns, his destination of the futon clear. Impulsively, I reach out and grab his wrist, stopping his momentum.

"You can sleep in the bed with me," I whisper. "It's not that big of a deal."

I'm a liar. It's a huge deal, but I want him to anyway.

"Are you sure?" he asks.

I nod. "Yes, it's fine."

He lifts the covers, and I scoot all the way toward the wall to give him some space as he climbs in. It's a small bed—twin-size, at most—and Finn is a big guy.

Nerves and excitement and a million other things flit around inside my belly. I never imagined I'd be ending the night in bed with Finn. It's like my body doesn't know what to do with itself.

I roll to my side with my back to the wall, and Finn rolls to his, facing me. Just enough moonlight shines through their window that I can make out his face in its entirety. It's beautiful, as always, but undoubtedly marred by the fight.

"That looks…bad." I wince as I gently touch my index finger to the broken skin on Finn's cheek, a spot that showcases one of many blows he took tonight. "Does it hurt?"

"Trust me, I've had worse," he whispers back, his eyes gentle on mine.

"You've had worse?" I frown. "What does that mean?"

He considers me carefully. "You have a good relationship with your dad?"

"My dad is awesome. Super supportive." Now, my mom, on the other hand, she's not even worth talking about.

His smile is soft, but mostly sad. "I'm glad to hear that, Scottie."

"What about you? What is—" I start to ask him about his family life, but when he reaches around my head and gently pulls the ponytail holder out of my hair, I lose my train of thought.

"There," he whispers softly. "That had to hurt to lie on."

With a tenderness I didn't even know was possible for a guy who just beat the shit out of an ex-UFC fighter, Finn pulls my body closer to his, adjusting us on the mattress so that our heads rest on his pillow. His brown eyes search mine for a beat before he presses his lips to mine.

The kiss is soft and sweet and everything I wish my first kiss as a thirteen-year-old girl would've been. But when he moves his hands into the strands of my hair, the urge to press my body tight against his becomes undeniable.

Chest to chest, I kiss him back. A complex warmth becomes rooted in my belly before it starts to spread to the rest of my body, and a delicious throbbing between my thighs makes a small moan escape my throat.

"Scottie," he whispers against my mouth, and my hips push into his until I can feel the growing hardness beneath his lounge pants. An intense, powerful feeling I've never experienced in my life overwhelms me.

If he asked right now, I think I'd let him put himself inside me. Which is fucking nuts, considering Ace and Julia are asleep ten feet away.

His hands move through my now-loose hair as he pushes his lips to mine again, so softly this time I barely feel them. Just like our voices, they're a whisper.

"Get some rest," he orders. "It's okay to sleep. I promise."

He punctuates that statement by turning me on my opposite side and pulling my back flush against his chest.

He's still hard and I can feel his arousal on my ass, but his big arms cocoon my body in a way that's not overtly sexual. It's gentle and caring and makes me feel safe and protected.

I thought it would take me ages to fall asleep—to let go enough to pass out. But there, in the warmth of Finn's arms, one second, I'm aware, and the next, I'm gone.

Fast asleep in Finn Hayes's bed.

Maybe I tugged hard enough on the rope of our hot and cold tug-of-war that the bad stuff is behind us.

20

Sunday, October 6th

Finn

The train rattles as we pull away from the station at the stop before mine, and I sink down in my seat and pull my jeans away from my knees. My knuckles are a mess, and my face doesn't look great either, but thanks to a dark basement room full of rich kids, I've got twenty-five hundred dollars in my pocket.

I rub my lips together to remind myself of the stinging split in the bottom one and catch the slightest hint of the taste of Scottie's lip gloss.

My jaw locks. When she wakes up in my bed alone and realizes I'm gone, I know she's going to be pissed. I didn't take her virginity—I'm not that big of a dick—but even the act of sleeping together is the kind of intimacy that deserves a "good morning" rather than an empty bed. Instead, I'm on my way to hell.

Willow texted me first thing this morning, upset from a confrontation with our father in the middle of the night. Both Trav and Jack stayed at a friend's house because they'd been drinking, and our mom worked the overnight shift at the factory—something she's apparently been doing a lot because of the two-dollar pay differential.

Leaving my siblings alone in that rotting house was my biggest fear about going to Dickson.

I lean my head back on the seat and close my eyes, allowing the lull of the train's motion to take me back to last night. To the sheer power I felt beating Donnie Marks and the way Scottie kissed me back on bleeding lips.

For the first time in his life, Ace even managed not to comment on it, and the night carried on almost as though it was the kind of life—the one with friends and few worries and college debauchery and a girlfriend—I could live. Scottie and I talked a little in the shadows of the night, though she didn't say much about home.

I didn't say much about home either, but now that I'm on my way this morning, I'm remembering why.

Scottie Bardeaux doesn't need to be mixed up with someone like me, no matter how good it feels to hold her while we fall asleep.

My phone buzzes in my pocket, startling my eyes open. When I pull it out and read the text, I know with certainty today isn't going to get any better.

> *Ace: Scottie just left. I tried to smooth things over, but she was upset. Pretty sure you're going to have to do some fast talking if you're going to have a prayer of salvaging that situation.*
>
> *Me: It's for the best.*
>
> *Ace: I hope you're sure.*
>
> *Me: Don't worry about it.*
>
> *Ace: Okay, buddy. Hit me up when you get back if I'm not in the room.*

Shaking my head to clear it, I scroll down to the messages Willow sent earlier this morning.

> *Willow: I can hear him breaking stuff, but I have the door locked and the chair under the knob, like you said.*
>
> *Willow: I think he's asleep. I don't hear anything anymore.*
>
> *Me: Keep the door locked.*

My blood boils and my heart races as I think about my sister being there alone and frightened. Maybe Trav and Jack taking her along when they go out drinking isn't such a bad option.

Knowing it's been nearly an hour since I heard from her last, I check in again.

> *Me: You okay?*

> *Willow: I heard the front door. I think Jack and Trav might be home.*

> *Me: Stay in your room until I get there.*

> *Willow: Okay, Finn.*

I look at my bloodied, broken knuckles again. I don't know what I'm going to do when I get there.

But there's a reason I didn't lose to Donnie Marks last night. And my siblings are an even better reason not to lose today.

21

Tuesday, October 8th

Scottie

The class is nearly full, and Professor Winslow is writing details about our first big exam on the whiteboard when Finn walks in. Everything inside me seethes as he walks straight for the front row and takes an empty seat next to Ace.

I'm on the side of the room, somewhere I never dreamed of sitting when I started the semester. But with Dane and Nadine cuddling in the back and Ace and an empty seat in the front, I had nowhere else to go.

No calls. No texts. I've gotten zilch from Finnley Hayes since we fell asleep in his bed together Saturday night and he disappeared Sunday morning, and I'm officially pissed off.

He kissed *me* at the Double C fight. *Twice. He* invited me to sleep in his room, and he's the one who kissed me after climbing into the bed. Not the other way around.

Ace tried to play the whole thing off like it was no big deal—tried to make me feel better about waking up in their room alone with him and Julia—but Finn's said more with his actions than Ace could have even dreamed of covering during his fast talk.

Finn may have wanted me Saturday night, but Sunday morning, his regret was swift and absolute, and I've got no option left but righteous anger.

I am *done*.

Professor Winslow is going through a study guide for our

Wuthering Heights exam, and no matter how hard I try, I can't hear a single thing he's saying.

My stupid gaze slithers back to Finn over and over, caressing each layer of skin in an attempt to peel him like an onion. I wish I understood him better.

At least then, I would know the best direction to point my wrath.

"I hope you realize I'm being nice here, giving you this awesome study guide that you should *definitely* utilize for your first big exam," Professor Winslow says, doing everything but a wink and nudge to tell us the questions on the exam will be at least similar to those on the guide.

Still, a guy in our class raises his hand, a frown on his face.

"Yes, Ben?"

"My study guide doesn't have any answers."

Professor Winslow frowns. "Shoot." He flips the paper over in his hands and then jogs toward Ben immediately. "Here. Try mine," he says as he hands Ben the paper.

Ben flips it around in his hands. "Hey! This one doesn't have any answers either!"

Professor Winslow offers an amused smile in Ben's direction. "That's right. The point of the study guide is to help you study. So, yes, your study guide doesn't have any answers because you're supposed to fill them out and *learn* while you do."

"That blows," Ben groans, dropping his head back and closing his eyes.

Professor Winslow laughs, slapping him on the shoulder. "Welcome to college, son."

Ace's laughter pulls my attention to the front of the room again, and Professor Winslow jogs back down to his desk to continue his explanation.

I stare with hard eyes at Finn as he smiles at something Ace says, and a bruise stands out on his face among the rest. It's on the top of his right cheekbone, and it shines in the stark auditorium-style lights. I know I watched half the fight with Donnie from behind my hands, but I don't remember Finn getting hit there. Not to mention all the staring at his face I did before I fell asleep in his bed. I would have noticed it.

My phone buzzes in my backpack, and I discreetly pull it out, expecting another "Hope you're having a good day, sweetie!" text from my adorable but cheesy dad, and end up frowning at the sight of more stupid messages from an unknown number.

Hey, skank.

A few seconds later, another populates the screen.

What's it like having an alcoholic mom who hates her daughter so much she drank her entire pregnancy?

Dread seeps into my gut, and an irrational urge to throw my phone across the room consumes me. I tried to block the number when they started sending messages, but they just send from a new number every time.

And now, the messages are escalating. This one is personal—so cruel that emotion clogs my throat and tears threaten to spill from my eyes. Whoever is behind this knows more than I wish they did.

Don't let this get to you, I silently tell myself and swallow hard against the discomfort in my chest. I shut my eyes until the tears stop threatening and shove my phone back into my backpack.

There are only two people at Dickson whom I can imagine sending me something like this and only one who would actually have the knowledge, but when I glance back at Dane and Nadine, they're so deep in their PDA they might as well be swallowing each other whole.

If it's not them, who is it?

I feel nauseated immediately by the uncertainty.

"Scottie?" Professor Winslow's voice startles me and pulls my gaze back to the front of the room. Everything he's said in the last three minutes might as well have been in Chinese for all the attention I've been paying.

"Scottie? You with us?" our professor questions gently. I know my face is the color of a tomato, and I can't help but check to see if Finn is looking at me.

He's not.

I should be thankful, but instead, I'm even angrier.

"Yes, Professor. Sorry." I frown, and my stupid lips quiver from the erratic game of ping-pong my emotions are playing.

I don't freaking understand how I got here. Obsessive and unfocused and desperate. So freaking desperate, it's pitiful.

"It's all good." Professor Winslow offers a smile that I can't match at all. "Just want to make sure you're prepared for the test."

On the outside, I nod appreciatively.

On the inside, I'm crumbling. My stomach is heavy, and my heart feels sick. I never dreamed I'd be the type of girl to allow myself such an intense longing for someone who doesn't deserve it.

I recognize that Dane wasn't good for me. I recognize that these messages I'm getting aren't right.

And yet somehow, I can't seem to make myself recognize the same things about Finn. He's not good for me, and the way he's treating me isn't right.

I don't want to care anymore.

I shouldn't care about the texts some coward is sending me from an unknown number. And I sure as hell shouldn't care about a guy who leaves me alone in his bed with no explanation or why he has a new bruise on his face I can't account for.

Too bad I do.

22

can't believe I agreed to this.

Honestly, a smarter girl would have backed out—*especially* after Finn snuck out of his bed and sent my whole psyche into a tailspin.

But Ace, despite his association with Finn, is the kind of friend you don't let down. He has your back, so you have his, even when it hurts.

And by God does this hurt.

It's three o'clock on a Wednesday, and instead of studying in the library, I am in full cheerleader glam in the middle of the Financial District in busy New York City. With practices every day and the course load I'm taking, I've been walking a tightrope to keep up with both at the same time. It's almost laughable that I thought I'd have spare time to find a hospital in the city to volunteer for, too. At home, I spent every second Saturday at St. Mark's Medical, volunteering in a few of the pediatric wings. I started doing it on a whim—Wren pretty much dragged me with her when she had to get community service hours to beef up her college application. But it only took one four-hour shift for me to find myself enjoying spending time there. It's…fulfilling and, honestly, still has me wavering back and forth on if should've gone premed or something in the medical field that would have me working closely with young patients.

Currently, I'm still undecided, but with my grueling schedule here at Dickson, I haven't had time to consider my actual degree path. A lame excuse, I know, but all I seem to have time for these days is staying on top of all of my core classes, cheerleading, and well…unfortunately, *drama*.

Oh, and Ace's pranks too, I suppose. *Insert eye roll.*

Thankfully, I'm not the only one getting strange looks from men and women sporting briefcases and smart suits as we walk toward the entrance of the building that bears the address Ace sent our way twenty minutes ago.

Five other girls from my squad—Kayla, Tonya, McKenzie, Emma, and Olivia—have joined me to engage in Ace's prank on his dad.

"Not going to lie," Kayla comments, her perfectly manicured eyebrows distancing themselves from her eyes. "I'm feeling a little out of place."

McKenzie laughs, rubbing a hand down her navy-blue skirt. "Girl, tell me about it."

A fancy doorman at the front of the swanky financial building pulls the gold-plated door open for us to enter, his smile suggesting he knows the plan better than I do. Kayla and McKenzie are first through the door, Tonya and Emma following, and then Olivia and I bring up the rear. Ace is waiting at the security desk in the lobby, dressed to the nines in a similar three-piece suit to the one he wore to the first college party I met him at.

He looks dapper as hell, and I wonder how Julia can act like his handsome face and tall, muscular body have zero effect on her. Like, I know they've been friends since they were little kids, but holy moly, when Ace isn't actively fucking around, it's impossible to miss how handsome he is. If he didn't want to do the college thing, he could easily be modeling for Calvin Klein.

Maybe there was some kind of roommate lottery where they grouped only the most attractive people together in Graham Hall.

Ugh. *Finn.* He's the last person I want to think about right now.

"Ladies, so glad you could make it." Ace grins, rubbing his

hands together in excitement. "Thanks again, Frank," he tells the security guard, sliding him a wad of cash I can only assume is the agreed-upon bribe amount.

Frank smiles and slides the money into his pocket, and Ace gestures for us to follow him toward the bank of elevators on the far side of the lobby. I look around as we move, unable to accept the sheer volume of marble floors and ceilings and sculptures I'm certain cost a bajillion dollars.

"Welcome to Kelly Investments," Ace announces with a shit-eating grin, spinning in a circle with his arms out wide. Kayla and the other girls laugh, but my nerves have gotten the best of me. I hate not knowing what's going on.

"You know, Ace," I chime in and nudge him with my elbow. "Now would be a good time to tell us what the actual plan is..."

"Yeah," Kayla pipes up. "Why do you need a bunch of cheer-leaders to prank your dad?"

"Let's get upstairs first, and then we'll get down to the nitty-gritty. I don't need any nosy fucks in the lobby ruining shit," Ace counters as he guides us toward a bank of elevators. One is already available, sitting idle on the ground floor, and the six of us file in while Ace plays gentleman and holds the door.

"How about you tell us now?" Tonya questions once the elevator doors shut.

"How do you ladies feel about changing out of your uniforms into something else?" Ace tosses out, completely ignoring Tonya.

"Something else?" Kayla retorts. "Ace, if you're trying to get us to wear thongs and pasties, I will kick you in the dick."

"No! No! Nothing like that." Ace cracks up, but he also covers his crotch with one hand. He tilts his head to the side. "You should meet my mom, though. The two of you think alike."

Kayla crosses her arms over her chest and settles into a hip, and Ace holds up two hands in front of himself. "It's a cheerlead-ing uniform like the ones you're wearing, but it's just a little more specific to the situation."

"If we agree, will it make this get over faster?" Emma asks. "I mean, this is our only day this week that we don't have practice, so I'm hoping to actually enjoy the downtime at some point."

"Yes, it will make this go faster," Ace answers.

"Fine," she agrees, followed by the rest of us nodding too.

The elevator dings its arrival on the thirtieth floor, and we follow Ace out of the cart and onto a completely empty floor that looks like it's under some kind of reconstruction. Plastic tarps and tools and buckets are littering the space, and the smell of fresh paint is thick in the air.

"Um…Ace?" Kayla questions as she takes in the bare room. "It's time to tell us the plan."

"Relax." Ace laughs. "This isn't our final destination. This is just the best place to get you guys ready for showtime." He glances around the room like he's looking for something but, eventually, just shouts, "Yo, Blake! Finn! Where the hell are you?"

My stomach drops. I don't know what I was thinking. I should have known he would be here. They're best friends.

Still, if I'd realized, I definitely wouldn't have come. I'm sure five cheerleaders would have been just as good as six.

Blake and Finn walk across the massive space with brown paper bags in their hands, and I have to remind my lungs how to breathe with each long stride he takes closer. I'm still so livid at him for making it be this way.

He smiles at the group but avoids my eyes, so I use the opportunity to look at him more closely. The new bruise on his face is yellowing now—it's healing definitely behind the rest, and the split in his lip is completely scabbed over.

"You got the goods?" Ace questions, and Blake grins, holding up the bags in his hands.

"You know it, buddy."

"Fuck yeah," Ace cheers, opening Blake's bag and handing Kayla the first uniform and set of poms. I stand back as Finn hands out his too, hoping to avoid talking to him directly, but when the other girls are done and there's only one left, Finn is the one to have it.

He holds it out for me to take, his eyes holding mine with all the same voodoo magic they've had since the first day I met him. If I let myself, I could fall directly into their warm brown pools and stay there.

When his lips part and it seems like he's going to say something to me, I snatch the uniform and poms from his hands and spin on my heel to face Ace. "Where are we supposed to change?"

"There's a bathroom over there," Ace answers, pointing down a small hallway near the elevators.

Kayla locks elbows with me and marches us that direction, and I don't look back.

If Finn Hayes wants to play it cold, I can be icy too.

23

Finn

"All right, ladies," Ace whispers as the elevator stops on the fortieth floor. "It's showtime!"

Blake lifts the two-thousand-dollar camera Ace handed him downstairs and starts filming, and all six girls file out of the cart on a synchronized jog, their Kelly Financial uniforms sparkling in the office lighting. The heels of their gym shoes tap their asses with each step, and their hands clap in perfect timing.

I trail behind, embarrassed, but unwilling to miss any of the action.

Frankly, it's impressive that they're this in time, seeing as Ace did no more than a ten-minute briefing of the plan on the thirtieth floor. The fucker had a notebook full of cheers and shit that he wanted them to do, but McKenzie—who is one of Dickson's cheer captains—told him to shut up and let them handle the cheerleading. It's beyond obvious now that Ace agreeing to it was the right move.

Ace is so damn amped I can practically see his body vibrating with joy. "Dude," I comment and grab him by the back of the neck. "Take a breath."

"Oh, Finnley, I *cannot*," he exclaims on a whisper as we walk down the marble hallway that leads to his dad's office. "I can't wait to see my dad's face when I one-up that fucker with something he'd never expect."

The receptionist waves to Ace as we walk past, not in the least surprised by the Kelly brand of shit, and we follow the cheerleaders down the hall and around the corner to the office he showed them on his hand-drawn map.

When the girls reach the desk in front of his dad's office door that's occupied by Thatch's assistant, the red-haired woman smiles so big it looks like her face might crack. Without hesitation, she gestures for them to go straight into the office behind her. A gold plate on the door reads **Thatcher Kelly, CEO Kelly Investments.**

McKenzie starts up as soon as she crosses the threshold. "Give me a K!"

"*K!*" Scottie and the other girls respond as they trail through the door, doing their little ass-kicking run thing again. I watch Scottie for longer than I'd like to admit, only stopping when Ace elbows me to stop at the assistant's desk.

"Give me an E!"

"*E!*"

"Tell me you planned this, Acer," Thatch's assistant begs, her glee not even remotely concealed. According to Ace's breakdown, she's been his dad's assistant since before he was even born.

"You bet your gorgeous ass I did, Madeline."

Madeline falls back into her chair, a fit of giggles consuming her, and Ace leans forward to high-five her when she puts a hand in the air.

"I've been warning him for decades that he would reap what he sowed with you and your brother. Goodness, I'm so thrilled to see it playing out in real time." She smiles at Blake and me before glancing over her shoulder into the office and then back at us. "Grab some popcorn, boys. This is going to be good. He's in the middle of a call!"

Ace's eyes widen in fear for half a second before Blake shoves him into the office and points the camera at Thatch, who's sitting behind a giant mahogany desk while all six cheerleaders dance in front of it, shaking their pom-poms.

"I looked at the projected reports, Thatch, and I can't deny they're good. Real damn good. But what are you going to offer us that our current investment firm isn't?" a male voice questions from the computer.

"We love Kelly Financial. Yes, we do! We love Kelly Financial. How about you?" McKenzie cheers, and Scottie and the other four girls don't hesitate to respond.

"We love Kelly Financial. Yes, we do! We love Kelly Financial. How about you!" They point their poms directly at Thatch at the end of the line, shaking their ribbons until the noise of it is so much, I almost have to cover my ears.

Thatch leans closer to his computer, trying to block it out and save the call. "Bradley, you *need* your money at Kelly Financial. I know it, and you know it—"

"Stronger than steel!" Kayla exclaims as she jumps in the air.

"Hotter than the sun!" Emma cheers and does a fucking backflip.

"Thatch won't stop!" McKenzie shouts, shaking her pom-poms.

"Until he gets the investment job done!" Scottie yells and jumps up to stand on Tonya's and Olivia's prepped hands. A second later, they toss Scottie into the air, and she does the fucking splits before landing perfectly in Tonya's and Olivia's outstretched arms. Thank fuck Thatch's office has twelve-foot ceilings.

I'd be lying if I said I'm not mesmerized or that I can keep my eyes off Scottie after that.

She smiles and cheers along with her friends, and the amount of pride I feel for her talent is insane. She's not *my* girl—I made damn sure of that. But she is *that* girl.

"Thatch?" a booming male voice echoes from the speakers of the computer. Thatch waves commandingly at the girls to stop, but they're ready for it, continuing anyway just as Ace's briefing suggested they should.

More voices filter from the speakers.

"What is going on?"

"Do we have a bad connection?"

"I can see him sitting there. I'm positive we don't have a bad connection."

"Then what is he doing? Some kind of gesture?"

"Everything but convincing us why we should invest our money with him, that's for damn sure."

Thatch's annoyed eyes finally break away from the cheerleaders and land on Ace, and for the first time since we entered the office, realization dawns. Ace gives his dad a big smile and two thumbs up, and I nearly choke on my saliva.

Holy shit, this family is crazy.

"You're doing great, sweetie," Ace calls toward his dad through cupped hands. "The Kelly Financial cheerleaders are so proud of you!"

In a split second, Thatch's face goes from ticked off to cool, calm, and collected. It's a face I've literally never seen my father make.

"Thatch? Hello?"

"Sorry, Todd," Thatch responds with a neutral smile on his face. "Your surprise arrived earlier than expected."

"Surprise?"

"Oh yeah. Just give me one second, boys," Thatch states and stands up from his desk chair. "Ladies, can I just say that you are looking very gorgeous today?" He winks, and I don't miss how all six cheerleaders smile at the compliment. *"And..."* He drops his voice to a whisper. "I would like to compensate you for your time."

"What the fuck?" Ace starts to complain, but his dad is too busy schmoozing his accomplices to turn against him.

"Compensate us?" McKenzie asks, her interest more than piqued.

"Wait a minute, I—" Ace tries to stop what is happening, but Tonya holds her hand in the air in a very obvious *shut up.*

"Five hundred dollars each," Thatch elucidates before winking at Ace.

"Hell yes," McKenzie agrees, followed by a "That's what I'm talking about," from Kayla.

Scottie glances back at us, avoiding actually making eye contact with me, of course, but ultimately agrees to the generous offer. Thatch, the charming bastard that he is, even strides around his desk and gets them in a little pow-wow huddle as he tells them what he wants them to do.

I grab Ace's shoulder and squeeze in support, and Blake continues to film as Thatch guides the now official Kelly Financial cheerleaders over to stand in front of the screen of his computer.

"Ladies, how about we show the boys at the Redstone Corporation how excited we are to have them on board." Thatch's grin is smug as his cheerleaders start up in another cheer.

This time, though, it's all about the Redstone Corporation. By the end of it, the sounds of claps and laughter echo from the speakers of the computer, his audience completely swayed.

"Sorry to break it to you, Ace," Blake comments on a laugh and wraps an arm around Ace's shoulders. "But I think your dad just one-upped your one-up."

Not only did Thatch run with being surprised by the Kelly Financial cheerleaders, but he actually *used* them to secure a deal with Redstone Corporation.

"V-I-C-T-O-R-Y," I say with a shrug.

Ace shakes his head as the cheerleaders collect their money from Thatch and leave the office in smiles. Scottie doesn't glance at me once on her way toward us at the door, and I can't blame her.

Still, that doesn't stop me from putting my body just slightly in the way of her exit.

"Sorry," she mutters as she bumps me, falling into my body enough that I have to steady her by the shoulders. When she looks up and glares, I release them and clear the discomfort from my throat.

"No big deal."

Silence forms a cloak over us and chokes the oxygen out of the air. I don't know what to say to her. I know my goal after going home Sunday was to stop leading her on, so she'd have the freedom to find someone else—someone she deserves—but I don't know that saying absolutely nothing at all was the way to go.

I don't want her to hate me. I just… I want her to know she deserves better than what I have to offer.

"You…uh…going somewhere?" I ask dumbly. Clearly, she's not planning to stay at Kelly Financial for the foreseeable future.

"I'm going back to school to study and catch up on the assignments I have to do. We have an away game in Ithaca this weekend, and the bus leaves tomorrow. I'll be missing all of my classes after our English test."

"How long is the drive?" I ask, unable to do anything but make lame small talk with her. It's so fucking pathetic, but I'm desperate to keep her talking to me at all at this point.

"Four hours on the bus." She shuffles a little on her feet, and she averts her eyes from mine to look down at her white gym shoes. But when her gaze lifts back up again, I'm shocked when she asks, "Why does it feel like you're always playing games with me?"

"I'm not," I refute, more offended than I have the right to be after everything I've put her through.

"Are you sure?" Her eyes narrow, and her normally gentle voice starts to rise with irritation. "Because *you* invited me back to your dorm Saturday night. *You* kissed me. *You* asked me to stay. But then, I wake up, and you're gone. No explanation. No nothing. No call or text or carrier pigeon after the fact. Why? Because if it's not a game, I want to understand it. Give me a real reason why."

Because I don't want to fill your head with the bullshit I've been dealing with since I was a kid.

Because I didn't want to wake you in the middle of the night to tell you I had to go save my baby sister from our father.

Because I came to this school to make my half brother feel the kind of pain I've been feeling ever since I was born.

Because I'm too fucked up for a girl like her.

I could tell her a million reasons, but I don't. I can't. Scottie shouldn't have to shoulder the bullshit hand the game of life has dealt me. She shouldn't have to think about the ugly realities my siblings and I have faced our whole lives.

And no matter how much I like her, no matter how drawn I am to her, she sure as shit shouldn't be close to a guy like me. She deserves better.

"You don't have anything to say, Finn?"

"I told you not to need me, Scottie. You're too fucking good to need me," I say like a total asshole.

"You know what, Finn?" she snaps, and a defiant hand goes to her hip. I feel proud of her and sad at the same time. "All this bullshit with you…it's worse than what I went through with Dane."

Her words have claws, and they slice through my chest until they draw blood.

I've had a lot of nasty things tossed my way. My dad's called me stupid and pathetic and weak. He's told me I'll never amount to anything. In the midst of one of his drunken rages, he said that I was a mistake he wished they would've aborted.

But right now, none of those words have ever hit as hard as this.

I'm worse than her asshole ex, whom I literally saw manhandling her with my own two eyes. That's how she sees me.

Scottie stands there for a long moment, but when I don't say anything to that, can't say anything to that, she walks away. Down the long hallway and out of sight, she's gone.

And I have the unshakable feeling that she won't be back.

Fuck.

24

nother day of English class and another day of sitting on the complete opposite side of the room from Finn. Only this time, it feels different.

More…final.

I don't know. I've been thinking about the way we left things in the Kelly Financial office all weekend in Ithaca and trying to make peace with it. Surprisingly, now that I've had time to process, I don't actually think Finn is ever trying to be hurtful. I think he's drawn to me just like I'm drawn to him, but the demons he fights inside are too powerful to overcome. It's why he plays me hot and cold, and it's why when we are together, everything feels so right.

Unfortunately, it's also why I know I have to find a way to get over him. The constant pull to be with him and the overwhelming urge to be his *fixer* is beyond unhealthy. I'm a freshman in college, for shit's sake.

I have to let it go.

Ace strides in just in the nick of time, as per usual, as Professor Winslow starts class by writing details of a new assignment on the board.

I take out my notebook and flip to the next open page, doodling a dog and a cat and a fish to pass the time—anything to supersede the urge to stare at Finnley Hayes.

Professor Winslow caps his marker and places it on the shelf below the board, turning to face the class and clasping his hands together after he does. I turn to a blank page and start paying attention.

"Okay, folks. We've reached the halfway point of our first semester—and you know what that means… It's time to get serious. We're going to be working on one of the most poignant works of self-reflection and the consequences of assumption I've ever read," Professor Winslow explains while I do my best to listen. I did okay on our test last week, but I wouldn't say my level of concentration was at its peak. And I really can't afford to let my grades slip.

"Starting this week and continuing for the rest of the semester, I'm going to be breaking you up into groups of three to work on an extensive project. There will be multiple parts. There will be tests. There will, hopefully, be teamwork."

I watch Professor Winslow's carefree smile closely and find myself overanalyzing it entirely. It's straight but still has character, and his jaw is stronger than most. It actually reminds me of Finn's smile in some freakish way, if Finn weren't so damn broody all the time.

"Before you leave today, you can pick up your copy of *The Winter's Tale* down here at my desk. It is on loan from Dickson, so please take care of it, but other than that, nothing is off-limits. I expect each of you to become intimate with Shakespeare's text."

"Ooh," Ace calls predictably. "Professor Winslow wants us to get intimate."

"With the book," Professor Winslow challenges with a wag of his finger. "But hey, since you're in the mood to be the center of attention, Ace. I'll start with you. You'll be working with…" He leans down to consult his clipboard. "Shawn Nevil and Joey Gonzales."

Ace frowns. "You want me to get intimate with guys?" Professor Winslow smiles. "Come on. Not even one girl? Like a male/male/female romance novel kind of thing?" Ace continues.

Even in my current mood, I snort. Finn's eyes jump immediately to mine, and I have to hold my breath.

On the night of the fight, as we ate pizza in Finn and Ace's dorm room, Ace mentioned that his mom's main career is photography, but that she also writes romance novels. I downloaded one online after that and actually got a chance to read it while we were on the bus to and from Ithaca.

It had a whole lot of freaky shit in it, including, but not limited to, service pig voyeurism—which isn't a surprise now that I've been around Ace and his dad a little bit—but it was also pretty romantic.

I just wish I'd stop turning whatever the hell is happening between Finn and me into some kind of romance novel of my own.

"Scottie Bardeaux," Professor Winslow calls out then, startling my attention away from Finn.

I raise my hand. "Yes?"

"You'll be working with…" He looks down at his sheet of paper again. "Finnley Hayes and Nadine Jones."

I nod and smile, but on the inside, I'm dying. I'm talking organ trauma, internal bleeding, sliced and diced.

I've talked a big game about getting over and moving on and rising above. But an intimate rest of the semester with the girl who hates me and the guy I wish I could get over? Sounds just powerful enough to prove the in-control-of-her-emotions me is a liar.

My head spins with equations and other math bullshit as I leave algebra on Friday. An electric vibe is in the air as everyone chatters about weekend plans and endless parties.

It's a bye week for the football team, and everyone is raring to celebrate our undefeated streak. Sigma Tau is having a luau, Beta Kappa is doing an Olympic-themed vodka luge, and according to two of the girls in algebra, there's a house party in one of the abandoned buildings just outside of campus.

My body rocks to the side in a violent push, and my hair ruffles while weight clings to my back. I stutter-step but catch my balance as Ace wraps himself around me like a spider monkey.

"What the hell, man?" I sigh, shrugging him off with a roll of my shoulders. He laughs, and my backpack slides off with him, landing in a heap and spilling some of its contents through the partially open zipper.

My dad's stolen journal—the one I acquired three Sundays ago, right before taking two or three fists to the face when I got between my old man and Willow—is the only thing I can see.

Ace, fortunately, is preoccupied with his own agenda as he climbs to his feet, and I put the contents of my backpack back inside. "Come on, let's go get dinner and figure out what we want to hit tonight."

"I don't know if I feel like going out," I hedge, making him guffaw.

"Yeah, okay, buddy. Good one."

"I'm serious."

"Too bad. I need a wingman, and now that you've royally fucked things with Scottie, you're the perfect candidate. I need you free to fondle the best friend of whomever I'm after anyway."

"Ace."

"*Finn.*"

I sigh, and he smiles. "See…you know how pointless it is to fight me on this, which means you know me. We're soul mates. I would have totally gotten intimate with you if Ty let me."

My jaw tightens at the mention of Professor Ty Winslow and our big group project. He makes it sound like Shakespeare is going to solve all our problems, but it'd be a lot more fucking helpful if he hadn't grouped me with the girl I'm not good enough for and a ditsy, promiscuous sidekick.

"At least you're not with Nadine."

Ace laughs. "What? You don't think her cast would feel good on your dick?"

I shake my head. "Fuck that."

"Yeah, I guess that would make Scottie's head spin. But you're already in hot shit, so what's the difference?"

"Ace."

"What? I'm just trying to ascertain where we are, dude. Are we groveling? Revenge-fucking her enemies? It's a broad spectrum, and I need all the info to be the best helper I can be."

"We're not doing anything. We're leaving everything exactly where it is, which is for the best."

He groans. "Well, that's boring as shit."

"I keep trying to tell you I'm a boring guy."

He laughs so hard at that he nearly scrapes his face on the sidewalk as he walks because he's bent over so far. "Right. The boring guy who's almost gotten expelled, has a brood of wild siblings he's seemingly in charge of, beat the shit out of a UFC fighter, and came very close to stealing the virgin cheerleader from her long-term

boyfriend within the first two weeks of school." He nods sarcastically. "Very boring."

I sigh. "Dinner it is."

Ace hollers and jumps on my back again, but I'm ready this
time, so I take off at a run with him still clinging to me. "Ayyyy!" he
yells, pulling the attention of a group of people standing in front of
the Logan Center. By the looks of things, both football and cheerleading practice just let out for the night.

Scottie's face is the first I notice, but I'm not surprised; it stands
out in a crowd.

I avoid eye contact even though it's hard, settling instead on
Blake Boden as he takes off at a jog toward us.

"Hey, girls," he says teasingly as he arrives to me pitching Ace
off my back yet again. "Did you see the text we just got?"

"What text?" Ace asks, appropriately summing up my response
too.

Blake looks around before answering like we're in the CIA on
a clandestine mission. "From my future wife, of course. It's a time
for the next Double C."

Almost as if summoned, Ace's phone chimes while mine vibrates in my pocket. I pull it out to read it.

Unknown: 10:15. Gyger Tunnel. Don't be late.

"I got the text before you guys. I bet she remembers me."

Ace snorts. "Lexi Winslow definitely remembers you, but don't
flatter yourself. She remembers everything. Her brain is like a fucking sponge."

My head whips up from my phone before I can read the other
text I have from my older brother Reece. "Lexi is a Winslow? As
in Ty Winslow?"

"Lexi is a Winslow, as in Winnie Winslow, Ty's sister. Her
dad, Wes Lancaster, is one of my dad's best friends and owns the
Mavericks."

"The New York Mavericks, pro football team Mavericks? Are

you fucking kidding me?" Blake questions emphatically. Ace nods and laughs. Blake holds both hands out to his sides before looking up to the sky. "Thank you. Thank you. Thank you."

My mind reels as I work through the sheer number of connections to my dad's other family I didn't know I'd be making so quickly. I don't know what my plan is or if it's a good idea, but immediately, my mind is made up. After reading my dad's journal for the past three weeks, looking for the perfect entry to pass along to Ty, I need to gather all the reconnaissance I can. Plus, maybe I can make some more money.

"Plans are set for tonight, Acer. It's Double C all the way."

"Fuck yes!" Blake yells, pumping a fist in the air while Ace shrugs.

"Works for me."

Ace and Blake chatter and fuck around as we walk toward the dining hall, and I scroll down to the message from Reece I didn't get to read before.

> **Reece: California is bullshit, as it turns out. I miss New York. Every time Jack or Trav texts me about some fucked-up thing they're doing while I'm powerless to stop it, one of my fairy brain cells loses its wings. I'm transferring to Dickson next year, and you can't change my mind. The paperwork is already filed.**

Reece doesn't know anything about my dad's other kids—fucking middle-aged adult kids, as it were—none of my siblings do. But if he's going to be here next year, I guess I better get busy bringing it all to light.

After all, what's a fucked-up family reunion without the whole fucked-up family?

26

"**M**ind if I borrow your curling iron? I need to fix a few curls." Julia says, leaning out from my half bathroom and shaking her blond hair side to side.

I laugh at her cute little dance and pull it out of the drawer in the white vanity at the side of the room that holds all my hair products, accessories, and devices like my hair dryer and straightener.

I hand it to her, and she smiles gratefully.

As she plugs it in and goes back to getting ready in the bathroom, I step back up to the vanity to continue working on my makeup.

All thanks to Tonya's elbow today at practice, my nose took an accidental hit. It hurt like I suspect any fist to the face does and started bleeding instantly—and hasn't stopped yet. I swear, it's been trickling on and off for hours. Even worse, though, I've got bruises forming under my eyes from the force of the blow, and they're an absolute bitch to get covered.

Julia holds a curling iron to her head at the front of her crown and peeks over her shoulder while still tethered to the cord.

"Did you get it to stop bleeding?"

"Yeah," I respond, pulling the wadded-up paper towel from under my top lip and throwing it into the garbage can under my desk. I go back to hiding the bruises under my eyes with concealer. "I thought I had it under control before you got here. I don't know why it started up again."

"Nosebleeds are so finicky."

"Where'd you learn that paper towel under the lip thing anyway?"

"One of my mom's best friends is the doctor on staff for the New York Mavericks. She knows all sorts of tips and tricks for sports-related injuries."

I bark a laugh. "You say that so casually."

Julia giggles and shrugs, taking the curling iron out from the back of her head now and letting a spiral piece of hair drop. "I grew up around all these people, so I don't even think anything of it, I guess. It's pretty cool, though, huh?"

"That your dad is a billionaire with a bunch of billionaire friends?" I mock with a wink. "Yeah, it's pretty cool."

Julia rolls her eyes. "Trust me, you'd never think my dad was a billionaire. It took my mom my entire childhood to convince him to drive something other than a Ford Edge."

"Honestly, I think that might make it even cooler."

Julia nods. "He's the best."

It takes everything inside me, but I somehow manage to ask my next question without a shaky voice. "What do you think Finn's deal is? Like his family and stuff?"

"I don't know, actually. Ace is normally such a blabbermouth, but he hasn't said anything about Finn or his parents." She laughs. "Probably hedging his bets to keep from getting beat up."

I force a laugh of my own. "Yeah. Finn's a pretty good fighter."

"Do you think that's what's happening tonight?" she asks about the Double C text we got about an hour before she got to my dorm. "Another fight?"

My lungs seize at the thought, but I play it cool, dabbing powder under my eyes.

"I don't know." What I want to say is *Yikes, I hope not*, but I'm afraid that'll give me away. And I've got a promise going to myself that we're not going to give in to the Finn Hayes feelings anymore.

Still, here I am, getting ready to go find out anyway. I'm not entirely sure if it's just fear—that I won't be able to bear not being there if there's another fight involving Finn—or if I'm stupidly hoping it'll lead to another kiss.

And yes, I'm aware. I'm hopeless.

I hear my phone ping with a new text message, but I'm too busy applying mascara to my lashes to check it immediately. It's on the other side of the room where Julia is curling her hair, and mascara application is a delicate process.

"What is this, Scottie?" Julia asks through a horrified gasp. When I turn around to look, my phone is in her hand.

Shit.

My shoulders tense as Julia walks toward me, concern swimming in her eyes. I take the phone from her outstretched hand and read the message to myself.

> *Hey, skank. Did you know that your ex-boyfriend was cheating on you the whole time you were together?*

It's a fucked-up message, but I'm just glad it's not about my mom. Unfortunately, another message pops up on the screen while Julia's still right there.

> *I'm going to celebrate the day you finally get what you deserve.*

"What the hell? What unimaginable asshole would send you something like this?" she questions, and a sigh leaves my lungs.

"I don't know. It's always an unknown number." I shrug and make a point to clear the notifications off the screen and shove my phone in my jeans pocket.

"Wait…you've gotten more of these?"

"It's no big deal."

Julia frowns. "Scottie, it feels like a big deal. This is legit harassment."

"Well, I did try to block the number once, but they just started using a new one."

"You think you should take this to the campus police?"

"Hell no." I laugh, horrified. "It's not that serious."

She's not convinced. A huge frown mars the usually perfect skin between her eyebrows. "It kind of feels that serious, Scottie."

"It's fine," I say and force a confident smile that I'm not even remotely feeling to my lips. "Plus, we don't have time to go to the campus police tonight." I check the clock and feel my stomach tense on itself when I realize we need to leave soon for Double C. "It's almost ten. Are you ready?"

"Yeah," Julia replies, running to the bathroom, yanking the plug out of the wall, and combing her fingers through her curls as she steps back into the room with me. "How do I look?"

I smile, and this time, it takes no effort. "Beautiful, as always. I've never seen you look anything short of perfect, though."

Julia smiles. "Look who's talking."

"I literally just stopped bleeding all over the place. And you can still see some of the bruising under my eyes."

"You look gorgeous, girl. Promise."

I glance at myself in the mirror and will myself to see what Julia is seeing. To be a confident, badass bitch tonight who doesn't need Finn Hayes or anyone else to notice her.

I need the bravado, even if I'm faking more than half of it.

"All right, let's go. Before we're late and we miss the whole damn thing."

Julia's eyes widen as I grab her hand and drag her, but she catches on quickly, snagging her tiny purse from my desk on the way by and jogging to keep up with me as my door slams behind us. I've opted to go bagless, just shoving some cash, my ID, and a lipstick in my pocket.

We laugh all the way down the stairs, passing Carrie at the front door of Delaney Place and pausing for a brief cordial exchange.

As soon as we start walking, I glance at my phone for the time—10:05.

The entrance to the Gyger Tunnel is under the football field and at least seven minutes away if we speedwalk.

"Come on. We have to hustle," I command, pulling Julia's hand again. She laughs but complies, and her phone chimes in her hand.

To her credit, she reads it and walks at the same time. "Ace says they're almost there."

"See? I told you."

"Don't worry. Ace will make sure they let us in." The way she says it is so matter-of-fact, I can't help but question her.

"You say that like he's never broken a promise."

She shrugs. "I guess that's 'cause he hasn't."

"Never?" I ask disbelievingly. All the guys I've ever known have slipped up at least once.

She shakes her head, the mottled yellow glow from the street-lights shining in her eyes. "Never. I know he's crazy, but he can't help that. It's in his genes."

"I just didn't know a man could be that reliable. I mean, my dad is incredibly reliable, but from my experience, he's an exception."

"Really?" she asks, and she seems genuinely shocked. "All the men in my life are unequivocally reliable."

"All of them?" I question, aghast.

"Yeah. My dad. My grandpa. My dad's friends, who are all my pseudo-uncles, I guess. Ace and even his little brother Gunnar, who's truly a crazy shit."

"Crazier than Ace?"

Julia's face actually startles. "Oh yeah. Ace is like a zero on a hundred scale compared to Gunnar's one hundred."

"Okay. That actually frightens me."

"It should."

I shove open the door for Wheaton Hall. It's the building that holds all of the professor's offices, and also, the safest, fastest short-cut for two ladies walking alone this late at night on campus. I pull Julia inside and startle when a large man appears at the other end of the hallway when we're halfway down it.

My scream echoes off the stone walls, and Julia's follows shortly after.

"Hey, hey," a voice I thankfully recognize calls over ours with authority. "It's just me. Professor Winslow."

I take several deep breaths to calm myself, and Julia covers her face with her hands. It's safe to say we both thought this was the start of our very own true crime special on Netflix.

"What are you girls doing in here so late?"

I nudge Julia with my elbow to get her moving with me—time is still ticking—and walk toward Professor Winslow with confidence. It's feigned, but whatever. "Just cutting through to the other side of campus. This is the safest route." He frowns, and I find myself questioning him. "What are *you* doing in here so late?"

He smirks. "Department meeting ran late, and then I got busy on some graduate papers. Turns out being the boss is busy."

Julia widens her eyes in an unspoken *We have to go.*

"Well, see you later...in class...I guess," I say awkwardly, grabbing Julia's elbow and dragging her by the professor.

"Hey," he calls, pulling me up short before we can get too far.

I grit my teeth and turn around. "Yes?"

"I noticed Finn had some new bruises in class last week. You wouldn't happen to know anything about that, would you?"

Julia squeaks, and I tighten my grip on her elbow. She thinks those bruises are from the Double C fight, but I know for a fact he had other bruises too. Bruises that weren't there that Saturday night he asked me to stay at his dorm.

Though, I haven't told Julia or anyone else that.

There are so many things I could say and so many I know I shouldn't, so I settle on the plain truth. It's hard to hear, even from my own lips.

"Finn Hayes makes sure I don't know a damn thing about him."

Professor Winslow's eyes narrow, but he nods. "All right, girls. Be safe."

We take off at a run, and we don't look back. We're late for Double C, and there's not a single thing that's safe about that.

27

Finn

Bodies sway at the entrance of the Gyger Tunnel underneath the football field. A pulsing vibe thickens the air, and Lexi Winslow stands at the front of the group with her sidekick Connor and a couple other nondescript students wearing long navy-blue robes like they're members of some kind of cult or the clergy collecting money from people.

There's a door behind them and a vent cover above it. Unlike the last meetup, there's no free betting going on—just a steady filing of bodies into the small space, handing over a set dollar amount when they're told. The robes make a permanent marker scribble on their hand to keep track of who's paid.

I glance down at my phone and watch as the time changes from 10:14 to 10:15. Lexi's booming voice over the crowd is immediate, and the din quiets.

"Welcome back, boys and girls, for another exciting event."

Ace looks between Lexi and the back of the crowd frantically, so I raise my eyebrows at him in question. "Julia's late."

"Why didn't she just come with us?" I ask. My question is answered before he even speaks, with just a look at his puppy dog face.

"Sorry. I'm sorry. But they're friends now, so Scottie is with her."

I hate myself for it, but I start looking to the back of the crowd too. Blake keeps staring at the supposed woman of his dreams as she continues to talk in front of us.

"Tonight's event has a flat fee of fifty dollars per person, and the winner will take the pot—minus some house fees, of course.

But it's not for the weak, so consider your balls carefully before agreeing to participate."

Ace must spot Julia and Scottie, because one second, he's beside me and Blake, and the next, he's shoving people out of the way behind us in a straight line until he makes it to them. I glance at them as he pulls them through the crush back toward us, but when they get close, I force myself to concentrate on…well, I guess in some fucked-up way, my niece, Lexi Winslow.

"Legend and lore speak of a labyrinth of tunnels that scale the entire campus of the university in a complicated maze of darkness. But we're here to tell you, they're not just fable. They're fact. Only the brave will make it to the other side." She turns to her left, ushering Connor forward, and he takes over.

"Behind us, through this vent, is the start of a maze of tunnels in scale and size you can't imagine. They sweep the entirety of campus, but their paths are far from direct. Your mission, should you choose to accept it, starts here, and ends at the tunnels' end under the Abrams Building on the far side of campus."

"You will get lost," Lexi states unequivocally. "In fact, some of you may be lost for days, with no one to help you find your way out. When I say this is a risk, I don't mean it lightly. You can work as an individual or as a group, but the winnings are the same. If you choose to work together, you win or lose together."

Ace shoves in next to me, pulling Julia and Scottie in front of us. Julia falls into place naturally in front of him, leaving Scottie with nowhere to stand but directly in front of me. She faces forward pointedly, and I grind my jaw in response. I know it's my fault, but I fucking hate that she hates me.

"If you panic, don't come crying to us. You either have the guts to do it, or you don't."

Ace, Blake, and I look at one another and nod, and, surprisingly, so do the girls. Ace notices at the same time I do. "You don't actually think you're doing this, do you, Lia?"

"Of course I am."

He shakes his head. "No way."

"Are you doing it?"

"Well, yeah." She narrows her eyes, and he puts his hands up defensively. "This isn't sexist, this is protective."

"Which is fucking sexist!"

"We'll still split the money with you," I add as a note of good faith, which, unfortunately, really pokes the Scottie bear in front of me.

"Like that makes it better?" she counters, but her gaze never meets mine.

Blake bravely wades in, though I'm not sure why. He could have held on to the safety of being a bystander pretty easily. "Of course it makes it better. You get the money, and you don't have to do anything."

"We're doing it," Julia says resolutely. "Scottie and I will be our own team."

"What? Fuck no," Ace counters again. "No way. If you're doing it, you're doing it with us."

Julia smiles, and Scottie keeps avoiding my eyes. Blake nudges me. "Looks like that whole discussion really came full circle."

Someone behind me shoves hard as Connor opens the vent and starts lifting participants inside, and I grab Scottie's hips to steady her as we both lurch forward. As soon as we're righted and she pulls out of my grip, I turn around and shove the person directly behind me, even though I don't know if it was their fault or not. Evidently, the kid recognizes me from fight night because he backs up and takes a few of his friends with him, apology in his eyes. It's only then that I notice Dane at the back of the room with a group of guys I don't recognize. He's not looking at me or even in this direction, but I wouldn't be surprised if he were the actual culprit of the shove.

Ace pulls my elbow and turns me around, and we make our way to the front as a group, handing over our money to a guy with jet-black hair when prompted and getting our hands marked.

"At least half of the people who came here tonight left through the door they came in…but don't worry, we still got their money for the pot," Lexi tells people as they step up to the vent to climb inside.

"I love her so much," Blake whispers so close to my ear, I have to wipe off some of his saliva.

"Down, boy," I comment, to which he smiles.

I study Lexi closely as she checks all of our hands and look for any sort of family resemblance. She's light to my dark, but I feel like there might be something there in the cheekbones.

I'm so fucking stupid for getting so involved with all these people.

"Really out here risking people's lives tonight, huh, Lex?" Ace asks her directly, a small smile playing with the seriousness of his words. "Not even supplying bottles of water for people who might get trapped for days."

She rolls her eyes and whispers, "There are exits all over the tunnel network. They might not be the right exit, but they're exits. If people aren't smart enough to take them, that's not on me."

It's an amazingly cutthroat attitude, but coming from a Winslow, I can't say I'm surprised. They're all in a privileged, self-serving bubble.

"Here," Julia says to Scottie and hands her a folded-up paper towel. "Just in case your nose starts bleeding again."

My eyes shoot to Scottie's face, searching it for evidence of an injury, and I immediately see faint bruises under her eyes. "What happened?" I ask, but she doesn't give me a response. Instead, she just takes the paper towel from Julia's outstretched hand and puts it in her pocket.

My chest tightens with irritation. I swear, if that fuckhead Dane did something to her, I will kill him.

"Scottie?" I step directly in front of her and gently slide my hand under her chin so she has to meet my eyes. "What happened? Who did this?"

"Tonya's elbow." She rolls her eyes at me and steps back so my hand falls away from her face. "It was an accident in practice, so you can relax."

"Don't worry, Finn," Julia chimes in. "Scottie and I didn't get into any brawls on our way here. Though, she did get some awful texts."

"Julia!" Scottie snaps, annoyed.

"What awful texts?" Ace asks before I can.

"It's some unknown number that keeps texting Scottie really nasty things," Julia offers, making Scottie frown even harder at her. Julia is unfazed. "Sorry, girl, but I still think you should show campus police. Or, at least, make sure these big dudes have your back."

Scottie sighs. "This really isn't any of you guys' business. I can handle it."

"Show me the texts," I demand as kindly as I can manage.

"No."

"Scottie, let me see the texts."

"It's no big deal," she says, and she makes a point to walk around me. "Now, come on, we need to get moving if we want to get through this maze before sunrise."

She might consider this dropped, but I sure as fuck don't.

Our group follows her lead, and when she steps up to the vent, I make a basket with my hands and nod for Scottie to step in it with her foot. She looks at my hands like they're snakes.

"Look, you're not getting up there on your own, so you might as well take the boost."

"Fine. I'll let you help me on one condition."

"And what's that?"

"You tell me where you went when you crawled out of bed without saying goodbye."

28

My whole body shakes as I climb through the tight vent after getting a lift up from Blake Boden.

I'm vibrating a little bit out of fear for what's ahead. But it's mostly anger.

I'm so mad at Finn—for being so willing to keep secrets even though there's an obvious pull between us—but I'm even more mad at myself for my inability to stop caring about him altogether.

Every push he gives me to get me to step away, I hold on tighter. Every conflict we have over whether we'd be a good idea, the more my heart aches to find out anyway. It's ridiculous and foolish, to say the least.

And yet…I can't seem to stop myself.

I scoot to the end of the opening of the vent and stick my head out, and it's only then that I realize it's a long way down to get out, just like it was a long way up to get in.

"Shit," I whisper into the otherwise empty and dark tunnel. I don't need to get injured this close to competition season, but I'm not seeing a lot of options for getting down otherwise.

There's a bump to my foot, and I startle, screaming in the small space so loudly my eardrums pulse. The grip on my ankle tightens, and Finn's low and reassuring voice follows. "It's okay. It's just me."

I swallow hard to stop the overwhelming wave of panic his words both push and pull against with equal force.

"I…I don't know how I'm going to get down. It's a big drop."

"Here," Finn says calmly, pulling gently on the ankle he's still holding. "Scoot back here, and I'll crawl over you and get out first."

"Crawl over me?" I nearly cry, the very real tightness of the space we're in seeming to get even tighter.

"I can do it, I promise. Just lie flat."

Out of options, as more and more people pile into the small pipe behind us, I steel my nerves and turn onto my back to make myself as small as possible. Finn crawls up my legs fairly easily, but when he gets to my body, he has to hold himself against me and shimmy to make it the rest of the way.

I hold my breath as he passes over my face. His hair and his eyes and his lips first, and then the tight muscles of his chest and abdomen, which are rigid beneath his tight black T-shirt. Then, of course, come his pants… I close my eyes as tight as I can manage and hold my breath as every inch of him passes directly over me.

I will myself not to think of us in this position for a different reason—will myself not to think of what it'd be like to taste him.

My self-discipline is, in this instance, unfortunately, pathetically weak.

I can barely move as I hear him jump down from the end of the vent.

"Scottie, come on," he calls then, just as Julia is making it to my feet. Her eyes are a mile wide, and I can only imagine mine match. Our bravado, it seems, is wearing off a little now that we're in the thick of it.

Scrambling to my stomach, I turn over and scoot back to the edge of the opening, but this time, Finn's mesmerizing eyes light up the darkness. "Come on," he urges again. "Just push yourself out. I'll catch you."

Flutters dance through my stomach like lightning bugs on a rural summer night. I take one big gulp of stagnant, damp air and do as he says, falling forward and directly into his arms. Our bodies slide against each other as he sets me down, and I don't take my eyes from his for any of it.

It's a mild consolation to my discomfiture if I can make him feel the same. His mouth opens and closes, and just for a hint of a moment, I think he's actually going to tell me something—to share something—important.

"Hey, guys! Can you help a girl down?" Julia calls, breaking the spell.

Finn steps around me and over to Julia, pulling her down exactly like he did with me. Though, I do note, there's remarkably less body contact.

Directly behind her, Ace scoots out, and then Blake. Once we're all out, we move out of the way so that the people after us can climb down. There's another tunnel that shoots off to the right, so while everyone else goes straight, the five of us convene in its opening to put together at least some kind of game plan.

"I've seen a map of these tunnels directly under the stadium before because Coach keeps a whole bunch of relic-type shit in his office. We have to start backward and go the opposite direction that we think," Blake informs us.

"I'm sorry?" Julia says, which is almost enough to make me laugh. I guess we really are committed at this point.

"Look, I'm telling you, everyone who just went straight is headed the exact wrong way. I'm not sure what happens when we get away from the stadium and start going toward Abrams, but I know, under here, it's like a giant loop, and the only way out is backward."

Ace nods dramatically. "So what you're saying is we can expect this to be just as fucking hard as Lexi said it would be."

Blake shrugs. "Pretty much."

"Well, come on, then," Finn directs, stepping quickly and naturally into the leadership role. "Let's go that way before the next group gets down here and sees us doing it."

When he takes my hand in his and pulls me straight into unthinkable darkness with him, I don't say no.

Maybe, just maybe, what happens in the tunnels under campus tonight can stay in the tunnels under campus.

29

Finn

"We're going to die in here!" Julia declares, officially flustered, as we end up back where we started the third leg of the tunnels again. I make a third mark on the wall with Scottie's lipstick next to the others and rub a hand through my hair.

"Relax, Juju," Ace coddles, breaking out yet another nickname for the girl he has no idea he loves. "It's going to be fine. We have a system. We just have to try the other tunnel this time."

Scottie lets her butt slide down the damp cement wall and takes a seat on the floor, her head in her hands, and I watch her closely as Blake starts to discuss strategy with me.

"Okay, so we know we took the left fork and the straight fork, and both brought us back here, so now we need to take the right fork. My Apple watch picked up the tiniest blip of GPS when we were at that point, and it showed us under Sorority Row."

"It makes no fucking sense to go right if we were under Sorority Row," I say with a snort.

Blake nods. "I know. Which actually kind of confirms it's the right move."

"I'm starting to hate this," Julia says then.

I seal my mouth shut, and Blake does the same, but Ace doesn't, laughing directly in her face. "You're kidding me, right? I tried to get you to sit this out, but *nooo*, you just had to do it."

"Shut up, Aceface. I didn't know it was going to be like this."

"Lexi literally said it was going to be like this!" he shouts, his voice echoing obnoxiously around us.

"Don't yell at me!" she yells back, making Scottie stand up from where she's sitting.

"Guys, calm down. We're close. We haven't seen anybody else in ages. If we just keep it together, we're going to win the money."

"Scottie's right," I agree, which actually earns me a smile. I don't want to get too excited, but after three hours of hand-holding and working together, she seems to be thawing toward me.

Julia takes a deep breath, and Ace pulls her into a hug. I bug out my eyes at Scottie, and she mirrors me with her own.

She dusts off the butt of her jeans as Blake waves us all down the dark tunnel once again, and I hold out an outstretched hand. She takes it so willingly, I can almost forget all the stupid shit I've caused between us.

Ace and Julia streak past us in a blurred run, and Julia's giggles trail behind her as they pass Blake too. I pick up the pace to keep up but meter myself based on Scottie's much shorter legs. When the group puts some natural distance between us, I chance bringing up a topic that could very well ruin all our progress.

Still, it feels too important to ignore it.

"I really do understand that it's none of my business," I hedge carefully, my voice a whisper. Her hand flinches in mine, but she doesn't pull it away. "I know I haven't earned the right to know very much about you, really. But I'm still going to ask you about the messages."

"Finn." Her voice breaks in unmistakable shame and embarrassment.

"I know. I get it." I laugh at myself. "I really do. Hell, I understand keeping shit to yourself more than anyone."

She glances toward me, and the glow from my phone's flashlight is just bright enough to see her features. They call me a hypocrite in more languages than either of us speaks.

"But Julia is your friend. She would not have brought this shit up without your permission if they weren't serious."

She sighs. "They're just mean. Smack talk, really. They haven't, like, threatened me or anything."

"I'll fucking kill whoever it is if they do."

"*Finn.*"

"I'm not kidding, Scottie."

She scoffs softly. "I know you're not."

"But you're still not gonna show them to me?"

She shakes her head. "I…I can't. I want to, but I just…"

"Can't," I finish for her. Fucking hell, do I understand her completely, even if I hate the shoe being on the other foot. "All right," I finally agree, letting her off the hook for now.

"Really? You're going to drop it?" she questions, pulling me to a stop just before we get to where the others are waiting.

"No," I say carefully. She frowns. "But I'll let it go for now if you promise to tell me if you get more."

"Finn—"

"Promise me."

She rolls her eyes. "Fine. I'll tell you if I get more."

"Hurry up!" Ace calls from the three-way split in the tunnel ahead of us. "We actually did it! There are no marks on the wall. This is a new split!"

Scottie and I speed up into a jog until we make it to them. Blake makes a mark on the wall with the lipstick and then steps back to consider our three options. "Abrams is one of the oldest buildings on campus, right?"

"I have no fucking clue," Ace remarks, making Julia laugh.

"It is," Blake says then, answering himself. "It was the original university building, back in the late eighteen hundreds."

"How do you know this shit?" I ask.

Blake rolls his eyes. "It was in the freshman orientation pamphlet I got last year. Obviously, none of you bothered to read yours."

"Wow," Ace chortles. "Blake Boden is a do-gooding dork."

Blake shoves him, and I put Ace in a headlock after he bounces away, ordering, "Stop making fun of the guy who actually knows shit, bud. He might leave our asses here and take the money for himself."

Ace wriggles away to bow down in front of Blake, actually striking a curtsy at one point, and we all laugh. "Please accept my humble apology, my dear sir, Your Football Royal Highness."

Scottie surprisingly settles next to me, and I drape my arm around her shoulders without even thinking. She grabs my dangling wrist and holds it to her chest.

My whole body aches with longing. I really wish I had a different life sometimes.

"We will follow your lead dutifully for this next leg of the challenge."

Blake picks Ace up to standing again, and Ace clings to him in an aggressive hug. "Security! Security!" Blake calls out playfully, and Scottie, Julia, and I all step forward to pull Ace off him.

"Come on," I say, pushing Ace forward into one of the tunnels with a shove. He bounces back like he's tethered to us, though, and Blake starts explaining his reasoning.

"The oldest building probably has the oldest tunnel, so I'm thinking it's this one."

I shrug. It's a good enough theory for me.

Blake waves us on, and we all follow him on the path, only revisiting one more split we have to mark before finding the right direction. At the end of the tunnel, there's a door, and Ace runs toward it excitedly. I don't know if it's the good news he's hoping for—the door that leads to Abrams—or another door entirely, but now that we've been at this for the last five hours, I'm convinced it's the door I'm leaving through, either way.

Whether we win here tonight or not, I at least feel like I won some ground with Scottie.

Ace tries the knob, and it opens without requiring a special knock. He charges through first, though Julia is plastered to the front of him as he does, and Blake follows closely behind. I usher

Scottie forward with a hand at the small of her back so she can exit first, and the smile she gives me over her shoulder will live rent-free in my head until the day I die.

Lexi is waiting on a table in the basement conference room just through the supply closet the tunnel lets us into. For as much beef as I have with the Winslows, after five hours in these fucking tunnels, I'm happy to see her.

Ace and Julia practically maul her, closing her in a group hug that nearly knocks her off her seat. Connor laughs at Lexi's discomfort. Blake takes Ace and Julia's place as they step away, Connor holding out the cash enticingly. Blake moves in for a hug, but Lexi stops him with a stiff arm to the chest. "No touching."

I hear Scottie choke to herself as she stifles a laugh in front of me.

As Blake steps away, his eyes even more googly than before, Lexi watches me closely, a small smirk on her face. I use Scottie as a human shield, pinning her to my front as I step toward my secret long-lost relative.

"Well, well, Finn Hayes is a winner again. I might have to keep my eye on you."

She's right, of course, but not for the reason she thinks.

"I think you're the one we need to keep an eye on," I challenge back. "Running an underground society at a prestigious university like this."

Her eyes narrow. "What makes you think I'm in charge?"

I laugh. "Maybe because you're always the one in charge."

She shakes her head and jumps off the table. "That's simple thinking, Finnley. And I'm pretty sure you don't have a simple mind."

She and Connor laugh together as they leave the room, and Blake stares after them, his mouth agape as always. "I swear I'm in love."

Scottie rolls her eyes and bumps him with her elbow to move him out of the way. Ace and Julia are counting the cash and splitting it up five ways. I take a stack from them as they hand them out, feeling the weight of it on the bulging anxiety that lives and breathes in my chest.

Blake smiles at his own stack. "Well, folks, you're stuck with me now. Consider this team officially formed for any and all group Double C shit for the rest of the year."

"Me too," Ace confirms, shaking his bills in the air while Julia nods. "Ditto."

Blake looks from them to me and Scottie—once again, we seem to have migrated toward each other. "What about you guys?"

"I'm in," Scottie says immediately, steering her gaze up and over her shoulder to me. But it feels like *my* answer is for more than one question.

Am I in the group?

But more importantly…

Am I ready to stop pushing Scottie away?

Power and pain and deep longing move from Scottie's green eyes to my gut as I hold them hostage. "You've got me." My heart thrums in my chest. "You've got me for good."

God help us all.

30

I flip through my copy of *The Winter's Tale* and wait for Scottie and Nadine to get to class and take the two empty seats next to me.

The ripped page from my dad's journal burns a smoldering hole in the pocket of my pants, and anticipation makes my heart race even though I'm sitting down. I spent last night while Ace was out with Julia pulling some prank on his parents reading through it again and again until I found the perfect page to leave on Professor Winslow's desk at the end of class.

The time has come for someone other than me to feel the pain of reality.

I want him to see the truth for himself and wonder, like I spent two years wondering, what it all means for his life. I want him to wonder who I am and how long I've known, and I want him to feel as helpless as I've felt my entire life living under the abuse of our asshole dad.

Scottie flops down in the seat next to me, and I jolt out of my daydream. It's one of the darkest parts of me—these horrible thoughts I have about people who don't know me at all—and it scares me a little that I can't rein it in immediately when Scottie sits down. I shift in my seat and swallow to clear my throat, but I still feel like I'm burning alive from the inside out.

"What's wrong? Are you okay? You don't look so good."

I shake my head and look down at my lap. "I'm fine."

She laughs. "Yeah, okay. Come on, Finn. Can we really not even manage to be friends? I mean, we worked together Friday night, and we're all two thousand dollars richer because of it."

"We can be friends," I say. Though, even to my own ears, it sounds against my will.

"Convincing," she says teasingly, bumping her shoulder into my own so many times, the tension in it finally leaves.

I crack a small smile. "You're right. We can be friends."

"Well, thank fuck for that. I was starting to think I was going to have to do this project with two people who hate me."

"I could never hate you." It's simple. It's fact. Scottie, for me, is the kind of person who lights up your soul. She's happiness and wholesomeness and the sort of girl you cherish. I just don't live the life of a guy who can give any of those things.

Nadine sits down before Scottie can reply, annoyed immediately. "I don't understand why we have to sit together just because we're working together."

"Probably so we can *work together*," I remark, saving Scottie the trouble of dealing with her.

"Then he at least should have let us pick our groups," Nadine whines, looking back at Dane. He's been paired with two other girls, and from the looks of things, he's absolutely eating up the attention.

"All right, guys!" Professor Winslow calls from the front, making the rest of the chatter stop and effectively saving Scottie and me from having to say anything back to our apparent hostage. "I can see that you've all taken seats with your groups like I told you to last class, which I appreciate. I've done this for a reason, but before I get started, I want to bring out a couple volunteers I've wrangled into helping me out today."

The classroom door opens, and my whole chest locks in on itself. Remington and Flynn Winslow—two of my other brothers—are dressed in jeans and blazers and sporting smiles despite the incredibly ridiculous fact that they're spending their morning at a freshman literature class.

I recognize them immediately and with ease after all the research I've done on all of them, but even if I didn't, the family resemblance is striking. In every feature of their faces, I see a little bit of my father.

I see Scottie watching me out of the corner of my eye, but I can't seem to steady my breathing. She reaches over and squeezes my hand.

My fingers tingle as she applies pressure, and I stare at the front of the room.

"My big brothers have agreed to be *my* partners for today, good sports that they are, even though I'm pretty sure neither of them has ever read *The Winter's Tale* before…or read anything, for that matter."

Remington and Flynn both laugh, and my whole body shakes with the need to get the hell out of here. Seeing three of my brothers here, in the flesh, with the irony of my dad's sick sense of fun names said out loud for all to hear, I want to crawl out of my skin. My dad probably thought it was poetic, starting all our names with the same letters as the kids we didn't know about, but it's not cute when the situation is as fucked up as this—it's bullshit.

Scottie squeezes harder, and I do the only thing I can do without making an obvious scene; I squeeze her hand back.

If I can make it through this fucking class, I can finally free myself from the powder keg of this secret. It's only one page of my dad's journal, but I know it'll be enough. The passage I've chosen is unmistakable.

"King Leontes has no trust for anyone in his life. His wife, his best friend, even his newborn by proxy—because of that, today, we'll be exploring the idea of the opposite with our group members."

Remington chuffs. "Pfft. Who wouldn't trust a baby?"

Ty laughs. "See. I told you he hadn't read it."

Flynn smiles at the floor, and I have to work to keep myself from grinding my teeth down to nubs. I hate that I feel this way, but I can't help it. Everything my siblings and I've been through has been for nothing. We could have been like this.

Scottie smiles at the brothers, but I don't miss how closely she's watching me too. I never wanted to put her in the position, but I can't seem to help it.

I'm unbearably jealous of the life I didn't get.

31

Scottie

Finn's skin is an ashen pallor the likes of which I've never seen before. He looks sick and distraught and like every bone in his body is being broken, one by one. Ten times worse than he did fighting an ex-UFC fighter in a dark, dingy basement.

He stares intently at Professor Winslow and his brothers, his jaw grinding with every word they speak at the end of class. He squeezed my hand so hard I had to hold my breath as they explained the trust assignment—meant to be the antithesis of King Leontes's treatment of his wife Hermione in *The Winter's Tale*—and never stopped glaring through the entirety of their trust falls. When we finally got up to do our own with Nadine, she said she could only be the one falling, not catching, because of her bum arm.

Finn finally broke character when I nudged him and laughed, but now, he's back to mean mugging.

"All right, guys. I'll see you Thursday. Don't forget to focus on the theme of trust in relationships as you're working on *The Winter's Tale* project for the next couple of days. We'll be moving on to something else when we come back."

"We won't be here," Remington, Professor Winslow's older, incredibly handsome brother, says, making Ty and Flynn laugh.

"Class dismissed!"

Nadine jumps up from her seat and takes off like her ass is on fire, but Finn sits there staring while everyone else is packing up.

"Hey," I finally whisper, now that we're without an annoyingly eavesdropping cheerleader audience. "Are you okay?"

Finn's gaze jerks away from the brother trio at the sound of my voice, and it takes a couple of seconds for his eyes to actually focus on me. "What? Oh. Yeah. I'm good."

I nod but slow my own backpack packing to wait for him. I might be late for communications since it's a haul to Hawkley, but that class is basically a joke anyway. I have a perfect grade in there from the one assignment we've done so far.

The room is pretty much empty by the time he gets his things together, and I can tell he's waiting for me to leave to finish entirely.

Something doesn't feel right, but without an actual reason, I can't insert myself any more than I already have. We're the opposite of friends with benefits. We're friends with intense privacy issues.

I zip up my backpack pocket and sling it over my shoulder, saying a firm goodbye in the hopes that it'll knock whatever this is out of him. "I better go because I have another class, Finn. I'll see you later?"

He nods, staring at the large desk at the front of the room, so with a sigh, I finally turn and leave. I get out the door and ten feet down the hall before the singing adrenaline in my veins pulls me up short, and I dive into a side hall to wait yet again. It's almost a full minute, but when he comes out of the classroom finally, his head is down and his steps are quick. He doesn't notice me.

I glance both ways after he goes out the door into the courtyard, and driven by insanity perhaps, I head back to the classroom to see if I can find anything.

No one is there, so I run inside and look around like I'm going to find something as obvious as a ticking bomb. My frown grows as nothing remotely resembling a red or blue wire stands out. Maybe I'm making all this up in my head. Maybe he's just mad that he's partnered with me. Maybe, I don't know, he thinks—

All of my thoughts pause as I spin around to the professor's desk in the front and see a piece of paper, torn, weathered, and folded on the edge of the desk. I check my surroundings again and then jog over to it and pick it up. When I unfold it, it takes me almost no time at all to see that it's a journal entry, but the writing is chicken scratch that'll take some decoding.

"Scottie?" Professor Winslow's voice asks, making me practically do a freaking herkie right there. "You need something?"

"Me? Oh. No. I just...forgot...something. So, I came back to get it," I scramble to answer. Of course, with the paper in my hand now, I can't leave it back on the desk like Finn obviously intended, or Professor Winslow will think *I'm* the one who left it there.

Shit.

This is not good. Definitely not trustworthy group partner behavior.

With no other viable options, I tuck the paper in my sweater pocket and smile, jogging out of the room without another word to the professor. I'm sure the exchange was weird on his end, but hopefully he'll chalk it up to something stereotypical like hormones.

Every fiber of me vibrates with anxiety and curiosity as I book it straight for my dorm room. Communications class is forgotten along with everyone else as I charge toward the privacy needed to do the unthinkable and snoop on this very private piece of paper.

Carrie looks like she might want to say hello when I pass her in our hall, but I smile and jerk my chin like a total dude and power forward, refusing to be stopped.

My breathing is ragged and my chest heaves as I unlock my door, shove through it, and slam it behind me. My full-length mirror on the wall directly across from it shows a haggard, flushed version of myself with unbelievably wild eyes.

I pull off my backpack and let it fall to the floor beside my desk and then take three deep breaths as I pull the paper out of my pocket. It's dampened with a thin layer of my sweat at this point, but no less readable, thankfully.

My hands shake as I hold it up and study the words. The first thing I notice is that it's dated well over forty years ago.

A week ago, I left my family behind. Wendy's snobby ass thinks I'm a deadbeat when I'm there, so I'm going to show her what a fucking deadbeat is. Pretentious bitch. Thinks she's better than me. I doubt she'll feel that way with five little fuckers on her own.

Remington looked like he knew I wouldn't be back when I left, but the others are too little to realize anyway.

I have a show in Reno tonight that should set me up to head to Vegas for a while, and when I win big there, I'll figure out my next move. I haven't been focusing enough on my music lately, so now's the time.

The first thing that stands out to me is that whoever wrote this is an unmistakable narcissist. The second is the name Remington. It's not that common, and I have a bad feeling it's not just a funny coincidence with the one we met today.

I skim through the rest and down to the bottom, where there are, at best guess, some shitty song lyrics.

Hard decisions, big priorities, save me from this drudgery
On my time, on my own, back to life I'll be
Whiskey neat and a Coke black, I'm on my own and I won't go back

What is Finn doing with this thing? And if the Remington from today is the Remington in the writing, how in the hell did he get it?

32

Julia and I cross the street on a half jog, and I adjust the tight corset of my vampire costume. I also try like hell to smooth the leather shorts over my butt so my ass cheeks aren't hanging out, but my bread basket is two buns too full.

I had planned to wear something a little less risqué, but when Julia showed up at my dorm to get ready and saw my boring costume of jeans, a black tank, and cat ears, she pulled an extra costume out of her duffel and told me to put it on.

Refusal wasn't an option. Julia can be bossy as hell when she wants to be. Her hips and ass are also a size smaller than mine, which is probably why I look so much like I'm on a Kardashian vacation right now.

Music pounds from inside the Alpha Pi house, the *Fang Bang*, as the genius frat bros have been calling it, in full swing. Black streamers and toilet paper litter the trees out front, and scary ghouls and goblins wander the dystopian sidewalk. People smoke and laugh and stumble over one another coming in and out of the house, but just outside the entrance doors of the big brownstone on Frat Row, a couple is arguing.

People coming out of the party laugh at them as they fall down the steps on their left, and for my part, I'm just glad I'm not part of the scene this time.

"I saw the texts, Davis! I saw the fucking texts!" the girl in a sexy Little Red Riding Hood costume screams into the face of the guy with a Solo cup in his hand and a face that's reddened from the effects of whatever's inside. "You cheated on me! *With my sister!*"

His eyes are a little lazy as he tries to focus on what she's shouting. Which, honestly, adds a bit of comedy to the clown makeup that's painted on his face. A giant smile in the shade of blood red doesn't budge when he says, "Babe. Calm down."

"Do not babe me, you motherfucker!" Sexy Little Red cries, tears streaming down her cheeks. "You fucked my sister, you piece of shit!"

She sprints away from him, and he tries with all his might to follow, but the big orange clown shoes on his feet make him waddle instead of run.

Julia and I exchange wide, unfamiliar eyes. She's wearing cat-style contacts to go with her Catwoman costume, and I've got irises the color of blood a la a hungry Cullen.

Her mom went the full mile on these costumes, evidently going so far as to consult a Broadway costume designer before dropping them off at Julia's room this morning along with a basket of assorted muffins, pastries, and fresh fruit.

When some of the other girls in Delaney saw it, they all commented on how nice it must be to be that rich. All I could think was how nice it must be to have a mom who cares so much.

"You think it's less dramatic inside? Or more?"

"Girl, I'm hoping the whole night is like this. It's very *vintage Jerry Springer with a haunted twist.*" She laughs and wraps her arm around my shoulders as we scale the stairs once occupied by Red Riding Hood and her clown. "Let's go see if Kayla's here yet."

A guy in a ninja outfit pulls open the door as I'm pushing it, standing back to hold it open for Julia and me when he sees us. His eyes linger on all our exposed skin, and I find myself dancing in a side step to point the cheeks of my ass in the other direction.

Julia notices and laughs. "You look fucking hot, Scottie. Own it." I shake my head, and she laughs again. "Well, then I hate to break it to you, but all you did by turning was show your ass to Finn Hayes instead of ninja boy."

"What?" My head whips around in shock. Finn is standing near the staircase, chatting with Ace and Blake, his face the most relaxed I've seen it, maybe ever, not looking sick at all. When he wasn't in English this morning, I assumed he was under the weather and had all but abandoned the idea that he would be here tonight. In fact, I was kind of counting on it since the journal entry I stole is still in my room, tucked away in the drawer where I keep my extra notebook paper, and I haven't had a chance to fess up to it yet. Seeing him here but knowing this isn't even remotely the right place to do it makes me feel sick to my stomach.

I don't want to lie to him.

Finn laughs and rolls his eyes at something Ace says, and I don't miss his obvious lack of costume. His dark hair fans over his eyes in the most delectable James Dean kind of way, and he's dressed in boots, jeans, and a black shirt that perfectly conforms to his muscles, as usual. In a sea of wizards and ghosts and ridiculous Harry Potters, he's an attractive apple, ripe for the picking. Every girl in his vicinity watches him closely, waiting for an opportunity to catch his attention.

Me included.

"I thought you guys were never going to show up!" Kayla exclaims as she barrels into us in her cute purple fairy costume. She pulls both Julia and me into a giggling hug. "A girl from my chem class just found her boyfriend is cheating on her, and holy hell! It was total drama for a minute there."

"Yeah, we saw her on our way in," Julia comments through a smile. "Screaming at the Bozo—no pun intended."

"I'm pretty sure he's trying to chase her down 120th Street without falling over his clown shoes."

"Not gonna lie, I kind of hope he eats pavement," Kayla says, but then she leans forward and drops her voice to a whisper only Julia and I can hear. "By the way, Nadine and Dane are here. They're both shit-faced, and I almost threw up in my mouth a little from the PDA."

Both of them meet my eyes carefully, and I shrug. "It's no big deal."

"Scottie, if that bitch tries to start any shit with you, I'll pull her fucking hair out," Kayla states. "Promise."

Kayla knows all too well the crap that Nadine Jones tosses my way on a daily basis at cheerleading practice. From tripping me on my way to get a drink of water to messing with my counts to try to get me to fuck up, she stops at nothing to make my life as uncomfortable as possible. The only saving grace is that her wrist is still sporting a cast from her drunken debacle at the Delta Omega house at the start of the year, and most days, she's working with our physical therapist or sitting on the sidelines. In English, she keeps herself in check, but I think it's because she's afraid of setting Finn off.

"Nadine is still giving you a hard time?" Julia asks, suspicious. I know she's thinking about the text message shit, but I really don't think it can be her or Dane.

"It's not a big deal. Really."

Kayla's narrowing eyes say otherwise.

"It's fine," I reassure both of them. "I'm so over Dane's rainbow, I'm with the leprechaun at the end. He and Nadine can ride off into the drunken sunset together—the sooner, the better."

Julia nods and Kayla grins.

Arms wrap around me from behind and sway me side to side, and I know who it is immediately. His smell is unmistakable and unlike the rest of the male Dickson population who cover themselves in cologne. Clean soap and deodorant and a little bit of male musk is all Finn Hayes needs.

"Vampire?" he questions, a barely there smile curling the corners of his perfect mouth on the shell of my ear. I shiver at the feel of his lips—lips I've kissed before—on my skin.

I shrug my shoulders into his chest. "Julia let me borrow it."

"So, she's the one I should blame for all these fuckers staring at you?"

I snort. "People aren't staring." I turn to look over my shoulder just as Finn shrugs.

His smile is mischievous and heartbreaking. "I was."

Finn Hayes is smiling and flirting and outright telling me I'm hot? I swear, in the two months we've been in school together, I don't think I've ever seen him this unrestrained.

"Lia!" Ace's voice booms as he and Blake join our group on their way out of the kitchen. "What the hell are you wearing?"

It's an ironic question, given his snake charmer costume. There's a cobra sticking out of the front of his pants—literally.

She scrunches up her nose and glances down at her costume before saying, "Uh…a Catwoman costume?"

"I can see *that*. But why do you have to be so…"

"So…?"

"Hot?" Kayla offers through a laugh.

"Sexy?" I add, making Finn chuckle into my hair.

Ace frowns, stepping toward her so his snake pokes her in the breasts. "I'm not leaving your side tonight."

"What?" Julia questions on a laugh. "I don't need a protector."

He narrows his eyes. Julia narrows her eyes right back at him.

Finn settles his hands on my hips, and my vagina tingles so hard I feel it in my throat.

Holy cow, what is happening tonight?

"I'm going to get a drink," I announce, even though I'm not thirsty at all. But a little distance from Finn feels like a good plan.

To my surprise, he says, "I'll go with you," and grabs my hand.

My head says *shit*, but the flutter in my chest says something else entirely. This…*this* is the Finn I've been dreaming about since the moment he wiped the tear off my face in the rain.

As he guides us deeper into the party with one hand in mine and the other at the top of my very small vampire shorts, I feel like

I'm in seventh grade again, mooning over Tony Gorassi as he held my hand.

When we get to the kitchen, the frat brothers, dressed like western robbers—or *bandoleros*, as they so helpfully keep yelling at random moments—point us in the direction of drinks. Finn lets go of me to rummage through the coolers on the island counter, and I have to wrap my arms around myself to ebb the feeling of emptiness. "Do you want a drink, drink? Or, like, a soda drink?"

"Soda. Definitely soda."

There's so much booze in this house, covering every surface, that I'm surprised he can even find a soda, but after rummaging for what feels like forever, he manages to hand me a Mountain Dew.

"Do the Dew?" he teases, and I'm overwhelmed by the sight of his face with an easy smile. It's even more handsome than I could have imagined.

"Thanks." The cold metal tab is sharp on my fingertip as I crack it open, and startled, I pull my finger away to the sight of blood. Finn grabs my hand and puts my finger in his mouth, sucking gently until the flow stops. My saliva is almost too thick to swallow as I stare into his sensuous brown eyes. Every fiber of my being is a raging fire.

"I'm pretty sure I'm supposed to suck your blood," is all I can think to say.

"There's still time," is Finn's absolutely unhinged answer. Holy moly, my head is *swimming*.

When I set the can down on the counter, he steps closer to me again and gently places his hands on my corset-covered hips. "Want to dance?"

"Dance?" I nearly laugh. If I'm dreaming right now, I swear someone had better wake me up before I make a WAP-inspired mess of my bed.

"What? You don't think I can dance?"

"Honestly?" I counter. "No. I didn't think you were the type to dance."

"What type do you have me pegged as?" His fingertips dig into the bare skin on my hips.

"I don't know." I push my teeth into my bottom lip. "The type that wears a leather jacket and rides around on a motorcycle?"

"I don't own a leather jacket or a motorcycle."

"Oh." My inhale is unmistakably shaky as he rubs the waistband of my shorts with his thumbs.

"Come on, Scottie," he says and takes my hand again to guide me back toward the big living room where a DJ is currently playing a remix of Sabrina Carpenter's "Espresso."

The section of the room that's been marked off as the official dance floor for the night is covered with bodies. Couples dancing close. Girls in sexy costumes giggling and shaking their hips and singing the lyrics to one another. And Finn leads us straight to the center of it all.

Which is crazy. I mean, Finn Hayes isn't exactly a social butterfly. He's a lone wolf who prefers solitary situations, not a golden retriever like Ace Kelly, who wants to be everyone's friend.

Chest to chest, he guides us into an easy rhythm with the best part of the song.

Sabrina talks about having a guy wrapped around her finger, and I channel all the power of her words into allowing myself to feel sexy. We move and sway together, and Finn's thigh cradles itself between my legs. It's erotic and intimate, and I can hear the sound of my heart deep inside my ears.

Finn can *dance*.

He spins me around with ease, leading me in movement until my back is flush against his chest. His hands find a home at the front of my waist, and I can feel his warm breath brush against my neck. My eyes fall closed of their own accord, and I relax into his embrace, savoring the feel of what it's like to be wrapped up in Finn's arms. I've dreamed of this kind of situation more times than I'd like to admit, and now that it's happening, my mind races with far too many questions.

Is he enjoying this as much as I am? Is he thinking about being with me as much as I'm thinking about being with him? Is he going to ask me to come back to his dorm again? What'll happen if he doesn't leave this time?

And maybe the biggest question of all…

Why is he so different tonight?

A new song pounds from the DJ's speakers, but my mind is too much of a mess to make out what it is as Finn spins me back around to face him.

I've never had the authority to study his eyes this closely, and now that I am, I can see the tiniest of golden flecks that make up a rim around the outside edge of his irises. I think, seeing it now, it's what makes them feel like magic.

I'm a live wire in the web of his sexy hair and stunning eyes and perfect lips, and I'm powerless to fight against it.

"Finn," I whisper as he slides one of his hands into my hair. My heart thrums and my adrenaline sings as he presses his lips to mine.

The kiss doesn't start off slow and hesitant like before. No. This kiss is deep and intense from the start. His tongue slides against mine while our bodies continue moving to the beat of the music, and my whole body melts into the kind of kiss I've never felt before.

It's consuming, but if I let myself think about it, I'm afraid I might realize it's only that way because I am. *Consumed.*

Body and soul and mind, I'm so deep in Finn Hayes, I don't know if I'll ever dig my way out.

I think…despite all the reasons I shouldn't be…I'm in love with him.

33

Finn

I t's two days after leaving that journal entry for Professor Winslow, and I finally feel free of the raging anger I've been carrying for two years.

I thought I'd be eaten alive with the drive to see Ty's reaction, to feel his pain as a balm to my own, but instead, my chest feels a thousand pounds lighter.

It's not my secret to carry anymore, not my burden to bear. We share DNA. It's a scientific fact, and for the first time since discovering it, I don't feel like it defines me.

I skipped class this morning to avoid popping the bubble and have been gliding on a high ever since.

Now, tonight, with Scottie tucked close as we dance to the heavy beat of Alpha Pi's DJ, I feel damn near like I can do anything.

Hands in her hair and her body pressed to mine, I explore her mouth like there's new territory to be discovered. She melts under my caress, giving her mouth over to me without hesitation. Right now, I'm convinced I could die without ever tasting another thing and still leave this earth satisfied.

I take a hard jolt to the back, jostling both of us forward on the crowded dance floor and bowling us into Kayla and Blake, who are dancing right next to us. It's a casualty of the tightness of the crowd—at least, that's what I assume at first. But when Kayla points over my shoulder with an uncharacteristic glare in her eye, I reconsider.

Dane and Nadine are there, dancing close, but his hard eyes

are on the ass of the girl he let get away, and they are on fire. I hold his eyes with mine, moving a possessive hand to flesh that sticks out just below the leather of her shorts.

Dane shoves Nadine to the side and storms away, and I smile to myself over the small victory. I'm not normally the type to flaunt a relationship for cheap thrills, but that motherfucker deserves every cocksucking thing he gets.

Scottie pushes away, unaware of the encounter.

Still, her abnormally red eyes search mine with a deep, undeniable yearning for something I'm not even sure exists. If it did, I wouldn't hesitate to give it to her.

"You okay?" I ask as she looks back at Kayla and Blake and then over to me. When she doesn't say anything—doesn't even seem to hear me—I try again with her name. "Scottie?"

"I'm going to head to the bathroom real quick," she rushes out. "Be right back."

She doesn't wait for a response or a reaction before spinning out of my arms and shoving through Kayla and Blake and then Ace and Julia behind them to get out of the pulsing crowd. Kayla's eyebrows draw together, but I nod and hold up a hand in a silent acknowledgment that I plan to follow her.

Several girls and a couple guys say hellos and call out for my attention as I make my way down the hallway, but I don't bother with more than a jerk of my chin for any of them.

Scottie closes the door to the bathroom at the end of another long hall, just as I'm rounding the corner. I walk slowly, stopping outside and resting against the wall to wait for her to come out.

She looks upset when she does and, more than that, absolutely shaken to see me. Her red contacts are out now, and her eyes look a little bloodshot. Maybe because she's upset or maybe because they were bothering her—I'm not sure.

"Finn?"

"Hey. Sorry I followed you. Just wanted to make sure you were all right."

Her eyes are a glistening green of unshed tears in an instant. I feel like shit immediately.

"Fuck, Scottie." I grab her hand and pull her down the hall to one of the bedrooms, closing the door behind us and locking it before ushering her over to the bed. She sits down on the end of it, and I squat down in front of her.

"Tell me what's wrong, and I swear I'll do everything I can to fix it."

Her breathing, already heavy, turns nearly ragged as a tear escapes, carving a path down her perfect cheek. I catch it at the bottom of her chin.

"Finn. It's…" She shakes her head. "I just don't know…"

In an instant, it hits me. *I'm* the problem. After everything I've put her through in the last two months, I've spent the entire night yanking her head in another direction yet again.

I haven't meant to. I just…feel different.

Sliding my hands into her hair, I tilt her head back enough that her eyes meet mine, pressing my lips to hers just once, softly. "I'm sorry," I say an inch away from her mouth, rubbing my thumbs on the gentle line of her jaw. "I know I've been unbearable."

She tries to shake her head, but I stop her with light pressure to her jaw.

"You broke my heart that day at Ace's dad's office…when you told me I was worse than Dane." She winces, but I keep going. "But you were right. Maybe I didn't put my hands on you or yank you around, but I've been rough with you too. With your emotions, with your peace of mind. I've been an asshole."

"Finn."

"I know I haven't given you a reason to believe in me." I shake my head, unable to explain it all properly. "But I finally feel…ready. I know it won't make sense to you, but for the past two years, I feel like I've been living in blackness. A dark so intense, I couldn't fathom it touching you. But I can finally…" I lick my lips and try to come up with the words to describe the end of an era and the beginning of a new one. A move toward the person I want to be, rather than settling for the one that I am. "I think I'm finally seeing the light."

It's out of nowhere and catches me completely off guard, but I swear, one moment, she's on the verge of tears, and the next, her lips are on mine.

They're hard but shaking, and the smell of her all around me hits me with an unnerving intensity. Fingertips pleading, I grab at her hips and pull her up off the bed and firmly against me, my mouth opening under hers until it does the same. With just a touch of my tongue, I taste her cherry lip gloss and fall into an onslaught of memories.

Of the kiss before the fight and the next one that came after. Of lying so close, our breaths mingled in my bed. Of her body under mine in the vent and our hands linked together as we ran through the maze of tunnels under campus. Of her hand on mine in class last week and the squeeze she let me give it. Of dancing with her tonight.

"Scottie," I breathe into her mouth, the skin of her arms around my neck sending a tingle down my spine. Our bodies push and pull against each other, and then our tongues tangle again, running against each other hungrily until I'm hard in my fucking jeans. I let myself absorb everything about her. Her touch, her mouth, the pretty sound of her gasp as I put my hands on her ass and lift.

"Come back to my dorm with me," she whispers, sending me off the edge of a cliff and into a free fall I can't stop.

"Yes."

I kiss her once more, hard and deep and unrelenting, before I grab her hand and drag her out the back door of Alpha Pi.

Scottie Bardeaux may not realize it yet. But tonight, she's officially mine.

34

Scottie

I unlock the door of my dorm room, and we tumble inside, fused to each other. Our mouths are a frantic mix of tongues and lips and teeth as we kiss like this is the last kiss we'll ever have. With the way things have gone in the past, and with the things I can't take back, maybe it will be.

Even knowing I should, I can't bring myself to stop.

Finn places his hands on my ass, lifting me up until my legs are wrapped around his waist, and presses my back against the wall. He never stops kissing me.

"Fuck, Scottie," he breathes into my hair as he rains kisses down my neck. He shoves my shirt out of the way to do the same to my shoulder and collarbone, and the feel of his lips on my skin makes my hips jolt forward and grind against him.

In a frantic twist, he moves us off the wall and falls forward to my bed, me underneath him.

He presses my back into the mattress, and I reach for his T-shirt, pulling it off him with a quick jerk of my hands. I go for his jeans next, my fingers shaking as they unbuckle and unzip his pants. I shove them down, along with his boxers, and even though Finn tries to stop their descent, I push his hands away.

"Scottie?" he questions, but I kiss him again instead of answering. The heat of his body on mine is indescribable. I feel primal and needy and irrational.

I push my leather shorts and thong down too, needing to feel his skin directly on mine.

At first, he doesn't realize how impatient I've been, too busy kissing and tasting at my neck, but when I climb over his body and straddle his hips, his eyes change from heated and hooded to wide and unsure.

"*Scottie*," he whispers, and he grips my hips, preventing me from pressing the apex of my thighs against him. "You don't have to do this. It's too big of a deal, too important—"

"Please, Finn," I beg. Despite the shame I'm feeling over the secret I'm keeping from him, I'm too far gone to feel any shame in pleading. "I want this. I want *you*. I'm ready."

"Scottie, I don't know—" He stops midsentence when I remove my corset, freeing my breasts and immediately peaked nipples. The way his eyes drink me in, taking in every inch of my naked body with dilated pupils and no blinks, emboldens me further.

"I *want* you to be my first."

Finn's breathing is ragged now, and his hands twitch into a hard squeeze on my hips. His eyes move down to where I'm wet and throbbing for him before slowly moving back up to lock with mine. "Scottie, I only have so much willpower."

"Let it go," I tell him simply. "I want you to."

Let me have this piece of you before I lose you forever.

Finn

"Take my virginity, Finn," she murmurs, and my hands have a mind of their own, loosening their grip on her hips. She takes full advantage of that and pushes herself against my cock, sliding herself up and down my length without putting me inside her.

Scottie Bardeaux is the most beautiful girl I've ever laid eyes on, the only girl I've ever had to make a conscious effort not to think about. And she's the only person I've ever wanted to see me for who I really am.

Every inch of her body is visible to me. Her delicate neck and collarbone. Her perky tits with the most perfect pink nipples. Her trim stomach. Her hips. Her firm, rounded ass is in my hands, and her gorgeous pussy is resting on top of my dick.

I'm not a virgin by any stretch of the imagination, but I've never experienced a moment like this. I've never seen anything more beautiful than a naked Scottie, and I know with certainty I'll take those words all the way to my deathbed.

I don't deserve her.

But for some reason, she thinks I do.

She knows I don't come from money, that I'm an emotional wrecking ball of baggage, and that I fix too many problems with my fists. And still, she wants me.

Trusts me.

With her body, her mind, and the most sacred gift a girl can give a guy.

Me. Finnley Hayes. The fuckup from the wrong side of the tracks.

My shitty childhood has hardened me. Turned most of my emotions to stone. I've seen too many things. Heard too many things. Witnessed too much violence and been on the receiving end of vile words too many fucking times to come out with a healthy view of love.

And yet somehow, this girl, this fucking girl, manages to make emotion clog my throat.

"Please." Her green eyes shine with desire and need. And her lashes look a million miles long with every blink she takes. "I need you."

I shake my head, willing myself not to let the sting in my nose turn to tears I don't want to fall.

"You're so beautiful," I whisper reverently. "The best thing I've ever laid eyes on."

Scottie needing me is the last thing I wanted to happen, but that doesn't negate the fact that it breaks open a part of me I've had closed off for longer than I can remember.

She needs me, but I need her more.

If I trusted myself to understand what love is, I'm pretty sure I would say I love her.

She kisses me and kisses me again, and with each greedy swipe of her tongue against mine, my hips move closer and closer to hers.

I groan when she starts to grind herself against me, and I damn near see stars when she starts to slide the tip of my dick inside her. *Fuck. Not yet,* my mind whispers, and it takes a Herculean effort for me to grip her by the hips and move her body back a few inches.

Her lips move down into a frown, but I'm quick to flip her onto her back and slide my body down the length of hers. I don't stop until my face is mere inches from her perfect pussy.

"Finn?" she questions, and I reach up to smooth my hand down her stomach. Her abdominal muscles shake with nerves and anticipation beneath my fingertips.

"There is no fucking way I'm going to rush through this." I slowly lick my tongue against her. "I'm going to taste you, Scottie.

And then, I'm going to make you come on my tongue. Again and again and again. And only when you're so fucking relaxed and sated will I slide my cock inside you."

"I…I…don't think it's possible for me to have…" She pauses, and her voice is barely there when she whispers, "Orgasms." Her cheeks are flushed the cutest shade of red, and her hazel eyes are wide—an adorable mixture of fear of doubt resting within them. "I've never really had one…with a guy…"

"That's because you've never been with me," I tell her confidently.

If it's the only good thing I do in this world, I will make Scottie Bardeaux come.

Her body is rigid, and I can tell by the way her hands are flexed into fists that she's nervous. I slide my hands beneath her ass and pull her closer to my face. Slowly, I start to lick at her, my tongue and lips delicate against her skin. Only when I feel her body start to relax against my hands do I pick up the pace.

Her eyes fall closed, and she reaches out her hands to grip my hair, tugging on the strands as soft mewling sounds fall from her lips.

I eat and suck at her, enjoying the way she's wet and swollen against my tongue. She tastes sweet like fucking candy and her curves are soft, and the more aroused she becomes, the more her scent surrounds me.

My cock only grows harder.

She moves her hands from her hair to her breasts, and I groan against her skin when I look up to find her lips parted and her fingers plucking at her perfect pink nipples.

"*Finn,*" she whispers. "I feel like I'm going to explode."

Her back arches and her body trembles, and when her hands end up back in my hair as incoherent moans spill from her lips, I lick harder and faster to match the pace of her hips. In one blissful cry, she comes on my tongue.

It is, hands down, the most beautiful fucking thing I've ever witnessed in my life.

And I'm only getting started.

Scottie

Every muscle in my body shakes as I come down from the highest peak of pleasure I've ever experienced. I've made myself come before, but what just happened with Finn is in another universe, another galaxy, another dimension.

His muscular body hovers over mine, and I reach out to grip his biceps with my hands. He poises himself at my entrance, a condom he got from his wallet covering his cock. I look down at where we are almost connected, and I'm shocked to see how big he really is.

He is long and thick and so hard that the tip is pink and swollen. I've never had even an inkling of an urge to study a dick before, but the sight of Finn's, aroused and ready for me, makes me want to write a graduate-level dissertation.

I wish I could wrap my hand around him. And wrap my lips around him. And suck on him until his pleasure finds its way into my mouth.

It's more than a fantasy; it's a craving.

I almost ask him to stop, to let me take the condom off his cock and put him in my mouth. But when I look up and our eyes lock, my breath gets tangled up in my lungs.

His dark hair hangs over his face in that mysterious way I always love, and his tongue sneaks out to lick his full lips. And his eyes. Oh my goodness, his eyes. The brown depths are filled with something deep and intense and meaningful that I can't even put a name to.

"It's still not too late to stop," he tells me then. It's the permission

I bet a million wronged girls wish for when they look back in time. The tip of his cock is just barely inside me, and if I said the word, I know without a shadow of a doubt it wouldn't go a millimeter farther.

But this is all I want. All I can think about. I have to have him.

"I want you," I whisper and grip his face with both of my hands to pull his mouth against mine. I kiss him hard, and as he kisses me back, I nudge my hips upward to move more of his cock inside me.

"You're so tight," he says against my mouth at the feel of my movement. "So fucking warm. So perfect."

The deeper he gets, the more powerful the combination of pleasure and pain grows inside me. It's unlike anything I've ever felt before. It's not just discomfort because he's so big and I'm a virgin. And it's not just pleasure because it makes me throb. It's all of it combined with the intimate significance of what this moment is.

I'm giving a part of myself to Finn that I can never get back. And he's chosen to savor every second of this poignant moment in time.

His cock sits at my barrier. My hips tense at the extreme feel of it, but Finn coaxes my mouth into another head-spinning kiss. He tastes and drinks at my lips until my body starts to relax again, and only then does he drive his hips forward to push himself all the way inside me.

A deep, visceral moan starts at my toes and shoots out of my lips like a rocket. Finn swallows the whole of it, working his mouth against mine. He slides his hands up my arms and over my breasts and doesn't stop until they're in my hair, caressing the strands in the most delicate way.

"This is everything," he whispers against my lips, and those words only make my body melt into his further.

Slowly, he moves himself in and out of me until I get too greedy to feel more that I try to urge him to go faster and deeper and harder with my hips.

I run my hands over his strong biceps and shoulders and the

muscles of his back, and the more he thrusts inside me, the more I feel his body tense up beneath my fingertips.

I am making him feel that way. Me. Instantly, I'm three sheets to the wind, drunk with power from the realization.

Finn starts to lose control, his movements becoming faster but more erratic at the same time as my body brings him closer to orgasm. His breaths come out in pants, and my body feels like it's drawn tight like a bow, ready to snap at any second.

"Fuck," he says on a whisper, the cords of his neck stretching so taut I can see them through the thick muscle there.

A raspy, guttural groan explodes from his lungs, and Finn pushes himself as deep as he can go. As he finishes inside me, I fall over the edge with him, into another spiral of pleasure that blurs my vision and holds every other part of me hostage.

His hands are tender, his lips precise, as he rains kisses all over the skin of my face before burying his head in my neck.

"I've never felt this trusted by anyone. This valued. I'll never forget what this means, and I hope you won't either, Scottie. This wasn't just something. It was everything."

I swallow hard around the growing knot in my throat as Finn pours out his well-fortressed heart to me. It's everything I wanted losing my virginity to be—he's everything I've ever dreamed of.

But it's only now that it's over that a bitter realization seeps through.

Finn Hayes is perfect. But I am a villain.

37

Finn

Scottie's hair feels like silk against my face as I nuzzle into the crook of her neck, the scent of wild flowers and rose hips overwhelming me. It's different from how she normally smells, but I think it might be her shampoo.

Besides the sounds of our slowly calming breaths, silence cloaks the room.

I feel like I'm on top of the world. The pleasure is secondary to the intimacy, and I think, if she lets me, I'll spend the rest of the night soaking it in.

I'm no choirboy, but I'm not impervious to the responsibility of what she just gave me either. It's more than the physical, too—it's a level of trust I honestly never saw myself being worthy of.

But fuck, Scottie is everything I don't deserve but everything I want.

Throughout my life, I've never felt the kind of peace I'm feeling right now. I've never felt so content. Never felt so…happy.

I look down at where our naked bodies are intertwined with each other and see the way her fingers dance delicately against the skin of my chest. The caress of her hands on me feels unlike anything I've ever experienced before. It's affirming and powerful, and I can't get enough.

Scottie leans her head back, and our eyes lock. Everything inside me melts. All the pretense and toughness and stubbornness. Whatever gentle version of myself it takes to stay here, I want to be it.

She starts to open her mouth, maybe to say something, but I take it as an invitation to kiss her.

I've never felt like I could spend hours kissing a girl without a single ulterior motive of moving things further, but kissing Scottie is the appetizer, the entrée, and the fucking dessert.

I'd be content to stay here for hours just doing that—it's all I expected to happen when we came back to her room tonight.

I'm so lost in the kiss that I almost don't feel when she starts to push me away with her hands at my biceps.

"Finn," she whispers. I have to work for it, but I manage to open my eyes and pull myself out of my aroused stupor.

Her eyes are sad—much sadder than I expect—and a bolt of unease runs through me. Did I do something while we were having sex that hurt her?

I push up onto an elbow immediately, reaching behind her bed to turn on her lamp so I can see her face completely.

"Are you okay?" I ask, gently cupping the line of her jaw. "I didn't hurt you, did I?"

She shakes her head, but that only eases my anxiety slightly. The corners of her mouth are turned down, and moisture shimmers in the corners of her eyes. Something is still wrong.

"What is it, Scottie?"

"I have to tell you something," she whispers again, her voice breaking this time.

Desperation sits heavy in my chest, the need to fix whatever this is overwhelming. I know I've left her wondering and unsure in the past, but I'm determined not to do that to her again. Whatever she needs, I'll be it.

"What is it, baby?"

She takes a shaky breath, her lips pursing as one tear breaks free and falls to the pillow. "I...I took the paper you left on Professor Winslow's desk on Tuesday."

I blink what feels like a hundred times, trying to make sense of the words. It's not only not what I'm expecting, it's...unfathomable.

I feel like I can't breathe. Carefully, I sit up beside her. "What did you just say?"

"I'm sorry, Finn."

I swing my legs over to the floor and scrub my hands into my eyes. "You...you took the paper?"

She scrambles to sitting too, pulling the loose sheet up and over her bare chest. Her face is a shattered mess of its normal beauty. I stare at her, unable to say or do anything else until she nods.

"You took it? Are you fucking kidding me?"

"I'm sorry." She reaches out to grab my hand, but I yank it away. "You were just so upset, and I wanted to know what was going on with you, and I care about you so—"

"Did you read it?"

"What?"

"You heard me, Scottie," I grit out, ice water in my veins making my whole body feel like it's under attack. "Did. You. Read. It?"

She swallows hard, and I know the answer.

Frustrated, I jump off the bed, scrubbing my hands down my face, and turn around to smash my fist into a lone armchair that's covered with her clothes.

When I spin back toward her, she scrambles back on the bed until her back hits the wall. She's scared. Of me. It's my worst fucking nightmare. With everything my mom, my siblings, and I have lived through with my dad, I've never, ever wanted someone to think I would hurt them unless they were actively hurting me.

Which, in a way, I guess she is.

"Where is it?" I demand, shaking with the effort it takes to make my voice calm.

"In my desk drawer," she whispers and slowly crawls off the bed. I watch, unmoving, as she drags the sheet over to her desk and pulls open a drawer, grabbing the sheet of paper and holding it out to me. When I reach for it, she yanks it back. Red-hot anger makes my eyes burn.

"Where did you get this, Finn?" she asks as she clutches it

against her naked chest. "It sounds like it was written by Professor Winslow's father."

"That's none of your fucking business."

"Finn, I swear you can tell me, and I won't judge you. I would *never* judge you. I promise," she pleads frantically, tears falling unchecked from her eyes now.

"I can't fucking believe this," I say, my hands in my hair. "You took my fucking property, hid it from me, and then what? Fucked me to distract me?"

"No!" she cries immediately, lunging toward me to try to take my hand. I pull myself away. She gathers herself in the sheet again, her voice as quiet as I've ever heard it. "It's not like that. The timing is terrible, I know, and the guilt was eating me alive, but I slept with you because…because I *love* you."

"Scottie, give me the fucking paper."

"No." She shakes her head, clutching my father's stupid words to her chest tighter. "Not until you tell me where you got it."

My jaw ticks, and my mind swirls. *Why is she doing this?*

"You know what, Scottie?" I say, my voice louder than I'd like it to be but completely out of my control. "I don't know shit about love, but this…*isn't* it."

My sobs are quiet but body-rending as Finn shoves his legs into his jeans and scrambles to grab his shirt from my bed.

I've pushed him too far, and now, everything is ruined.

"Finn, wait, please. I'm sorry. I'm so sorry."

I grab his elbow to stop him, but he spins around quickly, making me pull back into myself. His eyes are hard and cold. All his trust in me is gone.

"I'm so sorry, Finn. You were just so upset that day, and I wanted to know… I was trying to know why."

"You want to know where I got it, princess?" he snaps, a sardonic, malicious smile making him look all wrong. "My fucking dad wrote it. How's that for some fucked-up shit, Scottie? He's not just a deadbeat alcoholic who likes to beat on his wife and kids, but he's a deadbeat alcoholic who fathered a whole other family and left them behind. Professor Winslow is my fucking brother, and he doesn't have a goddamn clue because he got to experience a life without a father who likes to talk to his wife and kids with his fucking fists."

His words cut straight through me, and I have to move my hand to my mouth to stifle my sob.

"I didn't mean… My intentions were good," I insist.

Finn makes it clear with an angry raise of his hand that he doesn't give a damn about my intentions, good or not. I guess there's a reason they say they pave the path to hell.

"Give me the fucking paper, Scottie."

Tears stream down my cheeks uncontrollably as I hold out the journal entry toward him, and he snatches it so fast that I swear he takes my heart with it.

His movements are quick and choppy with anger as he grabs his wallet from the bed and storms through my door, slamming it behind him.

My body aches from where Finn and I were most intimately connected not even an hour ago, but my heart overpowers that feeling by tearing itself in two.

I knew Finn was complicated and complex and his past has made him hard around the edges. I knew he was flighty and difficult to make stand still for a reason, and yet, I pursued it time and time again.

Professor Winslow. Finn's *brother*. Instantly, more tears stream down my face, and guilt and shame tighten my chest.

I can't believe this is happening.

Finn's heart is shredded, and so is mine. And I only have myself to blame.

Monday, November 11th
Scottie

"Okay, everyone!" Coach Jordan announces. "Take five, and grab some water!"

We're only thirty minutes into our two-hour practice, and I'm already ready to go home.

A week and a half of calls and texts and, embarrassingly enough, showing up at his dorm uninvited one time, have all gone unanswered. Finn's become a ghost on campus.

On a basic level, I, of course, understand. I violated his trust in the worst kind of way. Taking the paper and not telling him about it was bad enough, but sleeping with him when he didn't know about any of it yet was the double down that nailed the coffin shut.

Finn Hayes wants nothing to do with me. I knew it that day by the look on his face.

But he hasn't been coming to class either, and the idea of what I've done ruining his entire college career is too much to bear.

I sigh and grab my phone from my duffel bag. While most of my teammates laugh and chat with one another, I busy myself with checking my phone for the millionth time today.

The only missed text is from Ace.

Ace: Don't worry, Scottie. I'm keeping an eye on him.

Fingers to the screen, I type out a quick response.

Me: Don't worry? I'm worried, Ace. He missed class all last week. He's going to fall behind.

Ace: I got him notes.

Me: Has he said anything about me?

I almost don't send the message, but my overwhelming need to know if Finn hates me for good is too much to deny.

Ace: Not really, Scottie. Mind telling me what happened between the two of you? I've honestly never seen him like this.

I'm not surprised Finn hasn't told Ace what happened. He isn't the type to talk about feelings.

But when I reread the part that says *I've never seen him like this*, I have to swallow down the urge to puke all over my white practice shoes.

Me: I messed up.

It's the only truth I'm willing to give. I've already done enough pushing and prying into Finn's life, and that hasn't gotten me anywhere but crying into my pillow every night. Any more explanation than that would just be another violation of trust.

Ace: Well, he probably just needs some space, then. Just give him some time to cool down, okay?

I'm terrified time isn't going to fix this.

I sink my head into my hands, willing myself to keep it together. But when my phone vibrates in my lap, I quickly glance at the screen again, fully expecting another Ace update.

But it's not Ace or anyone else I know, for that matter. It's a heavy fucking straw, tempting the camel's back to break.

Unknown: You think your mom gave you Fetal Alcohol Syndrome?

I shut my eyes and drop my phone into my bag, the cruel words starting a burn in my lungs. Who the hell is doing this? And how do they know so much about me?

I don't know what to do. Before, Finn would have wanted to know. But now? It feels so unfair to involve him at all.

Maybe I should go to the campus police, like Julia suggested. I mean, if I don't, is this going to go on all year?

"All right, girls. Let's run it through again," Coach Jordan calls, clapping at Nadine when she and a couple of the other girls don't stop talking when she does. "Come on, from the top. We only have three weeks until the qualifying competition for NCA Nationals, and we're nowhere near ready."

I set down my bottle and jump up, running back to our stunting formation that kicks off our routine. Kayla and Emma are my bases, and Tonya is my backspot. We work really well together so far, but I know we've still got a long way to go on taking this routine to the next level.

"I want full downs out of your liberties this time. We've got to get those clean before we move on to the doubles. Bases and backspots, I need you catching high, okay? No sagging butts scraping the floor. Flyers, I want your bodies tight, not loosey-goosey like some of you have been."

"Yes, ma'am," we all call out in unison. Coach Jordan nods to Nadine, who's stuck doing boom-box duty thanks to her messed-up arm. She rolls her eyes but hits play on the music, and the routine starts.

Two dramatic beats, and then Kayla counts it off, "Five, six, seven, eight!"

My hands under my chin, I clasp clap and set, and my bases do the same, ready for my foot. We bounce once, and Tonya gives my hips a shove, and I'm up in the air, hitting my liberty with the toll of the bell in the music. The other flyers beside us hit their marks, too, and then we all full down to cradle as the crescendo builds. I'm moving quick, ready to hit my mark for my tumbling pass, but the music scratches to a stop and Coach Jordan is yelling again.

"Back to the beginning! McKenzie, your hands were all over the place, and Beth looked like she was on a carnival ride with all that wobbling. We're not moving on until we hit this perfect!"

Kayla rolls her eyes as we get set again, but after a quick glance to Coach Jordan, shifts her face to serious. "Hey, are you okay?"

"I'm fine," I remark, rolling my shorts higher on my thighs so they stop riding up.

"Are you sure? You've seemed upset at every practice since last week. I just want to make sure—"

"I'm fine, Kay," I cut her off. I know she cares, and I know it's rude of me not to give her any credit for it, but if I think about the fact that I'm in love with Finn and he hates me and Finn's dad is Professor Winslow's dad and an obviously really shitty guy, I will most definitely start to cry. And that isn't going to help any of us hit this stunt well enough to leave practice at a reasonable time tonight.

I messed everything up. I have to deal with the consequences. Even if that means I have to plaster a fake smile on my face and find a way to carry this utterly devastating heartbreak that's had me crying myself to sleep every night.

"Come on," I say and force myself to look happy. "Let's do it again. Perfect this time."

Kayla nods, but I can tell by the look in her eyes that she knows something is up with me. Which means, to her, the matter isn't officially closed. She'll be asking me again, and frankly, I can't blame her. I'd do the same if our roles were reversed.

It's what good friends do.

But I have a feeling my mood isn't going to change anytime soon—I'm afraid there's no coming back from what I did to Finn.

"I told you I'm not going anywhere."

"Listen, Finn, you've been a mope-oppotamus for the last two weeks, and I'm done with it. I've never had a wingman like you, and I refuse to let you fall through the cracks."

"You've got Blake."

"He's busy with football and shit. And he's no Finnley Hayes, do you hear me?"

I roll my eyes and go back to changing the channel on the TV. Ace steps right in front of me to block my view.

"Get up, Finn. We're going out." I ignore him, so he waves his hands in front of my face. "It's not here at Dickson, so you don't have to worry about running into pretty, doe-eyed cheerleaders or any-thing, okay? My parents are having a Halloween thing with some of their friends, and they've insisted I attend. As such, you will be attending with me."

"A Halloween thing?" Nausea rolls my stomach immediately. "No way."

"Trust me, buddy, with the way you've been looking for the last little bit, it's not like you need a costume or anything. You look scary enough as it is." Ace misinterprets the situation entirely. "But my parents were in Cabo at the end of last month, and my mom's upset they didn't get to have their normal party. Now, get up, get dressed, put on some DO for your BO, and let's roll. Gary's down-stairs with the car already."

I sigh deeply and close my phone out of the text messages I've been staring at for the last hour. I'm not going to do anything with them anyway.

Scottie: I'm so genuinely sorry for invading your privacy, Finn. I realize you may never forgive me, but I don't think I'll ever stop caring about you.

Scottie: I know you think you know me and my whole story, but you don't. You'd be surprised how much we have in common.

I think I have a good enough bead on Scottie Bardeaux to know that she *is* truly sorry. But she played me—gave me her fucking *virginity*—knowing damn well what she'd done, and I can't seem to find a way to get over it.

I thought she trusted me…valued me. That the intimacy between us was a meaningful milestone for both us as a couple and me as a human being. Not some fucking cover-up for a mistake she made.

Not to mention the fact that I wasted days of my life thinking Ty Winslow had seen the damn thing when he hadn't. I don't know what I'm supposed to fucking do now. Leave it again? I don't even know what I'm doing anymore or what my plan is. I wish it would all just go away.

I shake my head, fucking annoyed all over as I get up and Ace pushes me toward the bathroom, a fucking clown grin on his face.

I run a quick brush through my hair and do some oral hygiene before throwing on a long-sleeved shirt and some jeans and calling it a day. When I come out of the bathroom, Ace's smile still stretches from ear to ear.

"Wow, honey. You're like a new man. See, doesn't that feel good?" I give him the finger, and his smile grows. "And you're being playful. Oh, baby, I think you're back."

"Shut up. Let's just go if we're going."

"I love when you get bossy with me. Keep it up."

Despite myself, I'm almost smiling by the time we make it to the car downstairs. Ace's raw magnetism is inescapable, and, I'll give it to him, he knows when to avoid a subject entirely. He hasn't asked what happened on Halloween at all, and he acts as though he intends to keep it that way.

My phone pings in my pocket again as I jump into the back seat of the Escalade and Ace gives Gary the go-ahead to head out. The glutton for punishment in me is hoping it's Scottie. The realist in me knows it's for the best if it's not.

> **Willow: Happy birthday, Finney! Thanks for being the best big brother in the world!**

I laugh at myself a little as I read it. I've been so lodged in the dumps of despair, I didn't even realize it was my own birthday.

"What's up, dude? What's funny?"

I briefly consider telling Ace the joke but decide against it pretty quickly. No doubt he'll make a big fucking deal out of it, and nineteen doesn't feel so much worth celebrating at the moment.

I shake my head. "It's nothing. Just my sister." He jerks up his chin, and I change the subject. "Where's Julia?"

"Oh shit!" he cries, his eyes widening. "I forgot to wait for her!" He only pauses for a second before winking at me. "Just kidding. She was getting her hair done or some shit. We're picking her up on the way."

I suck my lips into my mouth and nod. For the first time since he twisted my arm into doing this stupid thing, I realize he's not wearing a costume either. After how seriously he took his snake charmer getup for the Alpha Pi party, I'm shocked he isn't dressed to the gills. "Hey, why are you in a suit? I know I'm not into playing dress-up, but you are."

He tugs on the lapels of his suit jacket. "What? You don't think I look like a sexy beast today, Finnley?" I roll my eyes, and he laughs.

"All right, all right, you caught me. It's not actually a Halloween thing."

I throw both my hands up and scowl. "Then what the fuck are you dragging me to?"

"It's a surprise party for Julia. Her birthday is at the beginning of December, but her mom is using my parents' normal Halloween thing as an excuse. I just didn't want to chance you forgetting to be cool with all your brooding and sulking and shit and spoiling it."

I cross my arms over my chest, and he holds up his hands in defense.

"I can see now that was a big mistake because you'd never be uncool because you're the ultimate cool dude. So that's my bad." I sigh, but he keeps chattering. "Anyway, we'll be at the salon soon, so let's ixnay on the irthdaybay talk."

I give a thumbs-up. "No worries, dude." I won't be talking about any irthdaybays, mine included.

41

Finn

The penthouse elevator opens with a ding into an elaborate hallway of marble, crystal light fixtures, expensive-as-hell-looking wallpaper and a fancy-ass couch. There's a single door to the apartment that takes up this whole floor at the other end of the short hall, and the shiny lacquered-looking black paint and gold numbering on it looks like it costs more than my entire childhood house.

Julia looks beautiful as always, her hair swept back into a half-up mess of curls. She's wearing a cream-colored sweaterdress and brown leather boots and talking about the Daenerys costume her mom supposedly has for her inside.

I hang back while she and Ace pull ahead, not wanting to be involved in the big surprise.

Ace and Julia laugh as they run toward the door, having done it a million times in their lifetime. They're comfortable and happy and loved.

I don't have any fucking clue what that must be like.

Hands in my pockets, I slow nearly to a stop as Ace pushes the door open to the waiting crowd, all of whom yell, "Surprise!" with the kind of volume that seems like it would rattle the building.

Julia screams in response, covering her face and bursting into tears. Ace is the first to wrap her in a hug but is followed shortly by a beautiful, older version of Julia and a dapper dude in a suit I have to assume is her dad.

I feel incredibly out of place for about ten seconds or so, but as soon as the initial hugs are over, Julia turns and runs to me, throwing her arms around my neck for a hug of our own.

It's awkward and unexpected, but as Ace looks on with a giant grin, I extricate my hands from my pockets and hug her back. "Happy birthday, Jules."

She pulls away with a brilliant smile and then kisses me on the cheek. "Thanks, Finn."

I nod as she runs off again, back into the apartment where a whole host of people are waiting, and Ace takes her place, swinging an arm around my shoulders and dragging me inside.

It's just as elaborate as I imagined it would be upon stepping out of the elevator, but also ten times more surreal. Every edge of trim, every surface, every piece of furniture is perfect. Perfect in size and proportion to the place and in style and condition—the exact opposite of our hand-me-downs in Westchester.

The black cabinets in the kitchen stretch all the way to the twelve-foot ceilings, and candles burn in both the center of the fireplace to the left of the living room and on the mantel. Servers in bow ties circle the crowd, handing out appetizers from gleaming silver trays.

Floor-to-ceiling windows make up the entire back wall, the center of which contains two giant French doors. They're open to the patio, which is enormous on its own and adorned with more purple flowers than I've ever seen before, and fancy white sofas. Heaters run in the corners to keep the space from chilling too much.

I spin in a circle, trying to take it all in. "Hi, Finn," Ace's mom greets me warmly when I come to a stop facing her. My eyes are the size of saucers—I know they have to be—but she doesn't say anything. "I'm so glad you could come tonight."

"Hi, Mrs. Kelly," I reply.

She waves a hand in between us. "Call me Cassie, please." It feels weird, but so does everything else about being here. It's not worth it to disagree.

"Right. Cassie. Thanks for having me."

Out of nowhere, Ace is on my shoulders like a monkey—a regular occurrence in our relationship—yanking me around the couch and off to the balcony where all of the young people have evidently gathered. I wave to Cassie in apology, but Ace's shout overshadows it. "Come on, Finn. Stop talking to my mom and come meet the cool people."

I take a Coke from a waiter as we scoot out the door, and Ace grabs a Dr Pepper for himself. An uneasiness creeps back into my stomach as we approach the large group outside, but Ace keeps me close so Julia can introduce me to everyone.

"Oh! Mom, Dad, this is my friend Finn," she says excitedly, turning her parents around from the photo they were taking to face me. I hold out my hand for her dad, and he takes it and shakes it with a smile.

"Nice to meet you, sir." Julia's mom is beautiful as she offers a friendly grin and a wave. I nod. "Ma'am."

"No, need to be formal, Finn! I've heard all about you from both Julia and Ace. They speak very highly of you," Julia's mom says then. An undeniable warmth spreads in my abdomen and ends in a blush that radiates to my ears. "I'm Georgia, and this is Kline." She turns behind her and yells to the other side of the balcony. "Evie, come meet Julia's friend!"

Another blonde with bright-blue eyes and the boy who's with her—who is undoubtedly Ace's little brother, Gunnar—walk our direction at Georgia's call.

I'm introduced to them and a whole other group of men and their wives—members of his dad's book club, according to Ace's whispered info—and several other rambunctious children before things get really interesting.

On the far side of the patio, a TV is playing the Dickson away game against Duke, with a whole other group watching.

I notice Lexi Winslow immediately, standing with a pretty lady with a kind smile. Her hair is a dirty-blond color, and she's got her arm looped through the elbow of a man in an expensive suit.

"Lex!" Ace calls, getting her attention. "What's the score?"

"Fourteen to fourteen, tied up. Dickson has the ball in the red zone, and they just called the two-minute warning."

"No worries, then. Boden's got this," Ace says confidently, making Lexi snort.

"His two interceptions in the third quarter say differently."

"Don't be so hard on the guy," Ace chides. "He can't help it that he's in love with you."

"In love?" The man in the suit scowls. "He's several years younger than you."

Lexi rolls her eyes. "I hardly know him, Dad. You can relax."

The woman with them waggles her eyebrows, touching the man's chest. "You're going to have to stop being so protective at some point."

I lick my lips, my shoulders at my ears with anxiety. If my context clues are correct, the woman in question is my sister.

"Uncle Wes, Aunt Winnie, this is my roommate, Finn," Ace introduces then, confirming my suspicions beyond a shadow of a doubt.

I force a smile even though my nervous system is on overload. Fight-or-flight engaged, I'm mere seconds away from buzzing the tower, Maverick-style.

"Oh! Yay!" Winnie cries excitedly, pulling me into a hug so familiar, my heart races. "Roommates with Ace, huh? You must deserve an award for saint of the year!" Her smile is so bright, her eyes so kind, and her heart feels excruciatingly close to her sleeve. Her husband laughs at her joke and pulls her close, kissing her on the head before excusing himself and stepping away.

It's not rude, though. Thatch is literally crow-calling him from the other side of the patio.

I have to lick my lips to stop the sting of tears in my eyes as I answer her. "You know, surprisingly, he's not that bad."

She laughs and reaches out to touch my shoulder with a gentle hand, and everything I thought I knew about what I was doing at Dickson shatters in an instant.

It's easy to ignore the signs that Ty is decent or that the other boys have something to offer other than being stuck-up pricks. But it's impossible not to see some of Willow in Winnie, and the strongest part of my façade cracks just a little.

"Thank hell for that. All his mom talks about is figuring out a way to pay off the politicians to keep her two hoodlums out of jail!"

"Come on inside, everyone!" Georgia calls from just inside the apartment. "Julia's about to blow out the candles!"

"You coming?" Ace calls over his shoulder when I don't immediately head that direction with everyone else.

I nod. "I'll be just a sec. Just wanted to see the last play of the game."

He gives me an avid thumbs-up and takes off into the apartment, and I turn to the TV to make my moment of silence plausible.

Blake snaps back with the ball in his hands, poised at the two-yard line as he scours the receivers in front of him. He pump-fakes to the back side of the end zone once, but our tight end gets open just in the nick of time that he gets the pass off before the defensive line tackles him to the ground. The catch is good, and the crowd goes wild as Dickson seals yet another victory.

I watch avidly for any glimpse of the cheerleaders as our kicker puts in the extra point easily, and the crowd rushes the field.

Scottie and the cheerleaders mesh into a blob of football players, everyone hugging and jumping excitedly, but in the melee, the quarterback for the other team approaches her, saying something and handing her the football that we just put through the uprights. She blushes and accepts it, and my blood pressure hits an all-time high.

"Is that a show of good sportsmanship?" one commentator remarks.

But the other one answers, "I don't know, Don. I think Duke's

QB might just be smitten with one of Dickson's cheerleaders." They make another joke about star-crossed lovers, and I shake my head.

She's obviously really concerned with what happened between us still. Two weeks and she's taking footballs from stupid fucking—

"Finn!" Ace yells from the door again. "Come on, dude! My mom won't light the candles until you get in here for some reason."

Shoving down every raging emotion inside me, I jog toward Ace's call quickly and step inside as Julia takes her place behind a massive pink-and-white cake on the kitchen island. Cassie eyes Ace and me closely before giving Georgia the nod to light the candles and then Thatch to turn down the lights.

"Happy birthday to you. Happy birthday to you. Happy birthday, dear Julia. Happy birthday to you," we all sing in unison. Julia smiles brightly at us all before blowing out the candles, and everyone claps for her when she's done.

Meeting Winnie, seeing Scottie on TV, knowing my birthdays will never be like this—it's all too much.

I shove past Ace with the best smile I can manage, the hallway bathroom in my sights. I make it through the crowd and into the hall with only a little struggle and am just about to grab the knob on the bathroom door when a hand on my shoulder stops me.

The last person in the world I'm expecting is Ace's mom. I jolt at the sight of her, and she bites her lip in apology. A gift bag hangs from the fingers of her right hand.

I imagine she doesn't want me to miss the gift-opening either.

"I'm just going to the bathr—"

"Finn," she cuts me off. "I wanted to find a quiet moment because I had a feeling you wouldn't want me making a scene." My eyebrows draw together. "Fuck knows my family has a special flair for it." She lifts the bag in front of herself, directly toward me. "Happy birthday."

"How do you know it's my—"

She lifts her hand, cutting me off. "What are you, a cop? The *how* of how I know isn't important. Just take it."

Unsure what else to do, I take the bag from her hand and nod. She pats me on the shoulder and walks away, and I go into the bathroom as originally intended.

But now, I have a gift to open.

My hands shake as I pull the tissue paper out of the small blue bag, lay it on the sink, and dig around inside. One item at a time, I empty the unexpected gesture of its contents and study each of them closely. There's a brand-new pair of headphones and a card with a thousand dollars inside signed *with all our love*. There's also a pack of condoms, which is weird, but not outside the realm of expectation.

I have to sit down on the edge of the tub as a wave of awareness moves over me.

Dickson University isn't turning out to be what I thought it would be at all. There's conflict and pain and hard choices and everything in between, but there's so much more.

People *care* about me. People who hardly even know me but accept the things they do.

Dickson's not just a fucked-up family—it's also the good kind.

42

Scottie

All thanks to Blake Boden's second game-winning touchdown of the year, Dickson beat the Duke Blue Devils twenty-one to fourteen. The cheerleader bus is bustling with all the markers of perfect season excitement, Kayla and Emma even doing a rendition of "We Are the Champions" in the seat right behind the driver.

I'm trying really hard not to be a downer, but one more karaoke special from the Excitement Barbies and I'm going to have to put in my AirPods and drown out the happy noise.

My playlist titled "Sad Girl" I made a week ago and started listening to on repeat feels like just the vibe I'm looking for. Adele, Sam Smith, Lana Del Rey, Taylor Swift, Dua Lipa, Bon Iver, and David Gray, this playlist is a rite of passage for every pathetic girl trying to drown out thoughts of the boy who got away while she cries herself to sleep at night.

It's cathartic, in a way. Though, Veda, the therapist my dad had Wren and me go to when we were young to talk about our mom's addiction, might say listening to sad, depressing songs about losing someone you love over and over again could also hinder your ability to get over them.

Maybe that's the point, I think sardonically.

As much as it would improve my quality of life to do so, I don't *want* to get over Finn.

I want to get back under him. Being in his arms was still the most special experience of my life, even if I ruined it all shortly after.

After two full weeks of not seeing him at all, he finally came to Professor Winslow's class yesterday. He avoided me completely until we split up into our groups to work on our *The Winter's Tale* project, and even then, he only said what he had to to keep Nadine off our back. I tried to catch up to him to talk to him after, but he was gone, vapor in the wind, before I crossed the classroom's threshold.

I don't think he gave Professor Winslow the journal entry again, and I also don't think our professor knows that Finn is his brother.

It's all just assumptions from my end, but Professor Winslow is a guy who actually cares about his students. I've witnessed him on multiple occasions ask a student to stay after class because he could see they were having a rough time. He's known for that.

And I have a hard time believing he would've been that oblivious to Finn's surly mood if he knew they shared the same father.

"Where's your football?" Kayla's voice fills my ears, and I look up to find her leaving her seat beside McKenzie to cross the aisle and take the empty seat beside me. "C'mon, Scottie. Where's the football Hottie McHotson gave you tonight?" She waggles her brows at me, and I roll my eyes.

"It's packed away in my duffel."

She doesn't hesitate to jump up and locate my duffel above my seat, the dumb football clutched in her hands as she plops down into the seat again. She turns it over in her hands, and when her eyes spot the numbers Sharpied on the back of it, she squeals. "Holy shit! He gave you his number!"

"It's no big deal, Kay."

"No big deal?" she exclaims. "Duke's QB is smokin' hot. I mean, he's clearly not as good as our QB, but who cares about football skills when you've got a face and body like that guy, amirite?" She playfully nudges me with her elbow, and I snort at her antics.

"Down, girl," I tease. "Your horny is showing."

Kayla cracks up and shoves the football in my lap. "Call him." My head is already shaking my refusal. "No way."

"What? Why not?" Kayla searches my face like I've

grown an additional head. "I know you and Finn had a little something-something going on at the Halloween party." When my head whips toward her, she treads a little more lightly. "I mean, we all saw you dancing and making out, but I'm pretty sure you're still technically single…" She pauses and reaches out to grab me by the shoulders. "Oh shit! Are you guys, like, a thing now, and you're keeping it under wraps or something?"

Nausea floods my mouth as sadness the size of a boulder finds a place inside my stomach. I discreetly swallow hard against it. "No," I say, but my voice sounds half strangled. I clear my throat. "There's nothing going on between Finn and me."

"Wait…did something happen?" Kayla's mouth turns down at the corners, and she swivels in her seat to hold both of my hands. "I mean, I've been sensing that something's been off with you." She lowers her voice to a whisper. "But every time I ask, it feels like you're brushing me off…"

It's my turn to frown. I hate that I've been making one of my favorite people at Dickson feel like I'm brushing her off. "I'm sorry, Kay. Brushing you off was not my intention. I'm just…dealing with some stuff I'm not ready to talk about yet."

"Girl, no need to apologize. I get it. Not everything is peachy keen every single day of the week," she comments. "You know Nathan Hodges?"

My eyebrows draw together. "He's on the track team, right?"

She nods. "We were dating a little bit in October, but then he met some biology major with big boobs."

I wince, realizing only now that I'm not the only one with stuff going on. "I'm sorry."

I wish I could tell her the truth. I wish I could just word-vomit my tragic situation all over her lap. But I can't. It feels wrong to tell anyone. So I give her what I can.

"I was definitely hoping something would happen between Finn and me, but…" I pause and shrug. "You kind of need both people to want that for it to work."

"Damn, I'm sorry," she says and squeezes my hands. "You should have told me that was going on, Scottie. I would've been there for you."

"I know. You're right. Next time, you'll be the first person I call," I tell her, making a promise that I don't feel like I can actually keep.

"Well, if my opinion means anything," Kayla comments with a nod toward the football that's still in my lap. "Then I think you should call that man."

"You realize he goes to school seven hours from me, right?"

She waves her hand in the air. "I'm not saying date the guy. Just, like, have a little fun with him. Even if it's just some flirty texts back and forth."

I wish I could agree with her, but I miss Finn too much to talk to another guy. Which is probably insanely pathetic, I know, given how badly he wants me to leave him alone.

"Just consider it." Kayla takes the football from my hands and stands up to put it back in my duffel. "Good grief, Scottie," she groans when a pair of my gym shoes falls out of my bag, and she has to pull my bag down and set it in the aisle to get the football and shoes shoved back in it again. "What in the hell do you have in this thing?"

"Books," I admit. I've been sucked into reading Cassie Kelly's whole damn collection.

My phone vibrates in my pocket as Kayla shoves my bag even harder with a laugh, and I pull it out to check it.

As soon as I do, I wish I wouldn't have.

Karma called, bitch. And she's coming for your ass.

"Who is texting you?" Kayla asks as she plops back down in the seat, my duffel bag safely secured in the overhead bin above our heads.

"Just my dad," I lie and shove my phone back into my pocket.

Truthfully, I haven't really talked to my sister or my dad for any meaningful amount of time since before Halloween. And it's not for their lack of trying. They've texted and called, but I've only been able to offer them brief, two-minute phone calls or short and sweet texts back.

Getting out of bed every day and trying to focus on class and cheerleading is about all I can give right now, I'm so swollen with heartbreak.

"Oh my God!" Kayla bursts into laughter and startles the hell out of me. I glance over to find her looking at something on her phone. "You have to see what Julia just texted me."

She turns the screen of her phone toward me, and I scan through their messages.

> *Julia: Girl, it's a damn shame you and Scottie are in Durham because some wild shit has gone down here. (By the way, I saw you both on TV! You girls looked GORG.)*
>
> *Kayla: TELL ME EVERYTHING.*
>
> *Julia: Ace's dad just pulled the prank of a lifetime at my parents' surprise birthday party for me. He legit paid to close off city streets, bought a film crew, and even had police officers there to keep everything secure. Ace had no idea what was happening.*
>
> *Kayla: What the hell was the prank???*
>
> *Julia: Ace's dad and my dad pretended to be all panicked that his younger brother Gunnar got arrested and told Ace and Finn to get in the car to go bail him out. And that ended in a pretend police chase scene through the closed-off streets of the city. ACE WAS FREAKING THE FUCK OUT. Seriously, just watch this.*

Kayla clicks on the video Julia just sent over, and in an instant, I'm face-to-face with Finn's gorgeous face. He's sitting in the back of some kind of sports car with Ace, and in the front sits Ace's dad Thatch and an incredibly handsome guy I'm assuming is Julia's dad.

Ace looks petrified as his dad drives like a bat out of hell through city streets with no one on the road or sidewalk.

By the time police sirens sound from behind them, Ace is losing his fucking mind on the video while Finn tries to pin him down.

Kayla laughs her ass off at the clusterfuck.

Under normal circumstances, I'd probably find this hilarious too, but there's just something about seeing Finn's face this up close and personal that makes my chest become so tight I feel like someone has sucked all of the oxygen off the bus.

When Kayla can't stop laughing, other girls on the bus start to get interested, and she busies her attention with showing them the footage.

I'm thankful, to be honest, because every time she glanced in my direction and I forced an amused smile to my lips, I felt like my face was going to shatter into a million pieces.

Finn Hayes may be done with me, but I can't escape him.

Friday, November 22nd
Finn

"Come on, Finn. Churn those toddler-length legs," Ace chastises as we run past Brower Center. Blake laughs and looks back at me while I do my best to look at my phone, give Ace the finger, and run without dying at the same time.

We got another Double C text half an hour ago, just as I was settling in for a night in bed watching Netflix on my laptop, instructing us to be at the back of McKinley Library five minutes from now. I begged off—even with the potential for more money—but Ace was relentless.

Now, though, my sibling group message is in full swing, thanks to Willow, and if I don't answer, Jack and Trav will end up doing something stupid just to get my attention. Trust me, it's happened before.

> **Willow: *The dress is perfect! Thank you, Finney!!!***

I smile down at the photo of my sister in her homecoming dress and roll my eyes a little at the redheaded idiot who is standing beside her. His name is Crew, and he's my sister's newest boyfriend. Poor sap looks like he thinks he has a chance at longevity.

> **Me: *You look beautiful, Low. Have fun, but don't do anything stupid.***

> **Willow: *So, don't do anything Jack or Travis would do? LOL.***

Trav: Hey, I resemble that remark! ;)

Jack: Finn's the one robbing banks to buy dresses and shit.

Me: I'm not robbing banks.

Trav: Of course, Finney. Gotta keep this thread clean in case of an investigation.

Me: I'm not robbing banks.

Jack: Willow, how much did that dress cost again?

Trav: Maybe he's just rich by association now because of all his rich friends.

Willow: Shut up, guys. Stop making Finn feel bad.

"Finn!" Ace yells again, waving me forward from the bottom of the steps that lead into the basement of the library. "Look alive, would you?"

I tuck my phone back into my pocket and jog down to meet them, and Blake holds open the door while we hustle inside. We take a place at the back of the crowd as Lexi gets everyone up to speed on tonight's event. I don't see Julia or Scottie anywhere, and I'm a fucking idiot for looking in the first place.

How long is it going to take me to get over her?

"Texas Hold'em," she says matter-of-factly, lifting a hand to gesture at the green-felt-covered tables behind her. The décor is elaborate, as always, and I'm starting to wonder how they get these things set up without campus security noticing. They put a fucking fight ring in Nash, for shit's sake. *How?*

"Fifty bucks gets you in the game. Every table starts with five players, and you play until you're out."

Blake raises his hand, and I have to cover my mouth to smother a smile as an annoyed Lexi calls on him. "Yes?"

"What do we do when we're out?"

"Go home," she suggests. He smiles, the masochist. I swear, he loves getting owned by her.

Ace clears his throat at the two of us, whispering to Blake as Lexi shakes her head and looks back at her notes. "You have some kind of loser fetish or something? Like, is that what happens when you're as successful at something as you are?"

Blake waves him off, shushing him and pointing up at Lexi. His instructions are clear: *Listen to the love of my life.*

Ace and I share a bemused shake of our heads.

"We'll combine tables as people lose their asses. Only six people will make it to the final table," Lexi continues, oblivious to Blake all over again, even though he's staring at her like a serial killer. If the bastard trades in his souped-up Dodge Charger for a white economy van, we should all be concerned.

"How many people win the pot?" a guy from the back yells out.

"Only one," Lexi answers. "Winner takes all."

"Hell yeah," Ace comments and claps a hand on my shoulder, cocky. "They don't call me Ace for nothing."

I glance over at him. "Let me guess…you were playing Hold'em in the womb?"

"Pretty much. When my mom was pregnant with me, she loved crashing my dad's poker nights. She beat him and his friends so many times, they blackballed her."

"Give your money to Connor, and he'll tell you which table to sit at!" Lexi shouts over the crowd that's started chatting among themselves again. "Good luck!"

"What'd we miss?"

Ace, Blake, and I turn around to find Julia and Scottie standing behind us.

Fresh-faced and in a pair of tight jeans and a cream sweater, she looks fucking beautiful. Her dark locks hang down her back in a way that reminds me of Halloween, when she came on my mouth. My fingers itch to run through her hair, and my mind tries to fill my head with memories of what Scottie Bardeaux sounds like, tastes like, feels like when she's naked and chasing her pleasure.

And when our eyes lock unexpectedly, the contact shoves a dagger through my chest.

My realization is immediate.

She's not the kind of girl you get over—ever.

44

Scottie

"The name of the game is Texas Hold'em, Jules." Ace wraps his arm around Julia's shoulders and sways her back and forth playfully. "Maybe you should just cut your losses now."

"Get real, Acer." She scoffs and shoves him away with an amused smile on her lips. "I'm going to own your ass."

Both Ace and Blake laugh, but Finn and I are too busy trying not to look at each other to join in.

He's beautiful, as always, and my entire body aches with the urge to pull him into a magic hug. Something with spells and potions and the power to end all the pain and suffering between us.

Ace pulls money out of his wallet for both himself and Julia, and Blake tries to convince Connor to let him buy in twice. Finn pulls out his wallet to take out money, but a tsunami of insanity comes over me that's impossible to stop.

My fingers shake as I wrap them around his wrist and squeeze. Connor gets annoyed as Finn stops, turning to look at me.

"Are you in or out?"

My voice is a fraction of itself as I force the words out. "Finn, can I talk to you?"

Julia's eyes are wide as Ace and Blake drag her away to their assigned table, and Finn's jaw grinds.

"In or out, dude?" Connor prompts again, agitated even more.

Finn's chest expands. "Out."

My knees threaten to give out and take me to the floor, the

relief is so strong. Day and night, I think about Finn and all the things I want to say. Day and night, I've dreamed about the chance to clear the air.

Day and night for three weeks. I'm exhausted.

My bottom lip quivers as Finn jerks his head away from the tables toward the depths of the rest of the basement. I follow him into both quiet and darkness, the sound of my breathing like a hyena at a funeral—completely giving me away.

We make a right into the Dickson Archives, a stacked section of dusty books that smell like they haven't been touched in ages. Finn leans back against one of the shelves, crossing his arms over his chest, and I run my hands through my hair, trying to work up the courage to lay it all on the line.

The silence is almost unbearably heavy.

"I'm sorry," I say, the apology splintering the anticipation like a bullet to the heart.

I can tell by the firm set of his jaw and the shine of his eyes, he's right back in my room, naked and vulnerable and learning of my betrayal all over again, but I'm back there too. Hurting and desperate to make things right.

"I know that sounds hollow and trite and like some kind of fucked-up excuse at this point, but I swear, Finn, I'll be sorry about this for the rest of my life."

"I know you're sorry, Scottie. I saw your texts, I got your notes. I *know* you're sorry."

The knot in my stomach tenses as I force myself to confirm. "You know I'm sorry, but you're still avoiding me."

"Yes."

"Why?" The word is as broken as I feel. *If he knows I'm genuinely sorry, why can't he forgive me?*

"Because it doesn't change anything."

Righteous indignation makes my temper flare. All this time, all this heartache, everything we've been through and overcome, and that's all he has to say? "Wow, Finn."

His face ticks. "Don't go playing the victim just because you don't like what I have to say, Scottie. You wronged me. Not the other way around."

"I'm not saying I'm the victim," I refute, steeling my spine to ready myself to fight. I knew this conversation wasn't going to be easy. I hoped it would be, but deep down, I knew it wouldn't. "But I deserve the chance to speak my piece. To explain. To lay it all out there. Don't I?"

He holds out a dramatic hand. "Fine. Lay it all out there, then. Tell me what happened the day you took my property and kept it to yourself. Tell me what happened when you took me back to your room and begged me to take your virginity, knowing what it meant to me because I told you. *Tell me*, Scottie. I want to know."

The recap of all my poor choices falling from his beautiful lips sounds even more awful than I could have imagined, but I won't miss the invitation to explain, sarcastic or not.

"I saw you were upset that day in class—and not just a little bit. You looked like you were dying, burning alive from the inside out." He looks down to the floor and licks his lips as I continue. "I was…I was concerned. I know we were still a mess at that point, but Finn, I *care* about you. I did then and I do now, and I won't apologize for that. But the way I handled it… I know." I nod, my voice shaking. "I know I did a terrible job. All I wanted was a little insight into what was bothering you so I could help, but when I picked up the paper, Professor Winslow walked in, and I knew I couldn't put it back down. So, I panicked, and I took it."

"And read it."

"Of course," I admit with a shrug. "I wanted to understand you."

He shakes his head and shoves away from the shelf, but I grab his elbow and press on. "I knew when I read it how much I'd messed up, and I don't deny that. It wasn't any of my business, and it still isn't. I *know* that."

"And yet, here you are, bringing it up again."

I lick my lips and wipe angrily at the stupid tears that have managed to escape. "Because I want to fix it. Because I love you. Because when I begged you to sleep with me that night, it's because I wanted to be with you. Not because of the stupid mistake. Not because—"

He pulls away from my grip, his voice breaking as he gets close enough to me that I can smell him. His voice is raw and almost eerily quiet. "I loved you too, Scottie, pure and simple. But all the love I've ever known has been fucked up, and now, this love is too."

He pushes past me, and my heart cracks. "Finn, wait!"

"No, Scottie. If you need companionship that bad, why don't you just go call Duke's quarterback?"

Holy hell, he saw it. I can't believe he saw it. "I don't want that stupid quarterback who gave me the football! I want you! Can't you see that?"

"I want a lot of things too, princess. But reality check, in real life, you don't get them."

Hurt burrows deep inside my chest and stays there, effectively evicting the very last shred of my hope. Finn isn't going to forgive me for this. Not ever.

"You know what's crazy, Finn?" I ask. "I know that everything you're saying right now, you don't mean. I know that it's all bullshit. You know how I know that? Because I know what your eyes look like when you're telling me the truth."

His jaw grinds as he avoids my eyes, but I carry on. "One day, you're going to realize what you're giving up, but when you do, I'm going to be gone. Because from here on out, I'm going to make sure I stay as far away from you and your self-destruction button as I possibly can. How about that?" I laugh, but there's absolutely no humor there. "Looks like you finally got what you wanted. I'm leaving you alone."

I turn and run the path we used to get here, and I don't look back.

Finn Hayes and I are officially done.

45

Thursday, December 12th

Finn

English class is pretty full when I arrive for our midterm exam, and an excitement about winter break is in the air. I make a point not to sit beside Ace, who's been pestering me for the last two days about going to play poker at his parents' house tomorrow night, and find a seat on the left side of the room instead. I don't need him yapping at me while I'm trying to look through my notes one last time.

I open my backpack and pull out my notebook, but I don't even make it through one paragraph of notes before my phone goes off in my pocket.

> **Ace: Cute of you to think you can avoid me in such a technological age, Finnley. Listen, do you want to be in charge of snacks or drinks for poker night tomorrow?**

The urge to ignore him is overwhelming, but I can see by the way he's staring me down from across the room that if I *fuck around*, I'm going to *find out*. I sigh and type out a message.

> **Me: Can we discuss crudites AFTER the exam? Maybe? Just maybe?**

> **Ace: So, you're coming?? Do I have this as your promise?**

> **Me: Yes, dude. Whatever. I'll come to poker and bring**

juice boxes or whatever the fuck you want if you just let me
concentrate on studying right now.

I wait five full seconds in anticipation, satisfaction taking over when my phone doesn't buzz again. When I glance up at Ace one last time, he's waving a blank piece of paper in the air like a white flag.

I laugh. The motherfucker is so ridiculous. Ever since he won the Double C Texas Hold'em event three weeks ago, all he's wanted to do is play poker.

It's annoying as fuck, but truthfully, I'm not against going to his parents' place to hang out for the evening. His parents are a hell of a lot better than mine, and it'll give me something to do with my time on winter break rather than going home.

I look back to my notebook to read through some more notes, but Professor Winslow claps at the front of the room to get our attention, starting class ten insignificant seconds later.

I guess I know what I know at this point, and the exam will be whatever it is. I sigh again and shut my notebook as Professor Winslow starts to talk.

"Today is the day," he announces with a big-ass smile on his face. "Your English Lit midterm. I sure hope you studied because I didn't hold back when I had Doug help me create the questions. You think they'll pass?" He looks over at TA Doug, and Doug grins.

"I don't know, Professor. It's a mighty hard exam."

My brother—who still doesn't know he's my brother—laughs and rests his hip on the corner of his desk. He eyes the room for a long moment and then crosses his arms over his chest. There's still a huge part of me that resents him, but I'd be lying if I said it's as big as when I started this year. Meeting his sister—hell, my sister—Winnie broke down a truth barrier inside me I didn't even know existed.

They got the easy end of the deal, sure, but they didn't get it as the result of a conscious choice. They were abandoned.

"You know, my wife and my daughter are huge fans of Christmas. I'm talking, they've got my ass on a ladder stringing up lights and baking enough cookies to get diabetes kind of fans. And I don't know, I'm starting to wonder if all of their Christmas spirit has seeped into my pores or something…"

He pauses, and a grin stretches across his lips. "I'm feeling really generous today, and I'm thinking that, maybe, you guys don't need to take a midterm…"

"Yes!" one dude yells from the back. "For the love of everything, please!"

Professor Winslow laughs. "Oh, so you guys are a fan of that plan?"

More voices in the lecture hall shout out their agreement.

"Okay," he says and stands. He walks over to Doug's small desk in the corner and grabs the stack of midterms off his desk. And then he strides over to his trash can and drops them in with a loud thud. "Happy holidays."

The entire room erupts into cheers and applause and Professor Winslow lets it go on for a good minute, basking in everyone's happiness, before he holds up his hand to quiet the room.

"Now, even though you don't have a midterm, you *do* have a semester project to turn in to me today," he updates. "This final part of your project's point value will be double to replace your midterm grade, so I'm hoping you all put the team in teamwork and created a final thesis on *The Winter's Tale* that will blow my figurative load."

Girls squeal, guys high-five, and I shake my head. *Yeah, he's still a fucking douche.*

"Get together with your group one final time, and I'll come around the room to chat with you."

Everyone starts the process of relocating to their group, and I gird my loins to do the same. All the work on *The Winter's Tale* project for the last three weeks has been done by splitting it up or collaborating through email, and Scottie hasn't once tried to change that. There haven't been any in-person pleas or texts or calls, and I've tried not to let that get to me.

It has, of course, because for all the stupid shit I'm angry at her for, there's at least one other part of me that loves her. But I've tried.

Scottie's on the other side of the room, in keeping with her bid to avoid me entirely, staring down at her notebook in concentration as she jots something down. Shockingly, normally self-involved, makes-everyone-come-to-her Nadine is magnanimously on her way over to Scottie, so I grab my backpack to do the same.

I slump down into the empty seat beside her on one side, and Nadine takes the one on the other, but she doesn't look up at either one of us.

Again, I'm not surprised.

"Tell me someone printed off our final thesis," Nadine comments on a sigh, her beleaguered body melting into the seat like she just finished climbing Everest. "Dane had me up all night, if you know what I mean, and I didn't have time to head to McKinley before I came to class."

I'm not sure if Nadine thinks her mention of Dane makes Scottie jealous, but if it's possible at this point, I think she cares about Nadine and Dane's TMI even less than she cares about me. Her face, her body, her voice—they're all unfazed.

"I did," Scottie and I both say in unison. Scottie's eyes just barely meet mine, but they're quick to glance back down at her desk.

"Well, look at you two," Nadine purrs. "You're like the cutest little nerds. I love it."

I roll my eyes and pull out our printed fifty-page thesis from my backpack, and Scottie does the same thing.

"Uh-oh, which one are we going to turn in?" Nadine questions sarcastically, her evil little giggle making my ears bleed. "What a dilemma."

"Why don't we write Scottie's name on hers and my name on mine and turn our project in like that?" I offer, so annoyed with Nadine's never-ending shit I can't bite my tongue.

A stifled laugh falls from Scottie's lips. I hate how much I enjoy it.

"Don't be an asshole, Finn," Nadine scoffs. "I was just teasing you guys."

"Teasing. Right." Fuck, this chick is a waste of oxygen. She barely even responded to our emails about this stupid thing, let alone did her fair share of the work.

"So, Scottie," Nadine says, changing the conversation completely. "Any big plans for winter break?"

"No, not really," Scottie answers.

"You're not going home to spend time with your mom and dad?"

"I'm going home on Christmas Eve, but I'll come back to campus on Christmas Day. My dad and sister are supposed to be working anyway."

"What about your mom?" Nadine questions in surprise. "Surely she wants you to stay home for longer than a freaking night for Christmas."

Scottie shifts in her seat, clearly uncomfortable with Nadine's prying, but Professor Winslow stops in front of us and cuts off the conversation entirely.

It's the first time I've felt thankful to the guy. Because as much as I'd love to know more about Scottie's family dynamic, I'm all too familiar with being the one who doesn't want anyone to know.

"Are we ready to turn in our thesis?" Ty asks with a grin on his face. A Santa hat is now on his head, and he's switched out his normal gray tie for a red one.

Both Scottie and I hold out our printouts at once, and he laughs. "It looks like I finally found a group that is prepared. Maybe even *over*prepared." He looks over at Nadine. "Pray tell. Is there a third version of this group's masterpiece?"

Nadine opens her mouth, but Scottie beats her to the punch, making a sense of pride swell in my chest. I love seeing her stand up for herself to someone who's been nothing but shit to her. "Nadine said she didn't have time to print it out because she was with her boyfriend all last night. Right, Nadine?"

Nadine rolls her eyes, but an angry blush reddens her cheeks and mars the skin above her overly exposed breasts. "I didn't print it off because you and Finn said you had it covered."

"No," I chime in. "We never said that. You must have assumed since Scottie and I have done such a good job handling everything else. But it's all good, partner. Scottie and I made sure our project is getting turned in on time."

"Nadine." Professor Winslow looks directly at her. "The point of a group project is to work as a group. To work as a team. Should I be concerned that you didn't pull your weight here?"

"No. I swear, I did the work," she protests, sweating now. "I had a hard time typing because of my cast, but I *did* my share of the work."

Professor Winslow moves his attention to both Scottie and me, and for as much as I want to show Nadine's ass, I don't. I leave it up to Scottie.

"It was a group effort."

Clearly, I wish Scottie would have narc-ed, but I understand why she doesn't. She has to deal with Nadine at cheerleading on a daily basis for what will likely be her entire college career. The long-term consequences of selling her out in our freshman English class are extremely prohibitive.

Professor Winslow is skeptical, but he doesn't push it, accepting Scottie's paper while I tuck mine back into my backpack. "Okay, guys. Can't wait to read it."

"Thanks Professor Winslow," Nadine gladly crows, despite not having a single clue what the hell the paper is even about.

"Any big plans for winter break?" Professor Winslow asks, his eyes, unfortunately, on me. "Getting out of the city to spend some time with family, Finn?"

For the first time in what feels like forever, Scottie actually looks at me. Direct and without ire. It's rewarding and disconcerting at the same time.

Besides me and my deadbeat dad, she's the only person who

knows Ty Winslow is my brother, and I know without question she's kept it that way.

I know she has to be curious, has to wonder what the hell I'm going to do about my big secret. But that makes two of us. I still don't have a single fucking clue what I'm going to do.

"Yeah, something like that," I mutter, at a loss for any other option.

Professor Winslow smiles at all three of us. "Have a good break, guys. You are officially free to go, and I'll see you next year." He winks at his joke, like every token old person on the entirety of campus has done for the whole last week after saying the same exact thing, and I start gathering my things. Scottie is faster, though, and she's out of her seat and out of the lecture hall before I even have my backpack zipped.

She's keeping her word and leaving me alone.

Which is good. It's how things should have gone between us from the start.

I just wish it didn't have to suck so fucking much.

Friday December 13th
Finn

"I'm all in," Ace's dad declares, and his eyes are stone-cold as he stares down the only person still left in the game—Ace. "You in, Acer?"

Ace doesn't respond, and I eye the cards on the table, trying to guess what Ace and Thatch might have in their hands. I folded after Ace bet $25 in chips on the flop. Kline Brooks, Wes Lancaster, and two guys from the book club I met at Julia's party—Milo Ives and Caplin Hawkins—folded when Thatch bet $50 on the turn.

The five cards that sit before us consist of an ace of clubs, ten of hearts, nine of spades, five of spades, and nine of hearts.

I think the best possible hand someone could have right now is four of a kind, but that would mean they have the nine of clubs *and* the nine of diamonds sitting between their fingertips.

Next-best hands would include three of a kind with one nine, or a full house with one nine and a five, ace, or ten. Not so great but not terrible hands would include two pair, or a single pair with a king high.

I'm almost positive there aren't any straight or flush opportunities sitting on the table, but I'm not exactly a Texas Hold'em expert like Ace claims to be, and I'm not the best at math. Everything I'm thinking could be complete bullshit, to be honest.

"You gonna rumble, son?" Thatch taunts again, chewing on the butt end of his unlit cigar. Cassie came in just as he was about to light it and shut him down real quick. She wasn't mean, though—just whispered something in his ear that had him mumbling under his breath about titties for the next five minutes.

Ace still hasn't said a word, but his eyes are locked on his dad. His eyes narrow as he searches his face. Thatch grins. Ace looks down at his cards again before running a hand through his hair.

"C'mon, Acer. What's it going to be?" Thatch continues talking. "You gonna hold your nuts to the fire or let your mom honey-roast 'em?" Clearly, the name of his game is shit-talking.

Both Milo and Wes chuckle while Kline smirks over his glass of scotch. Caplin Hawkins, on the other hand, is almost just as much of a shit-talker as Ace's dad. Even being out of this hand, he can't stand not to be included.

"You better bow out, Aceface," he says. "Normally, all that comes out of your dad's big fucking mouth is bullshit, but I can tell he's gonna smoke you on this one."

"I'd tell you to suck my dick, Cappy, but we both know the Supercock is far too big to fit in your delicate little mouth," Thatch replies, blowing a kiss at Caplin right after.

"I fold," Ace says, disappointment rife in every long line of his Stretch Armstrong body.

"Uh-oh, boys. Better catch the falling star and put him in your pocket," Thatch teases as he makes a show of raking in the chips to his side of the table. "His poker skills are fading away." His smile is big and blinding from his clever change to the Perry Como song, so much so that I can see all of his pearly white teeth. If I took out my phone and started filming, I could submit the footage to a fucking toothpaste company.

He slides his cards toward Milo, who is the dealer for our next hand, and Ace reaches out to stop the cards' descent toward the discard pile.

"Hold up," he says, desperate. "You're not going to at least show me?"

"Take a look," Thatch says, and Ace turns the cards over to reveal two nines.

"I fucking told you, Acer!" Cap exclaims. "For once, your dad had a mouth full of something other than crap."

"Hey, Cappy, I'll have you know the thing my mouth is most full of at all times is pussy. Not crap."

Kline lets out a deep sigh. "You think you idiots might want to tone it down a little?"

"Oh, get real, Brooks," Thatch retorts. "This isn't a damn tea party. We're not deflowering virginal ears here. These fuckers have probably had more pussy this year than we have, and that's saying something. I have a very high sex drive."

"Yeah, Kline," Cap agrees. "Finn and Ace are full-grown college men now." He smirks. "I think I heard they spend a lot of time with your daughter."

Kline's eyes are daggers, spearing Ace first. Ace raises both hands in the air.

"Oh no, no, no," Ace refutes. "Don't look at me. I'm not dating Julia and have had very little pussy, if any at all."

Cap snorts, but Kline still isn't amused, his glare moving to me. I'm a little terrified at how such an easygoing guy can look so murderous. I shake my head, but Thatch's overbearing nature saves me from actually having to comment.

"You and Julia aren't dating?" he questions Ace, his face as serious as I've seen it.

"Good grief, Dad. No. We're friends. That's it. Hell, Finn and I are going to a sorority party after this, and I have plans to meet up with a girl named Scarlett."

We do? He does?

This is all news to me.

When Thatch smiles at Kline, raising his eyebrows in more disbelief, Ace gets agitated. "I don't know why the hell you guys can't seem to understand that men and women can be friends. Finn's been spending nearly every waking moment with a cheerleader named Scottie, and they're just friends."

Instantly, all the attention at the table is directed at me. The feel of bus tires is heavy on my back.

"A cheerleader named Scottie, huh?" Milo questions with a little smirk. "What's she like?"

Ace smiles nervously as he has a premonition of me strangling him. Cap is fully invested as he places his elbows on the table and rests his chin on his hands.

These old bastards are like the fucking FBI. "She's smart. Kind. Funny." I lick my lips. "Beautiful."

Thatch hums, and I sigh. "We had a little bit of a thing at one point, but now it's over. Definitely over."

"Uh-oh," Thatch mutters, his voice a lot softer than I'm used to. "I know that look."

"We all know that look," Milo says.

"Because we've all fucking experienced that look," Cap adds.

"Yeah." Wes chuckles. "We had to survive Cap's romance book club when he had that look."

"My book club, dude." Thatch points a finger in Wes's direction. "Cap just commandeered it like a real dickhead when he was trying to make Ruby fall in love with him."

"Can we not talk about book club?" Ace asks with a shudder. "Mom making me beta-read her manuscripts is enough romance for me."

"Don't shit on the romance world, son. It's a literary powerhouse, with the biggest readership of any genre on the planet."

"I'm not shitting on romance," Ace hedges. "I'm just scarred."

"I think we're getting a little off the rails here," Cap chimes in.

"Yeah." I nod. "Pretty sure it's Kline's turn to deal."

"Oh no, Finn," Cap responds with a smile I don't like one bit. "I meant that we need to get back to you and Scottie the Cheerleader."

I let my head fall back onto my chair. "Like I said, there's nothing to tell because we're not anything."

When I don't look up, Thatch's voice is the first to fill my ears.

"Like we said before, Finn, we've all been there," he says, and his voice doesn't hold his usual edge of teasing and sarcasm. "But from years of experience, I can tell you that you only get that look when it's someone who means something."

"Yeah, man," Kline agrees. "It's been decades since I almost screwed everything up with Georgia, but I will never in a million years forget how it felt during those moments that I thought I'd lost her for good."

Every single guy at the table voices their very similar experience. Even Wes, and he talks about Winnie—my sister—like she's the best thing that's ever happened to him.

The way these men talk about their now-wives is unlike anything I've ever experienced in my house growing up. I don't think I've ever heard my dad tell my mom he loves her. Or that she's beautiful. I've never heard him compliment her or say something just because he wants to make her feel good.

All I've seen is a man treating his wife like she's an object that doesn't deserve respect or love. I've seen my dad treat my mom so cruelly at times that, at the age of thirteen, I found myself on my knees beside my bed, praying to God and asking him to never let me treat a woman that way.

But I can't avoid that he's half of my DNA.

Kline starts to deal another round of cards, but my mind continues to race. I might be looking at my cards and doing my best to follow the table conversation, but I'm preoccupied with a startling new notion.

Did I push Scottie away because, deep down, I'm afraid I'm like my dad?

47

Scottie

As of three o'clock today, all my exams are done, and winter break is here.

How I survived the past month and a half while secretly nursing a broken heart—*while facing the boy who broke it no less than two times a week*—and still managed to keep a 4.0 GPA and not miss a single cheerleading practice or game is both a mystery and a miracle.

Our team even secured a spot at NCA Nationals at our competition in Alabama two weekends ago, and I didn't make any mistakes during our routine. Which, trust me, wasn't an easy feat. Some of the changes Coach Jordan made at the last minute put me into stunt formations I haven't been in at all before.

I run a brush through my hair and add a little hair spray to secure my curls in place. As I apply a fresh coat of mascara, I silently curse Julia and Kayla for convincing me to go out tonight. It's not that I don't want to celebrate the end of the semester with my friends—my body is just screaming for some actual rest.

Between the heartbreak of everything with Finn, cheerleading, more messages from unknown numbers, and exams, my stress steak is *way* overdone.

My phone vibrates on top of my nightstand, and I accidentally brush mascara onto my eyelid. Undoubtedly, at this point, just the sound of a text message causes a trauma response.

Still, more times than not, it's a friend, not a foe, which is why I make myself take the time to check.

Wren: I'm sorry I sprang the whole mom thing on you.

Oh yeah. I guess when I was listing my stressors before, I kind of forgot one.

My sweet sister.

Wren is five years older than me and a great role model in every way. She finished college last year and moved home with my dad and me to work at a local café while she takes online classes toward her master's. And while I know the transition she's going through being back at home has been hard, she's handled it beautifully.

She's always been better at the hard stuff than me.

Including our mom.

A couple weeks ago, while I was at home for Thanksgiving, she told me she'd started talking to our mom again. That she was sober, faithfully attending AA, and really turning a corner. It's a tale as old as time, though, and I've been having a really hard time believing in these particular fairies.

There are so many ugly memories and traumas tied into everything I've ever known with her. When I was two, she left me strapped in a car seat in a hot car, and the only reason I survived is because my seven-year-old sister—who had been left home by herself for hours—walked outside to look for me when Mom passed out on the sofa.

In the early days of our childhood, Mom hid her alcohol consumption from our father—which wasn't hard since he worked so much. But as we got older, it became too obvious for her to hide.

Me: I'm just having a hard time understanding while you believe her this time.

Wren: Well, there's always a risk. I mean, we both know that. But she really seems different.

Wren: I understand if you're not ready, tho. That's why I've been trying to give you some space to process.

Since my sister is five years older than me, I know there's a lot more shit that she can remember than I can—the only reason I know about the hot car story is because of Wren—and yet, somehow, she's finding a way to move on.

Maybe I need to find a way to move on, too.

> **Me:** *I'll think about it, okay? I've had a lot going on, and this on top of it feels like a lot.*

> **Wren:** *Take your time, Scottie B. Love you.*

> **Me:** *Love you too.*

I set my phone back down to finally fix my mascara, but the damn thing starts vibrating again with another message before I've even gotten the smudge wiped off.

> **Julia:** *Where you at? Kayla and I are waiting for you outside Delta Omega.*

I glance at the time on my phone and realize I've completely lost track of time. *Shit!*

> **Me:** *I'm running a little behind, but I'm almost walking out my door now.*

I'm using the term *almost* lightly here. The fact that I'm currently wearing only a bra and underwear is proof of that.

> **Julia:** *Okay! The party is super crowded, tho, so we're just going to wait outside for you to get here or I fear you'll never find us. Kayla says hurry so her tits don't freeze off. LOL.*

"Shit, shit, shit!" I mutter as I hop into action. I rummage through my messy closet until I find a pair of jeans, my favorite cream sweater, and a pair of boots that give me a few extra inches in height.

It's not necessarily the look I was planning for a Christmas-themed sorority party, but beggars can't be choosers.

I toss on my clothes, taking special care with pulling my cream sweater over my makeup-covered face, and take one ten-second glance in the mirror.

A little fluff of my hair and a quick reapply of lipstick, I decide this is as good as it's going to get, and I grab my purse and keys and jog out the door.

Luck is on my side when an empty elevator is waiting for me—I guess everyone else is already out for the night—and I don't waste any time stepping on and heading to the ground floor.

All stress aside, celebration is in order! And I've got a whole campus to cross to get there.

Scottie

By the time I speed walk up Broadway and make it onto 120th Street, I'm covered in a layer of sweat that gives the frigid December air a run for its money. Thankfully, I still have a few blotting papers left in my purse from my last outing, and I quickly dab one on my face as I cross the street toward the Delta Omega house in the distance.

I see Julia and Kayla standing outside, shivering in holiday-themed skirts and heels, and I cringe when Kayla shouts, "If my tits have frostbite, I'm sending you the bill for my plastic surgeon!"

"I'm so sorry!" I call toward them as I close the distance. "I was texting with my sister, and I lost track of time."

"How about we save the apologies for inside?" Kayla suggests, and I wrap my arm around her shoulders on a laugh.

"I can apologize and move toward the heat at the same time."

"Must be nice," she jeers good-naturedly. "I'm so cold I can't even think straight."

"Julia? You haven't even said anything. Are you okay?"

"If I were a chicken, I'd be begging KFC to put me in the fryer, okay?"

Both Kayla and I laugh as we hustle inside, stepping around a crowd of smokers just outside the front door. Music pounds so hard the windows shake, and the three of us cram inside and shove the front door closed behind us.

Drinks flow and hips shake in every available inch of space, and people chatter so loud, they're almost as deafening as the music. Everyone is in the celebrating mood now that exams are done.

In a way, it's almost infectious, and I find myself enjoying the sight of it all.

"You want anything to drink?" Julia asks, and I shake my head.

"No thanks."

"Is it bad if I have a beer?" Kayla whispers into my ear, and I lean back to meet her eyes.

"Kay, that's a decision you need to make for yourself. You and I both know there are other cheerleaders here tonight drinking, and I won't be mad if you do." I offer a reassuring, not-judgmental-at-all smile. "Hell, I spotted McKenzie playing beer pong in the living room when we first walked in."

"Okay, yeah," Kayla finally answers Julia's question. "I definitely want a drink."

"I'll wait here while you guys go," I reassure them when they both look like they're afraid to leave their puppy behind. "I'll be fine."

"Yes," a familiar male voice agrees. Blake Boden wraps his arm around my shoulders. "She'll be fine because I'll stay here with her."

Julia and Kayla get lost in the crowd, and I nudge Blake with my elbow. "Pretty sure I can handle standing by myself for a little bit, Blake. I'm a big girl."

"I know you can, small fry." He pats the top of my head playfully. "But you're my favorite cheerleader buddy, and I always look after my buddies."

He pulls two bottles of water from his Santa hoodie pocket and hands one to me. "Cheers to sobriety and beating the fuck out of Buffalo when we play them for the Big East Championship game in seven days."

"Now, that is something worthy of a cheers," I agree and tap my bottle to his before taking a quick drink. "Who did you come with tonight?"

He shrugs. "Myself."

"I guess it's pretty easy finding friends when you're the school's star quarterback, huh?" I tease, and he smirks.

"Ace and Finn are supposed to meet me here at some point tonight. Though, you know how Ace is about being fashionably late."

The sound of Finn's name still gets under my skin, but thankfully, it only takes a second or two for me to get my bearings again. I'm getting better...I think. It's still pretty fucking hard when I actually see him. One look into his brown eyes and my body is a swirling tornado of want and need and desire. My stupid, hopeless romantic heart can't seem to come to terms with the fact that he doesn't want us.

"Ace wouldn't be Ace without an entrance."

Blake laughs. "Last week, he brought his dad's accountant to our bookkeeping class. Made him sit through the lesson and everything. Our professor didn't even notice until he started working on Ace's imaginary books for him."

"Fucking hell," I chortle.

Blake nods. "I know. I nearly pissed my pants when he started waxing poetic about the importance of uncooked books. I swear he used the words 'raw dog' at least ten times."

"Yo, Blake!" someone shouts over the din, getting both of our attention. Blake strains to see who it is through the absolute crush of bodies, but I spot Dane almost right away, waving a friendly arm like he hasn't been an asshat for the entire semester. "Come over here! I want to show you something! And bring Scottie with you!"

Blake looks at me, a question in his eyes, but I let the notion of the end-of-semester party guide me. Maybe this really is the chance to bury all the damn hatchets and start next year on a clean slate.

"I bet he's going to let us watch him take seventy bajillion shots," I suggest sarcastically, shrugging in surrender.

"Talk about an honor," Blake muses with a chuckle as he guides us through the maze of people standing in the center of the house.

I spot Kayla and Julia near the kitchen, making their way back to us with beers in their hands, and gesture to them to follow us. By the time we get past the dance floor, Dane is bouncing on his toes waiting for us. "Come on, come on, slowpokes. We're gonna miss it if we don't hurry up."

Blake and I both roll our eyes but follow Dane down the hall to the back of the house where all the sorority sisters' bedrooms line the hall. He opens the door and waves his hand, dramatically gesturing for us to walk inside. "After you."

Blake goes first and I'm right behind him, but when he stops in his tracks, my face rams right into his T-shirt-covered back. My nose stings with the impact, and I rub at it as Blake tenses in front of me. "What the fuck?"

Curiosity makes me peer around him to see what's going on. *Oh my God.*

Nausea overwhelms me instantly, puke climbing my throat so fast I have to throw a hand over my mouth to prevent its escape.

"Oh, wait. Holy shit, Scottie. Isn't that your *mom?*" Dane comments, his taunting tone making it obvious he's getting actual enjoyment out of this sick and twisted situation.

"Wait. That's Scottie's mom?" Nadine joins in from the corner of the room, where she holds her phone toward my mom and one of the guys from Alpha Pi having sex in the pink-comforter-adorned bed. I recognize him immediately as one of the bandoleros from the Halloween party.

Blake turns and shuffles me, trying to push me out the door, but it's too late. I've already seen more than enough.

"Get her out of here," Blake orders Kayla and Julia, who've just arrived behind us.

"What's going on?" Kayla asks, just as Julia gets an eyeful for herself, crying, "Oh my God!"

Thanks to our commotion, my mom finally realizes she has an audience and sits up in the bed, her chest exposed and her hair a tangled mess.

"Scottie?" she says when her bloodshot eyes lock with mine. With just a look at her, I can tell she's shit-faced. After all, it's her most familiar look.

So much for fucking sobriety, huh?

"I think Scottie is ready to talk to you now, Mrs. Bardeaux," Dane comments snidely, his snakish charm so blunt, the only thing missing is a split tongue. Nadine continues filming and laughing from her spot in the corner, swinging the camera to me for a brief capture of my devastation.

The text messages, the torture, my mom somehow finding me at a random college party in the middle of my university—I'm surer than ever that Dane and Nadine are behind it all.

"Scottie, honeys," my mom slurs as she literally climbs off the guy's cock and starts searching for her clothes. She's completely naked and too drunk to make any attempt to cover herself with a sheet, instead walking right toward me like we're seeing each other at a sidewalk café somewhere. "I'm so happy you're here. I miss you. I want to talk to you."

"Aw, Scottie," Nadine chimes in. "Your mom misses you so much that she came to Dickson and fucked a frat guy just for you."

As gossip does what gossip does and starts to spread like wildfire, people flood in from the living room to get a look at my personal hell.

"Everybody get the fuck out of here!" Blake yells at the door, trying his hardest to manage the situation, but the nausea in my stomach becomes so intense that saliva floods my mouth, and I throw up, right there, all over the floor.

Nadine and Dane cackle like hyenas as I fight to standing again.

Dane forms a gun with his hand and points it straight at me, mouthing a single word of pure evil. "Bang."

This isn't some random guy I had a fling with or someone I hardly know. This is a guy I spent *two years* of my life with. A guy I thought was my first love.

I can't pretend I've got it together anymore. The phenomenon is over.

This is my breaking point.

49

Finn

Gary drops us off right in front of the Delta Omega house on the way home from poker, where winter-break-happy students swarm every available part of the yard and front steps.

It's a smart move by Ace, considering he would have had to stun-gun me to get out of our room had we gone back there first, but now that we're here, I'm at least moderately okay with it.

The state of things with Scottie has gotten entirely out of hand, and after some self-reflection forced on me by the billionaires, it'd be so fucking pointless to leave things the way they are going into the new year. She was trying to help me and made a mistake. Fuck knows I've done a lot worse, and it's time for the stubborn dick in me to let it all go.

A girl in a skimpy red dress runs down the stairs at the sight of Ace, barreling into his arms immediately, and my eyebrows draw together. *Is there really a Scarlett?* I thought Ace was bullshitting.

"Ace, you gotta get in here!" she orders, throwing a hand back toward the door as a stampede of people previously in the yard funnel through the door. My eyebrows draw together, but she keeps talking. "Something's going down in one of the bedrooms!"

It's only then that I notice the music has stopped too, the whole vibe of the house off.

Ace's face mirrors mine as he has a similar realization, and he sets Scarlett away from himself gently. "Did you see Julia Brooks in there? Or Scottie Bardeaux?"

She nods. "Yeah, they were both in there, last I saw."

Ace and I share a look, and I take off into the house. I hear him say, "Stay here, Scar," behind me, but I'm through the door and shoving through the herd of people before I have a chance to hear anything else.

Something going down in one of the bedrooms is one of the most terrifying things I've heard in my life.

Blake's voice booms over the din of chatter. "Get the fuck back!" My chest seizes, and I move through people without remorse, setting bodies out of the way with the bare minimum of care for their well-being and checking faces as I do. I don't see Scottie or Julia anywhere, and white-hot panic makes my chest burn.

I spot Blake blocking a doorway, still shouting at people to get back, and I make a beeline over to him. I'm no longer even minimally careful as I maneuver through students to get to that doorway.

"Oh, come on, Scottie. You should look a little happier to see your mom." I don't even have to see him to know those words came from Dane's mouth.

Laughter ensues, and the students outside the doorway are trying their hardest to get a look at whatever is happening in that room.

"Get the fuck back!" Blake shouts again, a vein popping at the center of his temple.

"Yo, Blake!" Ace yells, his voice at my back. Clearly, he took liberties with the crowd to catch up to me too. "What's happening?"

Blake's gaze jerks to me and Ace, his eyes wild and his jaw locked. He looks sad and fucking livid at the same time. My good-time, easygoing friend never looks like this. It does nothing for my sanity.

One by one, I pluck the rest of the bodies between us out of my way and into the wall and charge down the hall until I make it to Blake. He moves his body for me and Ace to scoot by and then blocks the space again, shoving the dude behind us with a hand at his throat. "I said, back the fuck up!"

Scottie is in the center of the room with Julia and Kayla, and their eyes are frantic as they try to keep her standing. A naked woman stumbles in front of her, trying to put on a pair of underwear, and a dude lies in bed with his hands behind his head. Dane's and Nadine's laughter provides a soundtrack to the whole gross scene.

"Come back to bed, Stephanie," the naked guy says, a proud grin on his mouth. "We weren't finished, baby. My dick is still hard." As if the words aren't enough, he moves one of his hands under the sheet to stroke himself.

"Scottie, honey," the woman slurs, still struggling with her clothes. "I wants-ed to see you."

"Yeah, Scottie. Your mom's here for you. She just fucked a frat guy to kill some time," Nadine comments, and the smile on her face is so vile it makes me sick to my stomach.

"Honeys, your boyfriend Dane told me that you wann to see me. I came here to see you," the woman, who is apparently Scottie's *fucking mom*, slurs.

"He's not my boyfriend!" Scottie shouts. "And I do *not* want to see you!" Her mom's face strains to understand what she's saying, but she's too fucking lit to understand anything.

"What?" she questions, coming toward her and abandoning her attempts at the underwear. "I jus wann to see you, babs. Wanna see—"

"Shut up!" Scottie screams at the top of her lungs. "Just shut up!" Julia and Kayla pull her back from the vomit on the floor in front of her, and her mom slips in it, falling to a hip right in the mess. She looks around, stunned and confused.

Dane's cackle follows immediately. "Aw, Scottie, don't be mean to your mom. She didn't even get to finish."

I stride over to the pathetic fucker and grip his shirt with both hands, shoving him into the wall. I may not know the exact details of how this whole mess started, but I know for a fact that he's behind it. "What the fuck do you think you're doing?" I shout into his face. "End this right now."

"What am *I* doing?" Dane laughs. "Scottie's mom is the alcoholic cougar who just fucked a college kid."

I shove his back into the wall again and put a hand to his fucking throat to choke the life out of him, but Ace puts a hand to my shoulder.

"Finn," he says, his voice edged with panic. "Stop."

"No." I shake my head. "No fucking way. I'm not going anywhere until I make sure this motherfucker chokes or bleeds out."

"Finn," he says my name again, putting force into the hand at my shoulder now. "Scottie needs you."

I hold my hand at Dane's throat but glance over my shoulder to see Julia and Kayla still struggling to get Scottie to stay on her feet. Sobs rack her body as her mom continues trying to talk to her from her puke-covered spot on the floor.

"My whole life, all you've done is ruin shit for me. That's all you've done," Scottie barely manages to choke out. "Why can't you just leave me alone for good?"

She turns around to run, but she trips and falls over Kayla's foot, splaying out on the floor right behind Dane.

I drop Dane to the floor, his legs crumpling like a house of cards, and spin toward Scottie as she gathers herself and jumps up again. Blake lets her through the door, and I chase after her, shoving anyone who gets in my way to the side.

It's not over with Dane—not even close. But Scottie, right now, needs me more.

50

Scottie

"Who is in there?"

"Scottie's mom!"

"Randy Evans bagged Scottie's mom!"

"Randy is a legend! He just fucked a freshman's mom!"

Laughter and chaos are all around me as I try to push through the crowd to get to the door.

Tears are streaming down my cheeks, and sobs I didn't even know were possible are bursting out of my lungs. Both Julia and Kayla call toward me, but I don't dare stop or turn around. *I just need to get out of here.*

Embarrassment and shame and anger and hate are balloons inside my chest, each one filling with air until I feel like my rib cage might burst.

Even once I'm out of the house, I don't stop running.

Every laugh or howl I hear from a student on the way triggers my panic further, and I pick up my pace. My side pinches from the exertion, my breathing erratic and shallow from the combination of running and crying. A car honks as I run directly in front of it on Amsterdam Avenue, and I twist my ankle trying to get to the other side and fall hands first into the sidewalk. I try to gather myself quickly, but the sting in both my overexerted lungs and ankle takes me directly back down. All I want to do is get back to my dorm and lock myself away forever, and I can't even do that.

A strangled scream escapes my lungs and my arms flail in front of me to fight off an unknown attacker as something touches my shoulder, but Finn squats in front of me and holds down my arms, his voice a whisper. "It's okay, Scottie. It's just me. It's okay."

His face is kind and patient, his eyes undeniably warm. He looks exactly like he did the day I met him.

This time, though, I'm gushing blood from my heart. I don't think he'll be able to stop the flow with a tissue this time.

"No." I shake my head, my face a mess of tears and runny makeup, and lock my gaze with his. "This isn't okay. Nothing is okay right now! Did you see what happened?" I choke on saliva again, my whole body shaking. "What did I do to deserve something like this?" I question the universe.

He answers even though the question isn't for him. "Nothing, Scottie. This isn't your fault."

"All my life, all my mom has done is fuck things up. That's all she's done. My whole life, Finn. My whole life has been affected by her fuckups. And Dane and Nadine?" The instant I say their names, I want to puke. "What the hell are they trying to do? Ruin my life? Like, is that the goal?" By the end of my rant, my sweater is wet from my tears and snot runs unchecked from my nose.

"You didn't do anything to deserve this," he repeats, his thumb wiping away tear after tear.

Carefully and gently, he picks me up to my feet again and pulls me into a hug.

A deep, guttural sob leaves my body as I bury my face and my tears into his shirt. He stands there, in the middle of the sidewalk, holding me with the tightest embrace.

"I'm here. Whatever you need, I'm here," he whispers into my hair.

I cry harder, his sympathy too much for my already shattered heart. I know he's trying to comfort me, but I don't know if I like the way it's making me feel.

Knowing he was there, knowing he saw it all happening in real time, is a crushing humiliation. After everything we've been through, everything he's done to push me away? I don't want his pity.

"I think I need to go home," I whisper, and he leans back to meet my eyes.

"Scottie, I'm so sorry," he says. His brown eyes are sad and apologetic, but I don't need his token apologies. I don't need empty words and confused affections. I need someone I can rely on, and sadly, right now, that's me. "I wish—"

"Stop," I cut him off before he can say any more. "It's too much, Finn. Another back-and-forth with you. I just can't handle that right now. I need to be alone," I tell him, pulling away from his embrace completely.

"I can't leave you alone right now," he surprises me by insisting.

"Finn, just go, okay? Let me be."

He shakes his head. "It's late and you're upset, and I need to make sure you get back to your dorm okay."

"I don't need you!" I yell, frustrated that he won't give me the space I'm asking for. "I don't need anything from you or anyone. I just want to be left alone." I spin on my heel and start walking back down the street, a small limp challenging my gait, but when I hear that his footsteps are right behind me, anger makes my legs churn faster.

"Go away!" I call over my shoulder, not even bothering to look in his direction. "Just go away!"

He doesn't respond, but he doesn't stop following me either.

My phone buzzes in my pocket, and I pull it out, thinking it's Kayla or Julia, but all I'm faced with are more social media notifications than I have ever had in my life. Morbid curiosity makes me look, and when I see all the tags on TikTok and Instagram and Snapchat, the nausea in my stomach is so strong that I have to stop in the middle of the sidewalk again.

All tags and comments and posts are about my mother. One on Nadine's TikTok is actual footage of the entire horrible scene.

All of the pizza I ate after practice comes up my throat and lands on the sidewalk right in front of me, my hands at my knees as every retch rocks me.

A gentle hand settles onto my back, rubbing comforting circles.

I hate that he's here, witnessing this. That this is how he's finding out he's been wrong about my perfect, privileged life, and I didn't get a say in any of it.

Like always. I didn't get a say in my mother's addiction. I didn't get a say when she'd go on a bender while my dad was at work and Wren and I had to fend for ourselves. I didn't get a say when she was supposed to be a caregiver and she neglected us time and time again.

I didn't get a say when Dane followed me to Dickson.

I didn't get a say in my mother showing up here.

I didn't get a say when it came to Finn and him constantly pushing me away.

And I didn't get a say in my heart's choice to fall in love with him.

Once my stomach settles and dry heaves no longer have me hunched toward the cement, Finn hands me a tissue to wipe my mouth.

I take it, but I don't say anything. Fatigue has now seeped into my bones, and I'm too tired to answer Julia's and Kayla's texts. I'm too tired to ask Finn why he's still here.

I'm too tired to do anything but put my head down and walk back to my dorm as Finn follows me once again.

51

Finn

Scottie sobs quietly in front of me as we cross Broadway and walk along the side of Delaney to the 116th Street Entrance. My jaw grinds in restraint as I give her space, looking both directions for any potential threats.

There aren't any, thankfully, because I know for a fact that she carries enough terror deep in her chest.

She doesn't even have to tell me the traumatic details about her mother for me to know what she's feeling. Because for as much as I've said we weren't—as much as I wish we weren't—Scottie and I are the same. We've dealt with the same vile behavior from our alcoholic parents, and we both carry trauma on our shoulders every fucking day.

I want to apologize for the things I've said and for the assumptions I've made about her life that were so clearly wrong. I want to tell her that, as much as I've denied it, I've loved her nearly every day we've known each other. I want to tell her that I love her now and intend to love her forever.

But I know the way she's feeling right now—the self-loathing that comes with a family you can't control—and how invalidating that is of your worth.

I know it because I've lived it. I know it because I *am* it.

I keep watch as she unlocks the door to Delaney and steps inside, waiting for it to fall closed behind her with a click.

And as the tension of her safety releases, red-hot fury comes flooding back. I turn back in the direction we came and pick up my pace to a run, sprinting across Broadway, past Wheaton, behind McKinley, and around Nash until I can see the Delta Omega house in the distance. I slow to a walk and steady my breathing, allowing anger to fuel my progress forward.

By the time I walk through the door, my back and neck muscles are flexing hard with each deep inhale of my nostrils, and my fists are clenched tight at my sides.

Ace, Julia, and Kayla are just inside the door, wrestling with people for their phones as they step up to leave the house. "What the hell is wrong with you?" Julia bitches at a girl who evidently has some kind of footage in her camera roll.

Ace is the first to spot me and drops what he's doing, stepping in front of me and taking his life in his hands. "Finn, hey, hold up," he tries, but I shove him out of the way with a hand to his chest and keep walking. Blake tries to step in front of me then, but I move him easily enough too, the kind of pissed-off-adrenaline I have flowing through my veins a tough match for even the strongest of football players physically.

They're both trying to help because I'm already on thin ice with the dean, but I don't care about the consequences anymore. I refuse to leave this house until I make that son of a bitch pay for what he did.

Dane is standing at a table playing beer pong with Nadine and two people I don't recognize at all. They're laughing and having a good old fucking time, like they didn't just do what they did to Scottie.

I have no idea where Scottie's mom is now, but I don't care. The dirty-blond-headed motherfucker with the ping-pong ball in his hand and a cocky smile on his lips is the only one I'm here for.

I shove all the red Solo cups off the top of their table with one aggressive hand, and they hit the floor, alcohol sloshing all over the place. Nadine shouts, "What the hell!" and jumps back to avoid the spill, but Dane doesn't do shit because he's already locked eyes with me. Fear seeps from his every pore as I move toward him, and he skitters back like the coward that he is.

This fight is entirely different from the one we had before, my patience for his bullshit more than already spent. I don't give him any time to prepare and land a hard punch to the center of his smug fucking face that makes his head jerk back violently.

Nadine screams.

"Shit," I hear Ace say before his and Blake's yells rend the air to say, "Get back!" to the approaching crowd.

As I hit Dane a second time, right on the cheekbone, the shouts of "Fight!" from several students around us reverberate through the house, and the DJ's music stops once again.

Dane stumbles on his feet as I land blow after blow to his face, his hands and arms as he uses them to block absolutely no match for my sheer determination.

"You feel like a big man for preying on a girl who's half your size?" I yell so hard that spit flies from my lips. I land another blow, and blood pours from his busted lip. "You couldn't stand that she broke up with you, huh? You and your pathetic ego couldn't let it go. So, what did you do, Dane? What did you fucking do?"

I punch him in the stomach before he can respond, a loud "Ugh!" flying out of his lungs.

"Only weak men prey on women. And that's what you are, motherfucker. You are a weak fucking, pathetic piece of *shit*."

Blood drips down his face from all directions, several open cuts gaping from my fist. He throws a punch at me, which I easily dodge since his equilibrium is all off. Nadine screeches again as I push him against a wall with my forearm to his throat, and Ace calls out behind me again. But I don't see anything but his cocksucking evil eyes.

As he starts to gurgle blood, my arm on his throat effectively choking the life out of him, Ace yells once more, and I drop him to the floor. He climbs up slowly, holding himself around his abdomen and fighting to open his swollen eye through the blood dripping into it.

"You're fucking done," he threatens, his voice gravelly and strained. "Say goodbye to college."

He might be right, but what he fails to understand is that I don't give a single fuck.

When he opens his mouth to speak again, I take it upon myself to shut him up. I punch him with all of my strength, landing a perfect uppercut that drops him to the floor like a rock.

He's out cold. Maybe, for all I know, dead.

I walk out the fucking door, and I don't look back. Either outcome is okay with me.

52

Saturday December 14th

Finn

Several pounding knocks to the door wake me up. With bleary eyes, I reach out toward my nightstand to check the time, and my swollen, still-bloodied knuckles hurt when I flex them to grab my phone. One tap to the screen and I see it's only quarter to six. Way too fucking early when I didn't go to sleep until four.

I lie back down, willing whoever is at the door to go away, but they just pound harder.

Ace groans in annoyance from his bed, and I'm on my feet, pulling a pair of discarded sweatpants over my boxer briefs and a T-shirt over my head.

I yank it open quickly, glancing back to Ace as he forces himself to sitting and then back to the man on the other side. "Are you Finn Hayes?" a man with a buzz cut in a Dickson Campus Police uniform asks.

I don't bother with denying it. I had a feeling this was coming; I just hoped I'd get a little more sleep before it did. "Yeah. That's me."

"I'm Officer Walters," he introduces himself and nods toward his partner. "This is Officer Marks."

I hear a thud from behind me, and without even turning around, I know Ace is now standing at my back, wearing nothing but his boxers. "What's going on, Officers?"

"Finnley Hayes, turn around, please, and put your hands behind your back. We have to take you into custody. Dane Matthews has pressed charges against you for assault," Officer Walters states.

A deep sigh escapes my lungs, but I turn around. That fucking prick is so predictable.

"What?" Ace pushes, standing out of the way but not stepping back by any means. "What do you mean, take him into custody? Are you arresting him?"

"Dane claims Finn assaulted him at a party at the Delta Omega house last night, and an eyewitness substantiated his claim."

"Who's his witness?" Ace asks, crowding the door as the cops pull me outside.

"Nadine Jones," Officer Marks says, affirming what we both already knew. It's textbook.

"Fucking rich!" Ace exclaims loudly. "Did those assholes bother to tell you what they did?"

"Sir, you're going to need to calm down," Officer Marks tells Ace as they pull me away from the door, but Ace isn't having any of it.

"Don't say a fucking thing, Finn. Don't answer any questions." He's already on the phone I didn't know he had in his hand. He obviously grabbed it before coming to stand beside me. "Dad," he says into the receiver. "Finn's getting arrested."

I comply as they guide me down the hall but stop halfway to ask a question. "Can I just check my phone real quick?"

Office Marks nods. "You have one minute."

Ace is still on a call with his dad, giving him the rundown of what happened last night at a mile-a-minute pace, but when I walk back toward him, my hands behind my back in cuffs still, he jumps into action.

"What do you need?"

I nod toward my bed, where my phone is plugged into the charger. "I just want to check my messages."

Ace holds up my phone in front of me to activate Face ID and then clicks open my message icon for me to scour it. The message I sent Scottie just before falling asleep is there, but so far, unanswered.

"You can bring your phone with you, if you want," Officer Marks says, but Ace is quick to negate that idea.

"Leave your phone here, man. I'll bring it up to you with bail money if I have to." He looks at the cops as Office Walters takes me back out the door, the phone call with his dad still to his ear through it all. "Where are you taking him?"

"Since this occurred on campus, we've been instructed to bring him to the campus station, and Dean Kandinsky is meeting us there."

"So, you're not taking him straight to County?"

"Not yet. No." Officer Marks shakes his head. "The dean feels strongly that he wants to have a conversation with all parties involved before we proceed further."

"Finn, do you want me to call anyone for you?" Ace asks, and I shake my head.

I don't want him calling anyone. "Keep this to yourself for now."

"Don't worry, Finn," Ace agrees as both officers lead me down the hall once again. "I got your back, man."

I know he does.

For the first time in my life, I know I have people I can count on.

53

Scottie

I wake up with a start to the bright overhead lights of my room, still blaring from last night when I finally cried myself to sleep. My face aches, my head pounds, and my eyes are a crusty mess of dried, salty tears.

There's no question that what happened really happened and that it wasn't a dream as I sit up slowly, last night's clothes and shoes pulling at my tender skin.

I glance at the clock above my door since my phone is still halfway across the room on the floor where I tossed it last night when the social media notifications reached an unrelenting buzz. For all I know, it's broken beyond repair. It's only six a.m., but it feels like I've been asleep for both a lifetime and no time at all.

I crawl off my bed slowly, my stomach pitching with upset. I threw up twice last night, and the lining feels nearly as raw as my emotions. My reflection in the mirror on the back of my door is horrifying—messy hair, red and splotchy skin, and mascara caked beneath my sad eyes.

I'm a mess. But who wouldn't be?

I grab a bottle of water from my mini fridge and nearly guzzle down the entire thing. My bladder screams for me to go to the bathroom and pee, so I stumble into my half bath and relieve myself.

I wash my hands, brush my teeth, and push myself back into my room, my entire body crying out for the scalding water of a shower.

I need to wash it all away, but the thought of leaving my room is beyond terrifying.

What if I run into someone who was at the party? Or someone who saw all the gory details on social media?

I have no concept of how far it's all spread, but I know how these things work. I wouldn't be surprised if the whole planet knows, not to mention everyone at Dickson University.

I know I shouldn't look at my phone—that it's the worst of worst ideas—but I can't stop myself from walking across the room and picking it up. The screen is littered with notifications. Missed calls and texts. Mentions on Instagram and TikTok. Snaps on Snapchat.

It's an overwhelming popularity I wouldn't wish on my worst enemy.

I have hundreds and hundreds of unread messages, a huge chunk of which are from Kayla, Julia, Ace, and Blake. All four of them are kind and consoling and worried—desperately. I'll never forget the way they all supported me last night and stood by me despite the ridicule from everyone else, but I'm not ready to face them yet.

I'm afraid I'll see everything I'm feeling in their eyes.

There's one message that stands out above the rest, however, making my heart ache for too many reasons to count.

> **Finn:** *I just want you to know that I'm here for you, Scottie. Always.*

He was there for me last night—silent and stalwart and strong without pushing. He was kind and calm and reassuring and everything I love about him. But I'm still not sure if that changes anything.

It's been a roller coaster of ups and downs with him, and the bottom of the last hill scraped the depths of hell.

Despite my better judgment, I keep scrolling, and when I spot the conversation I had with my sister last night, tears well in my eyes. She thinks our mom is sober. She thinks she's doing better.

She thinks she's on the road to recovery, for shit's sake, not fucking frat guys at college parties while she's too far gone to know her own name.

Wren would be devasted if she knew. I can't tell her the truth. At least not right now. *Maybe someday, but not today.*

Today, I'm going to crawl back into bed and cry until I can't anymore.

Yesterday, I was a cheerleader with a broken heart but the world in front of her. Now, I'm just the girl whose alcoholic mom showed up to a college party, got drunk, and had sex for all to see.

I'll never be the same again.

Finn

I am surprisingly calm when we arrive at the Dickson Campus Police station. Officer Walters leads me into a conference room at the center of the building. I sit down after he removes the cuffs, and he rounds the table to the door. "Would you like some water?" he asks, looking back at me.

I shake my head, and he files out of the room, leaving me to my thoughts. They aren't crisp or tangible, but a buzzing chaos just behind my eyes.

I know this is a big deal—I'm not an idiot—but I can't seem to find any remorse.

Moments later, he's back with Officer Marks, who's followed by Dane and Nadine.

Dane's face is a fucking mess. Dried blood is still evident on his skin and the stupid snowman sweater he had on last night, and bruises have settled into dark circles below both of his eyes. There are cuts on his cheeks, chin, and forehead, and his lips are both swollen and busted.

They sit down in two chairs on the opposite side of the room, against the wall instead of at the table, and the officers drop some paperwork on the surface at the other side of the table before stepping out of the room again. Nadine's eyes are both hard and frightened, but Dane is back within the bounds of his bravado. He's confident I won't beat his ass here. Though, I have to admit, I'm tempted to prove him wrong.

"You're going to fucking pay," he says on a hoarse whisper, the grip I had on his throat last night obviously having done a number on his voice.

I don't respond, but I also don't avert my eyes.

"Did you hear me, fucker?" he taunts again, leaning forward in his chair to use an angry pointing finger. "You're going to pay. My father's lawyer is already on his way, and you'll be lucky if you don't get prison time."

He's trying to goad me into losing my cool, but I don't give an inch. His scowl is brittle by the time Officer Walters comes back into the room with Dean Kandinsky, who's sporting jeans, a sweatshirt, and an old pair of boots.

I know it's not in my best interest that he looks like he just got out of bed. I've never seen him in anything but a pristine suit and tie before now, and this morning, his eyes are red, and his hair is ruffled.

He sits down in one of the chairs on the other side of my table, and Officer Walters sits down beside him. Officer Marks posts up by the closed door in a chair next to Dane and Nadine.

"Let's hear it. What happened?" Dean Kandinsky asks me through a deep sigh, his jaw flexed and rigid.

Dane, with absolutely no intention of letting me give my side of the story, rambles his bullshit behind him. "Sir, Finn Hayes assaulted me at the Delta Omega Christmas party last night." I don't miss the fake-as-fuck frown on his face or the trumped-up shake of his hands. This prick's plan is to milk this for all its worth as the dean spins his chair to face him.

"And you were a witness, Nadine?"

She nods several times. "Yes, sir. Finn just showed up and attacked him. It was terrifying."

"These are serious accusations." Dean Kandinsky looks back over at me. "Assaulting another student in this manner is an immediate expulsion from the university as well as whatever charges you face criminally. And since this is the second time something like this has happened with you on campus, I'm inclined to tell the judge this is patterned behavior. Do you have anything to say for yourself, Finn?"

"No, he doesn't have anything to say because he knows he assaulted me! He deserves to pay for what he did!" Dane chimes in yet again. Dean Kandinsky lifts a hand toward him without turning around this time, a silent *shut the fuck up*. But Dane, of course, doesn't listen. "Just look at my face. I probably should've gone to the hospital, but I felt it was my civic duty to come to the police station and press charges. No one on campus is safe with this lunatic around. That's why, once my father's lawyer gets here, I'm going to make sure I press charges and this guy is arrested."

"*Dane,*" Dean Kandinsky chastises, throwing a cutting look over his shoulder. "That's enough."

Two knocks sound on the door, and Officer Marks peeks his head out toward the disturbance. Not even five seconds later, he turns back around toward Dean Kandinsky. "There's a professor by the name of Ty Winslow here. He'd like to come in."

What the fuck?

Dean Kandinsky nods and sighs, sitting back in his chair and steepling his hands. "Let him back."

When Officer Marks stands and opens the door, Ty rushes into the room with frantic eyes, messy hair, fucking pajama pants, and a T-shirt that says NYU. If I thought Dean Kandinsky looked bad, I was sorely mistaken.

This motherfucker looks like he came here by way of a rope tied to a taxi as it dragged him through the streets.

"What are you doing here, Ty?" Dean Kandinsky asks as Ty takes the seat next to me. It's unexpected and, quite frankly, uninvited. My whole body tenses with the intrusion into my space. He touches my forearm, and my eyes jump to the spot like I've been zapped.

"Sir, I awoke to several phone calls this morning about the situation, a number of which came from students and some of this year's endowment donors." Dean Kandinsky sits up in his seat at that, the word "donors" hitting him in his metaphorical pockets. "There's more to this story than meets the eye."

Did Ace call Ty? Or Thatch? Maybe both of them did, for all I know. I don't want him here, but I know they're trying to help.

"What do you mean?"

"Dane and Nadine have been harassing Scottie Bardeaux. They set up an elaborate embarrassment, lured Scottie to the scene of it, and baited her friends, including Finn Hayes, to do something about it."

"We were not harassing Scottie," Dane tries to interrupt, but no one in the room gives him any attention.

"An elaborate embarrassment?" Dean Kandinsky asks. "What does that mean?"

"I think it's best if we step outside the room for me to update you. It's a bit of a delicate issue."

Dean Kandinsky frowns and stands, gesturing for Ty and Officer Walters to follow him out of the room. Officer Marks stays behind and, as the door closes behind them, sets up shop on the other side of the table, between Dane and me. I have no intention of starting anything at this point; I'd rather let Dane continue to dig his own grave. Plus, Ace told me not to say shit, and I've taken the directive seriously.

It feels like a decade before the three men walk back into the room, but when they do, Dean Kandinsky looks more pissed than I've ever seen him.

"The two of you aren't giving the full story here," Dean Kandinsky barks at Dane and Nadine, making both of their eyes go wide. Dane recovers quickly, though, spewing mock outrage right back at him.

"What? Finn Hayes assaulted me, sir. That's the story!"

"We'd like to see both of your phones," Officer Walters orders, his face stern too. Nadine hands hers over, even unlocking the screen with her passcode, a shit-scared expression shattering her normally cocky face. She looks like a little girl now, all of her normal persona eradicated.

"What the hell, babe?" Dane snaps, annoyed. "You didn't have to fucking give that to them without a warrant." Nadine looks helpless as the weight of what she's done crashes all around her. Her knees are bouncing up and down at a wild pace, and her fingers fidget with her clothes.

She fucked up hugely, but I don't think she's the mastermind of any of it. I think she got swept away in a plot concocted by her butthurt boyfriend and was too dumb to see it for what it was. That doesn't excuse anything, though. Shitty behavior produces shitty results, and now, she'll pay the price.

"I'm scared, Dane," she whispers, but her boyfriend is too busy worrying about himself to comfort her.

"I have rights. I'm not giving you my phone," he tells Officer Walters. "I'm not doing anything until my father's lawyer arrives."

His father's lawyer. It's all he keeps talking about, but I've yet to see actual proof this man exists.

Officer Walters scrolls around through Nadine's phone, unfazed by Dane's refusal. It only takes a few moments before his mouth turns down in a frown as he stares at the screen, nodding to Dean Kandinsky and Ty Winslow. Evidently, Ty's version of the events has been confirmed.

"Nadine, did you have the approval of both parties to post this explicit footage on the internet?" Officer Walters asks, and Nadine stutters over her words.

"I don't… I didn't… I didn't mean to do it! Dane told me to film it and post it, and I don't know…that's just what I did."

"I didn't tell you to post shit," Dane refutes, turning on his accomplice without a second thought. "You're such a liar, Nadine."

Officer Walters continues to look through her phone, and when he finds something else, he lets out a sigh. "Looks like the other students' claims of harassment toward Scottie Bardeaux are correct. We'll have to verify that this is her phone number, but it appears that Nadine was utilizing an app that scrambles her number and sends on a ten-minute delay to send harassing text messages as well."

"Dane was sending those messages!" Nadine cries. "He's the one who downloaded that app to my phone!"

Dane rolls his eyes. "She's lying, Officer. You heard her before. She's just scared to face the consequences of her actions. I had nothing to do with those text messages."

Officer Walters hums. "What about the ones with Ms. Jones where you two discuss a premeditated plan to bait Scottie Bardeaux's mother into coming to the university?"

Dean Kandinsky runs a hand down his face while he lets out a deep, exasperated exhale of air from his lungs.

"So what—we sent Scottie some text messages," Dane scoffs. "It's not our fault her mom is a drunk and had sex with Randy Evans in the middle of a party."

"By law, the text messages are a form of harassment," Officer Walters states. "And the posting of the explicit video footage to the internet and sharing it across every platform available without either party's permission is a cybercrime."

"Randy Evans won't give a shit we posted that," Dane says as Nadine cries into her hands, sobs making her body buck.

"I think we can all agree that you did not have permission from Stephanie Bardeaux," Officer Walters states.

"I take cybercrimes and harassment very seriously on campus," Dean Kandinsky says, his eyes fixated on both Dane and Nadine. "I'm appalled at both of your actions. It's clear that your goal was to do everything in your power to bully another student, and that type of vile behavior is not welcome on campus."

"Are you expelling us?" Nadine asks, her voice so small it might as well be a mouse.

"Yes," Dean Kandinsky states firmly. "I'm expelling both of you. But if you ask me, that's the least of your worries. These are serious crimes you've committed, Ms. Jones, and the legal system will do with those what it sees fit."

"Are you fucking kidding me?" Dane shouts. "What about Finn? He's the one who assaulted me! That's the whole reason we're here!"

"Finn Hayes faces his own set of circumstances, none of which are any of your business at this juncture as far as the university is concerned. Officer Marks and Walters will inform you of your legal rights on the matter, but for now, you're dismissed."

Officer Walters pulls Dane to his feet and escorts him and Nadine out of the room. Dane shouts about his father and his father's lawyer, but when the door shuts behind him, the sound muffles almost entirely.

Officer Marks gestures for Dean Kandinsky and Ty to step over to talk to him, and I listen intently, trying to catch all that I can of their hushed conversation.

"We were unable to reach Scottie Bardeaux, but we did get ahold of Stephanie Bardeaux. She lives upstate but is currently staying at a hotel nearby," Officer Marks updates. "She's coming in to give a statement and discuss the situation. It sounds like she's going to want to press charges against Nadine Jones and Dane Matthews. She was unaware of the explicit video that was posted of her, was very upset to find out about it, and is adamant she did not give permission."

"Let me know what happens once you talk to her," Dean Kandinsky states. Officer Marks tells them something else, but this time, it's too quiet for me to make out.

As Officer Marks steps outside, both the dean and Ty take a seat across from me.

"Finn, our university has a strong policy against violence of any sort," Dean Kandinsky says, and his mouth turns down at the corners. "I'm sure you can understand the position I'm in when it comes to you. You stood up for someone who was clearly being bullied and harassed by other students, but this is also your second transgression of the year, and I'm burdened with being the one who is in charge of keeping an entire university of students safe."

"I understand, sir." I nod. Everything he's saying is valid, and

I'm prepared to face the consequences. I know they're serious, but unlike Dane, I'm ready to face them like a man.

Officer Walters peeks his head into the room, interrupting the dean. "Jeff Hayes is here."

My father is here? My eyes jump to Ty as the reality I've been chasing for the last two years comes crashing down around me.

Our dad is here, and a family reunion is moments away from busting this scene wide open. As we saw last night, drunks aren't exactly known for making the best choices in intense situations.

Oh fuck.

Finn

"**Y**ou can bring Jeff Hayes back," Dean Kandinsky tells Officer Walters, completely oblivious to the mess he's inviting.

My hands shake in my lap as I try to control the dump of fresh adrenaline in my veins. "W-why is my father here?"

"We tried to contact your mom—the emergency contact you have listed on your university forms, but your father is the one who answered her phone and felt strongly that he would come down to discuss this situation further," Dean Kandinsky updates.

"I'm nineteen," I say, my voice rising with irritation and panic. "Why would you need to contact either of my parents? In the eyes of the law, I'm an adult, and I'm okay with that. I'm ready to face my consequences."

Dean Kandinsky's eyes shed a layer of sternness momentarily. "I appreciate that, Finn. I do. It's very mature of you. But parent involvement in an incident of this magnitude is protocol in the contract you signed in the student handbook at the beginning of the year."

"It's just policy," Ty says, and he offers a soft smile in my direction. "Nothing more than that, okay?"

He's trying to calm me down. He thinks he's helping. But what he doesn't know is that his world is about to be turned upside fucking down the instant Jeff Hayes steps into this room. I know it's been nearly half a century since he last saw his father, but the resemblance between the two of them is unmistakable.

"I don't want him in here," I say, but it's too late. Right on cue, my father steps into the room. He's wearing jeans and a stained white tank top that pop culture calls a wifebeater. Ironic, I know. His cheeks are ruddy, his eyes are red-rimmed, and I already know with just one look at him that he's had his favorite whiskey for breakfast.

"Hello, Mr. Hayes," Dean Kandinsky says candidly as my father enters the room. "Appreciate your coming down here. I'm Dean Kandinsky." He offers his hand, but my dad doesn't even acknowledge it.

"What did my fuckup son do now?" he questions instead, spittle flying off his loose tongue as he glares right at me. "I told you it didn't matter what fancy college you ran off to, and here we are. You sitting in a police station." He laughs. "Man, I fucking told you so, shit brains."

"Mr. Hayes, I don't think this—" The dean starts to interject, but dear old Dad is on a roll.

"You sure as shit weren't thinking when you let this idiot into your university. All he's going to do is cause you trouble. Just like the rest of my good-for-nothing spawn."

The dean's face turns hard and uncomfortable.

"I don't think you understand the circumstances at all, sir. Finn is in trouble, but it's not as clear-cut as it seems."

"Finn's a good kid and a good student," Ty hedges, standing from his chair to approach our dad.

I hold my breath as Jeff's face screws up in a nasty grin. "Oh yeah? And who the hell are you?"

"Professor Ty Winslow," Ty introduces, and my eyes fall closed. Two years and exactly one month and one day after I found my dad's journal, the truth has finally been set free.

My dad stumbles back, taking in Ty's face for the first time since entering the room. His expression isn't warm or welcoming—it's downright nasty. He laughs, the sound cutting like a knife as a tear falls down my cheek. "Well, look at that. Two of my fuckup sons in the same damn room. What a party."

"He changed his last name," I find myself saying, and Ty's wild eyes shoot to mine. "He used to be Jeff Winslow, but he changed it to Jeff Hayes." I nod, confirming all the questions running through Ty's desperate mind. We're brothers.

Watching Ty crumple doesn't feel even remotely like I thought it would. I don't feel power or satisfaction or vengeance.

Instead, I feel his pain.

"How the fuck do you know that?" my dad asks, rounding the table and pulling me out of my seat by the front of my shirt. I put my hands on his arms to shove him away, but Ty is already there, pulling him away from me by the denim of his jacket.

I don't even know how he got there so fast, but when my dad steps forward again, Ty puts a hand to his chest and shoves. "Get the fuck back."

"*Professor Winslow,*" Dean Kandinsky chastises, utterly shocked that one of his professors has just pushed a student's parent in a police station.

But Ty ignores it completely and ensures that our father can't look anywhere but at him. He crowds his personal space until their gazes lock. "I'm a little bigger than I used to be, *Dad.* So you'd better calm the fuck down before I make you."

"Oh no," Dean Kandinsky mutters.

For a split second, I swear I see shock and surprise and something else I can't translate on my father's face. But within a blink of an eye, it's gone and he's back to the cold, hard, mean-as-hell bastard I've known all my life.

He steps closer to Ty, gets right in his face, and I can imagine that the smell of stale whiskey is burning Ty's nostrils at this point. "You miss me, son? You feeling sad that I left you and your pain-in-the-ass siblings and mom to start a new family?"

Ty doesn't respond.

"What a great little family reunion we've got going on here, huh? Shall we get Wendy on the line? I'd love to know if she's still as big of a cunt as she was the day I left her."

Ty shuts his eyes, and his jaw ticks with each rigid breath he inhales through his lungs. He's tempted to throttle our father. He's tempted to make the bastard eat his words, but somehow, he manages to keep control. "You keep my mother's name out of your mouth."

"Ohhh, what are you going to do?"

"Whatever I'm going to do, I'm not stupid enough to do it here," Ty says, and his voice is so low I almost don't hear the words.

But our father takes those words as a challenge and shoves his chest into Ty's. "You're all talk, no action. Fucking weak. Just like Finn. Just like his brothers and sister. Just like his good-for-nothing mom."

I'm on my feet before I can stop myself, stepping right between the two of them to look our father dead in the eyes. "The only one who is weak is you."

His nostrils flare, and his breath brushes harshly against my face, the smell of whiskey and cigarettes and bad teeth violating my airway. He doesn't say anything, cocking back and throwing a punch right at my face that Ty somehow deflects.

Between one blink and the next, my father goes from ready to beat the shit out of me to completely restrained by Ty locking both of his arms behind his head.

Dean Kandinsky calls out the door for help, and Officer Walters arrives and takes over in a flash. He pulls cuffs off his belt and fastens them around Jeff's wrists before escorting him out of the room.

Ty's voice shakes with the all-too-familiar flight-or-flight adrenaline dump that happens when you're in Jeff Hayes's drunk presence as he follows behind, talking to Officer Walters. "He drove here. Make sure your officers are aware that he's heavily under the influence and should be arrested if he gets behind the wheel again."

"Finn, wait here for a moment, okay?" Dean Kandinsky requests, his eyes devoid of all their previous anger now. "Ty, a word."

The two of them step out of the room and shut the door behind them, and I can't hear shit from where I'm standing.

When they step back inside, Ty's face is more determined than I've ever seen it as Dean Kandinsky starts talking. "Finn, after evaluating the situation in its entirety, we feel strongly that expulsion would be the wrong reaction. Instead, I'm releasing you into Professor Winslow's custody and recommending a counselor." He turns to Ty, and my hands shake at my sides with an overwhelming surge of both relief and unspent anger. "Professor Winslow, I'm trusting you to handle this situation with the utmost care and consideration."

Ty nods.

"What about Dane? What about the assault charges?"

"I'll discuss the situation with Dane's father as soon as we leave here, and I assure you, the matter will be taken care of," Dean Kandinsky asserts.

My wheels are spinning, my heart on fire.

There's nothing left to do but leave the police station…with my brother.

Finn

"Here," Ty says, digging in the front seat of his car for both a long-sleeved shirt and my cell and handing them to me on the third floor of Dickson Garage. The walk here was made in silence, and unlike Ty, I'm not eager to break it. "Ace gave me these."

"I can't believe Ace called you," I grit out, shoving my arms into the sleeves of my shirt and dropping my cell into my pocket. I know he was trying to help, but I'm still fucking angry.

Ty shakes his head. "Ace didn't call me. Thatch did."

I nod but avoid Ty's eyes as he holds open the door for me to get in his car, and I step away from the vehicle instead. I'm not getting in, no matter how much he wants me to. Ty slams the door then, falling into step beside me as I walk. Everything about him is annoyingly sad and concerned, and I want to slap it right out of him.

"How long have you known the truth?" he asks, matching his pace to mine as I walk down the garage ramp toward the second floor.

I don't have to ask for clarification to know what he means. There was only one shocked brother in that police station conference room at Jeff's revelation, and we both know it wasn't me.

"Too fucking long," I answer honestly. "You're the whole reason I came here, to Dickson. I wanted to see how the other half lived. To see what it was like to be one of the lucky Winslow kids who didn't have to grow up with the world's shittiest father."

Ty's head jerks slightly at my words, just enough for me to

notice in my peripheral vision, but he doesn't stop meeting me step for step as we round a corner yet again, taking the ramp to the first floor.

"Finn, I'm so sorry that you've had to deal with him."

"You're sorry?" I retort on a harsh laugh. "Well, that fixes everything, doesn't it? I guess I can forget all about watching Jeff beat my mom more times than I can count or defending my siblings when he gets rowdy at night. Because you're *sorry*."

"Finn." Ty's lips turn down at the corners into a stupid fucking frown. "You and I both know that's not what I meant. I know how fortunate I am, and I know I can't take away your pain."

He's so sanctimonious. So fucking magnanimous. I can't stand it. I stop in my tracks and spin to face him, putting a finger to his chest and letting it all fly.

"You have no idea what my life has been like. You have no idea what my siblings' lives have been like," I tell him harshly, and I can feel the blood pumping to my forehead and neck and ears. "That's right! I'm not your only long-lost sibling from that fucking derelict drunk. There's also Reece and Jack and Travis and Willow. Reece is in California, but Jack, Travis, and Willow? They're still living under that son of bitch's thumb every day. Right now, I have to worry about what he's going to do when he gets home and takes this shit with me out on them!"

Ty's green eyes fill with unease and pity, and my vision tunnels. All I want to do is punch the sympathy right off his stupid face.

Impulse control officially spent for the day, I wing a fist right at him, but he blocks it with a startlingly quick catch. My hand trapped in his, I can't move, and he pulls me into a bear hug that makes it impossible for me to push him away. My feet scramble, but he holds steady.

"Get the fuck off!" I shout as panic overcomes me, but Ty doesn't let go. He holds on tight as I thrash the two of us all over that damn garage, whispering in my ear the whole fucking time.

"You can stop fighting, Finn. I've got you."

"Let me fucking go!"

"I've got you, Finn. I've got you. You're my brother now. I've got you."

I let out a scream as the dam breaks on my emotion, and tears stream down my face. Ty tucks me even closer, rocking me back and forth and shushing me softly. "I, and the rest of the Winslow kids, am your family now. You hear me? You're not alone anymore—we're going to fight like hell for you."

My whole life, all I've felt is that I was fighting for myself and my mom and my brothers and my sister. Fighting against a man who only wanted to make our lives a living hell. Fighting against all of the obstacles he purposely put in our way. Fighting. Fighting. *Fighting.*

I've *never* had someone to do it for me.

Tears still falling, I grip Ty's sweatshirt with my fists as he pulls me close.

"It's going to be all right, Finn. I promise." When he's confident I'm pulling it together, he gives one hearty pat to my back and then steps away to give me space.

I step back and swipe a hand down my face. There's a part of me that feels like a weak, pathetic fool for being so emotional, but deep down, I know that's just my father talking.

I have nineteen years' worth of being told I am useless and pathetic and weak by my father. Nineteen years of trying to protect myself and my mother and my siblings from a man who is so sick and twisted, he smiles when he makes his wife and kids feel pain. Nineteen years of being broken down as a man.

That takes time to get over.

"You're my brother, Finn," Ty says softly. "And everything you've had to live with until now stops right here."

An unexpected wave of relief washes over me, and I nod. Ty's face swells with pride.

"Okay, you said Reece is in California, but Jack, Travis, and Willow are still in the house, right?"

I nod, panic at what they're about to face gripping my chest.

"Okay, first things first, we need to get them out," Ty continues. "Your mom, too."

"It's not that easy. I've tried." I run a hand through my hair. "But he always ends up scaring or manipulating my mom into not pressing charges against him."

Ty shakes his head. "Don't worry about that. We'll find another way to pin down Jeff, but for now, let's get *our* brothers and sister out of that house."

It's a powerful statement—one I never dreamed would actually sound *good*. I can't believe how comforting it is not to be on my own.

He grabs his phone from his pocket and dials, putting it to his ear. "Rem," he says into the receiver. "Emergency family meeting. Meet me at Mom's, and call everyone else... Yeah, I'm good... but we all need to talk and pronto."

He hangs up without any obvious argument from Remington and meets my eyes. "Get on the phone with Jack, Travis, and Willow and tell them to get ready. We're getting them out of that house today."

"But he'll be back there any minute." I shake my head. "And they don't even know. I haven't told anyone about this—"

Ty grabs the tops of my biceps and forces me to focus. "You don't need to worry about anything but telling them to get ready and make sure they pack stuff for your mom. I will handle everything else. You have my word." He nods. "Now, Finn. Get on the phone with them now."

My hands shake as I dial Jack's number. Willow is the most likely to answer, but there's no way I'm dropping the responsibility of this on her shoulders.

Jack finally answers on the fourth ring. "'Lo?" It's still early for him, and his voice is filled with sleep.

But I don't have time to coddle him into waking up. I don't mince words. "Jack, it's Finn. I know this sounds crazy, but I need you to get as much of your shit together as you can in the next ten minutes. Get Trav and Willow, get Mom's stuff, too. Be ready to leave the house as soon as you possibly can. Leave and go to the park if no one is there in the next ten minutes to get you, and then call me."

"Finney, dude, are you high?"

"No!" I snap. "This isn't a joke, Jack. Do what I said, and do it now."

Jack's voice shakes, but he still manages a pretty kick-ass, "I'm on it." I don't blame him for being scared. I'm scared too.

Ty's smile is both loving and reassuring as I get off the phone, and he jerks his head in the direction we came. We both run back up the ramp toward his car.

Things are in motion, and there's no stopping now.

57

Scottie

When Julia knocked on my dorm room door two hours ago, I tried to ignore her, but she didn't stop knocking for fifteen minutes straight.

Other than ordering a pair of noise-canceling headphones on one-hour delivery, I didn't have any other choice than to let her in when I finally answered the door to half the floor out of their rooms, watching her.

She peels her banana on the futon beside me now, while *Love is Blind* plays on my television.

She hasn't asked me about my mom or anything, really. Instead, sitting in silence with me while the minutes tick the day away.

She's a good friend—probably the best friend I've ever had—but I'm in no mood to entertain. I'm hoping if I ignore her long enough, she'll finally decide to leave.

Julia's phone pings from her purse, and she stands up to grab it off my bed. She sits back down beside me and types out a response to whoever it is, but I don't bother asking about it. There's too high a probability that it's someone asking about "Scottie's alcoholic mom."

"You don't have to stay here," I tell her again when she drops her phone facedown in her lap. "I know that you're being a good friend and I appreciate it, but I'll be okay."

"You know," she says, her voice almost painfully soft, "I know you will be. You're a brilliant, capable, strong person whom I'm proud to call my friend. But it's also okay not to be okay right now."

I nod, tears spilling over in an instant while my lips quiver. Just as I feared, I can't hold back.

She wraps her arm around my shoulders and pulls me closer to her side. She runs her fingers through my hair in long, gentle strokes. "I'm so sorry, Scottie. I wish I had more to say, advice to give, but I have no idea what it's like to be in your shoes, so I'm not going to pretend I do. But I'm here for you. And I'm going to be here for you for as long as it takes."

The stupid tears soak into last night's sweater that I'm still wearing. I haven't gotten the courage to go shower, and without a clean body, it feels pointless to change. "Thanks, Jules."

We both stare at the television as another two episodes of *Love is Blind* play in their entirety. When a third episode starts to play, Julia is the one to break the silence.

"I don't know if you want to know this, but Finn beat the shit out of Dane last night."

My body freezes.

"The cops got involved. Even went to Finn's dorm this morning and arrested him because Dane wanted to press charges."

I sit up instantly and meet her eyes, panic making mine bulge.

"Don't worry, it didn't go the way Dane or Nadine wanted. They're being charged for harassment for the texts they sent you— using an app to scramble their number and delay their send time— and cybercrimes that include revenge porn because of the video Nadine posted online. They're also expelled from Dickson."

My head spins so hard I have to grip the couch to keep my balance. "H-how do you know all of this?"

"Ace told me," she says with a small smile. "Finn also texted me to check on you, but I haven't heard from him again since I texted him back."

"Finn texted?"

She nods. "I think he wanted to text you, but he didn't want to add any stress to your plate." I swallow a thick ball of saliva as she keeps going. "And I wouldn't be surprised if the campus police have tried to contact you. I know they contacted your mom, and she's already gone to the station and given a statement. Ace is pretty sure she's going to press charges against Dane and Nadine for releasing that video without her permission, and the officers are doing their best to scrub it from the internet too."

I scoff. She and I both know that getting something off the internet once it's on there is about as likely as witnessing a unicorn growing its wings.

It's fucking impossible, and for all I know, the damn thing is already viral. There's no guarantee Wren or my dad haven't already seen it.

My stomach sinks to my feet and then shoots back up like a rocket until it lodges itself into my throat. I feel sick and overwhelmed and anxious. *So unbelievably anxious.*

There's so much to process.

I scramble off the futon and over to my bed, digging through my messy comforter until I find my phone. I turned it off hours ago when it all became too much again.

I hold the button to power it on, and it only takes a few seconds to connect to the cell network. Notifications flood in once again.

Social media notifications. Texts from my mom and Kayla and Ace and Blake. A million calls and almost as many voice mails.

I don't dare click on any of them.

The whole world might as well be crashing in on me all over again. I turn my phone back off and toss it back onto my bed, and Julia watches with concern as I dart back into my half bathroom to throw up again.

The porcelain of the toilet feels cold against my hot, clammy skin, and I rest my forehead on the seat as soon as I'm done. Julia crouches beside me, rubbing at my back in soft, concentric circles. "It's going to be okay, Scottie. I promise."

I hear her. I do. But I'm having a hard time believing that anything will ever be okay again.

58

Finn

"Dad had a whole other family," Willow says, but it's more for herself than for anyone else. A musing of wonderment after the absolute whirlwind of the last twelve hours.

It's a little after nine in the evening, and I'm sitting in my dorm on FaceTime with all four of my siblings. Willow, Trav, and Jack are on one screen, and Reece is on the other. After everything that's happened today, I knew a face-to-face discussion was necessary, and because of Ty's request that I stay in my room tonight to ensure no more trouble with Dane while he packed his shit, this is as close as I could get to that.

"I can't believe he abandoned his wife and five kids," Travis says and shakes his head. "That is so messed up."

"Yeah, and then years later, he changes his name and starts a whole other family," Jack adds on a sigh. "He's a bigger dick than I thought. Which is saying a lot, given the guy broke my finger in three places."

"Could you imagine being his other kids?" Willow questions, and a disgusted expression forms on her face. "To find out that not only did your father abandon you when you were little, but he just went off and had a whole other five kids. It's gross."

"I think we can all agree that his other kids got the better end of the bargain," I interject. "I mean, they got a life without him. We got a life *with* him."

"Yeah, but that doesn't change the fact that their father left them when they were little," Willow counters. "I can't even imagine the kind of trauma that causes."

"Low is right," Jack agrees. "It's a miracle his other kids even want to help us. I mean, if my dad abandoned me and started a whole other family, I don't know that I'd be rolling out the red carpet for the kids who actually got a father."

I'm floored over my siblings' reaction to this. It's quite literally the opposite of mine and full of perspective and grace. Shame eats at me.

"How long did you know about this, Finn?" Reece questions, but Jack is quick to chime in right on top of him.

"What are the damn odds that one of your professors ends up being our brother from another mother?" His face gets this comical expression, and a laugh jumps from his lungs. "That has to be the biggest coincidence in history."

"Yeah," I say and avoid Reece's eyes. "Definitely a huge coincidence."

My eldest brother's spidey senses are engaged, but I refuse to get into the dirty details of how long I've known about our father's other family. It feels unnecessary at this point and, more than that, absolutely fucking stupid in a group setting such as this.

"How's Mom?" I question, and Willow shrugs.

"She's doing okay. I'm sure it's a lot to wrap her head around, her husband having a whole other family and all. She's also worried about missing shifts at the factory, but Remy told her she has nothing to worry about."

"Not to mention, this lake house is sick," Jack adds. "I feel like I'm in a damn Hallmark movie, bro. The Winslow siblings hooked us up."

After the state trooper that Remy called in a favor with picked up my brothers and sister from the park down the street from our house in Westchester, he took them to a lake house that's owned by their uncle Brad and aunt Paula. Ty was there to meet them. Apparently, Brad and Paula decided to spend the winter months in a rental in Florida, and they were more than happy to open their doors to Hayes strays. Then, Remy waited for my mom outside of work this afternoon and drove her up there to be with them after convincing her to come with him.

"The view here is unreal," Low says with a smile, even turning the camera to face the floor-to-ceiling windows that look out onto the water. "I can't believe we get to spend Christmas here."

"Ty even took Jack and me to this Christmas tree stand up the street to get a tree. I can't remember the last time we actually had a tree up," Trav comments. "You should've seen the look on Mom's face when we brought it in. I don't think I've seen her smile that big in years. Hell, probably my whole damn life."

"Damn," Reece muses. "I don't know how we're ever going to repay them for what they're doing for us."

"Dude. You're preaching to the choir," Trav agrees with a sarcastic grin. "I think I might like my new siblings better than I like you guys."

"I'm with Trav." Jack nods on a laugh. "If Winnie, Flynn, and Jude are anything like Ty and Remy, I might disown you fucks."

Low rolls her eyes, but she also smiles when she says, "All this time, I thought I was the only girl stuck around a bunch of stinky boys, but I actually have a sister. How cool is that."

"Are you going to try to come home for the holidays, Reece?" Jack questions, and Reece shakes his head.

"I wish, man. But I'm a broke-ass college student who can't afford a ticket. Plus, I need to save up for when I make the big transfer to Dickson next year."

"I still can't believe you're coming to Dickson," I admit.

Reece flashes a knowing smirk at me. "After all the fucking fights you've been getting into? I think it's safe to say I need to come to Dickson to keep your ass in check."

I shake my head. "I'm done fighting." Unbelievably, I mean it.

"Food's here!" another distant voice echoes in the receiver, and when Jack and Trav glance over their shoulders, it's apparent it's on their end.

"This has been a real lovely chat," Trav says with a wink. "But my new favorite brother Ty just brought a shitload of takeout, and I'm starved. See you fuckers on the flip side."

He's doesn't look back, and Jack follows his lead, only offering his middle finger and a laughing, "Love you assholes."

Low rolls her eyes and tells us she loves us, and Reece and I end the call shortly after that.

"So…I wasn't trying to eavesdrop, but it's kind of hard, you know?" Ace states, and I glance over my shoulder to find him eating a bag of potato chips on his futon. "Quite the turn of events, huh?"

"Yeah." I run a hand through my hair and drop my phone on my bed. "A fucking whirlwind."

"Don't worry, man, I don't even expect a thank-you or anything."

"What?" I furrow my brow, and he shoves a chip into his smiling mouth.

"For calling my dad, who called your—*who'd have guessed it*—brother to come save your ass. It's on the house. No charge. In fact, you can consider it a free service, complimentary with your roommateship."

I don't bother explaining that I've already known Ty is my brother for years. It'd mean having to explain the whole coming-to-Dickson-to-plot-his-downfall thing, and I don't think that would go over too big.

"I have a hard time believing you were starved for attention when you were a kid, but you sure as fuck act like it."

He laughs as I reach for my phone when it pings with a new text message.

> *Julia: Hey, just wanted to update you that I just left her dorm. I stayed all day until she literally made me leave, but she's not doing that great. Honestly, she's a mess. Embarrassed. Mortified. Doesn't want to leave her room.*

She wouldn't eat anything when I was there either. I'm worried about her, for sure.

I'm already on my feet, shoving my phone into my pocket and grabbing my keys.

"I'll be back in a few," I tell Ace, grabbing my jacket from the hook by the door.

He jumps to his feet, nervous. "Hold up. I thought you told Ty you'd stay in tonight."

I roll my eyes. "I'm not going to get into any trouble, I promise. But there's something I have to do."

He's reluctant, but he's also Ace. There's a reason I like him— he knows when it's not a good idea to cross a boundary. "All right, dude. But call me if you need something."

I nod and jet, running down the hall, down the stairs, and out the door, before anyone can spot me.

Thirty minutes later, I'm standing in front of Scottie's door with a bag of food from her favorite hoagie joint up the street. Every cell inside my body wants to see her, talk to her, but I know she's not ready for that.

So, I do the second-best thing. I set the food on the floor and knock three times before I jog down the hallway and out of sight.

I stay hidden, but I don't leave until I see her open the door and take the food inside her room.

Her eyes look sadder than I've ever seen, and her body is sunken and hollow. I wish I had the power to turn back time—to change the course of her fate.

But if I did, I would have changed mine and my family's a long time ago.

This is no *Aladdin*, and I'm no genie. Only time will heal this wound. But there's nothing to stop me from granting secret wishes while we wait.

Monday December 16th
Scottie

There is nothing like a New York City winter wind. Between the giant skyscrapers and the concrete pavement, it's as if each frigid gust has the power to freeze your bones. I pull my black puffer coat tighter around my body as I speed walk from the Logan Center to Delaney and burrow into its warmth.

It's only a little after six, but the sky is already dark, and the moon has set up shop for the evening.

Tonight's cheerleading practice went over by an hour, and it took every ounce of strength I had inside my body to plaster a smile on my face and show up. My focus was shit and Coach Jordan bitched at me quite a few times when I kept screwing up my scorpions, but I showed up, and for right now, that's all I can ask of myself.

Coach Jordan did pull me aside to ask if I was okay, but she doesn't need to know the gory, my-alcoholic-mom-had-sex-with-a-student details. Everyone on my squad knows—even the girls who weren't at the Delta Omega party—and that's more than enough trauma for me.

I lost count of how many hushed conversations stopped the instant I was within hearing distance at practice or how many times I caught Kayla giving someone a quiet vibing.

Coach obviously knows something happened with Nadine since she's off the squad and out of school, but the dean evidently felt he could leave it at that.

Thank everything.

My stomach growls as I pass the upperclassmen apartments, and I make a last-minute decision to reroute to Brower Center to grab a bite to eat. I've barely eaten anything since it all happened, save the sandwich that I'm pretty sure Julia made appear mysteriously at my door Saturday night, and a single apple first thing this morning. I cut through the alleyway between Delaney and the on-campus apartments and jog across Broadway when I find a break in traffic.

The lights of the Brower Center are still on, and a group of students wearing Santa hats and shaking jingle bells greets me near the door. I'm pretty sure they're part of Dickson's a cappella group who've chosen to spend the evening providing a Christmas-carol ambiance to any poor students who are still left on campus for winter break.

I start to offer a smile in their direction, but when a guy with red hair and a pirate's smile looks at me curiously, my current reality hits me like a ton of bricks. I avert my eyes, but it's too late. He knows who I am and spreads it among his friends hurriedly.

I run for the door and shove it open, but laughter interrupts their version of "Jingle Bells" before I can make it inside. I move quicker, letting the door fall closed behind me to separate us, but as I unwrap my scarf and trudge toward the double doors of the dining hall on the first floor, I hear them start a rendition of the song "Stacey's Mom"—though, my name takes center stage in the chorus. *Scottie's Mom.*

Tears well in my eyes before I can even pick up a tray, and when my breath gets shaky and my vision turns blurry, I forgo the whole dining experience, sneak out the back entrance of Brower, and don't look back.

The wind is still cold, but my body is an inferno of embarrassment. I run as fast as I can until I'm safely inside Delaney and take the stairs all the way to the fifth floor to avoid seeing anyone else.

My hands tremble from low blood sugar and I feel moments away from passing out, but I power through until I'm standing at my door, keys in hand. A plastic bag is hanging on the doorknob, and I pull it inside with me without looking because *the less time I'm out of my dorm room, the better.*

I drop my cheerleading bag to the floor and let the tears fall from my eyes unchecked. At this point, I'm so used to crying that I multitask while doing it.

I peer inside the bag and am surprised but grateful to see that it's filled with a boatload of my favorite snacks. Granola bars, trail mix, cookies, chips—you name it, and it's in here. I have no idea who dropped this off—I'm assuming Julia or Kayla—but I don't waste any time tearing open a bag of Chips Ahoy and shoving a cookie into my mouth. My salty tears mingle with the sugary treat, and I plop down on my bed to sob and eat the rest of the bag at the same time.

I reach for the remote to my television to drown out the silence, putting on a new episode of *Love is Blind* for consistency. But they're only just getting started on their blind dates when a soft knock sounds from my door.

Carefully, I tiptoe over and look through the peephole, half expecting to find an angry mob of *Pitch Perfect* wannabees, but all I see is a police officer in uniform instead.

"Scottie Bardeaux, it's Officer Walters with the campus police," his deep male voice announces. "I just wanted to chat with you for a few minutes."

Son of a bitch.

For the past few days, Office Walters has left me several voice mails, trying to get me to come down to the station, and I've ignored every single one, but this in-person visit has officially put the kibosh on my avoidance.

It's now or never. Time to get it over with.

I scrub a hand down my face to wipe away evidence of my sadness-snack-binge and answer the door.

"Scottie?" Officer Walters offers a soft smile, and I don't have the strength to return it.

Instead, I nod. "That's me."

"Sorry to bother you, but it's important that we get you down to the station to give an official statement about the events that took place on Friday night at the Delta Omega house."

I sigh. I almost ask him if it's necessary, but then I remember Finn's involvement in all of it and Dane's attempt at pressing charges for assault, and I know that I need to do what they ask, even if it feels like the equivalent of swallowing a cup full of nails.

"Okay," I agree and grab my purse, keys, and phone to follow his lead.

Even though the station is only a few blocks away, Officer Walters drives me in his patrol car and cuts our travel time to five minutes flat.

He escorts me inside, past the lobby area, through a hallway that requires a badge to scan in, and into the back area of the station.

"Scottie?" A female voice fills my ears, and I nearly trip over my own feet when I glance over my shoulder to see my mom standing there.

Her normally pretty face is an exhausted mess. She has dark circles under her green eyes, her clothes are wrinkled, and her long brown locks are in a messy bun on top of her head. She's me in about twenty years and a half million bottles of vodka. I hate how much I look like her.

"Can we talk?" she asks, and I shake my head. "Scottie, please, I know how awful all of this looks, and I'm so sorry, honey. I'm so sorry." She starts to step closer to me, and I lift my hand in the air.

"No." I look at Officer Walters. "Why is she here?"

"Mrs. Bardeaux is here because she wanted to update her statement with a few more details."

"If you want me to stay here and give a statement, then she needs to go. I refuse to be anywhere near her."

"Scottie, honey, don't say that," my mom begs, but Officer Walters is quick to abide by my request.

"Hey, Paul," he calls out toward an officer who is sitting down at the desk my mother is standing beside. "Please take Mrs. Bardeaux to one of the back interview rooms."

"Scottie, I just want a chance to explain. I know there's no excuse, but I want you to know the truth." My mom is completely ignoring Paul as he tries to lead her away, and the unexpected time with her is wreaking havoc on my nervous system.

Anxiety claws at my chest, and my knees buckle so hard that I have to reach out a hand to steady myself on Officer Walters's desk.

"Mrs. Bardeaux, please follow me," Paul urges, but it's clear at this point that nothing short of manhandling her is going to stop her from walking toward me.

"I thought you and Dane were still together. He told me he was your boyfriend. He told me that you wanted to see me. He—"

"Ma'am." Officer Walters steps directly in front of me to block her. "You need to stop. She's made it clear that she doesn't want to speak to you. You need to respect that."

"Scottie?" she questions, trying to peer around the officer to see me. I cower behind him, using him as my own personal emotional shield.

I don't see it, but I hear it when Paul successfully guides her toward one of the back rooms. There are retreating footsteps and any manner of a million complaints from her, but finally, a door clicks shut and a strangled breath escapes my lungs.

"I apologize for that, Scottie." Officer Walters offers me an understanding smile and gestures for me to take a seat near the desk I'm assuming is his. "Let's move through this quickly and get you back to your dorm."

My nerves are shot, and I feel like I'm seconds away from snapping in two. I nod and grit my teeth, forcing myself to power through.

"We found evidence on Nadine Jones's phone that she was utilizing an app to send you harassing text messages," he updates. "Were you aware they were from her?"

"No." I shake my head. "Though, after what happened on Friday night and the fact that she was filming the whole thing, I assumed it was either her or Dane Matthews who were sending me those messages."

"Have you seen the footage that Nadine Jones released on social media?"

Of course I have. It's my ongoing living nightmare and one of life's biggest mysteries that the explicit footage managed to get under so many platforms' community guidelines.

"Yes." I swallow hard against the bile that wants to migrate up my throat. "I've seen it. Too many times."

"I want you to know that we have successfully deleted the footage from Nadine's and Dane's accounts, and we are working hard to locate it anywhere else that a third party has shared it," he updates. "Once something is released on the internet, it's hard to remove it entirely, but our Digital Forensics Department is working hard to do exactly that." He slides a piece of paper and a pen over to me. "Now, I just need you to write down the events of Friday night from your point of view. Be as detailed as you can with names, places, and everything you saw."

This is the last thing I want to do, an actual crime against any of the very little progress I've made since it happened, but I make myself do it anyway. I know it's important, not only for me, but for Finn and all the other friends who've stood by me through the whole thing.

Once I finish, my face is wet with tears and my body feels like it's been squeezed through a lemon press. I can feel the exhaustion settling into my bones, and my eyes are heavy with fatigue as I slide my statement over to Officer Walters.

He hands me a tissue. "Thank you for doing that," he says. "I know it was hard for you, and I commend you on your strength. It's not easy reliving painful situations."

"This is one of the worst things that has ever happened to me," I verbalize my truth and use the tissue to wipe off snot that's trying to drip out of my nose. "And that's saying a lot because my mother has been an alcoholic all of my life."

"You're a strong young woman, and I'm proud of you." Officer Walters's eyes are kind and understanding. "And I hope there's never a next time, but if you ever receive harassing text messages or are put in a situation you feel is unsafe in any form, I want you to contact me directly." He hands me his card, and I put it in my purse. "Now, let's get you back to your dorm." He gestures for me to stand, and I follow his lead back out of the police station.

The ride in his patrol car back to Delaney is silent, but as we turn the corner onto 116th Street, the entrance door looming ahead, I can't stop myself from asking one thing. "Are Dane and Nadine going to go to jail?"

He keeps his eyes forward and his hands on the steering wheel. "I'm giving you all of this info off the record, okay?"

"Okay."

"Since they're first-time offenders, I don't think they'll get jail time, but they might have to deal with house arrest and a few years' probation."

I started the semester as Dane's girlfriend. And now, I've ended the semester with Dane facing house arrest and probation for crimes he committed against me and my mom. It all feels like a fever dream.

Now that I know Officer Walters is willing to share a little more than the standard byline, I venture another inquiry.

"Is Finn Hayes going to get in trouble?"

I've got more than enough of my own problems to occupy me into the next lifetime and beyond, but Finn is still one of the main things I've been thinking about since Julia told me he beat Dane up.

"The dean made some sort of pseudo-deal with Dane Matthews's father. Evidently, a number of the major donors of this year's endowment threatened to pull it if Dane pressed charges, and as Dane's father's company relies heavily on a lot of the construction and development business with the university, he found it in their family's best interest not to risk it. Their agreement will end up giving Dane a lesser sentence than he would normally face for harassment and cybercrimes, but I think it's the right thing to do, given the ramifications this would have on Finn's permanent record."

Relief's kiss is swift and intense as Officer Walters's words overwhelm me. Finn deserves a fair shot at everything good in this world—maybe even more than everyone else—and the thought that I might be the reason he didn't get it was unbearable.

For as much shit as I still have to deal with, this…this is still a win.

Friday December 20*th*
Finn

> **Ty: You and Ace watching the game?**
>
> **Me: It's not looking good. Ace is on the verge of a stroke.**
>
> **Ty: Ha. You should see his dad.**

That message is followed up by a photo of Ace's dad, Thatch. He's sitting in front of his giant television—the Dickson-Buffalo Big East Championship game on the screen—and a stress vein is prominent on his big head.

Both Ace and I were invited to watch the game at his parents' apartment—they had a bunch of people over, including my brother Ty, but Ace decided he'd rather watch at a diner that's not far from our dorm. Normally, he's a man of the crowd, but I guess there's too much riding on this game that he needed to watch it with as few people as possible.

I suspect the bastard put actual money on it.

Zip's Diner is practically empty, everyone else choosing hipper places like bars or frat parties than a mom-and-pop spot to enjoy the game. When I look over at Ace, it's almost disturbing how much he and his dad look alike, protruding forehead veins and all.

"Son of a bitch," Ace groans and slams his hand down on the table when Blake gets sacked for the second time in a row. "What is our O line *doing?*"

We're down by a touchdown, already on our fourth down, and

there're only fifteen seconds left in the game. The way I see it, there's no way they're going to be able to pull this one out. Boden would have to manage one hell of a Hail Mary pass to tie it up.

My phone vibrates several times in my pocket, and I pull it out to find a bunch of texts from my siblings.

Willow: Come to the lake house for Christmas, Finn?

Travis: Yeah, man, you gotta come here for Christmas. Mom's planning on making a whole fucking feast!

Jack: It's going to be the first non-shitty Christmas we've ever had. LOL.

Willow: There are actual PRESENTS under the tree!

For the first time in my entire life, my mom is happy, and my siblings are actually looking forward to the holidays.

And I'm relieved to know that our father won't show up and ruin it all.

Somehow, Ty has someone who has been keeping tabs on Jeff Hayes's every move. I don't know who and I don't know how he managed to make this arrangement, but whoever it is has confirmed that Jeff Hayes is currently staying in a shady motel just outside the city.

He took the train when he came to the Dickson Campus Police station, and he hasn't gone back home since. Hasn't even tried to come back to campus looking for me either. It's strange, to say the least. It's almost like he knows his shit is cooked.

With him MIA and my mom and siblings safe at the lake house, it feels like things are finally looking up for us. And I have Ty to thank for that. Which, considering how I started this year, is quite the turn of events.

My hate has been replaced by like, and it's even feeling as if I'm starting to develop an actual relationship with him. We've been in constant contact ever since that fateful day when our father showed up at the police station, and I actually look forward to hearing from him.

"Well, shit," Ace mutters, and I look back at the television to find Buffalo's student section rushing the field in celebration.

I give him a supportive pat on the back. "Maybe next year, man."

"Maybe?" he repeats, and his eyes turn wild. "There's no maybe, Finn. We're winning the Big East Championship next year and going all the way to the National Championship after that."

I hold up both hands in defense, my lips curling in a smile. "Okay, man. We're winning next year. No need to lose your cool."

He flips me the middle finger before excusing himself to take a piss. I stare mindlessly at the television until the camera turns toward the Dickson University cheerleaders, and Scottie's face is right there on the screen. Mindless turns to eagle-eyed focus in an instant.

I've sent her countless messages over the last week, including but not limited to:

Thinking about you, Scottie.

I hope you're okay.

I'm still here if you need me.

She hasn't responded, but that wasn't the point of sending them anyway. I'm content to be there for her any way I can while she works through a hell I know all too well.

One of the commentators mentions that she's the cheerleader Duke's quarterback gave the football to, and they proceed to dive into a conversation about how, back in their day, the cheerleaders never looked like her.

It's completely sexist and pathetic, and on any normal day, I'd probably be pissed off. But today, all I can see is her eyes. They're sad and distant, all the joy and charisma I fell in love with robbed by that fuckface Dane and his sidekick Nadine.

She plasters on a smile for the camera, but I know her well enough to know that she's crumbling on the inside. If I'm honest with myself, it's a look I've been responsible for putting on her face before.

The truth is a rusty knife, and it stabs me straight in the chest.

I wish I could take back so many things when it comes to Scottie. So many horrible words I've tossed her way. But I can't. All I can do is continue to support her from a distance.

Anything I can do to make her life easier, I do it. Leaving snacks on her door for when she gets back from cheerleading practice. Asking Julia to stop by her dorm and check on her. Asking Kayla to keep an eye on her at practice.

I won't stop until the joy is back in her eyes, even if I'll never be back in her heart.

61

Tuesday December 24th

Finn

"Cool your jets, Cass. I already told you, I'm leaving as soon as Julia gets here," Ace says into his phone, and a heavy sigh escapes his lips as he shoves three pairs of sweatpants into his suitcase. He adds another four hoodies, jeans, and a three-piece pinstriped suit that looks like a mob boss got ousted and ended up working at an accounting firm.

His clothing choices might be one of the world's greatest mysteries.

"Yeah… No… Yeah…" He pauses as he appears conflicted on whether to bring a T-shirt that has Britney Spears's face front and center or one that reads "I heart hot moms." He ends up shoving them both in his suitcase. "Relax. I'm listening…"

He's not listening, by the way. He's currently waving his hands in the air and mouthing something toward me. "Hold on, Mom. I think Finn needs something. You okay, man?" he questions, widening his eyes and pursing his lips, a silent "Please help me end this call" signal.

"Nah, dude. I'm good. No need to get off that very important call with your mother." The smile on my face makes Ace flip me the middle finger.

I shrug and go back to my mindless scrolling of TikTok until a new text notification pops up on the screen.

Jack: When you heading here, bro?

I start to type out a response, letting Jack know I'm planning to head up to the lake house—to spend Christmas with my mom and siblings—soon. My bag's been packed since I woke up this morning, but that's because my clothing choices don't include fucking suits and a hundred T-shirts like Ace's. I've got seven T-shirts, seven pairs of jeans, and two or three long-sleeves, and that makes my outfit planning pretty easy.

There's a knock on the door, and I toss my phone down onto the mattress to answer it. Ace is still too busy figuring out what hair products to bring and pretending to listen to whatever his mom is saying in his ear.

Julia is on the other side, a soft smile on her face, but when she spots Ace behind me, standing near a suitcase that's overstuffed with things he probably doesn't need to spend Christmas at her parents' house in the Catskills, she rolls her eyes. "How long has he been packing?"

"An eternity."

She laughs and steps inside, and Ace uses her presence to end the call with his mom.

"Jules is here. Gotta go. See you soon."

I can still hear her talking as he pulls the phone away from his ear, but he doesn't hesitate to hit end.

"You ready?" Julia asks him.

"I was born ready, Jules."

"Born ready?" She narrows her eyes on a scoff. "You're still packing."

His only response is to spin on his heel, toss a shitload of hair products and deodorant and cologne and I don't even know what else into his suitcase, and start to zip it up. But when the zipper gets stuck because the damn thing has too much shit in it, he walks over to Julia and lifts her up into his arms.

"What the hell, Ace?" She squeals and slaps at his chest, but he ignores her as he sets her down on top of his suitcase that's resting

on his bed. Once the zipper closes successfully, Ace smiles up at
Julia and waggles his brows.

"Born ready."

"Idiot." She snorts and hops off his bed, giving him a hard
punch to his stomach before heading back over to the door.

Ace laughs and pulls his bag off the mattress, setting it on its
wheels.

"What are you doing for Christmas, Finn?" Julia asks.

"Heading up north to a lake house my family is staying at," I
tell her, not completely sure what Ace has revealed to Julia about
my current situation. But the innocent smile on her face tells me he
hasn't told her anything, or, if he has told her anything, he's made
damn sure she keeps it locked tight. And that realization only makes
me trust Ace more.

He might be a fucking lunatic, but he's never once not had
my back.

"That sounds fun," Julia says, but then her face takes on a comical, terrified expression. "You should probably pray for us. We're
going to be stuck in my parents' cabin with Ace's parents, my grand-
parents, and our crazy-ass siblings."

"I hope your great-granny is in charge of Christmas dinner,"
Ace teases and Julia snorts.

"After she got Meals on Wheels for Thanksgiving when we were
little, my mom will never let that happen again. Georgia Brooks will
not accept anything but the kind of Christmas experience Hallmark
movies would be jealous of."

As they both start to head for the door, I can't stop myself from
asking Julia the only question that's been on my mind all damn day.
"Hey, Jules, do you know what Scottie's doing for Christmas?"

"I'm not sure." Julia's mouth turns down at the corners. "I think
she's just staying on campus."

"She's not going home?"

She shakes her head. "She's still having a hard time with..." She trails off because, clearly, it's a story we are all well aware of. "I tried to get her to come to the Catskills with Ace and me, but she refused."

"Shit," Ace mutters when his phone starts ringing in his pocket. He glances at the screen and rolls his eyes. "It's my mom again. That crazy woman is probably tracking my phone and can tell we haven't left yet."

"I bet she's desperate for other people to arrive because my mom probably has her crafting flipping ornaments and baking cookies."

"Yeah." Ace chuckles. "We better go."

They both offer a wave as they head out the door, but I barely even register it. I'm too busy thinking about Scottie.

Can I really let her spend Christmas by herself?

Christmas morning this year isn't filled with roasting chestnuts on an open fire or opening presents under a tree. There's no eggnog or cocoa or stockings hanging on the mantel, and my heart isn't filled with the spirit of Jesus Christ or the act of giving. Instead, I'm a shell of myself, my drive and determination to carry on completely depleted.

My dad and my sister are devastated that I didn't come home, both of them texting me this morning with sadness-laden Christmas wishes and thinly veiled guilt trips. But facing the truth at this point feels akin to skinning my family alive.

Coach Jordan is making us stay on campus for training, I told them. Meanwhile, Coach Jordan is probably having eggs Benedict on her parents' terrace in Boca Raton.

Do I hate myself for being such a coward? Yes. I do. But if my mom's not going to fess up to everything that's happened on her own, I'm not going to be responsible for total sibling destruction over a freshly carved Christmas turkey. What am I supposed to say? *Hey, sis, could you pass the potatoes before I tell you Mom's still a raging drunk?*

Thankfully, Dad and Wren are supposed to go to Aunt Carol's house for the day to celebrate with his side of the family. Once Uncle Shane starts doing his Christmas Walrus impression and placing bets on roll consumption, they'll forget all about my absence. At least, that's my hope.

I, conversely, plan to wallow in my loneliness.

Both Julia and Kayla left campus to spend Christmas with their families—you know, like college students who aren't bordering on agoraphobia—and I didn't even bother asking any of the other girls on my squad what they were doing. Truth be told, I've spent the last few practices trying to avoid any and all conversation as much as I can.

Fat flakes fall outside my window, exemplifying a clichéd white Christmas. There's not much accumulation yet, but the Weather Channel warned of a possibility of four or five inches.

It'll be pretty for an hour or two, before the city traffic turns the pure white to brown sludge.

I could take a walk right now, to savor it while it's fresh and soak in a little Christmasy ambiance, but the idea of running into anyone who might be lingering on campus is utterly prohibitive.

I pull my nose away from the cold glass and sigh. Time is moving at a snail's pace.

My fuzzy red socks cushion my steps as I grab a bottle of water from my mini refrigerator and a granola bar from my snack basket on top and plop down onto my futon. I grab the remote and pull up one of my streaming services to put on *The Holiday*. It's my favorite holiday movie, and if anything is going to be able to take my Grinch-y heart from ice-cold to lukewarm, it's Kate Winslet's cheeky humor and Jude Law's handsome good looks. Cameron Diaz has only just arrived in England and is dragging her suitcase down the snow-covered lane in high heels, when a knock on my door startles me completely.

My body in fight-or-flight, I pull my fuzzy pink blanket tighter around my flannel-pajama-covered body and shut my eyes. *Who the hell could it be, and whyyy are they knocking on my door on Christmas morning?*

When anxiety is at the helm, she always runs me head on into the fetal position.

They knock again, and I hold my breath. You know, just in case whoever is at the door can hear my breathing.

"Scottie?" a deep, husky male voice calls through the door.

Finn. I swear I'd recognize his voice before my own at this point.

Thanks to the paper-thin doors of Delaney and the fact that I have my television up way too loud to drown out my incessant, nagging thoughts of loneliness, I know he knows I'm in here.

I take a deep breath and climb to my feet, straightening my pajama pants where they've twisted at my waist. A few high-kneed steps later, I will my hand to turn the knob and swing open the door.

Finn is there, looking as good as always in a flannel button-down, jeans, and brown boots, but the kicker is that he's not alone. Three other people stand behind him—two guys, one girl—and they're holding bags in their hands. One of the guys has a small pine tree hanging over his shoulder and looks fit to be tied with excitement.

"Uh, hey," I greet nervously, self-conscious of my completely wacky outfit now. "What's going on?"

"Julia told me you were still on campus, and we were in the neighborhood, so I figured we'd stop by and bring you some Christmas stuff."

"Technically, Finn made sure we were in the neighborhood," the girl standing beside him says and drops one of the brown bags to hold out her hand. "I'm Willow, by the way. Finn's sister."

I start to take her hand, but she surprises me by pulling me into a tight hug. Her skin is cold from being outside, but her attitude is warm. "It's so great to meet you, Scottie," she whispers into my ear.

Finn runs a hand through his hair, looking almost bashful. I've never, in the entire four months I've known him, seen him look truly nervous. Until now. "Scottie, these are my twin brothers, Jack and Travis. And, yeah, this is my chatter-mouth sister, Willow."

"It's nice to meet you," I say, even though my mind is swimming with confusion and my heart is racing. *Finn is here? With his siblings? And they brought me a Christmas tree?*

"Not trying to be rude here, Scottie," Travis says with a cheeky grin. "But do you mind if we come inside? This tree is getting fucking heavy."

"*Trav*," Finn scolds. I shake my head and laugh. It's impossible to be upset with someone when they're being so damn honest with you.

"Uh…yeah…come on in…" I quickly glance over my shoulder to make sure there's nothing too incriminating lying around behind me. I'm instantly thankful I speed-cleaned last night at midnight when I couldn't fall asleep, when I remember the magazine art I'd made of Finn while I was watching *The Truman Show*.

I step back to hold the door open wider and gesture for them to come inside. Travis is the first one to clear the threshold, and Jack and Willow file in after him. Finn stops right at the entrance, his brown eyes probing mine with concern.

"Are you sure this is okay?" he asks, his voice a whisper. "Because we can—"

"Finn." I hold my hand up. "It's fine." *Good, even.*

It feels surprisingly nice to get some unexpected Christmas cheer and even better that the majority of my guests know next to nothing about me. I know Finn would never have shared what happened with them, and the safety of knowing people aren't making fun of me in their heads is thrilling.

Once Finn and I are inside and the door is closed behind us, I see that Travis has already found a spot for the tree—at the foot of my bed—and Willow has started putting ornaments on it. Jack is putting cookies and chips and other holiday-themed goodies on paper plates and setting them on my small coffee table. He's also eating them while he does it.

"Wow," I admit as I look around the already half-decorated room. "You guys came prepared."

"Isn't it great, Scottie?" Willow questions, a big smile on her lips as she puts an angel ornament on the tree.

"Yeah," I say and mean it. "It's definitely great. Thank you for doing this." *Thank you for making me not feel so alone.*

The Holiday is still playing on the television, and Jack and Travis have made themselves comfortable on my futon, their eyes glued to the screen.

"I love this movie," Jack says, and Travis cracks up.

"You would, dude."

"What?" Jack steals a cookie out of Travis's hands and shoves it into his mouth. "Kate Winslet is a goddess," he adds, but cookie crumbs shoot past his lips as he talks.

"You guys are cringe," Willow says, a scowl on her face. "Scottie is never going to invite us back."

Finn's eyes meet mine, and the smile that's on his lips is half amused and half apologetic. It's not my favorite smile of his, but I'd be lying if I said he had a bad one.

I want to ask him a million questions about his dad and Professor Winslow and how he's handling it all. When Julia was at my dorm the other night, doing another one of her secret well-being checks that she disguises as being bored or wanting to watch *Love is Blind* with me, she told me about Finn's dad showing up at the police station and everything that ensued after that.

Ace told her, of course, and then swore her to secrecy, which she then passed on to me. But I know no story is complete until you hear it from the primary source. There's a reason that game called Telephone always gets the message so fucked up.

Until Finn tells me about it himself, I don't trust any of the real details.

Mainly, though, I just want to know he's okay. After everything we've been through, I'm still not over him.

Finn

"He did what?" Scottie questions and bursts into laughter. This is the fifth time my brothers have made her laugh like that in the last three hours, and I'm positively vibrating with satisfaction.

After Ace and Julia left yesterday, I spent an entire five hours warring with myself about going home for Christmas while Scottie was here by herself. I didn't want to let my siblings down on the first real holiday for our family, but the thought of leaving Scottie here to rot in a bucket of sour feelings I've had the pleasure of marinating in my entire life seemed equally as cruel.

I finally compromised with myself on getting home a little late for Christmas with the Hayeses after making a quick stop at Scottie's dorm this morning, but evidently, making crazy decisions truly is biological.

My siblings all showed up at my dorm first thing this morning, ready to spread some Christmas cheer to the "friend" I told them about with me.

I didn't tell them any of the gory details—sharing something so personal is well outside my moral code—but they knew from our one million FaceTime calls about me being late that Scottie has been hanging out on the bottom rung of the down-and-out ladder.

Willow suggested that a Christmas surprise wasn't a Christmas surprise at all without going all out, so on our way over, we stole a tree and its ornaments from the courtyard behind my dorm and bought way too many Christmas-themed snacks at the store in Brower Center.

"Oh my God!" Willow exclaims and throws herself back onto Scottie's bed. She shoves a pillow over her face, and her next words are muffled. "Just shut up, Trav! Shut up!"

Travis smiles like a real bastard and continues telling Scottie about the night they found my sister's then-boyfriend Steve in her bedroom. "That's right, Scottie. Stupid Steve was so scared of Jack and me that he scaled the side of the house in his boxers."

"Of course, we didn't let him get away that easy," Jack comments with a smug grin. "Trav grabbed flashlights, and we stood outside shining them directly on him while he hung precariously from our gutter."

"You're lucky he didn't *die*," Willow says, sitting up to glare at our twin brothers.

"No, Low. Stupid Steve is lucky we didn't *kill* him," Travis says, and Scottie snorts, clearly amused by their overprotectiveness.

"I promise you, Low, if that fuckhead would've been naked in your bed, I would've killed him," Jack comments, his face pursed like it's puckered on a lemon. "It was already bad enough I found you two all cuddled up with him in his fucking boxers."

Travis holds up both hands. "Please, for the love of God, don't say anything else. I don't want to know."

"We were just sleeping," Low contends. "That's *all* we were doing."

"Again, I don't want to know," Trav repeats. Scottie looks over at me with big, comically wide eyes, and a flash of her and me in this very bed, very much *not* sleeping, catches me off guard. I have to swallow hard around the knot that's formed in my throat to breathe again.

"Poor Willow," Scottie says. "Her overprotective brothers are a permanent chastity belt."

"Thank you!" Low exclaims, tossing both hands in the air and letting them fall hard on the pillow in her lap. "Finally, someone who understands! They are boyfriend repellent, Scottie. Ninety percent of the guys at school are terrified of them."

"Good," Trav says. "That's exactly how I want it."

"You're lucky it was just me and Trav," Jack comments. "If Reece and Finn would've still been home, you would've been fucked."

"Dude," Trav says with wide, knowing eyes. "Stupid Steve's body would be rotting in the backyard as we speak."

"I'm not that bad," I counter, crossing my arms over my chest with a smirk. Trav and Jack and Willow burst into laughter.

"Please, you're the actual *worst*," my sister says.

"I'm not worse than Reece," I hedge, starting to feel a little embarrassed.

"Does Reece have a tendency to get into fights too?" Scottie asks, and all three of my siblings nod.

"Reece and Finn are straight-up brawlers," Willow states, and I roll my eyes.

"We're not that bad."

Willow laughs again. "Finn, you *are* that bad. But I will say, you're never the one to start fights. Only finish them. Reece, on the other hand…" She shakes her head dramatically. "He's a full-on hothead."

"Finn beat up my ex-boyfriend," Scottie offers, not to be left out of the conversation. I don't know if she even realizes what a big deal it is to bring it up like this when she's so fresh off dealing with the consequences, but I'm proud of her. "He deserved it, though."

Willow flashes a smile in my direction, matchmaking schemes in her eyes. She doesn't know the extent of ups and downs Scottie's and my relationship has already been through, and she doesn't need to. Honestly, at this point, if she can figure out a way to bring Scottie and me together, I might actually let her.

I miss her.

"And I saw him fight an ex-UFC fighter too."

Both of my brothers' jaws drop.

"What?" Jack questions, and Trav is quick to add, "Who?"

"It's nothing," I say, but Scottie smiles over at me like a little minx.

"Actually, it was something. He won the fight. And I think I died ten deaths watching it." She snorts. "It was terrifying."

"Who was it?" Trav asks again, and Scottie looks over at me as the realization of the NDA and the fingerprints on Special Agent Lexi's phone dawns on her.

"I probably wasn't supposed to say any of that, huh?"

I grin at her. "Probably not."

"What? Why?" Jack questions, desperate for more information.

"Uh-oh, Scottie," I tease. "I feel like you've found yourself in a little predicament." I make a show of pulling out my phone. "I should probably text Lexi and let her know that—" I start to say, but my words are cut off when Scottie literally dive-bombs into my lap and knocks my phone out of my hands.

"Don't you dare!" she shouts through a laugh. I wrap my arms around her body and hold her tight to my chest. With my free hand, I pretend to grab for my phone.

"Hold on, Scottie. I gotta send a quick text."

"Finn! Don't!" she squeals breathlessly, wrestling me to keep me from grabbing it. I take full advantage of our situation and hug her tightly to my chest, relishing the feel of her body against mine.

"What was that, Scottie? You want me to tell Lexi what you just told my brothers?"

She's laughing so hard she snorts, and I feel like the main character in a Marvel movie. To lift her from the depths of despair to this—coming here this morning has been a successful mission.

I know my historical record isn't great, but from now on, this is the only way I ever want to make Scottie Bardeaux feel.

When Scottie's laughter finally subsides, I unlock my arms, and she climbs off me and takes a seat next to Willow again. I watch her avidly, my fingers tingling with the need to touch her again.

The next two hours are filled with more funny chatter and my siblings making Scottie laugh with ridiculous stories about one another and me, and a boulder forms in my stomach when Willow checks the time and says we need to leave.

"You should come, Scottie," Jack says as he grabs a few cookies for the road. "Mom would love to have you for dinner."

"Oh no, I couldn't impose like that. I—"

"Trust me, Scottie, she made enough food to feed a hundred people. It's our first Christmas without..." Willow pauses, and everyone in the room, including Scottie, knows how to fill in the blank. Our shitstick of a situation definitely isn't secret anymore. "She's just going all out," my sister says, her voice soft. "I know she'd love to have you. Finn never brings anyone home. Like, ever."

"That's because he has no friends," Trav chimes in helpfully, momentarily pausing his lick of his lollipop to insult me.

"So, this would be a big deal for my mom. I know she'd love to meet you," Willow charges on, unfazed.

"Low," I chastise with a shake of my head. The last thing I'm going to do is push Scottie to do something she doesn't feel comfortable doing.

"What?" my sister asks, completely oblivious that her overenthusiastic offer is what I'd consider pushing.

"Scottie, you're more than welcome to come," I say and reach out to gently brush a piece of hair out of her eyes. "But it's also cool if you want to stay here."

"I'd really love to..." She nods, and her top teeth dig into her bottom lip. "But I don't think I can."

In an instant, Scottie's eyes go from bright emerald to a muddy green. Sadness has seeped back into her senses, and I'd do anything to make it go away.

But I know better than anyone that this is part of the process. Feeling your feelings is way healthier than smothering them down so deep you drive yourself to psychosis.

Scottie needs space and time and distance to process. And as hard as it is to do, I know I have to give it to her.

Scottie says goodbye to Jack and Trav and Willow, all three pulling her into a giant group hug before they head out the door.

I hang back for a moment while they go romping down the hall, and Scottie surprises me by placing a sweet kiss to the apple of my cheek. "Merry Christmas, Finn."

"Merry Christmas, Scottie."

I've never been much of a believer, but I have to admit, this Christmas, there's magic in the air.

Tuesday January 7th
Scottie

I was up before my alarm went off at seven this morning, already pacing my dorm room in anticipation of the morning ahead. It's the first day of second semester, winter break is officially over, and that realization only fills me with dread.

Rumors about my alcoholic mom and me have spread through campus like wildfire. Everyone and their roommate is well aware of what happened at the Delta Omega house that night, and no matter how hard the Dickson Campus Police have tried to remove all the footage of the video that Nadine posted on the internet, they haven't been successful.

Which isn't surprising. The internet is the seventh circle of hell, and rounding up something from every part of the fire-laden ring might as well be impossible.

Every time someone splices or edits the video or uploads from a new IP address, it gets harder to find, and if there's anything this generation is good at, it's burying their heads in technology.

They've made memes and posts and used sounds from the original video to make fun of the whole situation, but the original video is so broken down at this point, they'll never find it all.

I shouldn't know any of this, but the trauma bond I have with scouring social media to see how much people are still talking about it is real.

Funnily enough, Ms. Bartlett, one of the counselors at Dickson, reached out to me to see how I was doing and if I wanted to come in to talk, but I haven't answered her emails.

I should, of course. I just…can't.

So, for now, I have a choice. I can either attend my classes in the name of keeping my GPA for my scholarship, or I can crawl back under my comforter and let the consequences of my mother's actions consume me.

The latter would most definitely be easier, but I really don't like where it leaves me.

"Get your ass in the shower," I say as I stare at my just-out-bed reflection in a mirror. My hair's a mess, my eyes practically all dark circles, and my lips are set into a firm line. I look like shit, but it's nothing a little concealer, mascara, and hair spray can't fix.

If only Ulta sold products for the inside.

On a sigh, I grab my shower caddy, towel, and clothes, and slip on my flip-flops. I can do this. I'm *going* to do this.

Without giving myself time to overthink, I open my door and head down the hallway toward the main bathroom in the center of my floor. After some quick surveillance, I relax. For now, I'm the only girl in here.

I duck into one of the shower stalls, pull the curtain closed, and set my clothes and towel onto the little wooden bench in the corner. After I remove my clothes, I step up and over the threshold that blocks the shower area and turn the water on. It's cold as ice, and a little squeal escapes my lungs as I fidget on my feet, waiting for it to warm up.

Thankfully, since I'm one of the first ones to shower this morning, it doesn't take long for the temperature to reach the almost-scalding-hot that I prefer.

I shampoo my hair and rinse it out and savor the feel of the warm water against my skin, standing there for minutes on end. My muscles relax so much, my shoulders actually disconnect from my ears.

I'm so relaxed, in fact, that when I hear footsteps outside my stall just as I'm about to condition, I'm caught off guard.

"I can't believe winter break is already over," one girl says, making me startle. Another girl laughs, and I huddle under the water with a shiver. I've been in here too long, and the spray is turning colder.

"Kelsie, don't even try to bitch to me about break being over. Your ass spent two weeks in Hawaii with your family. I spent two weeks visiting my grandma's nursing home in Delaware."

"Uh-oh, Luna, your salty is showing," Kelsie replies, and her friend Luna laughs.

I don't think I've met Luna or Kelsie, but it only takes a discreet glance through the hole between my shower curtain and the wall for me to recognize their faces. I don't have any classes with them, but I've seen them at a few parties.

"Of course I'm salty. It snowed fourteen inches, and my parents' couch smells like feet. They turned my bedroom into a gym as soon as I left for college."

Kelsie laughs, consoling, "Hey! At least your mom didn't come to campus and sleep with Randy Evans!"

My entire body freezes as Luna bursts into giggles, agreeing, "You're right. That is something!"

Loud cackling echoes off the walls of the bathroom, and I find myself covering my body with both hands as tears flood my eyes.

"Doesn't she live on our floor?" Kelsie asks.

"Yeah," Luna replies, and I drown my head in the water. Conditioner runs into my eyes in stings, but I welcome the pain. It's a relief just to have a tiny distraction from the soul-crippling throb in my chest.

"Was it just one guy?" Kelsie questions. "I heard it was three."

I cringe. *Holy hell.* The truth isn't bad enough for people that they have to make shit up?

"Ew, *gross,*" Luna scoffs. "If my mom did that, I don't even know what I'd do."

"Oh shit, Lune. Did you see what time it is? We gotta jet if we don't want Murkowski to lose his mind that we're late. You ready?

"Yeah."

Hurried footsteps leave the bathroom, and the moment the door clicks shut, I step out of the shower and peer around the curtain. Once I know the coast is clear, I wrap my towel around my body, grab all my shit, and run toward my dorm as quick as I can.

My hair and body are still wet, and my tears flow unchecked.

Looks like crawling back under my comforter and letting the consequences of my mother's actions consume me isn't such a bad idea after all.

Finn

It's our first day back in English Lit after winter break, and Scottie isn't here. I knew things would be different this semester—not hating my professor anymore, him knowing he's my brother, and not having the huge burden of knowing my siblings are still trapped inside a house with an alcoholic abuser—but I didn't expect this change in the roster. Maybe in another class, sure, as our schedules are almost entirely different with the start of the new year, but because of the graduation requirements, Ty's class is year-round.

When I first got to the lecture hall this morning, I hoped she was just running a little late, but as time ticked by and Ty dove into class, I knew she wasn't coming.

I text Julia quick.

Me: Scottie's not in English. She didn't drop it, did she?

Julia: I don't think so. Last I talked to her, she was planning to be there.

Curious but temporarily satisfied with Julia's answer, I tuck my phone back into my pocket and *try* to pay attention.

I haven't talked to Scottie since Christmas Day, and I'm worried. I've tried, trust me, *I've tried*, but all my texts and calls have gone unanswered, and every time I leave snacks or food at her door after knocking, she doesn't answer. She's still having a hard time, and I feel helpless.

Even knowing what it's like to shove people away for the sake of your own sanity—been there, done that—I wish she didn't have to.

"I highly recommend that you start reading *Anna Karenina* now because this isn't the only book we'll be deep-diving into this semester," Ty announces, and a few quiet groans ring out in the lecture hall. He grins, eating it up. Now that I've gotten to know him, I appreciate his inclination to shit-stir. According to his mom, Wendy, it's been a part of his personality since he was a little kid. "You should save all of that excitement for the big semester project on *The Alchemist.*"

"Son of a bitch. Two books?" Ace complains, a scowl making him look like an ugly pug dog. I laugh under my breath as Ty picks his voice out in the crowd.

"Oh, Ace, please. Don't be upset. It's not two books."

"It's not?" the fool asks hopefully.

Ty smirks. "It's four." There's a groan heard 'round the world from just about the entire auditorium, and Ty laughs, assuring, "Have no fear, class. I'll make it fun. I always do."

He and his TA pass out papers as he explains in greater detail. "Make sure you get the packet from Doug. It outlines everything you'll need to prepare for this semester, and if you don't have it, you'll probably fail. Or, you know, you'll probably have to ask me for it, and I'll have to assign you a fifth book to read." He winks, and people all around me scramble to get their hands on this semester's syllabus packet. "Class dismissed."

Ace is like a rocket, jumping out of his seat, snagging a packet from Doug on the run, and speeding out the door. From what he told me this morning before class, he's supposed to meet Scarlett for brunch before his next class. I wouldn't say the two of them are serious, but evidently, they've been talking—and making out on occasion—since the night we saw her at Delta Omega.

It's stupid if you ask me since he's obviously in love with Julia, but we're men. Sometimes that means we're fucking idiots.

I stay in my seat until everyone else disperses, approaching

Doug personally. "I need an extra for a student who missed class today," I tell him, and he doesn't hesitate to hand over two packets. I shove them into my backpack and start to head for the stairs, but Ty waves me down, gesturing for me to come to his desk with a little lift of his head.

Doug packs up his briefcase and leaves the room, and Ty finally starts talking. "I just got word that he's been arrested without bail."

He doesn't even have to say his name for me to know he's talking about our father. Two days ago, Ty texted me with a vague update that he wasn't going to be a problem anymore, and if he meant anyone else, I'm sure his delivery would have been a little more dramatic.

When it comes to our dad, this is the best news possible.

"Without bail?" I question, my eyes searching his for answers. "He must have really fucked up somewhere along the line." I know all of my brothers have been calling in all their favors to do some digging into Jeff's past, even roping Thatch and Kline into part of it, but most of the shit was too minor or too old to meet the statute of limitations. If he's been arrested without bail, they must have found something really fucking awful.

"Bad shit, Finn." Ty's eyes turn serious. "Armed robbery... And he shot and killed a cop in the process."

The rug is pulled out from under my feet, and I have to reach out to steady myself with my hand on his desk. "When did he do that?"

"In Reno, about twenty-two years ago," he says gently. I may not be great at math, but even I can work out the timeline on that one. He fucking *killed* someone right before getting together with my mom. I knew my dad was a piece of shit, but it seems he left a few pertinent details out of his journal. *Murder.* I can't fucking believe I share DNA with someone capable of it.

"Listen, I know this is a delicate issue, and I'm sure it's going to be particularly devasting for your mom." I nod, and Ty grasps my shoulder. "Do you want me to tell your mom and siblings, or do you want to do it?"

"I'll do it," I answer honestly and without hesitation. Even though

Ty is our brother and the trust we have as a family unit is growing, I'd rather they hear this kind of news from me. I scoff. "No wonder he changed his name."

"Yeah." Ty lets out a deep sigh. "It's a real kick to the balls, isn't it? Knowing you share DNA with such a horrible human being."

Having him voice my thoughts aloud is a comfort. I never imagined I'd feel this way, but knowing Ty makes me feel less alone.

"Yeah. I just… I hope…" I pause, and Ty reaches out to clap a hand on my shoulder.

"Listen carefully, Finn," he says, holding my gaze carefully. "Just because he's our father doesn't mean we're like him. Just because he's our own flesh and blood doesn't mean we need to claim him. His choices and the way he's chosen to live his life don't mean shit when it comes to us and our lives, okay?" I nod, trying to take his words to heart. "I'm a good person. You're a good person," he says and releases my shoulder. "Hell, the only time I've ever seen you fight is to protect another student. Even when it threatened to give you severe consequences. That's not something our father would do. In fact, it's the complete opposite. Okay?"

"Yeah," I agree, and I even think I mean it. He nods and starts to pack up, but I pull him up short with a question on a different topic. "Is there any way you can get me a class schedule for another student?"

His brow furrows. "Who?"

"Scottie. She's still having a hard time, and I don't want her to fall behind for missing classes. Your stuff is easy to get, but I don't even know what she's supposed to be in other than this since it's a new semester."

He doesn't hesitate to open his laptop and log in to the university database to get the info for me, and I jot it down in my notebook. Now, I can get a plan together to make sure she has notes for everything when she's ready.

I want to do more for her, to be able to love her out loud and in person, but until she's ready, this will have to do.

Scottie

My face feels swollen and my mind groggy as I sit up in bed and look around my room. My hair is still damp, my towel wrapped haphazardly around me, but from the fading light of dusk outside, I can tell quite a bit of time has passed.

My stomach growls, and I rub at the thinning part of my waist in an attempt to quell it. I don't recommend the fucked-up parent diet, but it's pretty goddamn effective.

Still, if I have any shot at keeping up my ability to function at a high level for cheerleading, I'm going to have to stop skipping meals at some point.

Newly determined, I drag myself off my bed to my dresser for clothes and pull on the first thing I touch. A silver lining of total emotional devastation, perhaps—I'm not really concerned with my outfits.

I slide on my comfiest pair of Uggs and head for the door, key and wallet in hand. A small breeze blows in as I open the door to the hall, and a ruffling stack of papers on the floor catches my attention. There's also a cup of hot chocolate from the coffee cart outside of Brower and a brown bag of goodies, the steaming dragon logo on the side of both unmistakable.

I reach for the papers first, flipping through quickly. There are notes for all the classes I missed today and a white piece of paper at the back with a single quote printed across it.

What's gone and what's past help, should be past grief.

It's from *The Winter's Tale*, and I can't think of a single person in our friend group whom I didn't spam with it while reading it. I resonated with the powerful nature of how it reflects on how we encounter circumstances in life that are beyond our control and believed its notion that it's more productive to acknowledge what's happened and accept it so that we can heal and free ourselves from the burden of grief.

But the girl who loved that quote doesn't even exist anymore.

She was naïve and hopeful and endlessly romantic in the worst way. She thought she knew hardship and grit, but she had no freaking clue.

Friday February 7th
Scottie

I zip up my coat and walk out the doors of Brower into the dark, frigid wind with my cheerleading duffel and a bag full of sustenance—snacks in every form—in hand.

As the second month of the semester starts up, I'm finally starting to find a rhythm. It's clunky and well offbeat, but I don't spend every second of my life locked away in my dorm either.

As the whispers have dulled, I've found the strength to go back to class, and my performance at cheerleading practice is getting back up to snuff. With NCA Nationals coming up and my alternate expelled out of the picture, Coach Jordan has been on the brink of a breakdown, waiting for the old, capable me to show back up.

Tonight's practice was the first time she didn't make herself hoarse from screaming at me to get it together.

But missing nearly three full weeks' worth of classes has taken a toll. I have two quizzes to make up in calculus, an essay on abstract expressionism to write for art history, and about three hundred pages of reading in *Anna Karenina* for English Lit to catch up on—and not a whole hell of a lot of time in which to do it.

Julia and Kayla have been champs, though, checking in and getting notes from my classes without request or complaint. Considering we don't have a lot of classes together, I know it took a serious amount of coordination, and it's the one thing that's been keeping me afloat.

Thankfully, we have this weekend off from cheerleading, so I'll have a full two days to get as caught up on everything as I can.

Once I'm back in my dorm, I take a quick shower to wash away the practice sweat and plop down on my futon with my bag of snacks and another cup of hot chocolate that's been left anonymously at my door.

It's funny how when I first got here, I longed for the friendships I left upstate. Now, I know that *these* are the formative years—the ones that create friends for a lifetime. I'll never forget this group of people and the way they've stepped up for me, even at my lowest of lows.

I put *Perfect Match*—my new reality show that I'm watching but not watching—on in the background and grab my copy of *Anna Karenina*.

While everyone else is going out for the night, I'm tucking in. I don't have even the slightest interest in going back to sorority and frat row—even if Delta Omega did lose their charter over the whole incident—and the Double C event I got a text for will be swarming with the kind of company I'm trying to avoid.

The social media notifications have calmed down, but the sex heard 'round the world has hardly disappeared entirely. Kayla's been insistent that people don't actually blame me for any of it—even the sorority getting shut down—but I find that hard to believe. She and Julia have both been coddling me too hard to ruin it by telling the harsh truth.

I flip to page ten of *Anna Karenina* and will myself to concentrate. It's not going to do me any good to read it without paying attention.

Just as I'm finishing the thought, an ironically distracting knock pounds on my door, and I shake my head with a laugh. "Well, then. Maybe old Anna's not meant to be right now."

Familiar voices outside are a comfort as I climb to my feet and open it.

"Hey, girl," Julia greets as Kayla pushes inside with a pizza box and makes herself at home.

"You got any paper plates?" Kayla asks, and Julia flashes me a little grin.

"Kay is starving, so she doesn't have time for pleasantries."

"Yes!" Kayla exclaims, already opening the pizza box to grab a slice. "I'm starving, and after that practice this afternoon, I know you have to be hungry too, Scottie."

I shrug. My appetite isn't exactly back to normal, but I know it won't ever be if I don't make myself start eating regularly again.

"So...uh... I'm happy you guys stopped by, but, like, what's the plan?" I ask as Julia and Kayla get comfortable. "You going out after this?"

"No way," Julia answers around a mouthful of cheese and sauce. "We're here for a girls' night sleepover."

"It's been flipping years since I've had a sleepover," Kayla comments and pops the tab on a soda she got from my fridge. "Did you guys have sleepovers when you were growing up?"

"All the time," Julia comments. "Up until I was about eight, I even used to have sleepovers with Ace."

"You guys have the strangest relationship," Kayla responds, making Julia's head explode. I can't blame her, honestly, with the number of times she's gone over this.

"I don't know why everyone keeps saying that! Ace and I are best friends, and we've known each other our whole lives. Everything about us is *normallll.*"

Kayla looks over at me to garner support, but when she realizes I'm still hovering by the door, she frowns. "What's wrong?"

"Nothing." I shake my head and stare at my feet, trying to gather the courage to say it out loud. "It's just that..." I pause and lift my gaze to meet theirs. "You guys really don't need to keep babying me, you know?"

"Babying you?" Julia asks, confusion evident in her voice. "What are you talking about?"

"Making sure I have all of my notes, leaving me hot chocolate every night, dropping off dinner and snacks," I list off everything they've been doing over the past month. "The old-school Discman with burned CDs with very specific playlists. I appreciate it all, and I'll admit, the 'I want to break shit' playlist has really gotten me through some rough days, but it's not necessary anymore. I'm doing okay. Almost good, even. You don't have to keep going out of your way for me. Okay?"

"Um…Scottie?" Julia ventures, her eyes darting to Kayla and back to me. "That wasn't us."

I furrow my brow. "What?"

"That was Finn," Kayla answers. "I mean, we helped him with a few things, like getting notes from some of your classes when he couldn't make it to that part of campus, but it was all his doing."

Everything has been *Finn* this whole time?

"He's been really worried about you," Julia says, her voice soft. "I know you guys have had your *moments* in the past, but Ace says Finn's officially in his *emotionally healthy era*." She rolls her eyes and laughs. "I mean, you know Ace, he's dramatic, but every time I've seen Finn this semester, he *has* seemed different. Steady, you know?"

My body feels warm, my hands tingly. The idea of an emotionally stable Finn Hayes is…overwhelming. And frankly, seems a little too good to be true.

"Again, it's none of my business, and I know there's been some shit that's gone down between the two of you," Julia says, and her eyes lock with mine. "But when a guy is willing to do the kinds of things he's been doing for you, I think he might be worth talking to."

I can't say I disagree with her. He's always been special, and I love him for a reason. But my heart can't take another U-turn. I won't survive it.

Wednesday February 12th

Finn

"I feel compelled to give a toast," Wendy, the matriarch of the Winslow family, announces as she rises to her feet, her majestically silver bob of hair shining under the overhead lights.

The entire gang is here—both the Winslows and the Hayeses—for the first time ever. All of us, in one house. We've been together in parts and pieces ever since the big news first broke, but it's hard to get this many people's schedules to align. But tonight, we're all here, Remy having bought Reece a last-minute plane ticket so he could fly home from California yesterday, and thankfully, Wendy's New York brownstone is big enough to fit us.

"Reece, Finn, Travis, Jack, and Willow," Wendy addresses, "seeing you all here, so young and vibrant, takes me back to when my boys and Winnie were young."

"Hear that?" Jude teases, pointing to the Winslow kids. "We're old now."

Wendy shushes him immediately. "I didn't ask for crowd participation, Jude, but now that you've mentioned it…yes, you're old. And so am I!"

Jude laughs, and Flynn elbows him to calm down when he starts choking on spit. Wendy carries on, undeterred. I imagine she's pretty used to all their shit anyway.

"I'd be honored if you called me Aunt Wendy, and I want you to know that you always have me in your corner. I'm always here for you." She smiles toward each of us.

"Aunt Wendy it is!" Trav exclaims, and she laughs.

"Thank you, Travis," Wendy says through a small laugh. "And Helen," she says my mother's name and looks across the dinner table at her. "I feel like I've gained a friend. A friend I hope I get to know more and more as the years go by. A friend I hope knows that I'm always here for her too. A friend I hope will one day understand the same things that it took me what feels like decades to realize. You are strong. You are beautiful. And you can do anything."

"Thank you, Wendy. That means more than you probably realize." My mother's voice shakes, and a sheen of tears shines in her eyes. She's been emotional since I set foot in the door, and she greeted me by wrapping me up in a big hug. The past two nights, we've had long phone conversations—that she initiated—and I'm happy to see her taking all of this in for the gift that it is. She's going through a lot right now, and after spending years in an abusive marriage, it's almost like she has to retrain her brain.

Maybe I should be mad at her for staying in that situation as long as she did, but I've never seen my mom as the problem. When she married Jeff Hayes, she had no idea what she was getting into, and once the cycle of abuse started, his ability to manipulate and control was too much for a woman with five young kids. She was a victim like the rest of us, just trying to survive. How can I be angry at her for that?

"Let's raise our glasses to the Hayes family," Wendy starts to cheers, but Jude is quick to pipe up again. I have no idea how, but he loves to stir shit even more than Ty.

"And what about us, Mom?" he asks with a wry smirk. "You got anything sweet to say about your actual kids? You know, other than us being old?"

His wife Sophie doesn't hesitate to slap him on the back of the head. "Ignore him. Please."

"Hey now!" Jude retorts on a chuckle. "All I'm saying is she could've thrown us a bone, you know?" He looks over at Remy, who just stares back at him with annoyance. Then he looks at Flynn, who pretty much does the same.

His sister Winnie immediately says, "Don't even try to wrangle me into your needy bullshit."

"Yeah, Jude," Ty agrees. "If you need someone to suck your cock, ask your wife." The whole house devolves into an uproar, and Jack and Trav share a high five. One thing about putting all ten offspring of that asshole Jeff together is that things are going to get crazy.

"To the first official Winslow-Hayes Family Dinner Night," Remy announces, wading into the melee to calm us all down. His wife Maria raises her glass high in the air, and we all follow suit.

I cheers my glass of lemonade with the people closest to me—Flynn, Flynn's wife Daisy, Jack, and Willow—and allow myself a small moment of wonder.

From where I started to here had a really steep learning curve, but it's taught me an important lesson I'll keep with me forever. Hard things are worth it.

"Now, how about some fucking spaghetti?" Jude announces with a big-ass grin on his face. Wendy starts to open her mouth to chastise him, but her words turn into an outright laugh when Jude makes a show of walking the bowl of pasta over to his mom to serve her. "For my beautiful mother. The best mother in the entire world." He looks over at Helen. "No offense, Aunt Helen."

My mom just laughs, and Ty picks up a piece of garlic bread to toss at Jude's head. Jude dodges it on a chuckle.

My newest brothers might be middle-aged men, but they still act like kids. Not a single one of them is the uptight, better-than-thou persona I had imagined the first time I found out about their existence.

"You know what's crazy?" Travis questions as he serves himself a giant helping of spaghetti. "Jeff Hayes…Jeff Winslow—whatever you want to call that son of bitch—he might be a true piece of shit, but somehow, he managed to create incredibly good-looking offspring."

The sounds of cutlery clanking and people chatting stop on a dime.

"What?" Travis holds out both hands and shrugs. "I know I'm not the only one who sees that the Hayes and Winslow families aren't ugly. I mean, Winnie is beautiful with her blond hair and blue eyes. Flynn could be James Dean reincarnated. Remy might be in his fifties, but I swear, people probably confuse him with Superman. Ty could be Zac Efron's doppelgänger before his face got all fucked up." Our mom smacks him in the chest, but he keeps going. "And Jude looks like an old Abercrombie and Fitch model from back in the day." Everyone stares at Travis as he shoves a bite of spaghetti into his mouth and talks around his food. "My siblings aren't ugly either. Reece is a handsome fuck. It's annoying how attractive Finn is. Willow is so pretty that I feel like I spend most of my time beating high school douchebags off with a stick. And I'm *uberhot*, obviously, and since Jack is my twin, I guess he's okay-looking, too. It's just nuts, you know? Who would've thought an abusive drunk who's in prison for killing a cop could create such good-looking kids?"

When no one responds, Reece lets out a shocked laugh. "Bro, I think you might've taken that shit too far."

"Hey, I don't have any problem saying the silent part out loud." Travis just shrugs and shoves another bite of spaghetti into his mouth. "I know I'm not the only to pick up on that shit. Not to mention, how weird it is that all of our names start with the same letter—by birth order? Remy, Flynn, Ty, Jude, Winnie…Reece, Finn, Travis, Jack, Willow. It's fucking strange."

"Trav, honey?" my mom chimes in, and he looks over at her. "How about you just sit there and eat your food?"

Wendy lifts a hand to cover her mouth, giggles shooting up from her lungs in the process.

And pretty much everyone bursts into laughter. I'm not sure if it's out of actual humor or a coping mechanism. But all of us laugh for a good two minutes straight over Travis's observations that he probably should've just kept to himself.

"Has anyone heard from the kids?" Daisy asks once our laughter dies down, looking over at her husband—and my brother—Flynn. "I feel like they've all been gone a long time to pick up some pizza."

All day, my mom and Wendy have been cooking up a feast of spaghetti, garlic bread, chicken parmigiana, and sides. But when everyone started to show up and they realized how big the family gets when the Winslows and Hayeses are combined, they decided to send my sister Winnie's daughter Lexi out on a pizza run. Unfortunately, once she agreed to go, the rest of my new siblings' kids decided they wanted to join in on the fun too, which is a logistical nightmare because of how many of them there are. Wendy and her husband Howard offered up their Sprinter van for capacity.

Not even five minutes later, Lexi, Remy's girls Carmen and Izzy, Flynn's twin sons Roman and Ryder, Ty's daughter Emily, Winnie's son and Lexi's brother Wes Jr., and Jude's son Hawk and his daughter Meadow all piled into the fucker like the next act on this year's Circus tour.

Their ages run from eleven to fifteen—which is crazy because they're not much younger than Willow.

"Have no fear. I have Life 360 on Hawk's phone, and it looks like they're only a few miles away," Jude's wife Sophie says, and Daisy furrows her brow.

"You only have Hawk on Life 360? Not Meadow?"

Sophie laughs. "Have you met my son?"

"True," Daisy agrees, and Remy's wife Maria grins.

"I think Rem and I would be in an early grave if we had a Hawk."

"That's because, like Mom says, we're old as shit, honey," Remy teases, and Maria nudges him with her elbow. Wendy rolls her eyes. "Or, at least, I am. You, my beautiful wife, don't look a day over thirty-five. I look fifty-fucking-eight."

"That's because you are," Jude razzes. "You're old as shit."

"Yeah, but he ages like a fine wine," Maria says and presses a kiss to Remy's lips.

All this open affection is commonplace here, but it's the opposite of what I'm used to.

I grew up in a house where the only love that existed was the love my mother gave us. I never saw love between my mother and father. Only anger. Only violence. Only hate. Only fear.

Their DNA is shit, but the Winslows are like a flower finding its way through a crack in concrete. It makes me feel like maybe I can be a flower too.

"Hey, Remy," Maria says, and he looks over at his wife. "Don't you think now is a good time to…you know…"

He searches her eyes for a long moment, but when realization dawns on him, he nods in understanding. "Oh, right." He stands and raises his glass in the air. "I know Mom just did a toast, but I have some news that I think deserves another." He moves his eyes to my mom. "Helen, I know I'm not the only one here who is proud of you for having the strength to leave a man who has affected all our lives. A man who doesn't deserve a single person in this room."

A few tears stream from my mom's eyes. Wendy sniffles.

"Maria and I know the challenges that you face," he continues. "We consider you a part of our family now. And I'm not sure if you've realized this yet, but when you're our family, we have your back."

"Yes, we do!" Jude exclaims. Flynn, Ty, and Winnie all nod in agreement.

"And since the man who doesn't even deserve for us to speak his name is behind bars and awaiting a trial that will undoubtedly lock him away forever, we think you deserve a fresh start. A home that you can fill with happy memories and love," he explains.

"Uncle Brad wants his lake house back, doesn't he?" Jude teases, earning a flip of the middle finger from Remy.

"We've located a house in Westchester for you and Jack and Travis and Willow. It's a nice five-bedroom home, big enough for

Finn and Reece if they come home for the summers. It's within walking distance to the high school, and it's only a ten-minute drive to your job."

"Remy. Maria." My mother's head begins to shake back and forth in shock. "W-what are you saying?"

"We're saying that the house is yours. It's fully paid off and ready for you to move in," Remy announces, and Maria stands up to hand my mother a small white box with a pretty yellow bow.

My mother's hands tremble as she opens it, and when she pulls out a shiny pair of keys from the box, tears start to fall from her eyes. "W-what? No. I can't accept—"

"Yes, you can," Maria says, tears in her eyes now too. "You're family, Helen."

"Yes, Helen." Wendy stands up from her chair and walks over to my mom. "You're family. We love you."

Wendy and my mother hug, and everyone in the room is a mixture of tears, smiles, and outright surprise. Even Travis and Jack have slack jaws and wide eyes, little salty tear trails on their cheeks.

Remy just bought my mother a house. An entire fucking house. Because he wants to help us.

"Thank you so much," my mom says through her tears, and she walks over to Remy and Maria to wrap them up in her arms. "You have no idea what this means to me. To us. I just don't know how I'll ever repay you."

"You being a part of our family is payment enough," Wendy says, and fresh tears trail down my mom's cheeks. Willow is crying now too. I'm speechless.

I never dreamed it could be like this.

The door bursts open, and Roman, Ryder, and Hawk are the first ones to run inside with stacks of pizza boxes in their arms.

"Dinner is served!" Hawk shouts at the top of his lungs. But when he sees that the room is filled with people hugging and crying, his feet to skid to a stop. "What the eff?"

Roman and Ryder nearly barrel into him, and their reaction

is the peak of confusion. "Um, what the hell is going on?" Roman questions, and Ryder's brow furrows.

"Mom?"

"We're just happy, sweetheart," Daisy says, and Ryder's brow only furrows deeper.

"Happy?" he questions. "This looks like a scene out of a fucking funeral."

"*Roman!*" Daisy chastises through her tears.

"What? What'd I say?"

My brother Flynn heads over to his twin teenage sons, and he doesn't hesitate to corral them away from the dining room and into the kitchen. Hawk follows along voluntarily with a piece of pizza hanging out of his mouth.

Things may look and sound normal to someone else, but to me, my universe is rattled.

My mom and siblings are safe. My father can no longer hurt us anymore. My family, my support system, has tripled in size.

I'm not only worthy of love; I'm capable of giving it.

And one day, Scottie will be ready to receive it. Maybe I need to wait a little less patiently.

Scottie

I stop in the middle of a sentence of *Anna Karenina* and pause my TV, listening again to see if my ears are playing tricks on me. It's well after midnight on a Wednesday night, and I swear I just heard a knock on my door.

Another three more knocks, these harder than the first, I set my book down beside me on my bed and wrap my robe around my body nervously. A few seconds pass before my phone pings with a text message.

Finn: It's me.

My heart jumps to my throat, worry and curiosity swirling manically as I try to figure out what he's doing here at this time of night. Two more messages populate on the screen.

Finn: I know it's late, but I really need to talk to you.

Finn: Please, Scottie.

My lungs feel heavy as I labor over simple breaths. I haven't seen or talked directly to Finn since Christmas Day—which is my fault, I know. But after talking to Kayla and Julia last week, the depths of my guilt over that decision are more vast and expansive than ever before. He's been single-handedly keeping me alive, and all I've done is ignore him.

I slowly climb off my bed, heading for my door, anxiety and excitement and the fear of the unknown rolling through my veins.

Finn's face is as handsome as I've ever seen it. His jaw is firm and his eyes are intense, but just as Julia suggested, there's a peace about him that immediately puts me at ease.

"Tonight, I was at dinner with my family," he says, completely skipping over pleasantries and small talk. "My *whole* family. My siblings—even Reece flew in from California. My mom. Ty and his siblings and their wives and husbands and kids. Their mom, Wendy. Everyone was there. And everyone was getting along and having a good time. I honestly don't know if I've ever seen my mom and brothers and sister this relaxed and comfortable and *happy*. And I was sitting there, watching the interactions and listening to the conversations and thinking about how far everything has come. I was thinking about how our father is in jail for heinous crimes he committed prior to meeting my mom. I was thinking about how Ty and his brothers—my brothers—are happily married with wives and kids, and they are living healthy, stable lives. They don't drink too much or get violent with their families. All they do is love their wives, love their kids. They're all good men. Probably the best men I've ever known. And even though they have the same father as me, they are nothing like our father. And that reality shook me to my core. It made me realize so many things that I've been avoiding. And most of all, the only person I wanted to talk about it with was you."

I don't think I've ever heard Finn ramble on like this. He's not a talker or a conversationalist. He's quiet and broody, and it's a rare—pretty much nonexistent—occurrence when he is actually willing to let me see inside his head like this.

"Finn, I—" I stop when he raises a hand.

"Just let me finish first, okay? There's so much I want to tell you right now. So much I want to get off my chest. So much I need you to hear. So much you deserve to hear."

I nod and he takes a breath, his eyes moving down to the floor for the briefest of moments before meeting mine again.

"I've been a fucking idiot, Scottie. And I've thought about this moment in my head a thousand times, desperately trying to come

up with the right words to tell you. The right words to convey everything I want to say. But I'm not the best with words, and I'm shit
at facing hard feelings head on. But I want to change." He shrugs.
"I know I've pushed you away more times than I can count. I know
I've said ugly things to you that you didn't deserve, and I know I've
hurt you deeply." He grabs my hand and puts it flat to his chest, and
I swallow hard at the feel of his racing heart.

"I'm so fucking sorry for all the times I avoided you because
the way you made me feel was too much for me to understand."
His voice breaks, a tear falling to the floor between us. "I'm sorry I
blamed you for caring about me as much as you did, and I'm sorry
for all the times you needed me and I wasn't there."

His words are like bullets, hitting me one after another, straight
in the chest and shaking my entire equilibrium.

"For the longest time, I've feared that I would become just like
my dad," he continues, but his voice grows quiet. "But I'm more than
him. And you're more than your mom. And together, we're more
than all the mistakes we've made in the past."

He squeezes my hand, holding it on his chest with a ferocity
that makes my knees shake. "I love you, Scottie. Confidently and
completely and with the knowledge that my love is *worth* something.
And I know after everything that's happened between us that you
have every right to tell me to walk back out that door…but I'm hoping that you'll give me a second chance."

I have a choice. I can crawl back under my comforter and let
the consequences of my mother's actions consume me, or I can move
forward with Finn to the kind of love we both deserve.

I've been burned once before by stepping out on a limb, but
Finn's spent the last two months proving that his branch is strong
enough to handle my weight.

The first choice would certainly be easier. But sometimes, hard
things are worth it.

70

Finn

Scottie's eyes are big as they stare into mine, her hand on my chest the only thing keeping my heart inside. I have no idea what she's going to say or do, but I will myself to have the patience to wait it out.

"I know it's been you," she says, and her voice is so soft, so quiet, that I almost don't even hear her. "I know you've been the one who was making sure I had notes for all my classes. I know you're the one who has been leaving me dinner and snacks and hot chocolates to make sure I eat. And I know you're the one who left me that old-school Discman with all the playlist CDs."

"I didn't know what to do," I tell her. "You needed space, and well, I wanted to find a way to support you, to be there for you. I'm sorry if I—"

She doesn't wait for me to finish. "When Julia and Kayla told me it was you, I just about burst into tears. I almost called you. Texted you. Showed up at your dorm," she says, and I jerk my head back in surprise.

"You did?"

She nods. "I wanted to talk to you, but I...I don't know...so much had happened between us, you know?"

Fuck. "I know."

"I love you, Finn," she says, a sparkly sheen of tears making the green of her eyes mossy. "My feelings for you haven't changed. And after everything you just told me, forgiving you feels easier than breathing."

"Tell me I'm not hearing shit. Tell me you just said you love me and you can forgive me."

"I love you, Finn. And I think it's long past time we forgive ourselves and each other."

"Fuck, Scottie," I whisper, and I can't stop myself from stepping forward to lift her into my arms. My mouth finds her lips, and I kiss her with the kind of intensity that has us both gasping for air. But I don't stop. I *can't* stop. I feel like I've waited ten lifetimes for this.

"I love you, Scottie," I say, my mouth still pressed against hers. I can taste the salt from her tears as they slide down her cheeks and mingle with our mouths. "I love you so fucking much."

I walk us over to the bed, gently laying her down on the mattress, and I move to lie beside her, but she surprises me by gripping my T-shirt with both hands and pulling me directly over top of her. She wraps her legs around my waist, and her hips jolt forward to press against me. "Please, Finn," she begs. "I need you. I've needed you. I've needed this."

I stare deep into her eyes, wondering if this is the right thing, wondering if this is moving too fast. "Are you sure?"

"I haven't felt like myself in two months. Until now. Being here, with you, like this…I feel so much like me."

Slowly, I remove her socks and pajama pants and underwear. And when she sits up, I lift her shirt above her head. She leans forward to undo the button and zipper on my jeans, and I kick off my socks and boots so she can shove them and my briefs down my legs.

And when I start to climb back onto the bed, she drags my T-shirt over my head so that we're skin-to-skin.

"I love you, Scottie," I tell her again just before I press my mouth to hers. "I love you," I say between kisses down her neck. "I love you," I say as my lips make a path across her breasts. "I love you," I keep saying as I kiss every single inch of her body.

I don't know how many times I say it, but I know that I could say it a million more times and it would still not feel like enough.

By the time I'm rolling a condom over my hard cock and

kneeling between her thighs, we're both breathing hard, needy and desperate for each other.

And when I finally slide inside her, when my cock is filling her up and the warmth of her breasts is pressed against my chest and a little moan slips from her mouth and into mine, my truth is absolute.

Sometimes when history repeats itself, it's because it's supposed to.

71

"**H**appy birthday to me!" Ace cheers loudly when he steps into Zip's Diner, owning his role of birthday boy arrival pretty much exactly how I expected him to and entering a superhero stance as his eyes find us.

He wears a sash that reads Birthday Boy strung over his tuxedo—*yes, a tuxedo*—and a fake gold crown on his head. "Nineteen, baby! Let the good times roll!"

Julia smiles and rolls her eyes as she heads toward the table we reserved for the big night, where a few of us are already seated. The location, the vibe, and the decorations were all chosen by Julia, and the rest of us chipped in to help where we could. There are gold and black balloons everywhere and confetti on the tables, and still, Ace is the fanciest thing in the place. I'd say it's precisely how it should be.

Ace strides over with a big-ass smile on his face and stops at the only filled table in the entire diner. His eyes move over the streamers, the balloons that have his face plastered on the front of them, and the *Happy Birthday, Asshole* banner we have hanging from the ceiling.

He laughs his ass off at the matching T-shirts—with his face on them—that we're all wearing.

"Jules, you've really outdone yourself," he says and wraps his arm around her shoulders to tuck her closer to his side. He presses a kiss to her forehead. "Thank you."

Their affection combined with their just-friends status is either the biggest prank Ace has ever played on everyone or the biggest prank he's ever played on himself. The fact that he believes the two of them are just friends when he looks at her like he does might as well be the ninth wonder of the world. According to Finn, though, Ace had been on-and-off dating some chick named Scarlett for months now.

I wonder where she is tonight.

Blake and Finn stand up to give Ace a hug and a manly back-pat, and Kayla and I follow their lead, though our hug for the birthday boy is a little less macho.

When Julia told me her plans for throwing Ace a small, low-key birthday party like this, I questioned the whole thing. I mean, Ace is the social king. He loves parties and crowds and being surrounded by people. But with the way he's smiling and laughing and looking so damn happy, I guess Julia knows him better than anyone else.

Plus, it probably helps that his parents have some kind of mystery trip planned that has him and Julia and both of their parents flying out tomorrow. They have no idea where they're going or what they're doing, and knowing Ace's parents, I don't know if I'd be excited or terrified.

I can't wait to hear about all of it when they get back.

"You want a slice of cake?" Finn asks, his hand pressed gently against my back.

I nod, and he touches a kiss to my lips.

"I swear, the two of you are so adorable, it kind of makes me want to puke," Kayla teases and Julia giggles.

"I think I'm with Kay. No one should be allowed to be so damn cute together."

Finn doesn't balk at their words, instead, pressing one more kiss to my lips. This time, he adds enough tongue to make it nearly NSFW or public consumption.

I try to be strong, try to keep the kiss PG, but damn, I swear, whenever this man's lips are on mine, I kind of forget anything else exists.

I could kiss Finn for hours—days, weeks, months—and never get tired of it. Last Saturday night, after we got back from a Double C event at Dragon Stadium, we lay in my bed and kissed for I don't even know how long. Seriously. I woke up the next morning with my lips half pressed to his.

It's insane. *Indescribable.* And shouldn't be legal. But hell's bells, I'm so glad it is.

Kayla fakes a gagging sound, and Finn stops kissing me on a chuckle, heading over to where Ace and Blake stand near the cake.

"I just want you to know," Julia says, a soft whisper into my ear. "I'm so happy for you, Scottie. This is the kind of love you deserve." She gives me a gentle hug and then spins on her heel to stop Ace from shoving his entire face into the cake. "Ace! If you mess up that cake, I will stab you with this knife."

"Ohhhh, is that a threat?" he teases with both hands in the air. "Because it sounds kinky, Jules."

With a roll of her eyes—and a secret grin—Julia shoves him out of the way, and Ace smirks down at her as she cuts the expensive bakery cake she got for his birthday.

But before any slices are passed out, Blake's phone pings with a notification.

Both Ace's and Finn's phones are next.

Then mine, Julia, and Kayla's.

McKinley Library. Back entrance. 15 minutes.

"Looks like Double C is calling our name," Ace announces.

"You sure you want to go tonight?" Blake questions. "I'm happy to see that my future wife texted me first—clearly, she wants me there—but I think we need to let the birthday boy decide what we do tonight."

"Are you kidding me, son?" Ace retorts with a big-ass smile. "This is fucking perfect. Let's go!"

"What about your cake?" Julia asks, and Ace just slides the sucker back into its box and picks it up.

"Looks like we're taking it to go, Jules!" he exclaims and takes her hand. "Let's hit it!"

I'd question leaving the balloons and streamers and banner and all the other random birthday shit we brought to Zip's, but Ace is apparently besties with the owner. "Yo, Zippity-Doo-Da! We gotta jet!"

"No worries!" the gray-haired man I'm assuming is Zip calls back from behind the counter. "We'll handle the mess! You kids go have fun. Happy birthday, Ace!"

"Is it just me, or do you find it almost creepy how Ace seems to know everyone?" I ask Finn as we walk out of Zip's Diner. Ace is already striding up the sidewalk with Julia's hand still in his and the cake clutched to his side.

"I've given up on understanding it," Finn comments, flashing a little smile in my direction.

"Honestly, he might not even be a real human," I say. "He's probably, like, a robot or AI or an alien from an alternate universe. I mean, he managed to get you to be his friend, which is the equivalent of a miracle."

"A miracle?" he questions with a smirk. "You saying I'm difficult?"

"I'm saying you're, like, bad-boy complicated." I nudge his hip with mine. "Lucky for you, I love bad boys."

"Hey now," he says and surprises the hell out of me by lifting me up into the air and over his shoulder. He playfully slaps my ass. "I better be the only bad boy you love."

I'm giggling now, and he taps my ass again with his hand. "I promise!" I squeal when he tickles my side. "You're the only bad boy I love!"

"Good," he says, but he doesn't put me down on my feet.

"C'mon, Finn, you can't carry me all the way to McKinley like this."

"Watch me."

I shit you not, Finn carries me the entire ten-minute walk to

McKinley Library and doesn't set me on my feet until we're standing in front of the back entrance.

"You're a lunatic, Finn Hayes," I whisper to him and pinch his firm ass cheeks for good measure. He grins down at me and wraps his arm around my shoulders as Lexi opens the back entrance doors to let us all inside.

There are at least seventy or so people are here tonight, and Connor is at the door handing everyone flashlights.

Lexi stands guard until the last person is through the door, which is well behind us, and then shuts the door and puts the security system back on.

As she walks past us to the front of the crowd, Blake gets lost in his feels again. "What's her deal? Seriously? She's a grad student, right?"

I make wide eyes at Finn, while Ace does his best to be delicate. "Blake, dude, give it up already. She wants nothing to do with you."

I nearly laugh. To Ace, being blunt is being gentle.

"I don't get it," I whisper into Finn's ear, getting up on my tiptoes to reach. "Blake could have any girl on campus, but he's fawning over the one girl who continues to show that she doesn't want anything to do with him."

Finn's smile is unbelievably sweet as he shrugs. "I guess you can't help who you love."

"Hey, Lexi, how'd you get the security codes?" Ace heckles from our spot in the crowd as she's preparing to speak.

She doesn't bother giving him a response. "Tonight, you're going to try to find history," she announces. "Our university's founder, the late Harold Dickson, is rumored to have discovered a devastating truth about his pregnant wife in 1923. Per the century-long gossip mill, Harold found out that his wife Anastasia was having an affair with a high-ranking member of a royal family in Europe and that their baby was not his. Somewhere in this library are letters that reveal the truth."

Lexi looks around the room and flips on her flashlight. "Was his wife Anastasia really having an affair? Who was the high-ranking member of the royal family? Is Harold Dickson Jr. actually Harold's son? No one has been able to find the letters between Anastasia and her mystery royal lover, but they're rumored to be here, somewhere inside these walls," she announces. "Tonight, your mission is to find those letters. Find the truth."

Connor flips on his flashlight and steps up to take over for Lexi. "You have three hours, and you're in luck because tonight, there is no entry fee. Since no one was able to find the golden football in Dragon Stadium last week, we've rolled that pot over to tonight."

"What's the pot at?" someone in the crowd asks.

"A lot," Lexi answers with a grin. "I highly recommend you split off into groups. Three hours isn't much time to hit every inch of this library by yourself."

Ace, Blake, Kayla, Julia, Finn, and I group up without hesitation. We agreed a long time ago to work together, and after everything that happened over winter break, I petitioned to add Kayla to the Double C mix. We got in trouble with Lexi the first time we brought her, but now that Finn's her uncle, there wasn't much she could do.

The birthday boy guides us toward the staircase that leads to the basement of the library, ready to get started.

"Hold on." Julia holds up a hand and stops walking. "Wouldn't the basement be too obvious?" she questions, and Ace turns around to meet her eyes.

"You think you have a better place to start, Jules?"

She nods, but she doesn't voice it. Instead, she gestures for all of us to lean in closer to her so the rest of the crowd doesn't overhear. "I think we need to start in the attic."

"There's a fucking attic?" Ace asks, and she slaps her palm over his mouth.

"Yes, Ace. There's an attic," she whispers and stares at Ace with wide, knowing eyes. "But not a lot of people know about it, and I'm hoping to keep it that way."

"How the hell do you know about it then, Jules?" Ace whispers, and Julia shrugs.

"A guy from my history class showed it to me a few weeks ago."

"What guy?" Ace questions, and his voice is rising again.

"Just some guy I'm doing a group project with," Julia answers, and she's already heading toward a different part of the library, her eyes not realizing Ace looks like someone just shot his puppy.

"Jules, what's his name?" Ace asks, picking up his pace to catch up with her.

But I don't get to hear her answer because Finn grabs my hand and drags me toward the stacks. "Finn!" I whisper-yell, and he just grins at me over his shoulder. "What are you doing?"

"I want to show you something."

I giggle and follow his lead. As we're walking, I find myself thinking about how far we've come over the past month and a half. Ever since he showed up at my dorm that one night, things have been different. Amazing, actually. The first week after we got back together, we spent a lot of time having real conversations and talking about the things we both had missed when we weren't on speaking terms.

He told me everything that has been going on with his father. He told me about the Winslow family and what they've done for his mom and his siblings. He told me Reece is going to be transferring to Dickson next year. He told me what his reality was like when he was a kid living with an abusive drunk as a father.

And I told him what my life was like when my dad was still with my mom and what it's been like for me since she showed up at that frat party. I even told him more about my sister Wren and my dad.

It feels like we've talked about everything, but seeing Ace in his birthday boy sash tonight has me realizing there is one thing I've never asked him. "Finn, when is your birthday?"

"November 15th."

"November 15th?" A frown turns my lips into a crescent moon. "You mean I missed your birthday?"

"It's no big deal." He guides us through the rows and rows of books, and he doesn't come to a stop until we're so far from everyone else that I can no longer hear quiet chatter or see the glow of moving flashlights.

"It feels like a big deal," I say, sadness evident in my voice. "I missed your birthday, and I didn't even get you a present."

"Good news, Scottie. I don't want anything but you," he whispers and turns off both of our flashlights.

"What the heck?" I nearly shout when darkness consumes us. "I can't see any—"

His mouth is on mine before I can even finish my train of thought. He slides his fingers into my hair, and I don't hesitate to return the kiss with fervor.

Before I know it, my legs are wrapped around his waist and his big hands are gripping my ass.

Goodness, this feels amazing.

I lean my head back, and his mouth makes a path down my neck and between my breasts. My eyes have adjusted to the darkness now, and I watch as he pulls my shirt and bra down with his teeth so that his mouth can wrap around one pert nipple.

My hips jerk against him when he sucks it into his mouth.

And he's hard beneath his jeans, so hard against me, that my mind starts wondering what Finn's cock would feel like in my mouth.

Finn moves his attention to my other breast, and a deep, throbbing ache starts to form between my thighs. I press myself against him again and that only makes me think about his hard cock more.

What does he taste like? What would he feel like against my tongue?

Over the past few weeks since we officially got together, we've had a lot of sex, but I've never actually had him in my mouth.

The thought becomes all-consuming until I slide down his body and onto my knees. His hair falls over his eyes as he stares down at me. His eyes showcase a myriad of things—heat and confusion and want and desire. And it's all I need to see to get the courage to unzip his jeans.

"Scottie?"

"I want to do this," I say and pull him free of his boxers and jeans. His cock is so hard now that it juts out from his body, and the smallest drop of pre-come sits on the tip. I lick my lips. "I need to do this."

I don't give him any time to respond. I sneak my tongue out to steal a taste, and when the sweetness of him hits my taste buds, I slide my mouth over his hard length.

His hips jolt forward at the sensation, and it makes me feel powerful. It also makes me throb.

I suck, gently at first, and build up the pressure when his hands slide into my hair in the most affectionate but gently possessive way. He needs this as much as I need this, and I'm instantly high from it.

"Fuck, Scottie," he whispers through a moan. "I never want those lips of yours to touch any other cock but mine."

"Never," I hum.

"And my mouth will never touch any pussy but yours. Never. Fucking never."

"Yes."

I suck him deeper into my mouth and when I feel his body tense up with pleasure, I keep going. I suck and suck and suck and suck. And I don't stop sucking until the throb between my thighs becomes almost intolerable.

I suck until Finn tries to pull away before he comes, but I grab his hips and keep him right there, so I can swallow down his pleasure.

And I savor every single drop.

72

Fresh out of a shower, I walk into my room and find Ace lounging on his bed, watching an episode of *One Tree Hill* on the giant big-screen television that has no business being in our small-ass room. It's his newest binge show, and I've basically been forced into watching it with him.

"Dude! Shit is popping off!" he exclaims. "Lucas just revealed he knows who tried to kill Dan in the dealership fire!"

I kind of hate myself for even knowing what he's talking about, but I lie down on my bed with my eyes on the television because I'm a masochist.

My phone vibrates on my nightstand, and I check the screen to find a text from Scottie.

> **Scottie: Can you come over to my dorm? I have a bit of an emergency.**
>
> **Me: What? Are you okay?**
>
> **Scottie: Yeah, I'm okay, but can you get over here soon?**

Shit. I'm off my bed and sliding shoes onto my feet without hesitation. I slip my phone, wallet, and keys into the pockets of my sweats and toss a hoodie over my head.

"Where are you going?" Ace questions, but his eyes never leave the television.

"I'll be back. Scottie needs me."

He sits up in bed. "She okay?"

"Yeah." *I fucking hope.*

I'm out the door, down the elevator, and onto the sidewalk in two minutes flat. And I basically jog the entire way from Graham Hall to Delaney. By the time I'm standing in front of her dorm room door, I'm out of breath and in a full-blown panic.

"Scottie?" I call out as I knock my knuckles against her door.

She swings it open a second later, and I just about fall on my ass when I see her standing on the other side. My girl is completely naked, and her hands hold out a cupcake with a candle in the center.

"Happy birthday, Finn," she says, and her mouth quirks up into the cutest fucking smile I've ever seen. Her cheeks are flushed pink, like she's a little embarrassed, and her teeth dig into her bottom lip. "I know it's a little late, but I hope you'll forgive me."

I'm already walking into her room, gently shoving her back so I can shut the door and ensure that no assholes see my gorgeous girlfriend's perfect body.

"Make a wish," she says, and I don't hesitate to blow out the candle.

My wish—*let me keep this girl forever.*

"Did you make it a good one?" she asks, and I take the cupcake from her hands.

"It's the best fucking wish I've ever made in my life."

Scottie grins. "What was it?"

"I can't tell you that. I need that wish to come true more than I need fucking oxygen."

She looks at me curiously, but I'm already moving her back toward her bed. Once she's lying down on the mattress, I take the cupcake and smash the fucker all over her perfect tits and stomach.

"Finn!" she squeals, and I just grin up at her.

"I think it's time to eat some cake." I dive right in, licking my tongue across her breasts and sucking each nipple into my mouth. The cupcake is good, but it's no match for Scottie.

She moans and her hips squirm, and my cock is already so hard I could hammer fucking nails.

I lick the cake off her body, letting my tongue make a path from her breasts and down her belly, but when something black catches my attention in my periphery, I lift my head to look down at her left hip.

Finn.

My name. Tattooed on her perfect skin. Right below her panty line. It's small and delicate and so fucking perfect I don't even know what to say.

"It's not real," she says on a rush, and I lift my eyes to meet hers. "But I don't know…the more I look at it, the more I want it to be real." She smiles then. "I know I'm like six months late, but… Happy birthday, Finn."

I told her I wanted her for my birthday. And this is what she did.

I climb back up her body, not caring that cake is now being smashed against my clothes, and I press my mouth to hers. "I love you so fucking much."

I don't know what I did to deserve this girl, but I know I'll never stop loving her. Never stop protecting her. Never stop trying to be the man that she deserves.

Never.

73

"**J**ust so you know," Finn says as he stops right outside a pretty brownstone that makes my knees shake even harder than they already were.

Meeting the family is a huge milestone in any relationship, but meeting the family your boyfriend just found out he had in a house bigger than *Pretty Woman*'s Blue Banana is on a whole other level.

"My family has now tripled in size."

"Tripled?" I question incredulously, doing the quick math in my head. "How has it tripled? There were five of you before and five more now, that stands to reason that it would have doubled. The math isn't mathing."

He smiles. "You know what, you're right." I sigh a deep breath of relief, but he cuts it off to continue, "There *are* five new siblings, but they're all married, and they all have kids. So, it's not really tripled. More like quintupled."

"Finn Hayes, you are not helping!" I whisper-yell.

He winks and takes my hand to lead us up the stairs. "Relax, babe. It's going to be all good."

He seems confident, but that doesn't mean I believe him.

The door swings open before Finn even has a chance to knock, and a young teenage boy with bright-blue eyes and a stylish mohawk answers. "Yo, Finn. You're late." His eyes move over to me, and immediately, a small smile etches on his mouth. "And you've brought a friend," he states and says *friend* as if there's a far bigger meaning to the word.

Finn just claps him on the shoulder. "I did bring a friend. My *girlfriend*, Scottie."

"Hi, Scottie," the teenager says and holds out his hand. "It is my greatest pleasure to meet you." He makes a show of taking my hand in his and kissing the top of it.

Finn shoves him away from me with a laugh. "Okay, Hawk, that's enough flirting with my girl."

His name strikes me as completely odd, but somehow, it also fits the handsome teen like a glove.

Finn takes my hand again and walks us into the house, and he doesn't stop until we're in the dining room that's overflowing with people and bursting at the seams with chatter and laughter. *Holy hell, he wasn't lying.* It's a miracle everyone is able to fit in here.

"Finn's here, Grandma!" a teenage girl with brown hair shouts, and a woman with silver-gray hair, and who looks to be in her seventies, peeks in from the kitchen to smile at us.

"Hi, Finn!" she greets.

"Hi, Aunt Wendy."

"Would you like to introduce us to your friend?" she asks and steps into the dining room as she's wiping her hands on her apron.

"Yeah, Finn, why don't you introduce us to your friend?" a handsome man questions with a wry grin. Hawk is now standing beside him, and their resemblance is so uncanny I would gamble a million dollars that they're father and son.

My eyes scan the room, and a sense of relief settles in my chest when I spot Jack, Travis, and Willow. Finn's sister immediately comes over and wraps me up in a big hug.

"I'm so happy you're here," she says, and I don't have to pretend that I feel the same.

"Me too."

"Everyone," Finn announces loud enough to draw the attention of every pair of eyes in the room. "This is my girlfriend, Scottie. Scottie, this is…everyone."

It's dumb that my heart still zings whenever I hear him say girlfriend, but I can't help it. I'm proud to be Finn Hayes's girlfriend. Happy. Elated. Grateful. Sometimes I feel like we've been to hell and back and it's a miracle we managed to find our way back to each other. And sometimes I think it's no miracle at all because we're meant to be.

Everyone in the room starts to head our way to formally introduce themselves. I meet Finn's mom Helen, and she wraps me up in the kind of warm hug that only a mother can give, and Wendy Winslow's hug is just as warm.

I meet Remy Winslow and his wife Maria and their daughters Carmen and Izzy.

I meet Flynn Winslow and his wife Daisy and their twin sons Roman and Ryder.

I meet Jude Winslow and his wife Sophie and their daughter Meadow. I also find out that I was right about Hawk being Jude's son.

I meet Winnie and her husband Wes and their son Wes Jr. I'm also introduced to their daughter Lexi Winslow and offer a secret smile in her direction.

And I say hello to Professor Ty Winslow and meet his wife Rachel and their daughter Emily.

It's strange seeing Professor Winslow outside of the lecture hall, but it's even stranger to see how close he and Finn have become. Though, I guess it shouldn't be much of a surprise. Over the past two months, I've witnessed more text conversations and phone calls between the two of them than I can count. I knew if Ty had known about Finn, he would care, and he's more than proven me right.

"Winslow-Hayes Family Dinner Night is officially served!" Wendy announces as she carries a massive bowl of chicken fettuccini alfredo into the dining room and sets it on the table. Helen is right behind her with an Italian salad, and Winnie is right behind her with a tray of garlic bread sticks.

Finn pulls out a chair for me to take a seat beside Willow, and he sits down on my other side beside Ty. Everyone dives into the food like they haven't eaten in days, and the laughter and chatter don't stop between bites.

Finn looks so damn happy that I can't swipe the smile off my face as I watch him talk to Ty and Wes about Dickson's football team's prospects for next year.

"I'm impressed with Boden," Wes says. "He's only a sophomore and damn near won his team a championship. If he can keep his mind off my daughter, he might even live to see the NFL."

I widen my eyes at Finn as Lexi snorts and shakes her head, and he mouths that he'll explain how Wes knows about Blake's crush on Lexi later.

"I'm going to remember this conversation when you're trying to draft him," Remy states, and Wes doesn't even balk.

"He plays like Quinn Bailey."

"And Quinn won you a championship," Remy remarks.

Lexi surprises us all when she looks across the table to meet my eyes. "You know the Dickson cheerleaders are better statistically than Dickson's football team? They've won more NCA Championships that any school in their division, and it all started decades ago. If you guys win this year, you'll set a Guinness World Record."

Finn wraps a proud arm around my shoulders. "Oh, don't worry, Lex. My girl is ready for Daytona next week. You can get the record book ready."

His girl. Swoon.

Lexi shakes her head, refuting him. "I don't have any contacts at Guinness."

I'm surprised she took him so literally, but nobody else is, and for my part, I don't have time to dwell on it. The conversation keeps moving at a million miles per hour.

"Scottie, you're on the cheerleading squad at Dickson?" Wendy asks and I nod.

"Yes."

"Are you nervous for the competition?" Ty's wife Rachel questions. "That seems like a crazy amount of pressure."

"Oh, it is." A nervous giggle escapes my lungs. "I've never been on a stage this big, but I've been doing competitive cheerleading my whole life, so I'm hoping it's prepared me for this."

"You're going to do great, Scottie," Finn says and presses a kiss to my cheek.

I don't miss the way Willow and Helen watch or the smiles that spread across their faces.

"I can't wait for the day I get to be a bridesmaid at your wedding," Willow whispers into my ear, and I just about choke on my garlic bread.

"Slow down, girl."

My shocked reaction doesn't faze her in the least. "Mark my words, Scottie. You're going to be a Hayes one day."

I know Finn overhears that last comment, but the man doesn't clam up. He doesn't look like he wants to run for the hills. He just presses a kiss to my forehead and continues eating his food.

On the outside, I'm playing it cool.

But on the inside, my heart is marking ideal dates on the calendar five to six years from now and scouring the internet for the perfect wedding dress.

Which is totally insane, *right?*

Wednesday April 9th
Finn

Scottie: Are you awake?

I glance at the clock and see it's only a little after six in the morning. Ace is sound asleep in his bed, and the room is completely dark because the sun hasn't even attempted to peek above the horizon.

I scrub a hand down my face and adjust my pillows to rest my back against my headboard.

Scottie left yesterday morning for NCA Nationals in Daytona Beach, Florida. And today is the preliminary round. They are due to step on the mat at three o'clock this afternoon.

Me: I am now. LOL.

Scottie: Ugh. I'm sorry I woke you up. I'm just so nervous, Finn.

Me: I'm glad you woke me up.

Scottie: You're such a liar. No one would be happy to get woken up at six in the morning in the middle of spring break.

Me: Scottie, I know, in the past, I've given you quite the load of bullshit. But I promise you, I will never ever lie to you. Which is why I'll tell you now that you're right. I'm tired.

I send a tongue-out crazy emoji so she knows I'm joking.

Scottie: LOL

Me: BUT I'm also happy you woke me up. I wish I were there with you to tell you in person, but since I'm not, I'll tell you here. You are READY for this competition. Your team IS ready.

Scottie: I've never been a part of something this big, though. It's terrifying.

Me: All valid feelings. But use that nervous energy to your advantage.

Scottie: Okay. Yeah. I know you're right.

My girl is all up in her nervous feels, and I know exactly what I need to do—give a little fun distraction.

Me: Of course I am, Cheerleader Girl. And I'll be here to lick your pussy when you come home with the trophy.

Scottie: OMG. FINN.

I know her cheeks are full-on pink at this point, but I also know her perfect little pussy is probably a little wet too. I fucking love it.

Me: Hours, Scottie. I'm going to lick you for hours.

Scottie. FINNNNNNNNNN. STOP IT RIGHT NOW. I can't compete when I'm horny.

Me: Maybe you should touch my pussy for a little bit, then. I'll loan it to you since it's on your body and all. Just enough to take the edge off.

Scottie: You are a bad, bad man.

Me: You bring out the best in me.

Scottie: LOL. You mean I bring out the beast in you.

Me: Same thing. ;)

Scottie: Love you so much. Thank you for knowing exactly what I needed.

Me: Love you too.

I set my phone back on my nightstand, completely ignoring the fact that all the talk about Scottie's pussy has my cock taking notice, and lie back down on my bed.

I only manage an extra hour of sleep before a new text message notification pulls me back to reality. I figure it's another text from Scottie, but I'm surprised when I see my brother Remy's name on the screen.

Remy: You want to go see your girl in Daytona?

Me: What are you saying?

Remy: I'm saying that I pulled some strings, and if you can be at Teterboro Airport in ninety minutes, you can get to Daytona by this afternoon.

Me: How the fuck did you manage this?

Remy: Rich friends.

Me: You do realize you're rich too.

Remy: I guess that helps. LOL. And good news, you can bring a few friends. Though, I have a feeling since it's Kline Brooks's plane, his daughter Julia and Ace Kelly will be going with you.

That outcome couldn't be any more perfect.

Me: Thanks, bro. I owe you.

It feels weird to call him "bro" and yet normal, all at the same time. I can't explain it. It's as if I know what it used to be like—I lived it—but somehow, it feels like it's been like this forever.

> **Remy: Just go have some fucking fun in Daytona, and I'll consider us square.**

> **Me: That, I can do.**

Not even two minutes later, Ace's phone starts ringing, and he groans as he turns to his side to take the call. "'Lo?"

He rubs at his eyes and runs a hand through his mess of dark hair. "No shit? Hell yeah, Jules!" He sits up straight in bed. "Count me in… Okay… Me, you, Finn, and Blake… I know, I know… I'll be ready… Jules, I promise I won't fuck around… Fuck, woman, you're so bossy… Yeah, okay… See you in ten."

"Good news, Finnley. Julia's dad came through with—" He stops midsentence when he realizes I'm already dressed and have my duffel on my bed, smiling like a lunatic. "I guess you know the plan."

I nod.

"Daytona Beach, here we motherfucking come!" he cheers as he hops out of bed.

Looks like I get to surprise my girl.

75

Scottie

Kayla squeezes my hand, and I grip Emma on the other side, our cross-armed, pre-routine circle in full effect. It's a ritual we never miss before taking the floor, and my knees shake and my heart races as all of us ready ourselves for what lies ahead.

We're next on the mat, and Coach Jordan stands before us, her eyes serious but her lips set in a smile. "This is what we've been training for," she says. "The hours and hours of practices and training have brought us here. To this moment. And now it's time to show the world what we're capable of. Show them why we're the best. Show them why we're going to leave NCA Nationals with that trophy clutched in our hands."

"Hell yeah!" Tonya cheers, and a few other girls yell along with her without releasing hands.

"I believe in you. Each and every one of you," Coach Jordan states. "I know this is scary, but be brave and you'll amaze yourself. Dig deep and find your courage. The moment you step on that mat, I want you to show the judges just how good I know you can be. I want to see you smiling and having fun. I want to see you working hard. I want to see the kind of focus I saw last night when we were running through our routine one last time. It all comes down to two minutes and thirty seconds, and I know you guys are going to make every second count. Now, everyone huddle," she says, and we close our circle even tighter around her, letting go of one another's hands and grabbing our poms from in front of us as we do.

"Poms in the center," she says, and no one hesitates to follow her instructions. "One team!" she yells.

"One dream!" we respond in synchrony.

"One heart!" she exclaims.

"*We believe!*" Everyone shakes their poms in the center. "Dickson Dragons!"

"Let's go, girls!" Coach Jordan shouts at the top of her lungs, and my heart is already pounding hard inside my chest as we line up just outside of the main stage mat.

The team before us—the Stalwart Scorpions—have just walked off, and the MC steps onto the stage to announce us.

"I'm so nervous," I whisper into Kayla's ear, and she turns around to give me a tight, reassuring hug.

"You've got this, Scottie. We've got this."

"Damn straight," I say and swallow hard against the dryness in my throat.

"Plus," she adds with a wry grin, "we've got a little Dickson fan section out there in the stands."

"What?" I ask, but my eyes are already peering over her shoulder to steal a glance at the crowd. And it only takes me two seconds to spot Ace, Blake, Julia, and *Finn*.

Finn is here.

Wren and Dad wanted to be here, but they couldn't afford to take any time off work. Not to mention the money it would've cost them to get here.

It's an expensive trip for anyone, and I was prepared to be alone. But Finn somehow found a way to show up for me.

I want to cry from relief, but the visual of him standing there in a glittery Dickson Cheer T-shirt and a poster board that reads "Go, Scottie!" spurs several shaky giggles from my lungs. Ace and Blake and Julia are all wearing T-shirts that match Finn's, and their posters are held high in their hands.

It's a sight I'll never forget.

And just as the MC announces us and we start to file out onto the mat to take our places, I lock eyes with Finn. It's brief, but it's all I need.

Calm washes over me, and I kneel down in my position and wait patiently for the music to start, without nerves or anxiety or fear.

Just like Finn told me this morning, *I'm ready.*

76

Finn

We've been at the Daytona Beach Bandshell and Ocean Center for several hours now. The sun is brutal. The humidity is so thick I could cut it with a knife. All three of us—Ace, Blake, and I—have taken off our shirts to combat the heat, and poor Julia is trying to fan herself with her posterboard as we wait for the results of Scottie's team's division.

"If these judges don't push them through to finals, I will be so pissed," Ace comments as the MC of the competition steps onto the stage to announce which teams will be competing in the final round.

"Relax, Ace," Julia responds and wraps her hands around his forearm. "They're going to be in the finals. They were the best ones out there."

"That's what I'm saying, Jules," he says, looking down at her with a grin. "These judges better push them through or else."

"Or else what?" Blake questions on a laugh. "You gonna go down there and beat their asses?"

"Nah, dude," Ace comments and points his thumb toward me. "I'll send in Fight Club Finney."

Everyone laughs, including me, but that laughter is quickly cut off when the MC starts talking into the mic.

"The Advanced All-Girl Division IA finalists are," he announces and opens up an envelope, "in no particular order… Butler! Louisville! Dickson!…"

He's supposed to name off another seven teams, but the four of us are on our feet, screaming, shouting, and cheering so loud when we hear Dickson that there's not a shot in hell that anyone in our immediate vicinity heard the rest.

"Hell yeah!" Ace exclaims, and he lifts Julia into the air to spin her around. "I fucking told you, Jules!"

She just giggles and laughs and the two of them exchange their normal banter, but my eyes are too busy looking toward the area where all of the teams were waiting for their results. I spot Dickson's cheerleaders instantly, and their excitement is evident by high fives and hugs and jumping around in one another's arms.

My eyes spot Kayla. And then McKenzie. And a few other girls I know from Scottie's team, but I'm struggling to find my girl.

I search and search, trying to get a glimpse of the joy on her pretty face, and I don't stop searching until I feel something tap against my back. I glance over my shoulder and then proceed to do a double take when I realize it's not some random stranger in the crowd.

It's Scottie.

Her smile is downright blinding, and I don't hesitate to lift her up and into my arms. "You were incredible," I whisper into her ear, and she leans back to meet my gaze. "I'm in awe of you, Cheerleader Girl."

"We did it!" she squeals, and I lift her up higher in the air. Her cheeks flush pink when I garner a little too much attention our way.

"Way to go, Scottie!"

"Scottie! Scottie! Scottie!" Ace starts chanting, and Julia and Blake join him.

"Oh my God," she groans, but she also smiles as I slide her back down my body until her feet are planted firmly on the ground. Though, I do manage to steal a kiss on the way.

"I need to go back to my team," she tells me after giving Ace, Blake, and Julia high fives and hugs. "But I just wanted to come see you real quick. Honestly, I can't even believe you're here."

"All thanks to Remy."

She quirks a brow.

"He chartered Julia's dad's private jet."

"Damn."

"Tell me about it." I chuckle. "Now, go celebrate with your team. And maybe call me later?"

"Wait…how long are you guys staying?"

"Until finals."

"Yeah?" Her smile is equal parts hopeful and excited.

"Wouldn't miss seeing you guys get the championship for the world, Scottie."

"Well, then…" She pauses and shyly glances down at her feet. "You got any plans tonight?"

"No." I quirk a brow. "Why?"

"Because I was thinking that maybe we could hang out." She stands on her tiptoes to press a soft kiss to my lips. "But you have to be prepared to go full-on *Mission: Impossible* because our coaches have a strict no-boys-allowed policy."

"What? You going to sneak me into your hotel room?"

"Something like that." She kisses me once more. "Love you, Finn."

"Love you too, Cheerleader Girl."

She heads back toward her team, but on the way, she turns around to blow me a kiss.

"Yo, Finn," Ace comments and wraps his arm around my shoulders. "Not sure if you know this, but you're in love with that girl."

"Yeah. I most certainly am." And I don't even know if she realizes how fucking much.

77

Thursday April 10th

Scottie

It's just a little after one in the morning, and with a peek out into the hallway, I've confirmed that all of our coaches are in bed. I snag my phone from my nightstand and send a text.

> **Me: Are you in the elevator?**
>
> **Finn: Yes.**
>
> **Me: When you get to our floor, just wait there, okay?**
>
> **Finn: Okay.**

"He's on his way up," I update Kayla, and she already has her pillow and favorite fleece blanket in her arms. "Is Tonya ready to sneak you into her room?"

"Yes, but let me be the first one to tell you that you owe me. Big-time."

"I know! I know!" I close the distance between us to wrap her into a tight hug. "I'll do anything you want, I swear. And if Coach Jordan or any of the other coaches finds out about this, I will make sure you're not involved."

She groans. "Good grief, Scottie. You better not get caught."

"I won't. I promise."

"Wait…you're not a screamer, are you?"

"Kayla!" I blurt out in shock. And my face has to be as red as a damn tomato.

"Ha! You are too cute for words, Scottie," she comments through a laugh and gives me another hug. "And I'm just screwing with you, girl. I'm more than happy to sacrifice myself and my sanity to spend the evening listening to Tonya bitch about her ankle while stuffing candy in her face so you can get your freak on with your boyfriend."

Tonya rolled her ankle during prelims, and Coach Jordan and Darrell, our team's physical therapist, have instructed her to take it easy and rest it for finals on Friday. Fingers and toes and everything crossed she can pull through.

Kayla starts to walk toward the door, but she stops briefly to say, "Next Nationals, if I have a boyfriend, your ass is going to be the one rooming with Tonya. I don't care if you and Finn are married by then."

What the hell is with everyone saying crazy shit to me about weddings?

"Get real, Kay. I'm a little young for marriage."

"Says the girl who is basically living with her boyfriend at this point," she retorts on a whisper as she discreetly opens the door. "That man is always at your dorm these days."

She's not wrong. But that doesn't mean I'm ready to say "I do" anytime soon.

Five years down the road, however? That's a different story.

Kayla offers a little wave over her shoulder as she quickly sprints down the hallway to Tonya's room. I just barely make out the click of Tonya's door as it latches shut. Instantly, I pull my phone out of the drawstring of my favorite sweats and send Finn a text.

Me: Coast is clear, but, like, move your ass.

He doesn't respond, but in a matter of seconds, I see his face appear around the corner. He smiles at me like a man who can't believe I've talked him into illegally sneaking into my hotel room. But he also keeps walking toward me.

Once he reaches my hotel room, I all but shove him inside

and close the door so gently that you'd have to have the ears of an bat to hear it.

I turn around to find Finn sitting on my bed, and I don't hesitate to run across the carpeted floor to dive-bomb myself on top of him.

He laughs, but he also wraps his arms around my body and holds me tightly to his chest. "Excited to see me?"

"You have no idea," I say through a giggle and straddle his hips. I push his back down onto the bed and sit up straight on top of him. "All that talk about…*licking*…hasn't left my mind."

"Ohhh, so you brought me here with ulterior motives." He squeezes my ass with both hands, and I feign confusion with a tap of my index finger to my chin.

"I wouldn't say that. I mean, I thought it was pretty clear why I wanted you to come up."

"I'll be honest, Scottie, I thought you wanted to cuddle and shit. I didn't realize you're a horny little minx who snuck me into her hotel room so I can put my mouth on her pussy."

"But, like, I figured we could cuddle. *After.*"

He cracks up at that. And then, he flips me onto my back so that his big, muscular body is hovering over mine. "I don't know if it's safe, Scottie."

"Why not?" I ask as he moves down my body. He slides his fingers beneath the waistband of my sweatpants and pulls them—and my panties—off with a swift tug.

"I fear that once I taste you…" His eyes are on me now, right there, where I'm already wet and aching for him. "I won't be able to stop."

A little moan escapes my lips, and he rests his chin on my pubic bone to lock his gaze with mine. "You want to come on my tongue?"

I bite my lip and nod. *Holy hell, yes please.*

"What about my cock?"

My hips squirm and I nod again.

He leans back to look at me again, his eyes widening with heat and desire, and his hair just barely hovers over his eyes. He looks good enough to eat, and I'm starting to regret being so focused on my pleasure. The urge to pull out his cock and wrap my mouth around him is an insane desire I never knew I'd have for a man.

But goodness, I have that desire for Finn.

He sneaks his tongue out and takes one long lick against my center. My hips squirm and my nipples harden, and Finn just smiles as he does that move over and over.

It's the worst, most delicious kind of teasing, and I don't know how much longer I can take it before I start begging for him to make me come.

My back bows off the bed when he slides his tongue inside me and then slips it back out, wraps his lips around my clit, and sucks. *Holy moly.*

He moans against me, the vibrations causing zings of pleasure to shoot to my toes, and he just keeps eating at me. Sucking, licking, inhaling me whole.

And when I come hard on his tongue, he slides his cock out of his jeans and boxer briefs, slips a condom over his length, and spreads my legs with his big hands.

"I fucking *need* to do that again, Scottie, but I also need to put my cock in you for a little bit," he says and does just that. In one fluid motion, he slides himself inside me, and I instantly feel so full that I wonder if I'm going to explode from pleasure.

Thankfully, he has no mercy and starts up a driving, deep rhythm that makes my breasts bounce and my breaths come out in erratic pants.

This is different from the times before. It's raw and primal and animalistic. He is *fucking* me. And hell's bells, I'm loving every second of it.

My eyes fall closed and my back arches when I hear his moans turn deep and raspy. He's so close, I know he's so close, and it's only making me more aroused to know that I'm the one who makes him lose control.

But he doesn't let himself go over the edge. Instead, he slides his condom-covered cock out of me and flips me on top of his body so that his back is pressed into the mattress.

"Ride my face, Scottie," he says and lifts me up by the ass, spreading my thighs over his face.

"But…but…"

"I'm not giving you my cock again until you come on my tongue again." His mouth is already on me, and the feel of him licking and sucking at me like I'm the best thing he's ever tasted has my hands reaching beneath my T-shirt and grabbing my breasts.

And I'm so aroused. So insanely aroused that I just start grinding myself on his face.

"Yes. That's my girl." He groans and grips my ass, and that only spurs me on further.

All my inhibitions have left the room, and the only thing I can focus on is my pleasure. I ride Finn's face until my back bows tight as an arrow and my legs shake with my impending climax.

And I don't stop grinding myself on his mouth until waves of pleasure wash over me in such an intense, powerful way that I have to reach out and grip the headboard to hold myself up.

My head is lax and my eyes are closed, but Finn is not done. Before I know it, he's behind me and his hands are spreading my thighs out farther. And then, he's inside me. Still hard and big and oh-so deep.

He grips my ass with both of his hands as he drives into me with steady, deep thrusts of his cock, and my head falls forward from the delicious feel of it all.

"One day, I'm going to fill you up without a condom, Scottie," he growls into my ear, and that gets my attention. It makes my mind reel with need and desire and all the things I've never experienced.

"Do it. Now," I whisper, and he freezes behind me. "Finn, you know I'm on birth control."

"I know, Scottie, but…" He starts to shake his head, but I'm already turning around and removing the condom from his cock. "Scottie."

"Yes, Finn," I say and pull his body down on top of mine. "I want to feel you, *all of you*, inside me."

"Fuck." He grits his teeth. "I don't think—"

"Don't overthink it." I wiggle my hips beneath him in a way that makes the tip of his cock just barely slide inside me. He groans, and I wiggle my hips more so he's in a little deeper.

"I'm never going to be the same after this," he says and reaches down to gently caress his thumb over where his name has started to fade on my hip. And then he slides himself all the way inside me. Slowly, gently, he pushes his cock as deep as he can go.

We both moan at the feel of it.

And then, all hell breaks loose when the arousal becomes too strong to deny. My hands clutch at his back, and his hands slide beneath my ass as he thrusts himself in and out of me with heavy drives of his cock.

My nails dig into his skin when I can actually feel him getting harder inside me. There's no barrier, no condom, just him. Just Finn.

The reality of it becomes too much for both of us, and it's not long before he's pushing himself as deep as he can go and filling me up with his come. And my body throbs and clenches around him like it wants every single drop of him.

Holy hell. I never knew it could be *this* good.

78

My hair and T-shirt and jeans feel like they weigh a hundred pounds, and the vibe of the crowd is electric from the surprise rain shower that just moved through Daytona. Ace is bare-chested, swinging his wet T-shirt at Julia's ass as she wrings out the bottom of her navy-blue and gold sundress, and several people wearing official NCA gear are on the stage, drying the mat with large towels.

Louisville, Butler, and Nesco College have already competed, all nailing their routines and putting the pressure on Dickson and the other six teams left to go. I never realized how elaborate and difficult cheerleading at a competitive level was until I started paying attention to Scottie, but I'd spend my last breath defending their athleticism to anyone now.

This shit is intense.

Blake flings water off his hair, shaking like a dog right in Ace's face. Ace opens his mouth and sticks out his tongue like a goofball, and Julia rolls her eyes at me.

"Man, I bet all this waiting is making it ten times worse," she says, turning back to the stage as yet another stack of dry towels gets passed around.

"Anticipation can make things better too," I remark, thinking about making Scottie wait last night.

Blake smiles huge and waggles his eyebrows at me, and I swat him in the stomach when his gestures start to get out of control.

"What?" he argues. "As your Daytona hotel roommate, I can't help that I notice when you don't come back to the room until the sun is rising."

"Yo," Ace calls, pointing to the stage. "I think they're getting ready to start again."

Focus renewed, I jump down off the metal rung of the bleachers and take my seat again. An MC steps onto the stage with a smile on his face and puts a black microphone to his mouth. "We apologize for that thirty-minute delay and appreciate your patience. I'm sure there're quite a few of you who wish you would've brought some umbrellas, huh?" He jokes with the crowd, making Ace turn back to me and stick out his tongue.

I laugh and shove him forward, and he turns back around to pay attention.

"We'll be getting started again here in the next little bit, after our team does a final check for safety, and I'm sure the teams waiting back there could use your encouragement. Let's get loud for them, everybody!"

"Whoo!" I yell, shooting to my feet again. Ace, Julia, and Blake are a little slower, but when I pick Ace up under his armpits, the other two follow.

"Yeah! Come on, Dickson!" Julia yells, pumping her fist in the air.

"Dragons! Dragons! Dragons!" Blake starts to chant, encouraging the people around us to join in. Before we know it, half the crowd is calling out our mascot with us, and the MC's smile is huge as he returns to the center of the stage and puts his mouth to the mic.

"That's what I'm talking about! We've gotten final approval from the safety crew, and I'm thrilled to announce we're ready to go! Please welcome to the stage…the Dickson Dragons!"

Scottie and her team run out onto the mat, the sound of their stomps deafening as they approach the front of the crowd, waving their arms in the air and pumping us up. The atmosphere is electric, and my fingers tingle with excitement. "Hell yeah! Let's go, Scottie!"

Scottie's dark hair is in a high ponytail on her head, and a big gold bow sits at the top, matching her Dickson navy-blue cheerleading uniform with gold detailing. Her lips are painted bright red, and her mouth is etched into a big smile as she takes her position in the front of her squad, the point of the triangle with Kayla smiling brightly just off her shoulder.

The crowd quiets as the cheerleaders bow their heads, waiting on their music to start.

"I'm so nervous for them," Julia whispers to Ace, and he wraps an arm around her shoulders and tucks her close to his side.

"They got this, Jules."

"Go Dickson!" Blake shouts from between cupped hands, cutting into the silence like a knife.

"You got this, Scottie!" I add at the top of my lungs. I don't know if she can hear me from her spot on the stage, but I do see the slightest hint of a grin kiss her pretty mouth, so I choose to believe she can.

The opening notes of their competition song pound heavily through the speakers, and their heads snap up in unison.

It's go time!

Scottie's squad jumps into action, a synchronized unit of hips shaking and arm gestures. Each movement is perfectly timed to the beat of the song. The girls switch formation, and a path opens for three cheerleaders—Scottie included—to tumble toward the back of the mat.

She nails her tricks perfectly, and so do her other two teammates, and I unleash a yell I swear the captain of a ship off the coast can probably hear.

The squad moves into another formation that has the entire team doing a perfectly timed backflip and some kind of jump-leg thing where the feet of every single girl on the squad land at the same time. They hit every move with precision, and the hype running between Ace, Blake, Julia, and me makes us bob back and forth and bump into each other so much, we look like we're in a rugby scrum.

Dickson cheerleaders switch up their positions, and Scottie and two other cheerleaders are tossed into the air by their teammates who serve as their bases below. She stands on one foot, keeps her body perfectly straight, and holds one leg high in the air. The other two flyers mimic the same movements, and all three hit their marks without any issues. They all do two twists down into their bases' arms, but pop back up onto the top of their woven hands before their feet can touch the ground. Scottie and two other cheerleaders fly through the air in a full twisting flip, doing what she taught me last week is a basket toss.

I watch as Scottie completes her spinning backflip perfectly, my eyes so focused on her that I don't notice her bases are in shambles until Ace yells, "Shit!" when Tonya goes down to the ground, her ankle in her hands.

I feel like I'm watching in slow motion as Scottie drops like a rock toward a group of people who are in no way prepared to catch her from no less than twenty feet in the air. She hits with a sickening thud, her head and neck impacting the mat at a terrifying angle.

The entire crowd gasps, and I jump down between Ace and Julia, Ace holding me by my shirt to keep me from trampling the people in front of us. "Scottie!" My throat shakes and my voice is raw as the music stops, and silence descends around us. Scottie's teammates huddle around her and wave frantically for the medical staff.

"Oh my God!" Julia cries.

"Fuck, is she okay?" Ace questions, audible terror in his normally jovial voice.

Blake shoves his hands into his hair in distress, and I push forward again, not caring if I fucking have to step directly on the people in front of us at this point.

I haven't seen her move at all.

Medical staff slides Scottie's body onto a backboarded stretcher as I arrive at the front of the stage, but there are too many people in the way to make out anything else.

"Scottie!" I yell, jumping up onto the platform and shoving through cheerleaders carefully but quickly.

"Sir, you need to stay back," a security guard says as he tries to stop my progress when I finally get close, but he's no match for the adrenaline that's now rushing through my body. I move him out of the way and shove forward again, not stopping until I bump into a crying Kayla, who's holding Scottie's hand.

Guys in red jackets secure her waist, legs, and chest to the backboard, and a neck collar is in place right below her scared face. I step around Kayla until Scottie can see me.

When her eyes lock with mine, I'm immediately overwhelmed by the pure terror on her face. I seek out her hand desperately, taking her fingers in mine, and squeeze, wanting her to know I'm there.

"I'm here, Scottie. I'm here."

"Finn," she whispers. "I can't feel my legs. I can't feel anything." A sob bubbles up from her throat, and I squeeze her hand even harder with my fingers, willing her to take every ounce of my strength if she needs.

"It's okay." A tear trails down her cheek, and I reach out to swipe it off with my thumb. "I'm here, Scottie."

"Sir, you need to get off the stage," someone says to me, a hand gripping my shoulder and pulling me out of the way. "We need to get her into the ambulance."

"Finn!" Scottie yells, panic overwhelming her voice.

"I need to go with her," I challenge as they shove me out of the way again with a hand to my chest.

"I'm sorry, sir, but you can't. We have to go."

I lunge toward her as they carry her by and press my lips to hers quickly but gently. "I'm here, okay? I'm going to follow you to the hospital."

I grip her hand once more until her fingers slip from my own as they carry her away and load her into the back of the ambulance at the side of the stage.

She's been through so much already, and now this?

I know they say God doesn't give you more than you can handle, but the universe just told God to eat shit.

I don't know if it'll help or not, but hoping to swing the pendulum in our favor, I do something I've never done before.

I pray.

79

Sunday April 13th
Scottie

"We love you, Scottie," Coach Jordan says and leans over my hospital bed at Daytona Regional Medical Facility to give me a big hug. "I'll be thinking about you. Praying for you. And don't hesitate to reach out if you need anything, okay?" She turns to look over at my dad and sister Wren, who stand in the far corner of the room beside Finn.

As soon as Finn told Ty what had happened, he got my dad and sister down here on the first plane he found.

"Anything she needs, Mr. Bardeaux. You have my number."

"Thanks, Coach," my dad responds with a little nod.

Coach Jordan gives me one final hug and presses her forehead to mine. "Love you, girl."

As she steps away from my bed, every girl on my squad takes turns in her place, giving me hugs and well-wishes. They're all dressed in our navy Dickson travel sweats, ready to get on the bus to travel back to New York, and I hate that I'm not going with them.

I don't have all the final news about my injury yet—the doctor is supposed to be meeting with me today now that they have all the scans they needed—but for at least the foreseeable future, not winning Nationals and not getting on the bus to head back home are least of my worries.

I still have no feeling in my legs or feet, and my bowels and bladder aren't under my control either. I feel like half a person—like the scraps at the end of a magic trick gone wrong. I still feel like I'm going to wake up at some point and this all will have been a nightmare.

Tonya steps up to my bed, tears actively pouring down her cheeks. Her whole face is puffy and red, and I'm not sure she has stopped crying since the minute the whole awful thing happened. "I'm so sorry, Scottie," she says, and her voice shakes with grief. "I don't know what happened. I hate—"

"Don't do that." I shake my head. "This isn't your fault. It was a freak thing, Tonya. I know that. You know that. Everyone knows that."

No one really knows what exactly went wrong, but I do know that after the storms rolled through on Friday, there were still slick spots on the mat, no matter how hard the NCA staff tried to clean it up. I think between that and Tonya's already weak ankle, something just went wrong that no one could've seen coming or prevented.

I guess it could be argued they shouldn't have had us out on the mat if it was still wet, but I saw the NCA staff with my own eyes working their asses off to dry it, and the safety staff checked it comprehensively.

I could easily be angry, but no amount of righteous indignation is going to put feeling back below my waist. I just need to give it time.

Tonya hesitates to hug me, guilt still evident on her face, and I reach forward with both arms to pull her close to me. It's a little awkward because of my current situation—stuck in a hospital bed with an IV in my arm and legs that won't seem to wake up—but I do my best.

Kayla is the last one to give me a hug, and she squeezes me so tight that my lungs have a hard time accommodating air. "I wish I could stay with you," she whispers into my ear, and I lean back to meet her eyes. She's still visibly distraught, her lips quivering as she tries to stay strong for me.

"I'll be back in New York soon. You need to go with the team."

"I know. But…I just feel like I'm leaving you behind."

"No." I shake my head. "You have to go. End of story."

She nods and lifts one hand to swipe a lone tear that streams down her cheek. "Love you," she says and squeezes my hand, and I squeeze her hand back.

"Love you too."

Once my coach and teammates leave my room, heading for the bus that's waiting for them outside the hospital, I let out a big exhale and swallow hard against the urge to cry.

Being strong for them, when it feels like my entire world has been flipped upside down, is no easy feat.

Finn notices me fighting and shakes his head, giving me permission to let it all go. As emotion pours out, he steps away from my dad and my sister and takes a seat on the edge of my bed. His fingers rub gently at mine as I gasp at the void of the room, trying to take a breath deep enough to actually *breathe*.

"That was hard," I whisper to him shakily. With his free hand, he strokes my hair, tucking it behind my ear as it falls into the wetness of my eyes.

"You did good," he says. "But you don't have to be strong, you know? It's okay to be upset right now."

"Yeah, Scottie," Wren says and comes to sit on the other side of my bed. She takes my other hand in hers. "You're allowed to cry, scream, be mad."

I shrug, an unavoidable embarrassment making my cheeks heat when I can't make myself stop shaking. Finn reaches up to wipe the tears away from my face with his hand again and places a soft kiss to the apple of my cheek.

My dad stands at the foot of my bed, holding both of my bare feet in his hands, and I can't feel a damn thing.

I yank my hands away from Finn and Wren, scrubbing them over my face as I try not to panic. Surely this is just temporary. I'll start to get feeling back soon, and then it'll be a lot of rehab and other hard things, but I'll get better. Everything will get better.

Finn's phone pings with a text notification and I nod for him to check it when he looks at me in question. He reads it quickly, a sad smile curling the corner of his mouth. "It's Julia," he says. "They made it back to New York."

"Good." Julia, Ace, and Blake were all at the hospital Friday evening and all day Saturday, but they had to fly back home today. Julia was going to try to delay it, but I told her they needed to get back and not miss any classes.

I'm dealing with a setback, but I'll be back soon enough. And I don't want to be in college by myself because everyone else was too worried about me and flunked out.

"She says she'll try to call you later."

I nod. "Okay."

"Do you want anything from downstairs, honey?" my dad asks, digging in his pocket for his visitor's badge to put it back on. He's worked a lot of hard hours in his life, been a knight in blue-collar armor dealing with our mom, but I've never seen him looking like this. His hair is disheveled and sticking out everywhere, and the rims of his eyes are red with tears and fatigue. I know getting the phone call that I'd been injured while hundreds of miles away was probably the hardest thing he's ever had to hear.

So, I don't blame him when he offers up excuses to take breaks like this one.

"Good morning, Scottie," Dr. Stewart, the lead doctor on my case, greets with a friendly smile, surprising us as he steps through the door. I wasn't expecting that we'd hear from him until later today. "How are you feeling this morning?"

"Hopeful," I say with a smile as Finn takes my hand. "I can't feel anything yet, but I'm trying to trust the process, you know?" I mean it as a joke, having used humor with Dr. Stewart as a coping mechanism since my arrival. But his mouth doesn't curve upward like I'd expect, and the line of his jaw is rigid. It's an immediate hit to my swagger, and Finn's thumb stops moving on the back of my hand.

"Scottie, we need to discuss what lies ahead," he says, and the vibe of the room turns ominous.

I glance at my dad and back to the doctor, and Wren wraps an arm around my shoulders in support.

"Is everything okay? Have you gotten results back?"

All day Saturday, I was in and out of my hospital room for testing. X-rays and MRIs and CT scans and a whole bunch of other random exams were performed to give my medical team a more thorough view of my injury. I don't know what gave me the notion that everything would check out fine eventually, but right now, Dr. Stewart is scaring me that I might have been way off base.

"I have good news and bad news," he answers, turning on the light board and putting one of my images on it to show me. "This is an MRI of your spine, Scottie. And if you look right here at your lumbar vertebrae, you can see where your spinal injury is located between L2 to L4."

"So, she definitely has a spinal cord injury?" my dad questions, and Dr. Stewart nods.

"Sometimes swelling at the trauma site can give a false sense of damage. The inflammation causes pressure, and the pressure causes the paralysis."

"So, that's what it was? Just inflammation?" Wren hedges.

An angry impatience inside me wants to snap at my family to shut up and let the doctor talk, but deep down, I know they're just as upset and worried as me.

"I'm afraid not. Unfortunately, Scottie's injury is more severe." Dr. Stewart meets my eyes directly, speaking to me with a quiet kindness I know he's been practicing for years. "Your injury is what we call an incomplete paraplegia, Scottie. What that means in layman's terms is that your spinal cord severed but not completely, meaning some of the neural circuits between your brain and your lower body still exist."

"So, that means it's going to heal, right?" I ask, looking around the room at Finn and my dad and sister. "I mean, I'm eventually going to get feeling back in my legs, right?"

Dr. Stewart's eyes turn sympathetic. "While you may regain

some sensation or movement in the affected areas, the likelihood of anything more than that is low. Spinal cords don't heal."

My vision clouds and my hearing tunnels as he keeps talking, my chest seizing up in panic. "But the good news is the location of her injury is not considered life-threatening. Since it is located in the lumbar region of her spine, only her lower extremities are affected. If it were higher, say in the thoracic or cervical areas, we would be dealing with a lot more areas of risk and concern."

My mind races with another option of something that'll change what he's saying and make it all go away. "But what about surgery? Can't you fix it with surgery?"

He shakes his head. "The spinal cord is an extremely complicated part of the body. Injuries like these affect too many individual cells that are unable to be repaired or regenerate. But since your injury has only affected part of your lumbar spine, and because you're so young and physically fit, I *am* extremely hopeful that rehabilitation and physical therapy will be an amazing tool for you if you take it seriously. I can't make any promises—it's a horrible reality of my job that there are many uncertainties—but I believe you will be able to regain some control over things like your bladder and bowels."

"And I'll be able to walk again, right? I mean, of course, right? I'll be able to walk again," I ramble desperately, ignoring Finn as he tries to hold my hand and soothe me.

"As a rule of thumb, I never say never, Scottie." I hate the sympathetic frown on his face. "I've seen a number of medical miracles over the years that, for the most part, I cannot explain. But the likelihood that you'll regain the use of your legs is limited by the extent of your spinal trauma."

He keeps talking, saying something about keeping a positive attitude and working hard in rehab, but beyond that, I hear nothing but white noise. My brain is spiraling.

This isn't temporary. I'm not going to be back on campus next week, and I'm not going to rehab my way back into cheerleading.

Oh my God. Oh my *God*.

I'll probably never walk again. Never feel my fucking legs again. I'm actually paralyzed.

I fight for air through strangled sobs, gulping and gulping at the whole room around me. I scratch at my face and pull at my chest as the feeling of suffocation overwhelms me, and Dr. Stewart runs to the door to call for help.

Finn, my dad, and my sister all scramble at my bedside to help, but nothing makes me feel less like I'm dying. I sob and cry and wheeze for air, and Dr. Stewart finally pushes his way in to slide an oxygen mask over my nose. I take deep, desperate breaths, and Dr. Stewart nods at me over and over to try to help me find a slower, more oxygenating pace.

My dad cries at the foot of my bed and Wren tries to comfort him, while Finn grabs on to my hand and squeezes.

Dr. Stewart preaches of a new normal and taking time to acclimate while Finn holds tightly to me to try to keep me from spiraling out of control, but it's no use.

Nothing in the world will ever be the same after this news.

Monday April 14th
Scottie

I woke up this morning thinking I was the Scottie before my accident, but the harsh truth is that that girl doesn't exist anymore. My dad and Wren sleep uncomfortably on a pullout sofa, and Finn hunches over a chair, none of them willing to leave my room to rest anywhere else.

Time feels short and endlessly long at the same time. It feels like yesterday and ten years ago that I was walking out onto the mat at Nationals, completely naïve to the fact that it would be my last time cheering.

That it would be my last competition.

That it would be the last time I did stunts. Danced. *Stood on my own two feet.*

"You need anything from downstairs?" Finn asks, reaching out to tuck a piece of hair behind my ear. I have no idea what I look like at this point, but I can only assume it's horrible.

Wren was nice enough to brush my hair last night while she tried to distract me with reruns of *Grey's Anatomy*—one of our favorite binge shows—but I haven't had anything more than a sponge bath in over three days. I washed my makeup off myself in a water-filled bowl, but having done it without a mirror, I can still feel some of the dry, hard spots I missed every time I move my face.

"Scottie?" Finn questions again, his voice almost annoyingly gentle. I know it's his way of trying to comfort me, but the stark difference between his voice now and the one he used when he snuck into my hotel room Thursday night is just another reminder of what will never be again.

I fight to keep my voice from shaking with anger as I answer him. "No thanks."

"I'll be right back." He presses a kiss to my forehead and heads out the door, most likely to get lunch from the hospital cafeteria for Wren, my dad, and himself.

The lunch tray one of the staff brought in for me is still sitting untouched on my bedside table. It's hard to have an appetite for anything when you know that you can't control your bladder or bowels. I've never felt so much shame and embarrassment as I did this morning when a nurse had to literally clean me up because I soiled my bed.

Wren stands up from the sofa to come sit on the edge of my bed. "You doing okay?" she asks, but her eyes have a serious edge to them that makes my head tilt.

"Why are you looking at me like that?"

"Don't get mad, but Mom is here," she answers, and her mouth forms a self-conscious cringe. "I told her about what happened, and I didn't think she'd show up, but she's here. She's on her way up to your room."

I don't even know what to say other than *are you fucking kidding me*, but I don't have time because moments later, my mother's face appears outside the door.

She's hesitant and uncertain as she locks her gaze with mine, but Wren is so oblivious that she just gestures for her to come inside.

"Hi, honey," she greets as she closes the distance between the door and my bed. She has a stupid bouquet of flowers in her hands, and she finds an empty spot between all the other flowers and balloons and bears that other people have sent me.

"I can't believe you had the balls to come here," I say simply, startling a gasp from Wren.

"*Scottie.*"

It's not my sister's fault that I didn't tell her what happened before winter break, but I don't really give a damn anymore. It's not my fault that I fell out of my basket toss, but I'm paralyzed all the same.

Shit comes at you fast in life, and you'd better be ready for the changes.

"I'm not the bad guy here," I say with a shake of my head. "She's the one who's been lying to you about being sober. She's the one who hasn't told you the truth about what she did to me in December. If she's going to have the audacity to come here, knowing all the shit she's put me through, she's going to deal with the consequences."

"Mom, what's she talking about?" Wren questions as my dad climbs to his feet.

"What's going on, Stephanie?"

"It's nothing," my mom answers, ignoring every mangled bit of her responsibility again, and it's enough to push me over the edge.

"It's nothing?" I exclaim. "It's fucking everything, and you know it!"

"Scottie, baby, calm down," my dad comforts as the alarms on my monitors start to get excited.

"Mom?" my sister presses. "What is she talking about?"

Shame and embarrassment fold my mom in on herself, her mouth clamped shut as Wren and my dad look to her for answers. I don't feel badly for her at all. *She* did this to the both of us.

I don't hold back. "If she won't tell you, I will, Wren. Mom showed up on campus back in December—according to her, looking for me. But you know how college campuses can be, and hah, what do you know? She got lost and went to a party on sorority row instead, got wasted, and had sex with a college student."

"What?" my father exclaims. "Are you fucking kidding me, Stephanie?"

"Mom?" Wren questions, pain and discomfort and total shock evident in the stark lines of her normally beautiful face.

"I had the horrible pleasure of seeing it happen with my own two eyes, and everyone on campus found out about it when a particularly shitty coed of mine posted it online. I was officially labeled the girl with the alcoholic mom who has sex with college guys, and I lost fifteen pounds I didn't have to lose, rotting away in my dorm because I was afraid to go outside."

Wren's horrified eyes turn to me with concern. My mom has the nerve to start crying.

"I'm so sorry, Scottie. I am so, so sorry," she says through her tears. "I regret it every day. Every single day, I regret what happened. I regret it so much and I know I don't deserve your forgiveness, but I swear I'll spend the rest of my life trying to make it up to you."

"I want her out of my room," I say. "Now."

My dad doesn't hesitate to jump into action, stepping forward to gently grip my mom's arm and guide her to the door. But before she goes willingly, she pulls something out of her purse and sets it on my bedside table.

"I'm sorry, girls. I'm so sorry," she says one last time, and then, she willingly leaves the room with our dad.

"Scottie," Wren whispers, emotion in her throat. "Why didn't you tell me?"

When I see her tears, her sadness, it makes it impossible for me to stay strong. I'm an asshole for doing it like this, but I can't take it back. Tears of my own flood my eyes and flow down my cheeks. "I knew it would hurt you." I laugh sardonically. "Turned out a whole lot better with you finding out now, huh?"

Scottie

"You come first above our mother," Wren says. She sits on the edge of my bed, and her hands clutch mine tightly as I finish telling her the whole sordid tale of my freshman year at Dickson. "Always. Don't ever forget that."

Dane. Nadine. Finn and fights. It's a lot to take in, but at the end of it all, Wren is more determined than ever to prove her loyalty to me. I appreciate it greatly, but it doesn't change the colossal challenges that are left ahead.

"I can't believe Dane ended up being such a…" She pauses, and I don't have any problems finishing her sentence for her.

"Asshole?"

"Sis, I don't even think that's a strong enough word for him at this point." She shakes her head. "He ended up being way different than I envisioned when you first started dating him in your junior year."

"I know." I sigh. "Trust me, I know."

"I hate that I've been so out of the loop," she says, and a small frown etches across her mouth. "From here on out, I refuse to go that long without talking, okay? I want to know everything that's going on with you. All of the college parties and classes and boyfriends," she says, waggling her brows. "Or maybe boyfrien*d*," she emphasizes with a laugh. "He hasn't left your side, and I really like him. Normally the cute ones aren't this sweet."

Her words make discomfort wiggle inside my chest, and I look down to where my legs sit on the bed. Her talking about college parties and classes and boyfriends is a stark reminder of what I've lost. I'm probably never going to walk again. Definitely never going to cheer again. Everything that's been my identity for so many years can no longer be a part of my life.

I'm the paralyzed girl now.

A million questions roll through my head, none of which have a simple answer.

Will I still even be able to go to Dickson without my cheerleading scholarship? I don't have a job, and I know my father can't afford an expensive university like Dickson on his middle-class income. He worked himself to the bone to pay for me to go Ivy Prep, and that was less than half of the cost of college at Dickson.

And medical bills? How is my father going to pay for those? Surely those are racking up every second that I sit here in this bed. It's not like I'm going to be able to help him right away. I have to go through rehab and physical therapy, and who in the hell wants to hire a girl in a wheelchair who can't hold her bladder?

And Finn? How the hell can I even think about saddling a nineteen-year-old guy with the world at his feet with a paralyzed girlfriend in a wheelchair? I don't even know the logistics of how possible it is to ever have sex again. Surely having kids is out of the question too.

I'm spiraling by the second, but Wren is still busy with all the things a girl with two working legs thinks are important.

"So, this thing with you and Finn…is it—"

I suck my lips into my mouth, and she clams up as Finn and our father step into the room. They have bags of food from the cafeteria in their hands, and they're both smiling as they chat about something funny that happened when they were in the elevator.

Outsiders would probably think this is strange behavior from my dad, seeing as he just had to escort my mom out of the room. But I think after years of dealing with Stephanie Bardeaux—through marriage and then divorce—he's grown numb to any and all of her drama.

It's like she put him through so much stress and devastation in the past that he's learned to compartmentalize it all.

"Did you see this?" Wren whispers as our dad and Finn sit down on the plastic sofa in the corner of the room. I look over to see she has a small disc in her hand and quickly realize it's what our mom set down before she left my room.

4 Months, the sobriety chip reads.

"Is that how long it's been since...you know?" she asks, her voice still a whisper, and I force myself to nod.

It only makes me angrier that my mom thinks she's in the top fifteen on my list of things to worry about these days, four months sober or not.

Where in the hell am I supposed to go from here?

A week ago, I was staring toward a bright future, but now, all I see is a dark tunnel filled with obstacles and challenges I never in my life thought I would face.

"Scottie, do you want a sandwich?" my dad asks, and I shake my head.

"You're going to have to eat something, sweetheart," he urges, but I have no appetite at all.

It's hard to feel hungry when you're watching all your hopes and dreams go up in flames.

"I will," I lie. "But I think I'm going to take a nap first." I attempt to turn over on my side, but struggle with my body's new normal. Wren and Finn stand up to help me, and I have to bite down on my tongue to stop myself from crying.

It's demoralizing, to say the least.

They go above and beyond to make me comfortable with pillows and adjusting my blankets over the legs and feet that I can't fucking feel, and I stew on the pot of steam boiling deep inside. When they're finally finished, I shut my eyes and try like hell to fall asleep.

Unsolicited tears escape, and I discreetly lift my blanket to cover my face.

I don't miss that the lights of my room are turned off after that, Finn and my family trying everything they can to help me.

But every help they offer is a reminder of how much help I need in the first place, and I can feel anger seeping into all my cells one by one as they do.

What good is a light at the end of the tunnel if I have no chance of reaching it on my own two feet?

Wednesday, April 16th

Scottie

"Hey, Lonnie," I hear my dad's voice, and I open my eyes to find him on the phone. He stands up from the sofa to walk over to the windows. "Yeah, I know... I'm not sure when I'll be back at work... Scottie is still in the hospital in Daytona... The doctors want to transfer her up to New York soon, but they want to send her to St. Luke's in the city because they think their medical team is the best for rehabilitation."

He pauses and sighs. "How much PTO do I have? I didn't realize I was that low... Yeah, I hear what you're saying... Okay... No, Lonnie, I'm planning on getting back to work as soon as I can... I'm going to need it..." His voice drops to a whisper. "I know Scottie's medical bills aren't going to be cheap. I can't afford to miss paychecks right now..."

My heart breaks a million times over the stress and financial struggles my injury is going to put on my dad. My whole life, I've been focused on *me, me, me,* never really thinking too hard about all the sacrifices he's made to help my cheerleading dreams come true.

And what has all of that gotten him? A daughter who will probably be in a wheelchair for the rest of her life.

I don't think I've ever felt more worthless than I do right now.

My dad ends his call, and when he turns around, he sees that I'm awake. Thanks to all the feelings I'm having with literally no way to run away, I've been making excuses to sleep—or at least feign it—a lot. "Have a good nap?" he asks, his voice way too jovial for a man who's currently trying to figure out how to keep his job while his daughter is in the hospital. "It's getting late. I thought you might end up sleeping right through the night."

I can't even answer his question, my mind too focused on all the things I'm currently putting him through.

"I'm so sorry, Dad."

His brow furrows. "Sorry? For what?"

"For this," I say, and my lip quivers with unshed emotion. "For being here. For making your life harder. For all the times you've had to sacrifice I don't even know what to pay for training and gymnastics and everything else that comes with a daughter who wanted to be a competitive cheerleader."

"No, Scottie." My dad is by my side in an instant. "Don't do that. Don't say that. You got injured, sweetheart. It was just one of those freak things that no one could've prevented. I'm thankful that it wasn't worse. That it wasn't *life-ending*. I don't know what I would've done if I would've lost you." He grabs my hand. "You're my daughter, my little Scottie B. I love you, and there isn't anything I wouldn't do for you."

Tears stream from my cheeks, and my dad wraps me up in big hug. "We'll get through this, okay?" he says into my ear. "You're strong, Scottie. And I know this is hard and I know it feels like life handed you a bag of shit, but you can do this. You can get through this."

I nod even though I don't feel a single ounce of strength. Maybe if this year had been easier, I wouldn't feel so weak. Maybe I'd be ready to fight.

But I feel all used up and broken now, and I don't know if I have any strength left.

"You good?" he asks, clearly uncomfortable sitting in the emotion. My dad is the kindest, most well-meaning human. But he's not in touch with any of the feelings that start this deep, and I doubt he ever will be.

I force the fakest freaking smile to my lips. "Yeah."

"Good," he says and presses a soft kiss to my forehead. "You hungry?" he asks. "Wren and Finn ran to a burger joint across the street to get us some dinner. The nurses brought this tray about an hour ago for you, but it's meatloaf." He makes a disgusted face. "Personally, I don't think I'd test hospital cafeteria meatloaf, but that's just me."

"I wouldn't mind some fruit. Maybe a yogurt," I acquiesce, naming off things that seem the least likely to affect my stomach. I have to think twice about everything I put inside my body because I currently have zero control when it comes out.

I can't believe this is my life now.

The mere thought makes me want to break down all over again, but thankfully, my dad doesn't notice.

"I'll run down to the cafeteria and grab you a few things, okay?"

I nod. "Thanks, Dad."

He presses another kiss to my forehead, and I swallow hard against the emotion clawing at my chest. I'm trying to be strong. Trying to hold it together. But it's hard. So damn hard.

Once my dad is gone on his cafeteria mission, I grab my phone off the bedside table to give myself something to do other than think. There are so many notifications, it's almost overwhelming just trying to see them all.

Texts from Kayla and Tonya and a few other girls from my team.

Texts from Julia and Ace and Blake and all four of Finn's brothers and sister. Texts from Finn's *new* brothers and sister.

Texts from Coach Jordan and a few of the girls in my dorm and my RA.

Missed calls from aunts and cousins on my dad's side of the family.

Instagram and TikTok and Snapchat notifications.

Texts from my mother, all of which I delete immediately.

Everyone is sweet and kind and trying to show me support, but the reality is undeniable. The girl they knew isn't going to be the same anymore, and the things we did together won't be easily possible, if at all, for a very long time.

I have to ask for help to turn in bed, go to the bathroom, and put on clothes. I can't wash by myself or jump up to grab a door if someone needs it held open. I can't walk or run or wrap my legs around Finn's waist if I want to, and no one is ready to face that reality yet.

Nothing in my life is like it used to be.

At some point, someone is going to have to start facing the hard truth head on.

"Hey there," Finn greets as he walks into my room. He's carrying two bags of food and a drink carrier with four sodas. "You feel better after getting some rest?"

"A little." I punctuate the lie with a shrug. "Where's Wren?"

"She's taking a phone call in the lobby. I think it was someone from her job."

Another person who desperately needs to keep their job, but because they're here in the hospital with me, they're missing shifts.

"Ace texted me," he states as he sets the bags and the drinks on top of the sofa that he, my father, and Wren have been relegated to for the past few days. "Both he and Julia are working on getting notes for any classes we're missing. And I also called Ty when I was on my way to get food. He told me to tell you not to worry about anything. He'll talk with your professors and the dean."

I watch Finn as he grabs a soda, puts a straw in it, and brings it over to me. "Do the Dew?" he teases, and it takes me straight back to when he handed me a can of Mountain Dew at the Alpha Pi Halloween Party. The night we had sex for the first time.

It should be a happy memory. Finn and I got past all those demons and reached the other side despite the fact that I broke his trust and trapped him into taking my virginity.

Now, though, I'm in precarious danger of trapping him all over again. In a life with me holding him back.

"You should go back to New York," I blurt out, and his head jerks in surprise.

"What do you mean?"

"I mean, you shouldn't stay here. You need to get back on campus. You shouldn't be missing classes to stay here in the hospital with me."

"I disagree, Scottie," he says and sits down on the edge of my bed. "I don't think I should be anywhere but here. With you."

"No, Finn," I refute, and when he reaches out to grab my hand, I pull it away. "You need to go back to New York."

He doesn't understand it now, but eventually, he will. He'll find a way to move on, and he'll find a way to meet someone who can give him all the things I can't anymore.

His brown eyes search mine. "I want to be here for you, Scottie. I don't want or need to be anywhere else but here, okay?"

Finn has his entire life ahead of him. And prior to everything happening with his dad, his life enveloped him in hell and held him there. But now, he doesn't have to worry about his mom or Reece or Jack or Travis or Willow. He's even gained a whole new set of siblings who have shown him nothing but love and support and acceptance.

Unlike mine, his future is bright.

If he keeps doing this, sacrificing important things in his life because of his paralyzed girlfriend, one day he's going to wake up and regret it.

One day, he's going to realize that I was holding him back.

And I refuse to let it go that far.

I need to rip off the Band-Aid now and set him free.

Finn

"You need to go back to New York, Finn," Scottie says for the fifth time, and I try to grab her hand, but she pulls it away *again*. "You should've never stayed back. You should've left with Ace and Julia and Blake on Saturday. You're missing classes when you don't need to."

"I don't give a shit about my classes," I counter, standing over her and lifting her chin so she has to meet my gaze. Scottie is already petite, but right now, she looks so tiny lying here in this bed. She's defeated, and because of that, she's pushing me away. "I already told you, Ace and Julia are—"

"I know what you said, Finn, but I don't agree with it," she says, looking away so distinctly, it's a dismissal. "I think you need to leave."

"I can leave you alone for a bit. Go get some fresh air—"

"No, Finn. You need to *go*. I don't want you here anymore, okay?" She shoves at me as hard as she can, getting angry when I don't budge. "I said, leave! Go! Go back to New York and move on with your life!"

She's made up her mind, but she's made the wrong decision. I try to grab her arms to calm her down and Wren runs into the room in a panic, but Scottie's too far gone to stop.

"I want him out of here! Right now! Get security if you have to," she instructs Wren frantically.

"Don't do this, Scottie," I beg as she pushes the call light at the side of her bed to get a nurse. "I know you feel like everything is completely fucked right now. And that's valid. It's so valid. But don't push me away." I reach for her hand again, but she uses it to reach out and swing at me.

My throat is thick with pain and devastation, but I *know* this is just the hurt talking. She's lost all sense of control, but making me leave is something she can still do. I don't want to go, but I know she needs the victory. I know she needs to make something happen on her own just as much as I need her to know I won't go away forever.

"I love you," I tell her even as the nurse comes running into the room. "I love you, and I'll never stop. Do you hear me?"

She shakes her head, angry crying as the nurse tries to help, and then yells out again. "Get him out of here! Now!"

I hold up both of my hands as the nurse comes toward me, my last line of defense officially exhausted. "I'm leaving."

Scottie's face screws up on itself as she tries to fight the way I know she feels about me deep down inside.

She wants space. She needs time.

And I don't fucking want to, but I need to respect it.

Pushing through Wren and the nurse, I approach Scottie's bedside one last time and force her chin up to meet my eyes again. "I love you, Scottie. One day, you're going to realize just how much. I might be walking out of this room because I get that that's what you need, but I'm not fucking *going* anywhere. So, push me away if you want. But I'll be back."

84

Friday April 18ᵗʰ
Scottie

"We're all set to get you transferred this afternoon," Dr. Stewart updates, and his nurse Maureen sets down a few pieces of paper on my bedside table.

"Scottie, you'll just need to read and sign these affidavits, okay?" the nurse explains. "These give Med-I-Vac permission to take over your care during transport."

I don't even bother reading the forms. I just sign on the dotted line.

"I bet you're ready to get back home," Dr. Stewart says, a friendly smile cresting his lips. "I've already spoken with Dr. Hurst over at St. Luke's, and they're up to speed on your treatment plan." He gently squeezes my shoulder. "You're going to be in good hands, Scottie."

"Thank you." My voice is pathetically monotone, not at all matching the exuberance that Dr. Stewart and Nurse Maureen are showing. But that's probably because I don't have anything to be excited about.

Sure, I'm heading back to New York, but nothing about my life is going to be like it used to be.

I won't get to walk into my dorm room or attend classes. I'm going to be stuck in the hospital for at least another four weeks, and possibly up to eight, depending on how my rehabilitation goes.

"Mr. Bardeaux, you have my number." Dr. Stewart looks over

at my dad. "Don't hesitate to use it if you have any questions or concerns."

"Thank you so much, Doc," my dad responds and follows him and Nurse Maureen out of my hospital room. My guess is there's more paperwork for my dad to sign. More exorbitant medical bills that he has to say he'll pay, even though he probably can't cover all the bills I've already racked up in Daytona.

I'm starting to hate myself for how much additional stress I've just added to his life.

Wren sits down on the edge of my bed. "You okay?"

I shrug.

"You do know that you can be honest with me, right?" Her eyes implore mine. "Whatever you're feeling. Whatever you're thinking. You can tell me."

I know she's being kind. I know she's being supportive. But I don't think she wants her head filled up with the heavy shit that's running through my mind.

"It's going to be okay, Scottie," she says and leans forward to hug me. "You are surrounded by people who love and support you. And you're strong. Even if you don't feel like it right now, you are."

Being surrounded by people who love and support me is a fact. The problem with that is that I don't want to have to put anyone in that situation. I don't want my dad and my sister missing work shifts. I didn't want Finn to miss classes. And I definitely don't want anyone to have to change their life around to accommodate me.

I look toward the window, staring out at the sky. The sun is shining bright, and it's a stark contrast to the darkness that resides in my head. *I'm weak. So fucking weak.*

"Finn is still here." Wren's words pull my attention back to her. "He's in the waiting room. He's been in the waiting room ever since you told him to leave."

What can I even say to that? I told him to go back to New York two days ago. I don't know why he hasn't left yet.

"Why don't you want him in here?" she asks, and I stare down at the two limbs that no longer work.

"Because he should be back on campus, attending his classes. That should be his priority." Not a girl who doesn't even know what she has left to offer the world, let alone him.

"Scottie, I know this isn't my place, but I think you're wrong here. I think you have a guy who really loves you and wants to be there for you."

He loves me…now. But after months of dealing with this, dealing with me, and missing out on life because of my challenges, those feeling are slowly going to turn into regret and resentment.

When I don't say anything, she says, "I know the two of you have been through a lot. That's clear with everything you told me last night, but I think you're making a mistake."

Last night, when our dad was asleep, she grilled me about Finn. I guess after I told him to leave, and his response was to sit in the waiting room, that engaged her spidey senses a little too much. So, I told her all of the nitty-gritty details of our relationship. All of the ups and down and highs and lows. And where our relationship was before I got injured.

"You have a guy who wants to be there for you. Like, really be there for you," Wren says. "He clearly loves you, and I just don't understand why you're pushing him away."

The answer to that is easy. Because Finn Hayes loves the Scottie Bardeaux I used to be. A girl who I can't imagine will ever exist again.

Scottie

F our medical staff in jumpsuits with Med-I-Vac embroidered on their chests get the rundown from my nurses and Dr. Stewart as they turn my body from side to side to slide a backboard beneath me.

I can see my legs and feet moving, but I don't feel them. It's a strange feeling, having zero sensation from the waist down and not having control over my lower extremities. I honestly don't know if I'll ever get used to it.

Wren and my dad watch on from the corner of the room, and I silently wonder how much this transportation is going to cost.

"Is this really necessary, Dr. Stewart?" I ask him, and he steps over to the stretcher the Med-I-Vac staff has now relocated me to.

"Is what necessary, Scottie?"

"Transporting me like this," I answer. "I feel like my dad could've just rented a van and driven me back to New York." It would've been a hell of a lot cheaper. He could've just thrown my ass in the back of a U-Haul, for all I care.

"We've been through this, Scottie," Dr. Stewart says gently. "We don't want to cause any undue stress on your spine. The goal from here on out is to maintain as much function as we can. And since you haven't officially started rehabilitation and PT, we don't have a clear sense of your body's limitations."

My body limitations? My legs, my bladder, and my bowels don't work. I don't need a medical degree to know that. I'm living it every day now.

"This is the safest way to get you back home, okay?" He squeezes my shoulder. "I know it feels like a pain in the ass, and I get that. But this is all temporary. Once you start rehab and PT in New York, you're going to start getting your independence back."

Temporary. Independence. Those words don't feel like they will ever be a part of my reality.

"We're all set, Dr. Stewart," one of the female Med-I-Vac staff updates, and I remember that her name is Allison. She, along with the other three members of her team, introduced themselves when they first came into my room.

"Have a safe trip back to New York, Scottie," Dr. Stewart says with a smile. "Your father has my number. If you have any questions or concerns, don't hesitate to call me, okay? And I'll be in contact with Dr. Hurst and his team."

I nod.

"Thanks, Doc," my dad says and steps up to shake Dr. Stewart's hand. "Appreciate everything you've done for my girl."

My sister offers her thanks too, and I feel like a real ungrateful asshole for not saying anything. It's like I'm subconsciously pushing all my fear and anger about my injury onto him and his staff. People who have done nothing but treat me with kindness and have done everything in their power to maintain my dignity through some of the most embarrassing moments of my life.

"Thank you," I force myself to say, locking eyes with Dr. Stewart first and then Nurse Maureen, who stands near the doorway.

"It's been our pleasure," Nurse Maureen says, and Dr. Stewart nods.

"We'll be thinking about you, Scottie."

My dad and Wren step up to my bedside to give me hugs and kisses.

"We'll see you in New York, okay?" my dad says, and I don't miss the way emotion makes his voice all scratchy. "Our flight lands at eight this evening, and we'll head straight to the hospital."

"You guys don't need to do that. I'll—"

"Shut up," Wren says and squeezes my hand. "Don't be a martyr. We love you. And we'll see you in a few hours."

"That's precious cargo you got there. Take care of my girl," my dad tells the Med-I-Vac staff, and Allison reaches out to squeeze his forearm.

"She's in good hands," she says with a confident smile. "All four of us have the kind of medical transport experience that you can only get during war. We're going to take good care of her, and I promise we will get her safely to New York."

"You're all vets?" my dad asks, and all four members of the team nod. "Thank you for your service."

One of the male Med-I-Vac staff—I'm pretty sure his name is Ian—takes the front of my stretcher and guides my bed out of my hospital room and into the hallway. But we only get a few feet from my door when my stretcher stops in front of the nurses station so Allison can give the charge nurse a final rundown.

I startle when a hand grabs mine and squeezes.

I look up and to my left to find Finn standing there, dressed in the same jeans and T-shirt I saw him in two days ago. "See you in New York," he says. "I love you."

He doesn't wait for a response, and tears flood my eyes as I watch him walk down the hallway and out of sight.

I love Finn more than I've ever loved anyone, and if you love someone, if you *really* love someone, then you need to be strong enough to realize when you need to let them go.

I wish he would fucking let me.

'm halfway through today's assigned reading for my economics class when my phone vibrates in my pocket. I earmark the page, shut my textbook, and pull my phone out to check the screen.

> **Ace:** *You need anything? Julia and I are planning to stop by for a bit this evening.*

> **Me:** *Nah, dude. I'm good. Thanks.*

> **Ace:** *If you change your mind, you know how to reach me.*

I've been back in New York for almost week, and I've been at St. Luke's Hospital every single day, nearly every single hour, since I stepped off the plane that Ty managed to get me a last-minute flight on from Daytona.

The only time I've been on campus since I've been back is to run to my dorm to shower and change clothes. Other than that, I haven't been to class, haven't gone to any parties, haven't done anything but sit in the waiting room on Scottie's rehab floor.

She's still refusing to see me, to talk to me, but I won't let that deter me.

I'm not a mind reader, never have been, but I *know* Scottie. And crazily enough, we are so much alike it's not even funny. Her entire world has been flipped on its axis, and she's distraught and devasted—rightfully so—but she's also trying to push me away just like I stupidly did to her so many times before because of my own baggage.

Eventually, she's going to see the light, just like I did.

My love isn't conditional. It doesn't go away because she suffered a freak injury that's left her paralyzed from the waist down, and it doesn't shrink in value when things get hard. I know that life for her—and us—will come with limitations and challenges I'll probably never be able to fully understand because I'm not her, but none of that matters to me.

I love her. *All* of her. And there isn't a single fucking thing in this world that will change that.

So, I wait. In this dreaded hospital waiting room with the worst kind of chairs imaginable. And I also try to stay on top of my classes in the process.

"I had a feeling I'd find you here."

I look up to find Ty striding down the hospital hallway toward the waiting room. He doesn't stop until he plops his ass down in the chair beside mine.

"No luck yet?" he asks, and I shake my head.

"No luck."

"Is she letting anyone else back to see her?"

"Besides Wren and her dad, not really. She barely even let Kayla and Julia come in to see her when they stopped by yesterday afternoon."

"You're a good man," he says and nudges my knee with his.

"She makes me a better man."

"Isn't that how it always goes?" Ty questions with a smirk. "I was a real asshat before I met Rachel. She flipped my world upside down, and I shudder to think about where I'd be now if it weren't for her."

I furrow my brow. "You couldn't have been that bad."

"Oh, Finn." Ty laughs. "You have no idea. I was what you'd call a serial dater without any intention of commitment. I had so many fucking girlfriends that when Flynn brought his wife Daisy to our family dinner to meet us all for the first time, I honestly thought she was a girl *I'd* invited there but just forgot about it."

"What?" My head jerks back. "How is that even possible?"

"Like I said, man, I was a real asshat."

I laugh at that. "So, Daisy was just Flynn's new girlfriend then?"

"No, she was his wife. Though, if it helps at all, it *was* the first time we were meeting her."

My eyes damn near bug out of my head. "Wait… He married her before any of you met her? I'm going to need more details."

"Remind me to bring this up at the next family dinner," he says through a smirk. "And wait until you hear Remy and Maria's story. It's a doozy."

I laugh, and he shakes his head, gathering his thoughts. "Right. Yeah. Believe it or not, I did come here for an actual reason other than blessing you with my charming company. Two reasons, in fact."

I quirk an eyebrow.

"I've managed to get all but one of Scottie's professors to agree to pass her for the semester. She'll have the option to take the final or to go with whatever her grade was prior to the accident."

"All but one?"

"Professor Murkowski is being a bit of a dick, but I'll wear him down," he updates with an annoyed roll of his eyes. "Worst case, she'll have to take the final in order to pass, but I'm confident I can make sure he gives her plenty of time to catch up on anything she's missed."

Professor Murkowski has a reputation for being a hard-ass, so this revelation isn't that big of a surprise. Still, the girl's fucking paralyzed. If that's not enough to wear him down, I don't know what ever will.

Truthfully, Ty's the reason I've gotten approval from all my professors to work remotely. He's also been working behind the scenes with the Financial Aid Office to figure out what they can do about Scottie's cheerleading scholarship and figure out ways that she can keep funding for the next three years without being an active cheerleader on the squad. She's a good student and they have a couple of grants for some scholarships that are largely at their discretion, so he's pretty confident it's going to come through.

"I appreciate everything you're doing," I tell him, and he just claps a hard hand to my back.

"Of course." He rises to his feet. "Now, I gotta head out. Emily has a dance recital across town, and both my girls will ream my ass if I'm late."

Before he can go, I find myself standing and hugging him. I don't know why and I don't know how, but it just feels right. It's only been a few months since we've started working toward a relationship, but it feels like I've known him all my life.

"Thanks, Ty."

"I've always got your back, bro." He flashes a smile over his shoulder as he starts to head toward the elevators, but something dawns on me.

"Wait...what was the other thing you wanted to tell me?" I call out toward his retreating back.

He turns briefly to meet my eyes. "I'll text you." And then he disappears around the corner of the nurses station.

My phone buzzes a moment later.

> *Ty: The jurors found him unanimously guilty on all counts. And the judge has sentenced him to life in prison.*

Holy shit. With everything that's happened with Scottie, I completely forgot about my dad's trial. Normally, it can take a year after someone is brought into custody before they stand before a judge and jury, but since he killed a police officer and he's been a wanted man for many years, the court system fast-tracked that shit.

I don't hesitate to open up the group chat with my siblings.

> *Me: He got life in prison.*

Their responses come in seconds later, a variation of shock, surprise, and relief. All of which I completely understand. There's a small part of me that feels sad for my dad, but it's so small that if I blink a few more times, it'll disappear on the wind.

I don't know what I thought would happen when I set foot on Dickson's campus at the beginning of the year, but I know with certainty I never anticipated this. My mind rolls through everything that's happened over the past year, and I find myself scrolling through my other text conversations.

Ace and Blake, two guys I didn't know at the start of the year who have now become my best friends.

Julia and Kayla. Scottie's friends who have become my friends.

My group chat with all the Winslow siblings—who are my siblings too. It's been nonstop chatter since Scottie got hurt. Every single one of them wanting to stay updated on her condition. Every single one of them offering support in whatever way they can.

My separate conversation with Ty, whom I've grown so close with over the past few months that I actually feel like he's my own full flesh and blood. In a weird way, he's become a bit of a father figure that I've never had.

My siblings, of course. And despite the bomb I just dropped on them, our group chat has gone from ugly things happening within our house to peace and joy and happiness.

My mom. Ever since my father has been out of the picture, she's starting to find herself again and working through the guilt that comes with not leaving and getting us out of that house sooner. Hindsight is twenty-twenty, though, and she never had the support we have from the Winslows when she was trying to do it on her own.

Scottie's sister, Wren. Even her dad. For the past week, they've been keeping me updated on Scottie's condition and welcomed my loitering with open arms. Yesterday was the first day they left Scottie's bedside to go back to Westchester because they couldn't miss any more shifts from their jobs.

And of course, Scottie. I scroll up, past all my most recent text messages to her that have gone unanswered and look at the exchanges we had before she got hurt.

There are more *I love yous* than I can count. There's teasing and flirting and the kind of happy, cutesy fucking texts that probably would've made me want to puke a year ago.

I miss her.

She's the only missing piece to my happily-ever-after.

Thursday May 1st
Scottie

Sweat drips from my brow and my neck and my armpits and my boobs as I use all my strength to lift myself up from my wheelchair and into my bed. My arms shake and my hands cramp, and when my ass is halfway toward my mattress, my elbows start to buckle, but I force a deep inhale of oxygen into my lungs and muster every ounce of power I have to complete the distance. Once my butt hits the bed, I almost slip off the edge, but my physical therapist is there to help ease me back a few inches so I don't hit the floor.

"Great job, Scottie!" Pam exclaims. "I can't believe how strong you're getting."

"I don't feel strong." I blow out a breath of air from my pursed lips, and it forces a few pieces of sweat-drenched hair away from my face. "If you weren't here, I would've ended up on the floor."

"Scottie, it's been two weeks, and the progress you've made is unreal," she reassures with a soft smile as she hands me a glass of water with a straw. I take a sip. "Normally, you wouldn't be able to do any part of a transfer until the four-week mark at most. Usually, for most patients, it can take six to eight weeks, depending on their upper body strength. You're doing amazing. Don't get discouraged."

I try to take her words in and believe them as truth, but it's hard. Then again, everything feels hard these days.

My entire medical team has been excited about my progress. Dr. Hurst was over the moon this morning when he found out I had managed to successfully ask a nurse to help me to the bathroom without having an accident. Prior to that, I was either pissing myself without knowing or the staff had to catheterize me.

Now, I wouldn't say I've all of a sudden gotten feeling in my bladder, but I did feel the teeniest inkling of *something*, and when you combine that with the fact that I've paid enough attention to understand how often I usually go, it helped achieve that milestone. The me from three weeks ago never thought peeing in the toilet would be this exciting, but the me of today actually smiled over it.

It's at least a tiny shred of normalcy.

"Do you need anything before I go?" Pam asks, and I shake my head.

"I'm good. Thanks."

"I'll see you tomorrow, Scottie."

"See you tomorrow."

"And while I'm gone, do me a favor and give yourself a pat on the back, okay? You've made leaps and bounds that I honestly didn't think would be possible this early."

I make a show of reaching up with my right hand to pat myself on the back. "Way to go, me," I say sarcastically.

Pam just laughs and rolls her eyes. "One of these days, Scottie, I'm going to get you to say that, and you're actually going to believe it."

"Yeah, yeah," I retort. Pam grins before walking out of my door.

My rehab hospital room is different from the hospital room I was in at Daytona. And different from the first room I was in when I arrived at St. Luke's. About ten days into my rehab process here, Dr. Hurst felt I was ready to be transferred to a floor that requires less care from the nursing staff.

So now, instead of getting checked on every two to four hours by the nurses, I only see them around mealtimes. It's been a welcome change.

Though, if I had my way, all the flowers and balloons and cards and bears and everything else that people have sent me wouldn't have followed me here. It's not that I'm not thankful that everyone is trying to support me, but I'm trying to find a way to move on from feeling like a victim all day every day. When I look at it all, I get sad.

"Hey, hey, hey!" Wren greets as she walks into my room with her arms full of a duffel bag and a box, and I tilt my head to the side in confusion.

"I thought you weren't coming until tomorrow?"

"I switched shifts with Jessica," she updates and sets the bag and box down on the small dinette table near the window. "I'll be here tonight, tomorrow, and until, like, three o'clock on Saturday because I have to work early on Sunday morning."

She starts to pull items from the bag—a brush, a hair straightener, hair products, makeup, nail polish.

"What is all that?"

"I thought we'd enjoy a little girl time," she says and flashes a smile over her shoulder. "A spa day, if you will."

"You trying to tell me I look like a troll?" I tease. She shrugs, and I scoff. "Wow, don't spare my feelings or anything."

She laughs. "No offense, but you've been slacking on the self-care."

"Well, I don't know if you know this, but I recently became paralyzed."

"Oh shit, really?" She snorts. "I had no idea."

"Yeah." I smile, and this time, I actually feel like I mean it. The humor feels good. "My legs don't work. Like, at all. It's nuts."

"But...do your arms work?" she questions with pursed lips. "Because I'm pretty sure you don't brush your hair with your feet..."

"You really went there, huh?" I retort with wide eyes, but I also laugh.

Wren grins and carries the box over toward me. "By the way, Dad sent a care package of all of your favorite snacks. I hope you don't mind, but I ate half of the gummy bears on my drive here."

"Stealing the paralyzed girl's candy? That's a new low."

"Pfft. I guess now isn't the time to mention that I also ate your Oreos, huh?"

I know it's crazy, but this entire conversation is my favorite conversation I've had in I don't know how long. It's as if, finally, someone is treating me like I'm a normal person. Finally, someone isn't trying to bend over backward for me.

"Dad says he misses you and loves you and plans to come visit Saturday after his morning shift."

My happy balloon is instantly popped.

Ever since I was transferred to New York, my father has been spending all his time either working or visiting me. I hate it because I want some form of normal for him, too.

He's always been a hard worker, but this is another level, and that's all thanks to me and the financial debt my medical care has added to his life. I tried to tell him not to worry about it. I tried to remind him that I'm legally an adult and all the bills should be in my name, but he's the best kind of guy and refused to hear anything I was trying to say.

Wren grabs a chair and moves it toward my bed, and she gives me no option as she grabs my foot and starts to paint my toes a pastel shade of pink. Normally, I'd give her shit, but now, my mind is doing its typical spiral of all the things that weigh heavily on my shoulders.

Medical bills. My dad working himself to the bone.

My scholarship.

My classes that I'm missing every single day.

My squad and the fact that my injury caused us to lose Nationals. And all the teammates who have reached out, trying to come visit, but I just make up excuses to keep them away.

My friends—Julia and Kayla—who are the sweetest, kindest, most amazing girls I've ever had the pleasure of knowing, and for the past week, all I've done is avoid them.

Even Blake and Ace have tried to stop by.

And Finn, well…he texts me every day, all day long. Random

shit. Links to songs on Spotify. Funny memes that made him laugh. I love yous.

He also hasn't gone a single day without having a nurse come in and ask if I'm accepting visitors, but I always say no.

"Did you happen to see anyone out in the waiting room?" I ask Wren, my curiosity too damn piqued to deny.

"By *anyone*, I'm assuming you mean Finn," she says and just barely glances up at me as she applies polish to the pinkie toe on my right foot. "And yes, he's in the waiting room. Like he's *always* in the waiting room. All he needs is a bed and a family portrait, and I think they'd officially declare it his new home now."

"Get real. There's no way he's here all the time."

Wren eyes me seriously. "Scottie, he's here all the time. He never leaves."

"But what about his classes?" I question, and she shrugs.

"All I know is that he's here *all* the time. Sometimes, he *is* working on school shit, so I assume he's found some way to stay on top of things."

"I wish he wouldn't do that," I say, but my voice is so quiet that I don't even know if Wren heard me.

"You might be trying to push him away, but it's not working. I mean, he's always here. *Always.* Not to mention, I just found out today about that GoFundMe he started for you. If all those things combined don't scream love and devotion, I don't know what does."

"GoFundMe? *What?*"

"You didn't know?"

She pauses painting my nails to pull her phone out of her jeans pocket. A few taps to the screen and she hands me her phone. And right there on the screen is an actual GoFundMe page for *Scottie Bardeaux.*

And when I see how much money he's managed to raise for me, I drop Wren's phone into my lap. "Is that real?"

"Girl, it's real," Wren says. "When I showed Dad this morning, he burst into tears. I can't even begin to tell you how stressed he's been about keeping your medical care going, even though he doesn't have the funds to pay for it all. Last week, he spent hours on the phone trying to get payment plans in order. And now, because of Finn, all of that's been solved."

Big, fat, salty tears stream over my lips, and I pick Wren's phone back up to look at the list of people who have donated money and left kind words of support.

The Kelly Family—Thatch, Cassie, Ace, and Gunnar.

The Brooks Family—Kline, Georgia, Julia, and Evie.

All of Finn's newest brothers and sister—Remy, Flynn, Ty, Jude, and Winnie and their families.

Wendy Winslow and Howard.

Finn's mom and his siblings.

Coach Jordan.

Literally every single one of my teammates.

A bunch of my professors.

Dean Kandinsky.

Even Officer Walters from the Dickson Campus Police.

So many people and so much money and I don't even know how to feel about it.

When Wren sees that I'm crying, she stops painting my nails and climbs into bed beside me.

"I love you, Scottie," she whispers as she gently runs her fingers through my hair. "And I know this is all really hard for you. You're used to being independent. You're used to being the one who is helping other people, not the other way around."

"I'm such a fucking burden now. On everyone."

"But don't you see?" she retorts and leans back to meet my eyes. "You're not a burden, Scottie. You're important. You're special. You're loved. And everyone who is trying to help you is doing it because they love you. Because they care about you."

I shake my head. "But—"

"There are no buts." She cuts me off. "These are facts. This is truth. This is love. And the sooner you learn to accept that, the sooner you're going to be able to find closure with what you've lost and be able to move on to a future that, while it may not be what you pictured, can still be a future that is just as bright, just as beautiful, just as fulfilling. There are a ton of people here, right on this floor, you could help, you know? Other people struggling. Maybe helping them like you used to at the hospital at home will help you too. You have lots of gifts left to give. I promise."

Her words slice through my chest and open up a dam of emotion I didn't even realize was there. My entire being feels like it's at war—my heart and my head—trying to understand how I should feel and what I should feel.

I cry into Wren's arms until I'm numb from emotion.

I cry until I can't cry anymore.

I cry until I fall asleep.

But for the first time since I got hurt, they're not just tears of anguish—they're tears of possibility.

"**Y**our vitals look good, Scottie," Kimmie, one of my nurses, updates as she removes the blood pressure cuff from my arm. "Do you need anything?"

I shake my head. "I'm good, Kimmie."

"Promise me you'll eat a little dinner?" she asks and promptly puts my dinner tray in front of where I'm currently sitting at the little table by the window. "I'm leaving my shift a little early this evening, so Amanda is going to be the one taking over for me. And you and I both know that girl is too nice to press you like I do."

"Oh, trust me," I say through a laugh. "I know."

Kimmie grins and writes Amanda's number on the whiteboard below my television. "Call her if anything comes up before she does her final check tonight, okay?"

"I will," I say, good-naturedly exasperated. "I know the drill."

"You know, when you leave this place, you're going to miss me." She winks, and I don't argue. I know if there's one nurse I'll miss when I finally get discharged from here, it's Kimmie.

She's a ballbuster, to say the least, but she's exactly what a girl like me needs. She doesn't take any of my shit, doesn't sugarcoat anything, doesn't step in unless I specifically ask for help, and for that, I'm always thankful.

Kimmie knows how to make her patients feel independent, which is something I took for granted until I was faced with paraplegia.

It's amazing how much your perspective changes when something like this happens to you. Things that seemed like big things—gossip on campus, backstabbing friends, boyfriends, dating—feel trivial when you're faced with my reality.

Autonomy is at the core of everything.

"I'm off tomorrow, but I'll see you Tuesday." She grabs her clipboard and the little cart that has the blood pressure machine and other things to take my vitals. "Now, wish me luck. It's Mother's Day, and I best be walking home to flowers and gifts and dinner on the table. Otherwise, my husband is going to be in the doghouse."

"Happy Mother's Day, Kimmie." I smile.

I had no idea it was Mother's Day, but that shouldn't be a surprise. For most of my life, it's been a day I avoided. A day I tried to forget. I can remember being in elementary school and teachers having us make our moms little gifts. It was painful making a Happy Mother's Day card knowing full well I'd never actually give it to my mom because, at that point, my dad had fought for full custody of Wren and me in order to keep our mother's constant toxicity and reckless behavior out of our lives.

But seeing people like Kimmie and Georgia Brooks fill the role so well makes me think maybe I should pay more attention. Not for my mom, but for the real *moms*. The ones who mother everyone, not just their kids, with love and intention.

"Hey," Kimmie says then, pulling my attention away from myself and pausing her little wave as she's heading out the door. "I almost forgot, but I was hoping you could also find some time to go sit with Molly for a little bit."

I frown. Molly's another patient on my floor, dealing with a thigh-down amputation of her leg because of bone cancer. She's only in middle school, and her mom and dad both work two jobs to keep them afloat. As a result, she spends a lot of time alone.

"Why? What's up?"

Kimmie shrugs. "She's having a hard day. I think a visitor would help."

I nod gratefully. Ever since Wren suggested it, I've spent a lot of time cruising through some of the other rooms on the floor and chatting with other patients. Mostly, patients who are younger than me, and I have to admit, having a little company and some purpose has felt incredibly good. Empowering, even. "I'll go down there now."

Kimmie nods and winks, stepping out of the room and leaving me to do the transfer all on my own—a move I have very little doubt is intentional.

I roll my eyes at her and huff, but I also get down to business.

I reach out to grab my wheelchair where it's folded up against the wall, open it up with both hands, lock the brakes like Pam often reminds me to do, and set it at just the right angle so I can transfer with ease.

With two strong hands, I lift myself up from the chair and into my wheelchair.

I'm honestly pleasantly surprised with myself at how good I've become at transfers. Ten days ago, I was still incredibly shaky, and Pam or a nurse had to help me.

But today, not only can I do all by myself, but it didn't even feel like I had to use a lot of effort.

With a quick unlock of the brakes, I get my angle right and wheel out the door, into the hallway where there's relatively little activity. The nurses are busy switching shifts, and most of the patients are eating their dinner, so I have the hall to myself as I roll my way down the floor, stopping only briefly to push open Molly's cracked door and then cruise inside.

She's got a tray of untouched food in front of her and a frown on her face, but at the sight of me, she actually lights up.

Unexpected warmth spreads throughout my entire belly. It feels really good to cause a smile.

"Hey, Scottie!" she says excitedly, pushing up in her bed and swinging her tray over to the side. I wheel over to the far side of her bed and lock my wheels, settling in for a chat.

"Hey, girl. What's shakin'?"

She shakes her head, her jet-black bob swishing in the air, and jerks her chin at her absent leg. "Not much, you know?"

"Oh yeah. I know." I snort and glance down at my legs. "This morning, I realized I forgot to put on underwear. Thankfully, I remembered pants." I make a silly face at her. "Could you imagine if I would've had my butt cheeks out when Dr. Hurst came in to see me this morning?"

Molly howls with laughter. "He would have gone full tomato!"

I honestly don't know what it is about Dr. Hurst, but the man has some crazy skin. It's like any minor emotion—frustration, irritation, happiness, anger—makes the blood flow to his face like a faucet.

"So, it's not just me, then?" I grin. "Dr. Hurst's face gets really red sometimes, right?"

"So red!" Molly says through a giggle. "Like a lobster, Scottie. For reals."

We both laugh at that, and I cheer a silent victory that I've managed to put so much joy on her face. "Has your mom been by today?"

"Yeah, this morning." Molly nods. "I gave her the painting you and I did the other day since I didn't have a card for Mother's Day. Hope you don't mind."

I laugh. "If anyone should mind, it's your mom. You and I aren't the best artists."

Molly snorts. "I know. She still loved it, though. Said she was gonna hang it in our kitchen right over the table."

"An appropriate place for a painting of bacon and eggs," I hum with satisfaction, and Molly shakes her head.

"I still can't believe that's what you wanted to paint."

I shrug. "Listen, I had to give in to my cravings somehow, and I don't think my stomach is ready for the real thing." I jerk my chin toward her tray and then point at the banana on the right-hand side. "I am hungry, though. Mind if I have your banana?"

She shakes her head and hands it to me, and I peel it gratefully. "That chicken noodle soup is actually good, you know?"

"Really?"

"Yeah. Better than Campbell's, in my opinion. Not quite as good as the kind at my college, but pretty good. Try it."

Shrugging, Molly moves the tray back in front of herself and picks up her spoon, scooping some up and into her mouth.

I smother a satisfied smile and ignore the jolt of excitement. I know firsthand how hard it is to make yourself eat, but convincing Molly to do it now makes me feel almost superhuman.

"Mmm," she moans, putting a hand to her mouth frantically when a little bit of broth slips out. We both laugh, and when she goes in for another scoop, I have to fight the urge to pump my fist.

Molly and I babble for nearly an hour about celebrity news and Taylor Swift and nurse gossip while she eats, and as more light returns to her eyes, I feel more and more in tune with myself.

Not the Scottie who cheered or the Scottie who walked—but the Scottie who loved to help people even more than she loved to help herself.

I feel purpose and strength and, most of all…hope.

My life isn't what it once was, but if I let go of all the rage and hurt and stubbornness, it can still be good. Not having cheerleading on my schedule frees me up to do all the things I didn't have time for. One of Finn's many messages mentioned getting a different scholarship from some grant, which gives me freedom to succeed in school. And hell, I don't know, not being able to run away might make me face some of my problems so head on that I actually solve them.

As crazy as it sounds, the new Scottie isn't like the old Scottie… but she might be better. Stronger. Ready to save the world.

Wednesday May 14ᵗʰ
Scottie

I flex my stomach again, working at the core muscles I've been trying so hard to build up in PT, and drag myself up in the bed. I grab my notebook from the side table and jot down some of the other ideas I had for making Dickson's campus more ADA-friendly. It follows regulations already—it has to—but now that I'm thinking of things from a renewed perspective, I know there's a lot more that can be done to help students like me. *Future* students like Molly.

My phone buzzes with a text, so I drop the notebook back on the table and pick up my phone instead.

The message on the screen brings a smile to my face, so I quickly type out a reply.

> *Kayla: Remember how I was telling you about Sheila having the baby?? She sent a picture, and I think she looks like me!*
>
> *Me: OMG, KAYYY. Your niece is adorable! Which, yes, she looks just like you, so that isn't a shock! Her eyes are such a stunning color!*
>
> *Kayla: Thanks, girl! Julia and I have all the trashy magazines ready for tomorrow! See you then!*

A soft sigh escapes my lungs, the relief of letting the two of them come for a proper visit lightening the weight on my chest.

After I finish my exchange with her, I find myself scrolling my phone, looking through all the missed text messages and phone calls I've received over the past several weeks. It's hard to believe it's been over a month since I got hurt. A month since everything changed.

I have no idea what my mom is up to—I haven't spoken to her since I made her leave my hospital room in Daytona—but she still texts me often.

I don't know why, but it feels like I'm ready to read through some of them now, so I do.

> *I'm so sorry, Scottie. For everything. I know I don't have any right to ask for your forgiveness. But I just want you to know that you're always on my mind.*

> *Thinking about you today. Hope you're doing okay.*

> *Wren told me you're doing really well with physical therapy. And before you get mad at her, just know that I'm the one who asked about you. She didn't offer up any information easily, but I felt relief in knowing rehabilitation is going well.*

> *I love you. And I want you to know that I will spend the rest of my life taking accountability for everything I've put you through over the years. You didn't deserve any of it. It wasn't your fault, and it all falls on me. I was the one with the problem. I was the one who wasn't the mother that you deserved. That will always be the biggest regret of my life.*

All these years, I honestly think this is the first time she's ever said anything that resembles accountability or acknowledging the past.

I lift my fingers toward the screen and let them hover over the keypad. For the first time in what feels like forever, a part of me actually wants to text her back.

Thank you, I type the two words out. The only words that feel right in this moment. I stare at them for a long time before I end up hitting send, but eventually, I do.

I don't know what it means. I don't know if it will lead anywhere. I don't know if I'll ever respond to her again. But I guess
something is better than nothing.

I set my phone down on the table and stare out the window.
The sun has already set, and the sky is starting to turn to night.
Views of skyscrapers and light Wednesday evening traffic fill my
view. When I see an American flag blowing with the wind, a little
sigh of longing leaves my lungs.

I can't remember the last time I was outside. I can't remember
the last time I actually felt the sun on my face or the wind in my hair.

My whole reality has been hospitals for the past several weeks.
Even when I'm working with Pam, we always go to the PT room
on the fourth floor.

I look down toward the ground and note the little outdoor
courtyard that sits in the center of the hospital. It's completely empty,
and I decide that maybe, just maybe, I should try to go down there
for a little bit.

Technically, I don't have clearance from Dr. Hurst to leave the
premises, but…I'd still be on the premises, *right?*

Feels like a good enough explanation to me. Plus, now that I'm
wearing my own clothes and I'm no longer hooked up to IVs, the
only identifying information is my bracelet, and that's easily hidden
beneath my long-sleeved T-shirt.

I grab my wheelchair from its spot on the wall, lock the wheels,
and perform the transfer into my wheelchair like it's part of my routine now. It's not a struggle physically, mentally, or even emotionally—which is maybe the most shocking. It just is.

When I wheel past the floor-length mirror just outside my en
suite bathroom, I realize I'm smiling. It's a sight that's becoming
more and more frequent these days, and a surge of pride bolsters
me as I wheel toward my door.

Slowly, I peer out toward the hallway and the nurses station.
When I don't see anyone in sight, I make a break for it. As quick as

my hands will let me, I wheel down the hall and toward the bank of elevators.

Every few seconds, I glance over my shoulder to make sure no one is there to try to stop me, and I'm relieved when I manage to reach the elevators without a single staff member noticing.

If Kimmie were on shift, she might be pissed if she found out I did this, but Amanda is my nurse again this evening. She's sweeter than pie, and the most I'll get is a disappointed look on her face if she ends up noticing my absence. The risk is most definitely worth the reward.

Once I'm on the elevator, I hit the button for the ground floor, and the cart whizzes to life. And when I reach the lobby level, I wheel over the threshold without much difficulty and head toward the hallway I'm pretty sure leads toward that courtyard.

I offer a confident smile to the woman working the main desk in the center of the lobby, my expression conveying, *I'm just a random girl wheeling around. Nothing to see here.*

The woman doesn't think anything of my presence and goes back to looking at whatever is on her computer screen.

Phew.

When I reach the automatic doors, I stop in my tracks when I realize I'm not heading toward the courtyard. Instead, I'm heading straight out the main entrance of the hospital and right into the busy city.

Shit.

I almost turn around, but then I remember the lady at the desk, and since I don't want to raise any red flags before I can feel the wind on my face, I keep heading straight, through the automatic doors and toward the sidewalk.

For a Wednesday evening, the sidewalks aren't that busy, but anxiety has my heart racing at record speeds. I've never had to maneuver through pedestrian traffic like this. Hell, I've never even navigated anything but smooth hospital floors.

The concrete makes the wheels of my chair vibrate, and I force myself to breathe through the stress. *This is no big deal. You can do this. And more than that, you can enjoy it.*

Anxiety and fear of the unknown try to wreak havoc on my mind, but I keep reminding myself that I am capable of doing hard things. It's what Pam always tells me during our therapy sessions. *I can do hard things.*

I'm a half a block from the hospital entrance at this point, and when I reach a crosswalk, I let myself stop for a long moment, out of the way of foot traffic, just to take it all in. Spring is in the air, and the breeze is lukewarm against my face. Trees and flowers are blooming from planters on the sidewalks. And there're a lot of people already enjoying outdoor dining at restaurants.

The crosswalk light changes, giving me the go-ahead, and I do my best to navigate the curb as I wheel onto the street. People walk around me, but I keep my eyes forward and focus on maneuvering my wheelchair.

This is good. This is normal. This is…invigorating.

I'm doing this completely on my own, without the assistance or guidance of anyone, and I'm doing it because of my own longing to do it.

I'm living. I'm happy. I'm Scottie.

I get across the street and onto the sidewalk, and a few drops of rain fall onto my face. I can't believe how good they feel—how good they *could* feel. And to think, on that first day of class, I was doing a shrieking run to get away from them. I tilt my head up to the sky to savor it, and the pace of their timing picks up, pinging me quickly from the dark storm cloud above.

If it weren't for getting my chair soaked, I think I'd stay out here forever.

Thunder rumbles in the distance, and I decide that now would be a good time to head back to the hospital. I've had my fun, but there's no need to go overboard. Being a rod for lightning would really put the icing on this year's cake.

I have to wait again for the crosswalk, and as the seconds tick by, the raindrops come faster and harder. By the time I cross the street and reach the sidewalk, it's pouring down from the sky. My hands slip against my wheels, the water making it hard to get a good grip, and people on the sidewalk are running around me as I try to head back to the hospital entrance.

I stop in the middle of the sidewalk to try to wipe my hands on my T-shirt, but it's no use. I'm soaked—my hair, my shirt, my sweats, even my bra and underwear and socks and shoes are drenched. And the rain doesn't let up or give me a break.

I start to laugh maniacally, the dam of every emotion I never thought I'd feel again bursting inside me.

I don't have my phone. I don't have my wallet. I have nothing but myself, my wheelchair, and my hospital bracelet. And I can't move. It's not funny, but for some reason, it also is.

I may have convinced myself I don't need anyone helping me, but I sure could use a knight in shining armor right about now.

"Scottie!"

The sound of my name urges my eyes forward, and I see Finn running toward me.

"Scottie!" he calls out, and it only makes me laugh more. I call out to the universe for a knight in shining armor, and it sends me one. Maybe my luck has finally taken a positive turn for a change.

"What are you doing? The nurses are looking for you," he says when he stops right in front of me. The rain has drenched his hair and white T-shirt and jeans, and his brown eyes implore mine as he kneels down in front of me. His face is gentle, as gentle as I've ever seen it, and another flashback to our first encounter in the rain steals any decorum I have left.

"Man, this is something!" I say, my laugh almost hysterical now. "You and me, meeting in the rain like this."

"Let me help you," he says, and I shake my head. I don't want to go. I know it's dangerous, and I know I'm soaked, but I've never felt more in a moment of kismet than I do right now, and I don't want to let it pass me by.

"You remember the day we met, Finn?" I ask, looking up to the sky again and putting my arms out to my sides to soak in the rain.

"Of course I do."

I nod, a run of tears joining the rain on my face now. They're not sad, though. They're just me. "Here we are again, the damsel in distress and the mysterious man of her dreams." He smiles, and I reach out to touch his handsome face. "I didn't know anything about you that day and I don't know where you came from now, but I don't care. I love you. And I know I should let you go, but—"

"Don't."

"Don't what?"

"Don't let me go." His voice is the most determined I've ever heard it, and his eyes never break contact with mine as he shoves to standing. "I don't want you to, Scottie. Can't you see that?"

"Finn—"

"I love you, Scottie. I choose us. I choose you. Do you hear me?"

Between one breath and the next, he lifts me out of my chair and up and into his arms. Rain pounds from the sky but all I can feel is the warmth of his skin as he cradles me close to his chest. "I love you. I love you more than anything in this world, and I refuse to let you push me away."

It feels like it's been forever since I've felt his arms wrapped around me. Forever since I've felt his touch. And it's all so powerful, so intense, that I bury my face into his chest and sob.

"I love you," he whispers and kisses my forehead and hair. "I love you. I love you. I love you."

"I choose us," I whimper. "Because I'm ready to choose me, too."

"**Y**ou have me, Scottie. You have all of me. And there isn't a single fucking thing that will ever change that." I grab her hand and put it right above my heart. "You're special, Scottie. You were before, and you are now," I say, and more tears stream down her cheeks. "And fuck, I'm going to spend the rest of my life trying to be a man who deserves you."

"You don't mean that."

I yank down the neckline of my soaked t-shirt, lift her hand up, and purposefully take her index finger to trace over the black ink that sits above my heart. **Scottie**. In her handwriting. From that first note she passed to me in English Lit class all those months ago.

"Finn?"

"When I say I love you, I mean it. When I say you have me, I mean it," I whisper. "Nothing has changed for me. Nothing will change for me. Because, Scottie, to me, you're not defined by that fucking wheelchair. It's a part of you now, but it's not *you* any more than my dad's bullshit is me. We're kindred. Meant to be. And I refuse to move forward without you. You have me. Period. End of story."

"I can't believe you did that," she says, and her eyes well with more tears. "Tell me it's fake. Tell me it's like the silly temporary tattoo I did for you that one night."

"It's permanent. It's forever. Because it's how I see you and me."

"We're young. There's no way you can know that."

"Scottie, that day in Daytona, when I saw you fall, when I saw you get injured, I feared the worst. I feared I'd lost you. I feared that I would never get to hold you. That I would never get to kiss you. That I would never get to see your smiles or hear your laughs or see how fucking cute you look when you get all flustered and your cheeks are stained red."

I lean forward to press my lips to hers, and I feel tears in my eyes when she actually lets me do it.

"When you fear you've lost the person you love, it puts a hell of a lot of things into perspective," I whisper against her mouth and lean back to meet her eyes. "Sure, we're young. Sure, we have a lot of growing up to do. I agree with all of that. But I know with every ounce of my soul that you're the girl I want to grow old with. The girl I want to one day marry. You're the only girl I want to be by my side for the rest of my life, and nothing will ever change that."

91

Scottie

"I love you," he tells me again. "I'm here. And whatever obstacles and challenges and hard times lie ahead, I'm here. It's me and you against the world. That's how I see it. That's how I'll always see it."

He kisses me again, harder this time, more passionate, and the rain mingles with our tears and tongues.

And I kiss him back. I don't stop kissing him until the urge to say I love you is too much.

"I love you, Finn," I whisper against his lips. "I love you. Period. End of story," I repeat his words, and he leans back to meet my eyes.

"Me and you?"

I nod. "Me and you."

He kisses me again, and I wrap my arms around his shoulders to savor the feel of it.

We've been through hell. We've been through ups and downs. We've been through a lot of shit. But each time we face something, it makes us stronger. And even when we tried to fight against this thing between us, this all-consuming love that's grown, it didn't matter because we always ended up right back here.

Us. *Together.*

"How about I get you back inside before your nurses end up calling the cops?" he asks, leaning back again to meet my eyes.

"Pretty sure the cops wouldn't be too fussed," I answer with a smile. "I mean, how hard is it to find a girl in a wheelchair?"

Finn laughs and shakes his head. But he also presses another kiss to my lips before grabbing my wheelchair off the sidewalk and heading back toward the hospital. His strong frame carrying both me and my chair without any issue.

By the time we're through the automatic doors, a question pops into my mind.

"When did you get that tattoo?"

"About a week ago." He smirks down at me. "And don't laugh, but Ace's dad is the one who did it."

"What?" I blurt out on a shocked laugh. "Ace's dad gave you that tattoo?"

"Yeah." Finn grins. "Not only is he the financial king of New York, but he's also a certified tattoo artist."

"Holy smokes." I giggle. "That family is, hands down, the craziest bunch of people I've ever met."

Finn doesn't say anything, but he doesn't have to. It's facts.

Once we're out of the elevator and Finn gives my nurse Amanda a moment to see that I'm okay, he carries me back into my room.

Once inside, he sets me on the bed and grabs a fresh pair of clothes from the small dresser that has all my belongings in it.

"I can get dressed myself," I tell him on a laugh, slapping his hands away.

But he shakes his head. "This isn't for you," he says and starts to remove my socks and shoes. "This is for me."

I stare down at him, completely incredulous.

"All I've wanted to do is be here for you. For days and weeks, I've sat in hospital waiting rooms just so I could be close to you, and now I finally am," he answers like it makes total sense. "I need this right now. I need to help my girl get out of her wet clothes and get dressed, and because you love me, you're going to let me."

It's almost reverent, the way that he removes my jeans and underwear and bra and T-shirt. And his touch is gentle and affectionate, and it urges more emotion to spill onto my cheeks.

But I don't stop him. Instead, I lie there and let him help me.

I let him put fresh clothes on me. I let him brush my hair.

And after my nurse Amanda drops off a pair of scrubs for Finn to change into, he climbs into bed with me and pulls my body close to his chest.

"I love you," he whispers into my ear, and I don't hesitate to respond.

"I love you too."

We fall asleep like that. Finn's body wrapped around mine.

And for once, my heart and mind agree.

It's taken us forever to get here, but it's an amazing feeling to know that nothing could ever be big enough or wrong enough to make us leave.

We've already been through it all, and, together, we've come out the other side—*this is love.*

EPILOGUE

Friday July 25th
Scottie

"I have great news," Ms. Bartlett, my counselor here at Dickson, updates as she leans across her desk to hand me a paper. "Your schedule has been updated."

"How many of my classes did you manage to switch?" I question, glancing down at the sheet of paper with a cup half full of hope. I know Ms. Bartlett will try, but with the semester starting soon and open enrollment happening nearly a week ago, I don't expect her to be able to perform magic.

Studying the paper more closely when Ms. Bartlett doesn't say anything, I run quickly through the dream schedule, double-check twice that all the psych classes I needed are on there, and then gape. "Wait...you got me in all of the classes?"

"All of them." She smiles, and she's not the only one. If my face were a spaceship, it'd be picking up humans at an astonishing rate.

"You're a miracle worker!"

"I'm glad you're happy, Scottie." Ms. Bartlett grins and blows imaginary dust off her fingernails before subsequently polishing them on her shoulders.

"And—" A soft knock on her office door grabs our attention, interrupting her.

A scruffy curled head pokes in and locks eyes with her, and she gives me an apologetic smile. "Give me a second, Scottie?"

"Of course," I say with a nod as she steps out of her office to talk to her colleague.

Silence and solitude seep in around me, and I pick at my

cuticles as thoughts of excitement and anticipation for my new career path swirl through my mind.

A career path inspired by Molly and me and Luke—another teenager from St. Luke's Inpatient Rehabilitation who was diagnosed with retinal detachment syndrome and is mentally and emotionally struggling with his new reality after a failed surgery attempt on his right eye. A career path inspired by the millions of young adults like us, dealing with unforeseen circumstances or unfair hands and doing their best to navigate in a world that wasn't designed for them. A career path born of one pivotal conversation I can still remember word for word, weeks later.

"You know, Luke, maybe being blind won't be so bad?" Molly had chimed in. *"You're really cute, and I bet there will be a lot of girls who will want to help you out, you know."* She waggled her brows and giggled, and Luke burst out in laughter.

"You think being blind will get me girls, Molly?"

"Probably." Molly giggled more. *"And maybe I don't have to stop running track because I lost my leg. Maybe I can get one of those cool legs and run in the Paralympics."*

"That'd be so cool, Molls," I said, and Luke agreed.

"That's definitely something I want to be there for in person," he said. *"But you'll have to save me extra tickets, though, because I'll need a bunch of seats for all my new girlfriends."*

Luke's doctors have given him a dismal prognosis in regards to his vision, and they've estimated that, in a few years' time, it's likely he will go blind in both eyes. Molly is still dealing with adjusting to her amputation, but she's also experiencing a significant amount of phantom limb pain. Per Molly, *it sucks big time.* And I'm not sure what the future holds for me. I may or may not walk again, and I can't put my life on hold in hopes of a miracle.

But the three of us are a mere drop in the bucket of people like us, and there's a space for me to help provide light at the end of many a dark tunnel.

We need space to vent our frustrations and the tools to fix

the things we can. And we need someone advocating for that outside of ourselves and our families, during the most vulnerable time in our lives.

As Luke and Molly spoke and I listened, I realized that the *someone* advocating for the bucket of people like them and me could be...*me*.

After I left the hospital that day, I sent Elizabeth—aka Ms. Bartlett—an email. Ever since then, she's been helping me get my course load updated to reflect my new major—a bachelor's in Developmental Psychology that will hopefully lead to a masters of science in Child and Adolescent Developmental Psychology.

My end goal is to be a therapist who specializes in counseling and being a supportive resource for children with disabilities. Especially, children and adolescents who are faced with tragic, life-changing situations like Molly and Luke and me. I want to help advocate for them. Help them and their parents deal with the numerous difficult emotions you face. Help them find their path to acceptance, and more than that, their path to not just surviving but *thriving*.

"Sorry about that, Scottie," Elizabeth announces as she walks back into her office and sits down behind her desk. It's crazy how all those months ago—when everything had happened with my mom—I was purposely ignoring this woman. But over the past two weeks, I've been in contact with her so much that we're on a first-name basis.

"No problem," I say.

"So, we're happy with the schedule changes?"

"Happy?" I question on a laugh. "More like ecstatic. Thank you so much, Elizabeth. I know it wasn't easy, getting all of this switched last minute."

"It's what I'm here for, Scottie. I'm glad to do it." She smiles. "So...do you think you'll want to get a PhD in Clinical Psychology?"

"A PhD?" I furrow my brow. "That sounds like a lot of work."

"Of course it is." Elizabeth chuckles. "They don't call you a doctor for nothing. But I've seen your grades, Scottie. I also see your passion. This is the kind of career you were made to do. So, don't write it off, okay?"

"How about I'll start with my bachelor's and go from there?" I toss back, and Elizabeth grins.

"And how about I'll be here for you every step of the way?"

"Sounds perfect."

"Oh, by the way," she adds. "I had an interesting meeting with Connie over at the Disability Services Office. She wants me to assist her in creating a survey for all students to fill out every year so that the university can be aware of any disabilities and provide them with resources that will help accommodate them. And I heard that you are the driving force behind this incredible change… Is that true?"

I can't hide my smile. "It's true."

After some serious research on ADA accommodations on college campuses, one of the things I found out was that most universities—including Dickson—have students self-identify their disabilities. Every university appears to have a different process of self-identifying, but the commonality of them all was that it ends up putting students in a situation where they have to strongly advocate for themselves rather than having the university trying to advocate for them.

Insert me looking out for them instead.

And it appears that Dickson is taking my suggestions to heart. At a pretty rapid pace, to my utter surprise.

"I swear, Scottie, you can take on the world." Elizabeth smiles at me from across her desk, and the only thing that comes to mind is… *Hell yeah, I can.*

My phone vibrates in my jean-shorts pocket, and I cringe a little when I meet her eyes, but she just waves a hand at me. "By all means, check your messages. I don't mind."

I glance down at the screen and see a text that makes me smile all over again.

Finn: Are you coming home soon, birthday girl?

"Well, with the look on your face, I'd say, it's a good text," Elizabeth comments, and I laugh.

"It's my boyfriend."

"Let me guess, he wants you to get this boring meeting over with so you can celebrate your birthday?"

I snort. "Pretty much."

"You got big plans for your birthday, Scottie?"

"Just spending time with my boyfriend."

Honestly, it feels weird to call Finn my boyfriend. With how far we've come, that word feels weak. It feels like it doesn't come close to encompassing what he is to me.

"Well, I'm not going to keep you here any longer. You need to go enjoy your birthday instead of sitting here talking to me about career paths."

Funnily enough, I love talking about my career path. It feels like my destiny. It feels like everything I've been through has been for a reason. Like, this is how my life is supposed to be.

Would I love to get out of this chair and walk again? Of course.

But am I going to spend the rest of my life feeling sorry for myself? Hell no.

I have so much to give, so much to offer, and if my freak accident of an injury has proven anything, it's that I'm strong. I can do hard things.

I can do _anything_.

"Thanks for everything, Elizabeth," I tell her again as I start to wheel out the door.

But when I make it down the hallway and to the elevators, I pause to send Finn a quick text back.

Me: Honey, I'll be home soon. ;)

And his response comes in a second later—*I can't fucking wait.*

———

Finn

Today is Scottie's birthday. She's officially nineteen, and she has no clue that I have quite the bash planned for her.

Everyone in our friend group has her under the impression that they're either back home or on trips for the summer, as per my orders to keep it a surprise.

Ace is in the Bahamas with Julia and her family. Kayla went back home to hang with her folks in Texas. Blake is in California for the next two weeks.

At least, that's what we've told her.

All of it's bullshit, but my girl has no clue.

I hold the door for her as we head out of our new on-campus apartment. That's right, we're officially living together, and while these apartments on Broadway are generally reserved for juniors and seniors, Scottie milked her injury for all it's worth, and Dean Kandinsky gave us an exception.

Sometimes, being the paralyzed girl ain't so bad. Those are her words, not mine, and they were said when the housing office handed over the keys to us about a week ago. We wasted zero time moving in, and the past five days have been the kind of bliss I never thought was possible.

Scottie tries to act stubborn when I start to push her chair, but I roll my eyes and keep moving us down Broadway toward Zip's Diner.

This place is our go-to these days, and all thanks to Ace's friendship with the owner, Zip helped me get everything arranged this morning when Scottie had her meeting with her counselor.

"I'm just so freaking happy that Elizabeth was able to help me add all of the psych classes I needed to stay on track to get my bachelor's in four years," Scottie rambles, still excited about her meeting this morning.

"I'm proud of you," I tell her.

"You're proud of me?" she asks and looks over her shoulder to meet my eyes.

"You're the strongest person I know," I say and mean every word. "The way you face your own challenges and the way you've made it a priority to help other people? You're amazing, Scottie."

Her lips twist up into the most adorable grin. "Why'd you stop? Keep going," she says through a giggle. "Tell me more about how awesome I am."

I laugh at that, but I also give in to her easy demand. "You're beautiful. You're kind. You're smart. You're funny. And you have the most perfect tasting puss—"

"Okay!" she exclaims on a laugh. "That's enough."

"Hey, you asked, babe." I chuckle and squeeze her shoulder. "And you know how it goes when you ask me to do something, I'll always come through."

"Speaking of class schedules, you horny beast, did you check yours?" she asks, and I shake my head.

"Nope, but I have a feeling you already did."

She giggles. "Yeah. I did."

"And how's it look?"

"Like calculus is going to own your ass, but it's all good. I'm sure Lexi can help you out."

She's not wrong that Lexi will be my go-to for all things numbers. She's the smartest person I know, and lucky for me, she's family.

"And what about you? How's your schedule looking?" I ask. "I know you managed to get all of the psych classes you wanted, but what about your other classes?"

"Mostly good," she says. "Though, I have to deal with Murkowski again." She rolls her eyes, and I know exactly why.

Professor Murkowski was the only professor who made Scottie take a final in order to get credit for the semester. Every other professor allowed her to keep the grade she had prior to her injury and just gave her some busywork that involved reading and writing a few essays.

Murkowski, though, the hard-ass, had Scottie studying for two weeks straight. Thankfully, she passed, even managed an A, and has zero classes to retake her sophomore year.

And all thanks to a Kelly Financial grant, she also has a scholarship that covers her tuition, housing, and other fees for the next three years.

By the time we reach Zip's Diner, Scottie is too busy talking about her class schedule to notice all the people who sit inside the restaurant. You can see them all clear as day through the windows, but she's too busy looking over her shoulder and talking to me.

She's obsessed. What can I say?

The entire room erupts with "*Surprise!*" as I push her inside, and a smile lights up her entire face.

Ace and Julia and Kayla and Blake all stand at the front, smiling and laughing when Scottie notices them and starts freaking out.

"What?" she exclaims. "I thought you were all out of town!" She looks over her shoulder and meets my eyes. "This is your doing?"

I grin. "Yep."

"You're diabolical."

"I know." I wink and lean down to press a kiss to her mouth. "I'm also going to let you know now that this isn't your actual birthday present from me," I whisper into her ear, and she tilts her head in confusion. "There's another surprise for you when we get home tonight. And involves you being gloriously naked."

The past few weeks have been...a revelation for my girl and me. She's started to get...feeling...in the best kinds of places, and I've pretty much spent the last fourteen days figuring out all the ways that I can make her come. It's fucking fantastic.

"Finn." Her cheeks turn red, and I just press a kiss to her lips.

"Happy birthday, Scottie."

I step back to let everyone come up and hug her and tell her happy birthday. And I'm in awe at everyone who showed up. Scottie's cheerleading teammates. Her sister and her dad. Her mom, whom she's been in some contact with lately and is still sober. Both of Ace's parents and Julia's parents. My entire family—Winslow and Hayes.

Zip's Diner is literally packed to the brim.

Julia wheels Scottie over to where her team stands, and music starts to play from the speaker. I look up to find Zip smiling over at me with a thumbs-up. His wife starts to bring out a buffet of burgers and hot dogs and other sides, and a few of his employees have trays of sodas and waters that they set on tables for everyone to grab.

And my girl is smiling like the fucking sun. She looks so damn happy that I have to swallow against the emotion forming moisture in my eyes.

She's been through so much over these past few months, so to see her now, here, happy and having fun, well, it's everything to me.

"You pulled it off," Ace says and claps a hand on my back. "She didn't have a fucking clue."

"Nope." I smile, but my smile turns to confusion when Blake comes over to stand beside us, an angry look on his face.

Ace and I both follow his line of sight to where Lexi stands beside Adam, one of the PTs at Scottie's long-term rehab clinic, at the other end of the room.

"Who's that guy?" he asks me, and I shake my head.

"What guy?"

"Seriously?" he questions, frustrated, and Ace laughs. "The one talking to Lexi."

"You're fucking intense right now, Boden."

"I don't care." He meets my eyes again. "I need to know who he is."

"He works at the Hodge Clinic, dude. He just came because he's been working a lot with Scottie."

Blake nods.

I laugh. "You know you sound a lot like a jealous boyfriend right now, right? For a girl who won't give you the time of day."

Blake smiles, the freak. "We must not allow other people's limited perceptions to define us, Finnley. There are things known and there are things unknown, and in between are the doors of perception."

"The fuck did you just say?" Ace asks, and I laugh.

Blake shakes his head. "Never mind. I'm going in."

"You're going in? What does that mean?" Ace tosses back, but it's too late, Blake is already striding across the room and heading straight for Lexi. "What is he doing?"

"I think he's asking her out."

"Oh fuck," Ace mutters. "Why do I feel like he's going to crash and burn?"

"Because he is," I say through a laugh.

We both stand there, watching from a distance as Blake interrupts Lexi and Adam's conversation. His mouth is moving a mile a minute, like he's nervous as hell, and his hands are joining the party.

Lexi's face is neutral, hardly offering anything at all. And we're too far away to hear what she says, but when Blake turns back around and heads in our direction, he has a big-ass smile on his face.

"Holy shit, did she...?" Ace questions, and I shrug.

"I don't know, man, but he looks thrilled."

Once Blake is standing right in front of us, he lets out a big sigh of relief.

"So...?" Ace urges, and Blake just shrugs and slides his hands into his jeans pockets.

"I obviously asked her to share our love with the world, and she very graciously said no."

"What?" I blurt out on a snort. "Get real. You got rejected."

Ace is nearly wheezing. "Why do you look so happy about that and please, even more than that, why are you talking like a fucking poet tonight?"

Blake smiles. "Because it's only a matter of time."

Ace and I both look at each other in confusion.

"Mark my words," he says. "That girl will be mine."

I can't decide if it's complete delusion on his part or if he actually is in love with Lexi.

"Finn. Help me out here. Bring this man back down to earth." Ace looks at me again, hoping that I have something to say in this situation.

"Dude, I can't judge," I answer honestly. "I spent four weeks in hospital waiting rooms for Scottie."

"That's what I'm saying." Blake wraps his arm around my shoulder. "When you know, you fucking know. Right, Finn?"

I look across the room to where Scottie is laughing over something Ace's dad is telling her. And seeing that joy and smile on her face and knowing how fucking much I love her makes it impossible for me to refute Blake's claims.

"When you know, you know."

And, oh baby, do I know.

THE END

The next book in the highly addictive Dickson University Series is coming soon!

Mark your calendars for February 7th, 2025 to see if Blake Boden's delusion of ending up with his dream girl Lexi Winslow comes true. ;)

Preorder Playing Games today!

Sign up for our newsletter, and we'll keep you up-to-date on any Dickson University Series news AND a lot of times we share fun teasers and excerpts!

Plus, our newsletter is hilarious! Character conversations about royal babies, parenting woes, embarrassing moments, and shitty horoscopes are just the beginning! If you're already signed up, consider sending us a message to tell us how much you love us. We really like that. ;)

Need EVEN MORE Max Monroe before our next release?

Never fear, we have a list of nearly FIFTY other titles to keep you busy for as long as your little reading heart desires!

Want to know more about the handsome Winslow Brothers? Start with The Bet!

Want to know more about Ace's (wild and crazy) dad Thatch and his billionaire friends?

Grab Tapping the Billionaire!

Check out our Suggested Reading Order on our website!

www.authormaxmonroe.com/max-monroe-suggested-reading-order

Follow us online here:

Facebook:www.facebook.com/authormaxmonroe

Reader Group: www.facebook.com/groups/1561640154166388

Twitter: www.twitter.com/authormaxmonroe

Instagram: www.instagram.com/authormaxmonroe

TikTok: m.tiktok.com/ZMe1jv5kQ

Goodreads: goo.gl/8VUIz2

ACKNOWLEDGMENTS

First of all, THANK YOU for reading. That goes for anyone who has bought a copy, read an ARC, helped us beta, edited, or found time in their busy schedule just to make sure we stayed on track. Thank you for supporting us, for talking about our books, and for just being so unbelievably loving and supportive of our characters. You've made this our MOST favorite adventure thus far.

THANK YOU to each other. Max is thanking Monroe. Monroe is thanking Max. We always do this, and it's because we *love* writing books together. P.S. What is happening with us? Holy drama llama, these books are starting to get intense. Are we going through something??

THANK YOU, Lisa, for being you. We don't know what we'd do without you. We are one hundred percent certain no editor on the planet other than you (the love of our lives) would accept a manuscript that is double the size it should've been with a smile on their face when the deadline is tight enough to make your asshole pucker.

THANK YOU, Stacey, for always making the inside of our books so pretty and always, always, always being so flexible! We love you!

THANK YOU, Peter, for always going with the flow with our wild cover ideas. We know you worked your ass off on this one and we are forever grateful!

THANK YOU, Rick, for having the best poker face in the business. Though, we'll never forget the day we told you what happens in this book, and you were like *insert the widest eyes we've ever seen*. If we had it on video, it'd be all over social media by now. Also, thank you for helping us navigate all of the numbery stuff we loathe so much.

THANK YOU to every blogger and influencer who has read, reviewed, posted, shared, and supported us. Your enthusiasm, support, and hard work do not go unnoticed. We love youuuuuuuuuuuu!

THANK YOU to the people who love us—our family. You are our biggest supporters and motivators. We couldn't do this without you. Literally. The next few months are going to be bumpy, but man, your love and support make it so easy for us to strive for our wildest dreams.

THANK YOU to our Awesome ARC-ers. We love and appreciate you guys so much.

THANK YOU to our Camp Love Yourself friends! We love you. You always find a way to make us smile and laugh every single freaking day. You're the best. Let's keep hanging out, shall we?

As always, all our love.
XOXO,
Max & Monroe

Made in United States
Orlando, FL
11 March 2025